PORTRAIT IN BLACK AND GOLD

PORTRAIT IN BLACK AND GOLD

a novel by

CAROL DAMIOLI

INANNA PUBLICATIONS AND EDUCATION INC.
TORONTO, CANADA

We gratefully acknowledge the support of the Canada Council for the Arts and the Ontario
Arts Council for our publishing program.

We are also grateful for the support received from an
Anonymous Fund at The Calgary Foundation.

Note from the publisher: Care has been taken to trace the ownership of copyright material
used in this book. The author and the publisher welcome any information enabling them
to rectify any references or credits in subsequent editions.

Cover artwork: Self-portrait, 1556, Anguissola, Sofonisba (c. 1532-1625) / Muzeum Zamek,
Łańcut, Poland / The Bridgeman Art Library.

All poetry, except that of Louise Labé, is from *Women Poets of the Italian Renaissance: Courtly
Ladies and Courtesans*, edited by Laura Anna Stortoni and Mary Prentice Lillie (New York:
Italica Press, 1997). Copyright © 1997 by Laura Anna Stortoni. Used by permission of
Italica Press. The Louise Labé poetry is the author's translation.

Bible quotations are from *The Holy Bible*, King James Version (New York: American Bible
Society, 1999); Bartleby.com, 2000. www.bartleby.com/108/.

Library and Archives Canada Cataloguing in Publication

Damioli, Carol, author
　　Portrait in black and gold / Carol Damioli.

(Inanna poetry and fiction series)
Issued in print and electronic formats.
ISBN 978-1-77133-064-0 (pbk.). — ISBN 978-1-77133-067-1 (pdf).--

　　I. Title. II. Series: Inanna poetry and fiction series

PS3554.A487P67 2013　　　　813'.54　　　　C2013-905397-2
　　　　　　　　　　　　　　　　　　　　　　　　C2013-905398-0

Printed and bound in Canada.

Inanna Publications and Education Inc.
210 Founders, York University, 4700 Keele Street, Toronto, ON, Canada M3J 1P3
Telephone: (416) 736-5356 Fax: (416) 736-5765
Email: inanna.publications@inanna.ca　Website: www.inanna.ca

To the memory of Kathleen D. Hughes
— herself an artist.

Table of Contents

1.

The Master

Among the wisest souls who live among us,
You bear away the prize and boast of all.
      —Lucia Bertani dell'Oro (1521-1567)

APRIL, 1554

She had long ago set her sights upon Rome, eager to follow the path traced by so many painters before her, to see for herself the powerful ancient carvings that had inspired her own time, and to leave her own imprint on the city's muddy streets.

Yet the city held another even greater lure, and now, at last, she moved toward it. She crossed damp and cracked paving stones, moved among carriages and stray dogs, passed fruit sellers, fish-mongers, beggars, and running children.

Her maid and companion, a woman older and half a head shorter, stopped and scratched her head. "'Raven's Slaughterhouse'? What kind of a name is that for a street?" the maid asked. "It sounds horrible."

"I think it sounds intriguing," the young woman said. "Maybe *il Maestro* will know what it means." Her pale blue eyes scanned the street. "According to his letter, that must be his house right over there."

"Ach, watch your step, love," said the older woman, lifting the hem of her plain grey dress. "The Romans seem to clean the streets even less often than we do in Cremona. Or else they have many more horses."

They paused across the street from a wide two-story house. The younger woman was attracted to its symmetry and the purity of its lines: the towering central door was framed by a white stone arch, and the same white stone framed two smaller doors, two arched windows, and two statue niches. *How odd*, she thought, *that of all houses, the niches on this one would be empty.* Flat grey trim formed rectangles to contain each element, and the grey and the white contrasted splendidly with the beige brick. She found charming a balustrade across the top that served only to delight the eye.

When they crossed the street and stood at that central door, the younger woman hesitated, shifting her weight from one foot to the other.

Everything that had led to this moment cascaded through her mind — the painting lessons, the innumerable drawings, the struggle to excel in her early portraits, her father's encouragement, the taste of fame in her native city. Now, she was about to meet Michelangelo Buonarroti, the Florentine sculptor and painter so magnificent that he was called *il Divino*. She knew that any painter would beg to be standing on this particular doorstep, more than any other in Europe.

Yet doubt, an old friend, clawed at her. Was the Master granting her a meeting out of mere courtesy, a perfunctory encounter filled with formalities but without substance, just to fulfill his curiosity about the rare wonder of a woman painter? Or would he, as she dared imagine, let her into his sphere of genius, long enough that she might absorb its radiance? And what of his *terribilità*, his emotional intensity?

"I know," her maid said, seeing her hesitation. "But you're ready, Sonia. You've prepared well. Maestro Buonarroti holds out a gift to you — take it. Never mind about what *might* happen, love."

The maid touched the white linen cap over her grey hair to make sure it was straight.

"And do I look all right?" the younger woman asked. She had reached twenty-two years, but still was not used to wearing her hair in an elaborate twist pulled onto the crown of her head. "You look lovely, dear. Forest green velvet is very becoming on you," the maid said.

The younger woman looked gratefully into her maid's kindly brown eyes. She relaxed her tense shoulders and lifted the knocker ring, confidently letting it crack against the coffered door.

"Good morning. I am Sofonisba Anguissola, from Cremona," she said to the man of middle years who opened the door. "I hope we're not too early."

"Not at all. I am Tommaso Cavalieri. Maestro Buonarroti is eager to meet you." A smile enlivened his fine-boned face.

"Signor Cavalieri, it is such a pleasure to meet *you*, finally, after corresponding for so long," Sofonisba said as she stepped inside. "This is my maid, Rosa Marco."

"Good day, Signora Marco. Let me take those for you," Tommaso said, taking the parchment roll that Rosa carried. "Drawings, I see." He ushered the women into a whitewashed formal sitting room that showed the same clean austerity as the house's façade. Two large wooden chairs and a small table flanked a fireplace where a low log fire burned.

From a side door, with no preamble, came the Master, wearing the plain, long black tunic of a common merchant. Sofonisba noted an undeniable dignity in his bearing.

"Signorina Anguissola, at last."

"Maestro Buonarroti. This is indeed an honour." She extended her hand and he held it briefly in both of his thick, highly-veined ones, and she saw that his green-flecked light brown eyes regarded her up and down.

Sofonisba assessed him in return. At seventy-nine years, Maestro

Michelangelo Buonarroti stood in every physical way in sharp contrast with his pupil and friend Tommaso. Tommaso reminded Sofonisba of the lithe figures in the many Greek and Roman sketches she had studied. The Master, although his back was still straight, had the stocky body of a stonecutter, not an athlete, and his height reached only to Tommaso's shoulders.

"May I present my maid, Rosa Marco."

"Signora, welcome. Both of you, please sit down. It was so good of Signor Vasari to bring us together." The Master led them to a long table set with wine and almonds. The women carefully arranged their skirts as they sat. Sofonisba noticed that the master lowered himself to the bench very slowly, under Tommaso's vigilant eyes.

"Now, Signorina Anguissola, pray tell me, how are your mother and father?" the Master began.

There was something behind his cordiality that Sofonisba could not fathom — a darkness, or a mere tiredness?

"Papa is quite well, and Mama, she is also well ... I do thank you for asking. They send you their highest regards ... and great regrets that they could not escort me here, and meet you."

The Master gestured to Tommaso that he should fill the wine cups. The thin spring sunlight came furtively through the front windows.

"But by sending you here on your own, with Signora Marco," he said, "they are showing their pride and confidence in you. You are here as an accomplished and much-admired painter, and not as your parents' daughter."

Sofonisba smiled warmly at the Master and settled more comfortably on the bench as he continued.

"And when I say you are beautiful, it is not the self-serving flattery you've no doubt heard many times before. God denied me beauty" — Sofonisba had indeed noticed his flat nose and heavy brow — "so I seek it everywhere, and I've tried to pour it into the creatures I've painted and sculpted."

"Maestro Buonarroti, no one can doubt the beauty of your creations, but not only in the physical sense. Their beauty is spiritual, too. When Rosa and I saw your *Pietà*, the one from your early years, of course we first noticed the loveliness of the Virgin's face. But the sense there of calmness despite inexpressible grief is what I will always remember." She paused, worried that her words were presumptuous. "Forgive me if I'm repeating something you've been told a thousand times."

"Ah, the *Pietà*," The Master gazed toward a window. "That was so long ago, when I saw things much differently."

Tommaso turned toward the Master and said, "Signorina Anguissola brought a bundle of sketches all the way from Cremona. Why don't you take a look at them?"

The Master snapped back to their little group. "Certainly." Tommaso fetched the bundle and spread several of the drawings on the table.

The Master leaned intently over the works, revealing nothing in his face, making no sound or gesture, just reverently lifting the drawings and setting them down, one by one, occasionally nodding his head of still-dark brown hair or touching his short beard or moustache. In the shattering quiet, Sofonisba could hear carriage wheels on the street and church bells ringing somewhere. Hope and fear fought inside her. She inhaled deeply, then let the air out slowly, trusting no one could hear her. She forced herself to take a sip of wine. *Is this where he decides? Is he giving me a Last Judgment, just as he painted in the chapel of Pope Sixtus? How will I hold my head up in Cremona if I must leave for there tomorrow?*

"I know it was mentioned in your letters, but an old man forgets things," The Master was saying. "Tell me again, who taught you?"

"Well at first, Signor Bernardino Campi, son of the goldsmith Pietro Campi. Then Signor Bernardino was called to Milan by the governor to do some commissions, and I continued my lessons with Signor Bernardino Gatti, the one they call *il Sojaro*, after the wine vats his father makes."

The Master nodded. "I can see from these sketches that both your teachers did a good job. These are excellent, as I might have expected, from all I've heard about you. They're even better than the drawings you already sent me. You, too, have successfully taken on the *Pietà*," Michelangelo said, holding up one sketch.

Her heart fluttered with joy at his praise.

"Thank you for your kind words, Maestro Buonarroti. That drawing was for a canvas I did in oil, an assignment from Signor Campi to copy his *Pietà*. You can see your influence on us — we studied drawings of your early *Pietà* before doing anything." *Oh Holy Virgin, let this journey not be just a foolish dalliance.*

The Master examined the sketch further. "I've seen drawings of Signor Campi's work. I see his influence here — the elongated fingers, the light and shadow."

The two artists went on talking, about style, technique, and the art markets in Cremona and Rome.

"...And this one is very special," the Master continued, picking up a drawing of a boy crying as a crab pinches his finger, and a girl trying to comfort him. "I remember asking for it. You had sent me a drawing of a laughing girl, a self-portrait, I believe, and I had said that you should try to portray a crying boy, which would be more difficult. And you have drawn this boy quite sympathetically. The emotional tension between his pain and the girl's calm is exquisite. And how inventive to show an informal scene, instead of the usual stiff arrangement."

"Thank you. Oh, Maestro Buonarroti, your praise means so much. I took the face of that boy from my brother, Asdrubale, and the girl is my sister Minerva."

The Master regarded the drawing further, in yet another chasm of silence, while Sofonisba tightly interlaced her fingers. Rosa reached for some almonds, and her wide sleeve knocked over her wine cup. "Acch! Oh my, what a mess I've made! I'm so sorry, what! Oh Lord...." Sofonisba dared not raise her eyes to Rosa's. She stifled a smile, knowing that dear Rosa's intention had been to break the tension somewhat while they waited for the Master's decision.

Tommaso deftly placed some rags over the pale red puddle on the white tablecloth, murmuring, "It's not so bad, Signora Marco, there we are, and none of the sketches were stained!"

The Master slid the drawings into a pile, then turned to Sofonisba.

"Signorina Anguissola, I have always thought that painting was inferior to sculpture. But when I saw my work on the Sistine ceiling, I came to appreciate painting more. Although, these days…" His face lengthened and darkened. "Well, never mind. If your skills as a painter are what I've heard they are, then anyone who guides you will take a worthwhile journey. And so, I'd be pleased if you could come here for instruction, if you can spare any of the time you'll have in Rome."

Sofonisba shot up in her seat. "Maestro Buonarroti, I — I can hardly say how happy that would make me." She paused for the slightest of moments to regain herself. "Yes, certainly I can spare the time."

The Master smiled slightly. "Let's begin at early morning, so we can finish before the others get here. I seem to have attracted a band of rowdy young boys, some claiming to be art students, they're always hanging around here — sometimes they even listen to what I have to say."

"I am honoured, Maestro Buonarroti. Again."

The Master stood up and winced. "Tommaso—" he gasped, and the younger man leapt up to support him and help him move away from the table.

"There go my gouty knees again. I would say it's a curse of old age, but I've had it too long for that." Tommaso stepped away. "There. Well. Where were we?" The Master tried to smile.

"I won't keep you, Maestro Buonarroti," Sofonisba said as she stood up, "but pray, what is the meaning of your street's name — 'Raven's Slaughterhouse'?"

The Master and Tommaso exchanged troubled looks. Tommaso ran one hand through his mass of curly brown hair.

"That, signorina, I will reveal at the end of your time with me," the Master said.

Puzzled, the women made their farewells, then stepped back into the turbulent Roman streets. When she and Rosa were many steps from the house, Sofonisba, forgetting the Master's hint of melancholy, sighed with relief and joy: "Ah, Rosa, lessons from Maestro Michelangelo Buonarotti! I just want to dance! And that was rather sly of you — knocking over that wine cup."

"Are you saying I *meant* to do it, love?" Rosa feigned, as she and Sofonisba linked arms and laughed. As they walked, they traded impressions of the Master, who had loomed so large in their imaginations for so long.

The faces of Rome that swirled around them were mostly serious — priests and bankers in dark clothes and expressions — but a harlot caught their attention when she called and whistled for customers from an upper window. It occurred to Sofonisba that she had never heard a woman whistle before. Rosa frowned at the display, but Sofonisba smiled.

The bustle of Rome lessened when they turned down a side street toward their accommodations, and Rosa's voice took on a sympathetic tone. "I noticed, love, how you hesitated when you mentioned your mother," she said.

"Oh, Rosa, you know about Mama, how hard it is."

Rosa patted Sofonisba's hand. "I do understand."

Tommaso began to clear the table while Michelangelo sat down in a chair beside the fire. "Are you really going to tell her?" Tommaso asked him.

"Only if, in the coming months, she proves herself capable of handling it."

"That's doubtful. The Anguissola nobility is new, but her polished manners, and her dress — you'd think she came from a long noble line," Tommaso said. "Young women like that are too delicate for that story."

"Maybe you underestimate her. Now bring my wine over here."

The next morning Tommaso led Sofonisba and Rosa down a white hallway that opened into the Master's large studio. At one end a stone fireplace contained a small blaze. Wooden tables lining the walls held stacks of drawings, chunks of white marble and plaster, and chisels and hammers. Sofonisba noted an unmistakable smell of walnut oil; the atmosphere was of uninhibited creativity.

The Master entered silently and alone, but it was an entrance nonetheless, with his proud and vital gait. He greeted Sofonisba and Rosa warmly. He showed Rosa to a chair where she could keep her usual discreet but watchful distance. The Master pushed pieces of charcoal out of the way to give the two painters room at one of the long tables. Looking around, Sofonisba felt instantly curious about a bulky, unrecognizable form that stood under a canvas drape in a pool of marble dust.

"So, what would you like to know?" the Master asked Sofonisba.

The question threw her into a panic. *I must say something, but Holy Virgin, don't let me sound like a fool.*

Before she could say anything, he chuckled. "Never mind, that's a horrible question," he reassured her. "Of course, you want to know everything about painting. So did I, when I first joined Ghirlandaio's studio. That was so long ago."

"Actually, Maestro Buonarroti, before we talk about painting, there is something I would like to know about your house," Sofonisba said. The master fixed his eyes on her curiously. "There are two statue niches in the façade, but they're empty. I am surprised that they are not filled with some of your great sculptures."

"A good observation. I have debated what to do with those niches," the Master said. "The dilemma is, if I place a different statue in each, that would destroy the lovely symmetry of the façade, and I just can't bear to do that. In theory, two mirror-image statues would solve that problem. But I cannot make two statues that are perfectly similar, it's just impossible." He shaped two invisible statues with his hands. "Every piece of carved marble or stone is unique. So I leave the spaces empty."

"I see." She was newly impressed.

"Now, Ghirlandaio told me he couldn't teach me everything, because he didn't know it, and that learning to paint is a lifetime process. That's my first lesson for you. Now hand me that stack of drawings." The Master had drawn sheet after sheet of faces, hands, feet, arms, torsos, old people, and beautiful young women and men in a variety of postures.

"Leonardo, my fellow Florentine, may he rest in peace, well, we had our differences, you may have heard, but he painted the most exquisite hands I've ever seen, in the portrait called *La Gioconda*. I'm sure you've seen sketches. But don't try to imitate him exactly, or any other painter for that matter, including me. I can help, but it's better to find your own way."

"Oh, but hands are so difficult," Sofonisba said. "If you could teach me the secret of painting hands, Maestro Buonarroti, that would be a tremendous help."

"The secret. Hmm." His forehead furrowed. He told her to draw as if she were doing a study for a painting of one of her sisters. She concentrated, wanting to make a strong impression, focusing completely on the tools before her.

Michelangelo showed her how to shorten the fingers, to make them more solid. Sofonisba tried again.

"That's better! You were already moving in this direction with your sketch of the crying boy. Keep going. But for now, enough talk, enough drawing. Let's paint."

She returned the next day for her next lesson, and again for many days and weeks after that.

Sofonisba was alarmed one day when the Master gave her a prepared wooden panel about the length of her hand, and half again as wide, and told her to paint a self-portrait. Anything on a panel that size could almost be called a miniature. *Doesn't he know I've done many large portraits? Surely Papa told him.*

"You may be wondering why I've handed you such a small panel," he said. "It is a challenge to paint a portrait in a small space — to get the perspective and detail right."

She painted a three-quarter pose similar to her last large self-portrait, but turned in the other direction. She showed herself in a simple black gown with brown sleeves. In her left hand she held open a small book. On one page she signed her name and the year, 1554.

The Master praised the balance between the light of her complexion and hand, and the dark of her gown and the background. He admired the subtle variations and the texture in the background colour. "And the detail in that lace collar — superb!"

He placed it on an easel and took a more distant view.

"And now may I be a little more, if you will, *personal*. I see here a woman who is already well-known, but who remains modest and sincere. Those eyes — so direct, so piercing, and the colour of the sea — such large, observant eyes that show that you look at the world, and yourself, with great intensity. Then there's the hair — a rich auburn color, pulled into a plain net. I'm afraid you don't do yourself justice, signorina. You are more beautiful than that. Why such a serious expression, pray?"

"Because I want to be taken seriously as a painter," she said. "So I portray myself in an unembroidered gown, with an austere style of hair, no jewellery, and with a book in hand. I found out, painfully, back in Cremona that too many men think that any woman who can paint is a freak of nature, or a miracle. You are most generous in your understanding and encouragement, Maestro Buonarroti, but I'm afraid most men are not."

"Then most men are fools." He looked down at his knee and winced a little, then suggested they sit down.

"I was a close friend of the poet Vittoria Colonna, may she rest in peace. Perhaps you have read her work?"

"Indeed I have, Maestro Buonarroti, her sonnets are splendid, so moving," Sofonisba said. "How fortunate you were to know her!"

"It was through her that I came to know well that a woman can be highly accomplished. So it is not a surprise to me, signorina, that you, a woman, show great ability and invention in your work."

His words thrilled her, but she suppressed a smile. "Thank you, Maestro. Now, in this painting I showed myself holding a book, a common enough object in a portrait," Sofonisba said, "but for me it means intellect, knowledge, and striving." She paused. "Is that too much to put into one small self-portrait?"

"Not at all," Buonarroti said. "*Brava*, signorina! But there's one thing. Let's look at the way you did the hand, and how to make it better next time. Hands!" he snorted. "They are *always* troublesome."

Michelangelo's gout meant that he rarely ventured into the city. He saved his energy to show Sofonisba three places that were most important to him. The first was the basilica of San Pietro, where he was superintendent of the works and his mighty dome was still unfinished. The second was the Sistine Chapel, where the turbulence of the painted scenes leaped out at Sofonisba. Noting the richly muscular figures, she understood why the Master considered himself a sculptor first and a painter second. His *Last Judgment*, on the altar wall, took her breath away with its drama and emotional force. Sofonisba tried not to dwell on the fact that she would never paint frescoes.

Their third stop, a short walk across the Tiber River, was the church of Santa Maria sopra Minerva, its façade oddly draped with hides that tanners had hung out to dry. The Master led Sofonisba to the left of the apse to show her his marble of the *Risen Christ*. The naked figure stood in a proud and defiant posture that reminded Sofonisba of the Master's *David*, but without the tension. Sofonisba admired the work for its natural and realistic appearance, and because it was completely without shame.

Sofonisba treasured each day, aware of the rare privilege of standing beside Michelangelo while encountering his work.

The Master was so courteous, so generous with his knowledge, and so even-tempered that it puzzled Sofonisba when, from a look of his or the tone of his voice, she sensed in him a gloom, almost a note of tragedy. She could not fathom its source, even after taking instruction from the Master for many months.

2.

The Awakening

So when the father has a little daughter,
Let him set her to tasks just like his sons',
And not consign her to a lower station
In terms of noble wit or deeds of daring.
                    —Moderata Fonte (1555-1592)

CREMONA, 1542

While the true beginning of anything can be difficult to know, Sofonisba's memory always led her back to the church of Sant'Agata, in a working class district of Cremona. There, when she was ten years old, she stood near the altar, watching a man paint the sky.

She barely moved, as fascinated as if the man were applying the actual celestial blue that sheltered Cremona. But Bernardino Campi was painting the *Madonna with St. Lazarus and St. Mary Magdelene* high on the wall inside Sant'Agata's main door.

The sight of the painter's apprentices beside him on the scaffolding, many of them mere boys, also caught Sofonisba's interest. They stirred mysterious mixtures in buckets, applied messy liquids to the ceiling, and handed Campi clean paintbrushes. Each wore a loose apron, moved in careful steps and sidles on the small platform, endlessly joked but always quickly obeyed the painter. It seemed incomprehensible to Sofonisba that these paint-spattered, sweated-stained boys were part of an unfolding tableau of splendour.

After some time, the painter, a slender man of twenty, descended the scaffolding, carrying a water bucket. He approached Sofonisba.

"Signorina, this is the third time this week you've come here, watching me with the intensity of a young hawk," Campi said as he set down his bucket. "If you're going to do that so pointedly and so often, I think I deserve to know your name." Sofonisba saw friendliness in his brown eyes.

Before her maid could respond to the lowly painter who dared to address a nobleman's daughter, Sofonisba replied, "I am Sofonisba Anguissola. My father is Amilcare Anguissola and my mother is Bianca Ponzone. And this is my maid, Rosa Marco."

"Pleased to meet you both. I am Bernardino Campi, son of Pietro Campi."

"I know," Sofonisba said. "My father sells art supplies to all the painters in Cremona. Sometimes he tells me where they're working."

"Ah, so that's how you found me. But why, pray? Why do you care what I'm doing here? It seems an unusual interest for a young girl."

"I watch because…" she squinched up her face. "Well, because you're making beautiful pictures. Just with paint." She thought some more. "Oh, and this is the biggest church in Cremona where a painter is working today."

"I see," the painter replied, and chuckled. "So you find beauty in my painting. Thank you for the compliment. Hmm… Would you like to see these pictures up close? Of course this work isn't finished, but…"

"Signor Campi, could I?" Sofonisba's face lit up and she bounced on her heels, but Rosa cut in. "Now wait, Signor Campi, is that safe for a child? Painters fall from scaffolding all the time. I've heard tales. Sonia!"

The child was already skipping beside the painter when Campi looked back to say, "The signorina and I will be very careful."

In the pleasant stillness of the late afternoon light Sofonisba shivered, sensing grand adventure as she lifted her skirt with one hand and held on with the other.

When she was not quite to the top of the ladder, about thirty feet above the church's stone floor, she was already distracted by Campi's ever-nearer work. She climbed on. A sharp cry from Rosa pierced through the hush. Sofonisba's foot had slipped through the ladder, and she swung crazily to her right. Campi reached up and grabbed her around the waist, steadying her. "Are you all right, signorina?" he asked.

"Yes, yes, let's go!" She could almost touch those lovely paintings.

"*Madonna*, Sonia, come down right now!" Rosa yelled.

"Rosa, I'm almost there." Two more steps, and Sofonisba stood on the platform, hugging herself, giddy with joy. She smiled down at Rosa and smoothed her black silk skirt.

"Signor Campi," Rosa hissed. "She's not one of your ruffian apprentices, you know."

"We won't be long, Signora Marco," Campi called down.

Sofonisba quickly lost herself in the scenes before and above her. "Reds, blues and golds, and they're all so — so soft."

"Oh, I learned those from Titian of Venice, a truly great painter. When he was working in Mantua on the ducal palace, I was one of many painters who went there to learn from him." He reached up and flicked a speck of dust off the image. "Cremona is small, so a painter must travel, you see."

Sofonisba nodded. "And how do you do this work, signore?"

"This is called *al fresco*. Painting on wet plaster."

"But how? How can a person paint on wet plaster?" She had turned away from the images to look at him.

"Oh, you don't want to hear all that."

She bounced on her heels again. "Yes, signore, I do, I pray you."

The painter raised his eyebrows. "All right." There was no gliding past her. "First, we spread a thick coat of plaster to fill in the cracks between the stones. Then I sketch out the picture with charcoal. We paint over the charcoal with red ocher pigment. Over that I set a patch of new plaster, on the part I will paint right then. While that patch is still wet, I apply the paint."

"You put paint on wet stuff? Doesn't it run all over?" Sofonisba asked.

"Ah, that's the hard part. I have to wait until the plaster is just right, not too wet or too dry, and then paint like a madman. You see, if I don't move quickly, the colour in one part of the patch will look different from the rest. And if two or more patches bear the same colour, I have to work them in the same way."

Sofonisba considered that. "What if you make a mistake?"

"Ugh," the painter grimaced, and stroked his clean-shaven chin. "Then I have to chip out the old plaster and put on new, fresh plaster."

"Why don't you just paint over a mistake?"

"Because that new paint would eventually fall off the wall. It has to be stuck — bonded, we say — to the wall with wet plaster."

Sofonisba giggled, then glanced back at the work. "Could a madman do this?"

Before Campi could reply, Rosa called up: "Sonia, love, it's time to go now."

They descended, and as Campi, Sofonisba, and Rosa walked out of the church, each was absorbed in their own thoughts.

He's so lucky to be a painter. He gets to make things that last forever, Sofonisba mused.

Signorina Anguissola is very intelligent — Amilcare is lucky, Campi reflected.

Sonia's lucky she wasn't killed, Rosa thought.

When they reached the church door, Campi pointed across the piazza to a compact red-brick lump of a building with six pointed, open arches.

"Do you know the Palazzo Cittanova?" he asked Sofonisba.

"Sure, Papa goes there for meetings all the time," she replied in a bored tone.

"The arches open onto that inviting loggia, and on the second story, there are those delicate windows. See them, with the three lobes?" Campi pointed. "Even the crenellated roof dignifies the building, though it was meant for defence," he said.

"Cren-ell-ate-ed?" Sofonisba pronounced. "You mean with those square-shaped things that stick up from the top?"

"Yes, that's what I mean. Ah, there I go, seeing everything through an artist's eyes!"

Sofonisba looked at the building again. The three-hundred-year-old palazzo that she had passed by many times took on an entirely new appearance. She felt a vague awareness of a vast unexplored world all around her, one full of designs, shapes, textures.

"Most important, Palazzo Cittanova is the home of the merchant's guild," Campi was saying. "The merchants — men like your noble father — take care of the religious buildings, and they are open to art, so they provide me and my fellow painters with lots of work!"

"Painting must be the greatest thrill in the world," Sofonisba asserted.

"For me, yes, it is, and any skill I have is a gift from God," Campi said. "Come back any time, signorina. Please give my regards to your father and mother." He turned to Rosa. "Signora Marco, good day."

"Good day, Signor Campi," Rosa said, and Sofonisba repeated the farewell.

Sofonisba sat with her father in the soft evening lamplight of his study, a room lined with books and a few small devotional paintings on wood. "I went to watch Signor Campi at Sant'Agata again today. This time I talked to him. He sends his regards."

Father observed daughter with blue eyes identical to hers. "Ah yes, Signor Bernardino comes into the shop often. So what did he have to say?"

"He told me how a fresco is done. And he said that painting is the greatest thrill in the world," Sofonisba said.

"Sounds like quite a serious conversation," Amilcare said. "Did he say anything about the 100 florins he owes me?" He closed his ledger.

"Papa," Sofonisba said impatiently. "He was kind, and friendly, and…" She stopped herself from telling her father about her climb up the scaffolding. "It was so exciting."

"Hmm…" Amilcare tapped a quill on his writing table, and his grey beard twitched.

"Pray what, Papa?"

"How would you like to learn to paint, my dear?"

"Me?" Sofonisba stretched the word out in surprise. "*I* couldn't. Signor Campi said his skill is a gift from God. I don't have that gift."

"How do you know you don't? Since you could walk, you've been, we've all seen it, Sonia, scribbling little pictures on any scrap of paper you could find. And anyway, Bernardino was being modest, and pious. Yes, he has God's favour, but his skill also comes from good training and years of practice. You could have those things." Sofonisba gave him a doubtful look. "Well, it's something to think about. It's time for supper now — tell Mama I'll be there in a moment."

"All right." Sofonisba left the study.

Amilcare opened a leather-bound journal.

April 20, 1542

Sonia met the painter Bernardino Campi, and seems quite taken with him and his work. A daughter who can paint would bring some glory to our family name, and some funds into the household. And her talent as a painter could be part of her dowry. She is too young now, but it will not be long before lessons could start, if she's willing. Tomorrow I will bring her paper and chalk from the shop.

The moon had just begun to rise when Rosa helped Sofonisba out of her long-sleeved black silk bodice and long skirt. The maid removed the underskirt of whalebone hoops that gave the dress its stiff, bell-like shape. She lifted Sofonisba's lace-trimmed chemise over her head and placed it carefully on a chair, then untied the girl's corset.

"Papa said I could learn to paint."

"Oh? And do you want to?" Rosa asked, handing her a linen nightgown.

"Yes, I think I do, though it seems a bit daft," Sofonisba said. She sat down at her dressing table, and Rosa removed the brown velvet band and the pins that held up the girl's long hair.

"It's a dream, love, and there's nothing wrong with just a little dreamin'," Rosa said.

In the mirror Sofonisba caught the maid's faraway look. "Rosa! You've had dreams — what were they, pray tell?"

"I'm an old servant. We have no time for dreams."

"But you were young. What did you dream about then?"

Rosa stopped the hairbrush in mid-air, above Sofonisba's head, then continued brushing, but more slowly. "Yes, I did dream, long ago. There was a young man, well-spoken, handsome. His name was Federico Mariano. And I was pretty then, really, I was. But my family was poor, and his family wouldn't hear of our marrying. Still, we clung together." A smile emphasized her high cheekbones and hinted of lost beauty. Then Sofonisba saw the look of reverie vanish, to be replaced by one of pain. "Then he got the blame-fool idea of joining the imperial militia to go fight the French at Pavia," Rosa continued. "I told him he'd make a poor soldier, ach!" She set down the brush. "He's buried at Sant'Agostino. I put flowers on his grave every Sunday."

"Oh, Rosa!" Sofonisba turned and embraced her tightly. Rosa returned the hug.

"Could I come with you sometime, to put flowers on the grave?"

"No, love," Rosa said firmly.

"Why not?"

"You just can't, that's all." Rosa straightened the brush, comb and other objects on the dressing table. "You know, love, it was all for naught. So many dead young men, and still, wars go on. Now France is fighting Spain. Your father's told you about that."

But the girl did not want to talk about war. "So your dream — "

"Came to nothing. But don't give up on one of your own. And besides, I'm happy here," Rosa said as she opened the velvet drapes around Sofonisba's bed and tied them to the bedposts. Then she pulled back the matching bedcover. Sofonisba climbed into bed, her head heavy, but not with sleepiness. "Good night, my dear Sonia."

"Good night, Rosa."

Sofonisba treasured the story of the lost lover-soldier, and turned the tale over in her mind again and again with wonder, as one might do with a well-cut gem, to study all its facets. She felt privileged that Rosa had entrusted the story to her, and deep sorrow for Rosa's pain. But it was Rosa's firm "no" that stuck most profoundly in Sofonisba's mind; the unmistakable "no" meant to keep her away from a certain grave at Sant'Agostino.

But the girl could not forget. The following Sunday, while the Anguissolas sat in the family pew for Mass at San Giorgio (all except her mother, in confinement as she awaited the birth of her fifth child), Sofonisba began to plot. She returned home with the others, but when no one saw her, she slipped out. She pulled her lace veil down her brow and took an indirect route. At first the sight of all the tombstones at Sant'Agostino made her despair of ever finding Federico Mariano's. She walked around slowly until she saw it, beneath a cypress tree. It was an ordinary stone that told the years of his birth and death and nothing more. She wondered why Rosa had been so adamant about never showing it to her. Then she noticed a second stone, a tiny one close by Federico's with the simple inscription: *Baby Mariano and Marco*. She had barely read it when a sharp voice caused her to jump.

"Sonia!" In dread she turned and faced Rosa, who carried a bunch of flowers.

"Sonia, what *are* you doing here? I said you were not to come here!"

"I — I thought I would be gone before you got here. I'm sorry…"

Rosa stiffened and clutched the flowers tighter. "Sonia, go at once to the cemetery gate and wait for me."

Sofonisba turned and did as she was told. When Rosa met her a quarter of an hour later, the flowers were gone.

"Come on, Sonia, I'll walk you home."

Sofonisba dared not look at Rosa's face, fearing reproach and scorn. Neither said a word as they walked.

When they reached the landing above the first flight of stairs, Sofonisba's mother called to them from the sitting room.

"Sonia, come in here. Where have you been? Nobody had any idea!" Her voice rose and her brown eyes widened. "Was a daughter of mine gallivanting through the streets alone? Or were you pestering Rosa on her day of rest?"

"Please, I beg you, signora, don't be angry," Rosa said before Sofonisba could speak. "I took our Sonia for a walk, to show her my family's parish church, that's all. I should have told you. I am sorry."

Bianca's face softened. "Well, all right. Aaaagh!" Bianca grabbed at her huge belly.

"Mama! Mama!" Sofonisba yelled.

"I'm giving birth, dear daughter, not going deaf," her mother said. She moaned miserably. Rosa offered to help her up to her room.

"I've had enough babies" — *gasp* — "to know there's no time for that. Oooooh!"

"Sonia, run and fetch the midwife," Rosa commanded.

She headed back into the city streets, running through them for the first time in her life. Her corset and long dresses had always discouraged it, and besides, in normal times it was not proper for a young lady. People stopped and stared as she passed. She felt a wrenching in her chest. *Did I bring this on, with my foolish little outing?*

When she returned, her mother, the midwife, and a neighbour woman sequestered themselves in the sitting room. "The others are in the garden," Amilcare said. "Go join them."

But Sofonisba wandered up to her room in a terrified and exhausted daze. It was not long before Rosa found her.

"Rosa! It's my fault that Mama…"

"Sonia, love, it's not your fault. It's the baby's time to be born, that's all." She stroked Sofonisba's hair. "Let's say a prayer. Dear God, please protect the signora in this needful time…"

Later, Sofonisba wrote in her journal.

April 24, 1542

I have yet another little sister, Europa. I call her the Little Bird, because she makes chirpy sounds, and now everyone calls her that. So now I have four younger sisters: Elena, Lucia, Minerva, and today, the Little Bird. If this baby lives, I will have someone else to draw. One of our neighbours, a hardy young woman, just lost her newborn after only two days. It was fearsome because it happened so close to Mama's lying-in… Let Europa thrive, dear Lord, and keep Mama strong, I pray!

CREMONA, SEPTEMBER 1546

Amilcare mounted his horse after morning prayers at San Giorgio. He rode at a slow trot over the cobblestones through his native Cremona, sitting taller on his mount as he dwelled on the city's ancient glory — the place where the poet Virgil had first studied. Now, Cremona stood second in regional importance to Milan, but one thing countered any feelings of civic inferiority — Cremona's pride in the achievements of its painters, sculptors, and architects.

He skirted the main piazza, built when the Romans were drawn to Cremona for its strategic site on the Po River, between Genoa and Venice. The open market bustled. Amilcare inhaled the scents of fruits, vegetables, meat and fish, spices, flowers, and wine. He heard the vendors' songs: "The freshest eggs!" "Get your sweets! Right here!" "Fine leathers for all the family!" At other stalls on the piazza, or in shops that opened onto the market, one could find wool, silk, brocade, fustian, linen, soap, candles. *God provides for us well*, Amilcare thought.

He waved to the banker who had helped him in business and who now sorted and stacked coins that glinted in the sunshine. He called *"Buon giorno!"* to the jeweller and to the pawnbroker — one had served him in good times and the other in days of struggle. Remembering occasional periods of famine, Amilcare felt a certain reassurance when he heard the grain merchants call out in their bartering, and when he caught the aroma of bread from the communal ovens.

He looked up with pride at the Torrazzo, the tallest tower in Italy, with nearly five hundred steps. Standing guard over all, visible for miles, the landmark loomed in the mind of every Cremonese expatriate, like a finger that forever beckoned the native home.

City and countryside lived entwined like choral voices (and this day, at least, in harmony). Amilcare slowed the eager mare so he could better savour the day's beauty. The land surrounding Cremona yielded a prized red clay that formed most of the city's buildings, the same type of clay that had built Siena, so that Cremona was called "the Siena of Lombardy." *Ha* — Amilcare scoffed whenever he heard that — *let Siena be the Cremona of Tuscany!*

He rode by orchards, vineyards, and fertile fields of rye and wheat, where sinewy men and women worked on the harvest. Flax would supply Cremona's linen weavers, and the mulberry trees would feed the worms sent to Venice for the silk trade. Amilcare rejoiced in his good fortune to be riding in comfortable warmth, after the oppressive heat of August but before the autumn rains would turn the road into a sodden mess.

As a superintendent of the church of San Sigismondo, Amilcare often made this short trip to see the progress of the church's decoration. But it was a different and uncommon mission that called him out to the Via Marmolada on this singular morning.

He stopped at the site of a long-gone, primitive chapel where a hundred years before, Bianca Maria Visconti, daughter of the Duke of Milan, married the powerful knight Francesco Sforza. When she died in 1468, Bianca Maria left in her will the money to build the imposing San Sigismondo, where the chapel had stood.

This church is deceptive, Amilcare thought, as he always did upon entering. The building's plain grey stone façade made it look like a simple country chapel, recalling its humble beginnings and befitting its rustic setting. But one step inside swept the visitor into quite another realm.

The nave spread far ahead, so far that the altar and pulpit appeared to form a tiny stage set in an immense theatre. The vaulted ceiling soared fifty feet above on bold Romanesque arches. Lofty round windows lit a scene of quiet diligence: groups of painters and their apprentices were adorning the walls and ceiling with scenes of virgin birth, the multiplication of loaves and fishes, water becoming wine, figures ascending heavenward, resurrection from the dead, and other assorted miracles.

Amilcare removed his velvet cap and spotted Bernardino Campi high up on the scaffolding in the chapel of Saints Filippo and Giacomo, depicting the two on the chapel's vault. *Fresco painting is hard enough without interruptions*, Amilcare thought. *I'd better wait.* He carefully studied the church's other decorations, noting their progress or lack of it, until Campi called a break in his work. The painter let his apprentices descend the scaffolding first; once back on the church's stone floor, they started in on a jug of wine. Then Campi wiped his hands on a paint rag and headed down.

"*Buon giorno*, Amilcare. So good to see you."

"*Buon giorno*, Bernardino." Amilcare gestured into the church's vastness. "This place will be magnificent when it's finished. I'm always awestruck by the skill in here — you, the other Campis, and Boccaccino. And how is the work on the chapel vault going?"

"For once, we're right on schedule. I think that Filippo and Giacomo are watching over me, making sure my portrayal of them does them justice. Would you like to take a closer look?" Campi pointed to the scaffolding ladder.

"Oh, that can wait, Bernardino. I came here to ask you about something — well, about something else." They went into the sacristy, away from the eyes and ears of the apprentices and other painters, and sat down at a small table. The painter unbuttoned his brown smock.

"My eldest daughter, Sofonisba, whom you've met, is quite talented at drawing," Amilcare began. "She took to it like an expert as soon as I handed her chalk and paper. I know you will say this is just a father talking, but she is mature for her age, studious and bright. She was very young when you met her, but she's fourteen now, and I feel she's ready to move on. I want you to take her in hand now."

Campi straightened his back and looked wide-eyed at Amilcare. "Why, I'm already married, Amilcare."

Amilcare rocked back from the table and a great laugh erupted from his noticeable gut. "Good God, man, I'm not offering my daughter in marriage. I want you to teach her to *paint!*" He burst into laughter again, then wiped his eyes with a silk handkerchief. "Oh, Lord in heaven."

Campi laughed, too. "Yes, I remember Sofonisba. She is quite intelligent — used to watch me paint at Sant'Agata all the time. But it's unusual, to say the least, for a woman to paint. And most women painters learn from their fathers."

Amilcare fidgeted in his chair. "She has learned all the usual things a girl of her station is expected to know — reading, needlework, music — she plays the clavichord brilliantly. And she can dance. In fact, her dance master said she dances with such vigour and grace, it's 'like a shower of ladylike sparks.' And there is no better young horsewoman in all the region. I've also provided her with tutors for literature, rhetoric, Latin, French, arithmetic. Some say that's not appropriate for daughters, but I just ignore them. I want her to learn more than I ever did, to never be embarrassed about her mind, as I —" He glanced at the closed door and scratched his grey-haired head. "I couldn't teach her those things myself, and there's no way I can teach her to paint. So I turn to you, Bernardino. You're a young man, and I trust you will not put on airs if I say you're one of the best painters in Cremona. And Sonia admires you." He stopped squirming and sat back with an expectant look.

"Amilcare, you flatter me. But I don't know, I do have plenty of commissions, to take on a student now, really, I don't think —"

"My dear Bernardino," Amilcare said coolly, with a half-smile, "maybe you've forgotten how much you owe me for painting supplies from my shop." He looked Campi in the eye.

"You know I'm good for it!"

"Yes, I know, but if you teach my daughter to paint, the debt just might — vanish."

"So that's it." Campi sat back, hands on hips. "You want to make an arrangement." He let a tense pause grow. "Anyway, you still haven't said *why* you want your daughter to paint."

"I want to do the right thing for a talented daughter. She's too young to marry, and in a convent her talent could wither away. That would be a tragedy. And…" Again Amilcare looked around uneasily.

"What now, pray?"

Amilcare leaned toward Campi. "Although the shop and my investments are going well now, Bernardino, I do have six daughters—"

"Six! I must have lost track of one sometime."

"Yes, daughter number six was born late last year. Anna Maria. My wife and I finally ran out of historical and mythological and family names for the children, so we named this one after the grandmother and mother of Jesus."

"Congratulations. So, go on."

"I love them all beyond words, you understand, but it's expensive to keep them in silk, and later will come the matter of their dowries. But if they can paint, I can bargain for lower dowries, even though the Anguissola nobility is still new. And another reason for Sofonisba to paint is that wealthy people will pay a lot for their portraits, you see…"

"Yes, I do see," the painter sighed.

"So there's something in this for both of us, Bernardino."

The painter gave the father a skeptical look. "And what if I take her on, and it becomes apparent that she is quite incapable of painting?" Campi challenged. "As her father, you can't fathom such an outcome, but what if?"

"Then our arrangement is cancelled, and you'll have to pay your debt in florins instead." Amilcare sat back and crossed his arms. "But I'll have you know I sent one of her sketches to Michelangelo Buonarroti, the Florentine."

"Amilcare! You sent one of your daughter's sketches to *il Divino?*" Campi's mouth gaped open. "You really might be getting ahead of yourself, my friend. Has the Master responded?"

"Not yet," Amilcare said confidently. "Well, will you do it?"

Campi grunted, placed a hand on the back of his neck, and looked up. Then he faced Amilcare. "All right, I'll do it." He sighed again.

"Oh, and did I say you must teach her sister Elena, too?" Amilcare said. "The two of them are inseparable. You'll find she's also good at sketching."

"Two noble young women to teach to paint," Campi said, false brightness in his voice. Then he noticed the small wineskin looped through Amilcare's belt. "Pray, what do you have in there? We simply *must* toast our agreement."

Over Amilcare's wine they settled a few details, then stood and shook hands.

Campi returned to the chapel and clapped twice to rouse the languid apprentices. Some of them were bewildered to hear Campi mutter as he climbed the scaffolding ladder: "The saints are indeed looking out for me."

For Amilcare, a peculiar sensation teased as he remounted his horse. It was not even a complete thought, more like the barest flicker of the mind: that he had just set into motion a force whose overwhelming effects he could not even begin to predict.

"So how much longer, pray, do I have to pose here?" Elena asked Sofonisba as they sat in the garden.

"Just one more minute. I'm doing the lips now, so if you don't talk, it will go faster," Sofonisba replied. She quickly wielded a piece of charcoal in short, careful strokes over handmade paper.

"Every time you want me to be quiet, you say you're doing the lips," Elena said.

"And every time, you keep talking anyway, so if this sketch doesn't resemble you, it's not my fault." She made one final stroke. "There," Sofonisba said, setting down the charcoal and regarding the sketch at arm's length. "I can fill in the rest myself."

Elena relaxed and leaned back on the stone bench, then stretched her legs out in front of her, beneath a sky-blue silk dress. "Sofi, ever since Papa brought you a stack of paper and bits of charcoal from the shop, you've been drawing everybody," she said.

"And what about you? When I started drawing, you did, too. But when I'm your model, I don't squirm half as much as you do." Sofonisba picked up another sheet of paper and began to draw a bed of purple asters. "I'll draw the garden," she said to her sister. "It doesn't move or talk at all."

"Here. Draw *this*." Elena scooped up some dry leaves from the ground and threw them at her sister. Sofonisba, gasping in mock rage, gathered up more and launched them right back. Twigs, dirt, and more leaves flew in both directions as the girls shrieked, until Sofonisba yelled, "Papa!"

The rare sight of Amilcare walking briskly into the morning garden made Sofonisba and Elena pull the foliage out of their hair and brush it off their skirts. "Papa, has something happened?" Sofonisba asked.

"Something wonderful has, my dear." Amilcare settled himself on the bench between his daughters. "I've just been to see Bernardino Campi, the painter. You met him a few years ago, Sonia — you were awestruck by his painting at Sant'Agata. Now you're old enough to learn to paint, and Signor Campi will be your teacher. You'll both take the lessons, because I wouldn't dare try to pry bread and jam apart. Now, this is something you want, isn't it? Both of you?"

Sofonisba jumped up and threw her arms around her father's neck. "Oh, yes, Papa, thank you!"

"Of course, Papa!" Elena said.

"I can see it now," Amilcare said with a faraway look. "When you two are able, you'll train your younger sisters. The Six Painting Anguissola Daughters — it's a magnificent prospect!"

"Uh, maybe *someday*, Papa," Sofonisba said.

"Well, I must get back to the shop, and Mama says your dancing master is arriving soon," Amilcare said, and left the garden.

Sofonisba and Elena laughed at their father's ambition.

"And I'll be the leader of the Six Painting Anguissola Daughters," Sofonisba joked. "Finally I'll get some respect from you and the others."

"Yes, telling us all what to do should come quite easily to you," Elena teased.

Sofonisba and Elena formed a lovely, if contrasting, picture as they walked with Rosa to the home of Bernardino Campi. Elena, with her dark-blond hair uplifted and held by twisted braids and gold pins, and wearing a lavender silk dress, smiled gaily to the friends they passed: *"Buon giorno!"* Sofonisba, wearing a simple black dress, her auburn hair in a single braid wound around the back of her head, just smiled distractedly.

"What's wrong, Sofi? You're so tense. It's so good to get out of that house, even for just a few hours a day. And this could help the family," Elena said.

Ah, Elena, always so practical. "I'm happy, of course, but I'm worried about disappointing Papa."

Elena took her sister's arm. "That's impossible. Papa thinks you can do anything, and besides, you'll be a first-rate painter."

To distract herself from the burden that Elena had unwittingly placed on her, Sofonisba decided to concentrate on the unfolding city. She knew that nearby Milan far overshadowed Cremona, that Ferrara and Mantua had their courts, and Pavia its university. But none of that mattered. Cremona was comfortable, and to walk its narrow streets was like seeing a friend she had known all her life. Sofonisba took in the graceful decorations of the grand churches, patrician houses, and small chapels. She saw elegance in the curves of fountains, in rows of columns, even in the miniature Madonna statues of tiny street-corner shrines. Cremona's beauty meant that a morning walk across the city was worth the frequent annoyance of having to step around garbage, mud, and horse droppings.

That morning, their mother had made herself clear. Bianca impressed upon her daughters that they did not have to learn to paint, and that it was merely a trade, after all.

"But we want to, Mama. And Papa —"

"Oh yes, your Papa. He's got some grand notions, that's for sure. I just don't want you two to be pushed into anything." Bianca sighed. "Well, just behave like the noble young ladies you are."

They passed the church of Sant'Agata. The scaffolding that Sofonisba had climbed had long since been dismantled, and everyone admired Campi's completed frescoes. The sight of Palazzo Cittanova reminded her of that day: *Signor Campi helped me "see" that old building for the first time. That was truly my first art lesson.*

As they walked, the trio inhaled the aroma from a baker's window, heard a troupe of actors sing an off-key invitation to that evening's performance, and silently asked for God's mercy when a funeral procession went by.

They came to a busy piazza, where two young men stood facing each other, sneering and trading insults. The right ankle of one was tied to his opponent's left. A small crowd egged them on.

"Come on, lovies, let's go," Rosa said when Elena and Sofonisba stopped.

"Oh please, couldn't we just watch for a bit?" Sofonisba asked. The crowd at that moment roared when, at a signal from a third man, the two bare-fisted fighters began to pummel each other, their feet locked together all the while. They fought in a fierce little circle, grunting and panting until one of them, the victim of a savage blow to the forehead, fell backward to the ground. The other whooped and raised both his sweaty arms in victory. As half the crowd collected their winnings and the other half grumbled, Sofonisba laughed. "And Papa thinks that we sisters fight hard!" she said to Elena as they walked on.

"So, it took a couple of rowdy young toughs to relax you," Elena said. They had reached Bernardino Campi's doorstep, just as the deep notes of the Torrazzo's bells sounded the hour of nine.

Sofonisba introduced herself, Rosa, and Elena to the woman who answered her knock.

"Oh yes, you must be the two for the painting lessons," the woman said. "So it's today. Do come in. I am Anna, Signor Campi's wife." She led them into the back of the house, where Campi had his studio.

Campi was standing before an easel, engrossed in some portrait detail, and he did not look up until Anna said, "Dear, your students are here. Sofonisba and Elena Anguissola."

"Oh." He set down his brush, wiped his hands, and said, "Come over here," gesturing to a long table. He swept it clear of drawings, chalk, palette knives and paint rags, and Sofonisba, Elena, and Rosa sat down. Anna left the studio, but not before meeting her husband's sullen eye.

"Learning to paint starts with sketching," Campi said, standing at the head of the table. "Forget everything you think you know about that." He looked around the studio. "Here, draw this." He set a large, plain wooden bowl on the table, and gave Sofonisba and Elena parchment and pieces of charcoal. Then he left the room.

Anna found him in his study.

"What are you doing in here, pray? You've got students! You didn't even tell me they were coming today."

"I've given them a drawing task."

"How do you expect to teach them if you hide in here?"

"How, indeed," Campi said indifferently, leaning back in his chair, glancing around the room.

"I know you don't like the idea, but we are in debt to their father, and with another child coming…"

"Ah yes, their father," Campi said. "He thinks his daughters consort with the angels. Especially the older one, Sofonisba. So now I have two dilettante, high-born daughters to try to make painters out of. It's impossible."

"Eh, Nardo, you don't know that. Set aside your childish wounded pride and give them a chance. And don't hold their nobility against them."

"Hmmpf." Campi ran his hand along his short beard. "The Anguissola nobility *is* quite new, after all." He rose and sauntered to the studio.

⌒

That night, Sofonisba recorded the day's events in her journal.

September 16, 1546

Today Elena and I had our first lesson with Bernardino Campi. He is still a young man, but in appearance he has added more than the four years since I met him. He now has a brownish-black beard, the same colour as his moustache and his straight short hair, thinner than before and receding at the temples.

He sat his wife, Anna, down by the fire and told us to draw her. She has a round, full face, and just a bit of black hair showed between her forehead and white cap. I'm afraid a case of nerves overtook me, and my drawing was quite poor — I made Anna's head too large and her eyes too close together. Elena, on the other hand, did a perfectly charming drawing of Anna, capturing her features rather well. At least, that's what I thought. Signor Campi was mild in his criticism of my work, for which I was grateful. As for Elena's drawing, he nodded, said "uh-huh," that it was an adequate likeness. But he could have said more, given her some genuine words of praise.

Next, he arranged some figs just so on a plate and told us to draw that, and he lectured us on perspective and proportion. I do not believe any plate of figs ever received so much attention! I'll never look at figs the same way again, and that, I suppose, is Signor Campi's great wish.

CREMONA, LATE OCTOBER 1546

It was exhilarating for Sofonisba to ride at a determined gallop across the meadow on a black mare, a Barbary horse that Amilcare had ordered from North Africa especially for her. Elena kept up on a roan stallion, while Amilcare and Bianca rode a good stretch behind. The sisters eventually slowed down enough to appreciate the golden glow of the autumn sun, then stopped in the shade of a cypress grove.

"Oh, you're both getting to be too swift for me," Amilcare said when they regrouped.

"Sofi's the clever one on a horse," Elena said. "Go ahead, Sofi, show Papa and Mama something."

"See that hedgerow over there?" Sofonisba said, relishing the prospect. She pointed to a row of shrubs down the meadow. "I'll jump that."

She took off before her parents could issue the usual tedious cautions. As the horse's hooves drummed along, she revelled in the wind, the mare's growing speed, and the moment of flight when she cleared the hedge with an easy grace.

"*Brava*, Sonia! Beautiful, Sofi!" Amilcare and Elena said.

Her mother was silent, her face blank. "Mama?" Sofonisba asked.

Bianca looked tensely into the distance, twisted the reins of her horse, and then looked at Sofonisba. She said stiffly, "Well, you made it," and flashed a tight smile. Then, briskly, she suggested they all head over to the woods to hunt for mushrooms. Turning her horse around, Bianca did not see how her oldest daughter had slumped in the saddle.

When they had a leather bag that bulged with earth-fragrant mushrooms, the foursome began to lope back toward the city. This time the sisters let their parents get a fair distance ahead.

Listening to the larks' song, Sofonisba tried to shake off her mother's coolness. She wondered whether her mother's attitude went beyond the riding of horses. She was comforted when Elena said, "Sofi, don't be too downhearted about Mama. She is always full of misgivings."

Sofonisba nodded. She only half-listened as Elena then chattered on breezily about nothing in particular, but Sofonisba did hear her ask, "Well, Sofi, what do you think of our lessons with Signor Campi now, after six weeks?"

"Sometimes it's hard to know what to think," Sofonisba began. "You did a fine drawing of Signora Anna that first day, and he didn't praise you hardly at all. Then I thought, well, learning to paint is new and strange for us, so maybe it's strange for him, too, to teach us." The city's Porta Nova came into view in the distance. "I feel a certain, I don't know, an indifference from him, not the friendliness I knew when I first met him. But that was years ago, after all. Now he has several small children, and more work and responsibilities." The city gate loomed larger.

"And I do look forward to picking up a paintbrush sometime soon," Sofonisba added.

Elena burst out laughing. "You mean, if you draw one more lemon, loaf of bread, wine flask, or one of Signor Campi's children, you'll scream? Me, too! He said at the beginning that drawing comes before painting. But he knows we've been drawing on our own for years now. When do we get to paint?"

"Yes, we've been drawing a long time, but in just a few weeks he's made us better at it," Sofonisba said.

"Still, we're older than most boys are when they start their apprenticeships," Elena pointed out. "Signor Campi started when he was about ten, right? For us, time is racing by."

The talk was all around Cremona — in the market square, in the grand drawing rooms, in the artists' taverns. Amilcare Anguissola had arranged for painting lessons for his daughters. Some derided it as a waste of time and money, that "everyone knew" women were not capable of painting. Others bemoaned Amilcare and Bianca as parents, saying they had always been too indulgent. Sofonisba and Elena would not get far without a proper apprenticeship, and clearly an apprenticeship was forbidden for daughters of the nobility. The painters of Cremona, however, knew better than to underestimate Bernardino Campi — he was an excellent teacher. A few observers pointed out with malicious pleasure that a woman painter, no matter how skilled, could never create frescoes — of course, they required too much physical labour for a woman.

Campi ground his teeth when Anna entered the studio and told him that Amilcare Anguissola had arrived and wished to see him.

"Amilcare, *buon giorno*, sit down," Campi said, forcing joviality. "I have not seen you in quite a while."

"*Buon giorno*, Bernardino. I know you are busy. I will not take much of your time." Amilcare pulled a letter from inside his jacket. Campi could read the flowing letters of the red seal: MB. "I just received this letter, from Michelangelo Buonarroti, the Florentine," Amilcare said casually.

Campi's eyebrows shot up. "Maestro Buonarroti?"

"The same. I told you some time ago that I sent one of Sonia's sketches to him," Amilcare said. "Now he has responded. The sketch I sent showed a laughing girl. Buonarroti has asked her to try to draw a crying boy. He says that would be more difficult."

"Could I — could I read this letter, pray?" Campi asked.

"Certainly." Campi took the parchment carefully and handled it like a holy relic. He read, then looked squarely at Amilcare.

"The Master is indeed taking an interest in Sonia's development as an artist," Campi said with a touch of awe.

Amilcare smiled with paternal pride. "And how are my daughters doing in your classes?"

"Um, well, they have both improved their drawing skills quite rapidly," Campi said, returning his voice to a businesslike tone. "They may be ready soon to actually try painting. Though I couldn't say exactly when."

As soon as Amilcare had left, Anna approached her husband. "What did Amilcare want?" she asked.

"He wanted me to know that Michelangelo Buonarroti, the greatest of all, is interested in his Sofonisba," Campi said. "It's not just a matter of a proud father's bragging. She must truly have some great gift."

"Couldn't you tell that from looking at her work?" Anna asked.

"Yes of course, her work is quite good, but…"

"But that pride of yours got in the way," Anna finished.

"How could I have … I suppose I overlooked… " Campi said, sitting down. "God sent her to me, and I…"

"Never mind that now," Anna said. "You are a great teacher, when you want to be."

"The Maestro…" Campi said, and shook his head in wonder.

A monstrous odour assailed Sofonisba and Elena at their next lesson, a smell like something that had died in the forest and had been left to rot. Anna chuckled and told them they would get used to it. The sisters were further discouraged when Campi said he suspected that they were eager to try to paint. *"Try?" Why didn't he just say, "to paint?"* Sofonisba wondered. Campi told them they first had to learn how to prepare a wooden panel or a canvas. Sofonisba asked why they could not just start painting on a bare canvas, and Campi replied that the surface was too rough and porous for that. Usually, apprentices or assistants would do such work, but a painter needed to know the steps, he added.

The first layer of preparation was the source of the frightful smell — a glue base called liquid size, made by boiling sheep parchment or dried rabbit skin with powdered white chalk. Campi gave Sofonisba and Elena large brushes and had them apply the mixture in a thin layer onto a stretched canvas. Five more layers of liquid size would follow. Once the liquid size dried, the smell went away.

Next came the priming, a layer of white lead ground in oil. Campi used linseed oil, and it had to be "cooked" until it was just the right consistency. It was thick, and though it was called black oil, it was really dark brown. Sofonisba and Elena brushed it on in a thick, smooth layer.

The oil was also mixed with pigment to make paint. The oil could not be too dark or too light; it had to be mixed with the pigment in a certain proportion, and the leftover oil poured into bottles and tightly sealed. Campi showed the sisters his cabinet of pigments, made by a druggist from minerals, berries, flowers, metals, even insects. Ultramarine, the most precious colour, came from the costly lapis lazuli stone. Campi showed them how to grind the pigments and mix them with the oil. It was hard work, but worthwhile, because it made the glorious colours appear.

While she listened, Sofonisba vowed to herself to paint Campi's portrait some day. *He is much different now from when our lessons started. Somebody has to record those kindly brown eyes.*

On the way home, Elena thought she saw Ercules Vizconti, a man about Sofonisba's age, looking at Sofonisba in what Elena called a "curious" manner.

"Curious? Do you mean curious-strange, or curious as in wanting to know more?" Sofonisba asked.

"Heavens, don't make this a language lesson, Sofi! His look showed great interest in you, that's all. Complimentary interest."

"He was probably looking at you, Elena. You're the beauty."

"No, no, it was you. I'm sure of it. Did you see him, Rosa?"

"I did, but I couldn't say which one of you he was looking at," Rosa said.

"Well, *I'm* sure," Elena said. "Forget it if you want, Sofi, but there it is. And I know very well that you're more excited about learning to paint than about any young man in the world."

"On that, at least, you're right."

At the end of their next lesson, Campi asked Sofonisba and Elena not to come to his house the next day, but to meet him in front of the cathedral. "It's time for a new phase of your instruction," was all he would say.

Sofonisba, Elena, and Rosa crossed the market square the next day and found him waiting under the portico of the cathedral, as promised. He carried a large, flat leather bag. "We'll go inside later. First, let's step back and have a good look."

They moved back to the middle of the square and silently studied the cathedral's façade. The heat of the day soon made Sofonisba impatient. Finally Campi asked her, "Now, Sofonisba, if you were going to paint a picture of this cathedral, what colours would you use?"

Painting! Could it be about to happen at last? "White, of course."

"And what else?" Campi prodded.

"Rose pink, grey, violet, brown!"

"That's better. And what shapes, Elena?"

"Squares and rectangles for the building stones. A circle for the rose window. Verticals, long and short, for the many columns. A triangle for the pediment, like our Greek forebears."

Campi smiled. "Very good. You have been listening while I've droned on about design and form. Now look at this lion." He pointed to one of the marble lions holding up a pillar in the portico. "What is the lion grasping?"

"A snake!" They had never noticed.

"Yes, and your noble family name means 'the lone snake'. Your father once told me that the Anguissola motto is, 'the lone snake is victorious…'" Campi said, "um, but the lion seems to have gotten the better of this one…"

Sofonisba and Elena giggled tentatively, and Campi let out a big laugh. "Sofonisba, Elena, please, from now on, call me Signor Bernardino," and all the icy formality between teacher and students melted away.

"Now let's go in. I want you to see the artistic tradition you're joining."

After the lively market square outside, the cathedral's majestic silence slowed their feet and heartbeats. The three women followed Campi part of the way down the nave.

"So many painters left their mark here," Campi said. "These scenes above the arches, of the lives of the Virgin and Jesus, were done by Boccaccio Boccaccino, Altobello Melone, Girolamo Romanino and others. But there is one work I especially want to show you." He pointed back toward the entrance, at a fresco above it depicting the Crucifixion.

"That's by Giovanni de' Sacchis." Sofonisba noticed that Campi did not so much say the name as breathe it out with reverence. "We always called him *il Pordenone*, after his hometown in the Veneto. With Giorgione and Maestro Buonarroti for inspiration, he in turn influenced all the painters of Cremona. Look at that roiling sky, and that crack in the earth, which that soldier and a horse are in danger of falling into, and the way the three crosses stand at discordant angles. What drama and unease *il Pordenone* projects!"

Sofonisba found herself caught up in Campi's enthusiasm. She listened closely as he led them around the cathedral, pointing out other great frescoes, and altarpieces in the side chapels. When they had made a circle and returned to the entrance, Campi fetched some chairs from the vestibule.

"I'm sure you're both tired of drawing household objects and my children. So now, choose some figure or detail within this fresco, and draw it," he said, pointing toward *il Pordenone's Crucifixion*. He pulled drawing tools from his leather bag. Sofonisba and Elena placed the boards on their laps and began to work, while Rosa went off to light a candle.

Sitting on the edge of her bed, holding a drawing board on her lap, Sofonisba held the black chalk tentatively above the bluish white paper. "Sometimes you just have to plunge right in," Signor Bernardino had said. Occasionally glancing in the mirror, Sofonisba began at the top, outlining the crown of her head, then the curve of her right cheek, her chin, and finally her left jaw. Next, she drew her centre-parted hair and her left ear. She wanted to show some maturity in this self-portrait, so she gave her face a serious expression and large eyes. The bodice of her dress had a high neck, allowing a bit of lace from her chemise to be visible above. The stylish sleeves were full at the shoulder and tapered to cuffs revealing more lace. The book she placed in her left hand further conveyed dignified maturity — at least, that was what she intended.

She usually worked with Elena in their studio in the afternoon, but for this self-portrait assignment, Sofonisba wanted solitude. She struggled with the hands, finding them hard to outline. After a few muddled attempts, she set the drawing board aside and leaned back against the headboard. From that angle her window allowed a narrow view of Cremona, just a bit of rooftop below a patch of sky. *Ercules Vizconti*, she mused. *Is he my destiny? Papa wants us to paint because we can make money, and the skill would be* part of our dowries. But what if a husband forbade us from painting? We would have to stop. Our love for painting may mean we wouldn't want to marry, because marriage just might yank the paintbrush out of our hands! Mama doesn't want us to paint unless we like it, or maybe not at all, I'm not sure. Oh, it's all too complicated…

The tolling of the bells of San Giorgio signalled the time for evening prayers.

Sofonisba and her father were sitting in his study late in the afternoon, talking about her painting lessons, when her mother appeared in the doorway. "Sonia dear, I need to talk to your father," Bianca said.

On the landing outside the study, Sofonisba glanced back and was surprised to see that her mother had not closed the door.

"I'm not sure I like this at all," Bianca was saying to her husband. "All of Cremona is chattering endlessly about the strangeness of young noblewomen being taught to paint. I don't want my daughters to be objects of curiosity."

Sofonisba knew she should continue down the stairs, but she could not.

"No, I don't want that either," she heard Amilcare say. Then there was a soft *whump* as he closed his ledger. "But we can't let that stop us. As long as they carry themselves with dignity, the town busybodies will soon find something else to gossip about. Both girls have some talent. Can we let that go unexplored?"

"Amilcare, my lord, we've been married for fifteen years. I know you too well to believe that you're only concerned about developing their talents. You also want them to make money," Bianca said, her voice taking on an edge. "If only you — if only our finances were better…"

There was a short silence. "I wish that the thought of my daughters earning money had never entered my mind, and in a mere trade at that," Sofonisba heard her father say. "But I'm afraid we must think of it. I worry every day about how I'll provide them with dowries."

"I worry about that too," Bianca said, and Sofonisba thought her heart would break at the sad tone of her mother's voice. "But that is not my biggest worry. I am afraid that something will *happen* to them. Not just their own safety, but their reputations. If those are ruined, there will be no dowries to worry about."

"Other women have painted. A few, anyway."

"I don't care. They were not my daughters." A pause. Her mother's voice strained higher: "My lord, can't you see it? For women to paint is … well, it's just *unfitting*. It's just plain wrong."

Sofonisba covered her mouth to stifle a gasp. *Mama — oh, please no —*

Her heart pounded in anguish as she stumbled down to the garden. She sat on a bench and buried her face in her hands. Minerva and Europa, playing with the dog at the other end of the garden, paid her no attention.

Bianca's words stung deeply. *"Unfitting." So I am letting Mama down, as I thought! But Holy Virgin, I cannot stop painting now.*

Soon she was aware of the sudden absence of shrieks and barking, and she lifted her head to see Minerva and Europa standing before her with frightened looks. "Sonia, what's wrong?"

Sofonisba straightened and tried to smile. "Come here, my loves," she said, and pulled her sisters close, one arm around each. "Nothing's wrong, nothing at all."

"Then why is your face all red?" Even at just seven years, Minerva's grey eyes could pierce a brick wall.

"I was thinking about some silly grown-up things, nothing to trouble you," Sofonisba said. "Now where's that dog run off to? Let's find him!"

Campi told Sofonisba that she seemed distracted, but she calmed him with a joke and put on a show of diligence. She did feel as if a shadow had fallen across her efforts. She wanted to grab her mother and force her to understand, to accept, to turn away from disdain. She longed for her mother to feel the thrill of painting that Campi had once described and that Sofonisba had already sensed for herself. She tried to win over her mother by showing her some small practice paintings she had done, explaining how she did them, and while Bianca was attentive, Sofonisba sensed a reserve, a distinctly noncommittal tone: "Yes dear, I see. My, you certainly do work hard" was her mother's cool response. Sofonisba then tried the opposite tack, telling her mother nothing about the lessons. She could not be sure, but she thought that her mother seemed happier that way. For Sofonisba, however, the deep unease remained.

Sofonisba and Elena sat in the studio, each at her easel, struggling with Campi's latest assignment—a portrait of the Virgin and Child. "Signor Bernardino's had us painting portraits of his wife, his children, our parents, our sisters, each other, ourselves, and now the Virgin and Child. Before that, it was objects." Sofonisba set down her brush. "But did you ever take a good look at his *San Giacomo* in San Sigismondo, or Bernardino Gatti's Christ figure in his *Resurrection* in the cathedral?"

"Yes, what about them?"

"Well, what is it you remember?"

Elena, her brow furrowed, said, "Well, in the *San Giacomo*, he is holding a huge book, and he's all draped in huge folds, and in the *Resurrection*, Our Lord is also heavily draped, arms uplifted as he floats to heaven. But what a dull game this is, Sofi! Pray why are you asking?"

"They're not entirely wrapped up," Sofonisba said, and smiled mischievously.

"No, they're not. The *San Giacomo* fresco reveals his bare back, and the Christ figure shows his chest."

Then Elena, too, began to smile. "Flesh, and muscle," she said calmly. "Is that what you're getting at, dear sister?"

"Exactly. Signor Bernardino has never shown us how to paint flesh, or even to draw it, except for faces and hands."

Elena giggled. "Well, how could he? Who could be the model? I can just see it. One day we walk into his studio, and you say, 'Signor Bernardino, we'd like to learn to paint human flesh and muscle, so please take off your clothes.'" They both dissolved into gales of laughter.

"So we can't wait for Signor Bernardino to teach us," Sofonisba said. "There's only one other way." The sisters looked into each other's eyes for only a moment. And then Sofonisba bolted the studio door and closed the shutters, while Elena lit two lamps.

They unlaced the back of each other's bodices and drew them off, then stepped out of their brocade skirts and underskirts. Their white chemises popped over their heads and to the floor. That left only their corsets, and neither hesitated.

They took turns posing and sketching each other's bodies: breasts, bellies, buttocks, backs, and thighs. They observed the curves and valleys, and shifted poses to vary the light and shadow. Sofonisba told Elena that she had the loveliest breasts in Cremona, and that she hoped to do them justice. Elena said that her drawing was the only way Sofonisba would ever see the roundness of her behind.

As they were looking over each other's work, a knock at the door made their faces light up with identical horror. "Sonia, Elena?"

"It's Mama!" Elena whispered.

"Why do you have this door bolted?" Bianca asked. The sisters could hear her jiggling the door handle.

Sofonisba, still naked, spoke through the closed door. "Mama, Signor Bernardino gave us a difficult assignment, and we didn't want Lucia and the others wandering in here," she said.

"Oh. All right. I just wanted to remind you two about your French lesson this afternoon."

"Yes, Mama." Sofonisba and Elena heard their mother walk away. Then the gales of laughter blew once again.

After that, feeling refreshed, they dressed, and sat down once more at their easels. Still, neither moved to pick up a brush.

"Now I wonder what good it is," Elena asked. "What use is it for us to know how to draw the curve of a woman's breast, or the slope of her calf? We'll never paint nudes. The scandal would ruin us."

"Always the practical one," Sofonisba said. "No, we may never paint nudes, as Titian does, but we still need to know about the human body. Even if everyone we ever paint is fully dressed. To get the drape of a garment right, it helps to have drawn what's underneath. And we can paint nude infants, like the Christ child, for instance."

"Infants don't have a lot of muscles for us to worry about," Elena said.

"Who knows? The church might change its attitude, and you and I will be able to paint bare-breasted Madonnas some day."

"Sofi! That would be blasphemous," Elena said. "So what do we do with these?" She pointed to the pile of drawings.

Sofonisba stoked the coals in the small fireplace, making the flames jump. She took a last glance at her depictions of Elena's pulchritude, then rolled up one of the sheets and twisted it. She placed it in the fire.

"Awww," Elena said softly, then carried her own forbidden drawings over to the fireplace. When the day's efforts were ashes, Elena opened the shutters and returned to the unfinished but fully clothed Virgin on her easel. Sofonisba remained in a chair by the fire.

"Sofi? What is it?"

Sofonisba pinned up a loose strand of hair. "Well, drawing each other's nudity was helpful, but we've still never sketched nude *men*."

"Oh Sofi...."

3.

Cremona

Within my breast I feel alight,
A new delight,
Because I hear the summons of the Muse,
And I must follow; if I fall
(Heeding her call)
My eagerness must be my excuse!
　　　　　　　—Isabella Andreini (1562-1604)

CREMONA, JANUARY 9, 1549

The Cremonesi had always been exceedingly proud to have the tallest bell tower on the peninsula. But the full beauty and advantage of that fact had never been so vivid as on the day the sacristan cried from the top, "I see them! They're almost here!" and the excitement level in the streets below leaped up another notch.

On that signal, two hundred *cavalieri* rode out of the city, all wearing red velvet berets with white feathers, red jackets, stockings and boots, and gold medallions around their necks. Along with a band of pipers and drummers, they went to meet Prince Philip of Spain, heir to the Habsburg throne that ruled Cremona and the rest of Lombardy. He would stay briefly in the city as part of a long tour of the European domain he would one day rule but had never seen — at age twenty-one he had never been outside Spain and knew nothing about European geography. This ignorance disturbed his father, the well-travelled Holy Roman Emperor Charles V. His remedy was a long journey for his son, from Valladolid, where the future king was born, to Italy via Genoa, then on through Milan to Germany and the Netherlands. Philip would join Charles in Brussels, capital of the Habsburg Netherlands, and there Charles would continue the careful cultivation of his heir.

The announcement of the royal visit months before had convulsed Cremona. As Philip had never seen his inheritance, so his future subjects had never seen him. The city plunged into plans for lavish festivities. Although some Cremonesi harboured impatience if not resentment over Spain's control of Lombardy, local pride and royal protocol demanded that the city present to Philip an impressive spectacle. Besides, everybody loved a good joust.

An army of artists was recruited to design and build many splendours, including triumphal arches for Philip to pass through on his city tour. Bernardino Campi would paint large military scenes as backdrops for the pageants planned for Philip's entertainment.

"I'll need you both to help me," he told Sofonisba and Elena. "All my other commitments must wait. We'd better start now."

"Now? The prince doesn't arrive for four months!" the sisters protested.

"Yes, now. We don't want to create anything less than stellar work. Every artist's workshop in Cremona is trying to outdo every other."

The horses in the prince's entourage of fifty wore nearly as much silk and brocade as their riders. The sound of fifes and drums set the tempo as the city's welcoming delegation, Amilcare Anguissola among them, led the royal group into Cremona through the Porta San Luca. The simple stone portal was wide enough for five horses and riders to pass through side by side. Artists had transformed it by adding equestrian figures of Philip and his father, life-sized portraits of their patron saints, various angels and cherubs, and the Habsburg coat of arms. A dozen Castilian flags in red and yellow framed the arch, but hung limply in a desultory winter breeze — the rare, flat note in a song of enthusiasm.

The prince and his horsemen and the Cremonese *cavalieri* rode past façades draped with red and yellow bunting and balconies full of the cheering and the merely curious. In the city's San Giorgio district, the Anguissola sisters, their mother, and their servants crowded onto the third-floor balcony and tossed flowers as the prince rode by in stately cadence on a white horse. Their observations tumbled together: "Oh, there he is ... He looks more Nordic than Spanish ... Did you see that he's blond and has a strong chin ... He's fairly handsome ... A king doesn't have to be handsome ... Well, he's not king yet!..."

Running down to the street, the household joined the crowd that flowed with the procession under a triumphal arch and into the cathedral square before finally rolling to a stop. The crowd completely filled the piazza and packed every available balcony. A few even tried to see and hear from the top of the Torrazzo.

The piazza was adorned, like the rest of the prince's route, in yellow, red, purple, and gold. A silver-painted pyramid two stories tall, to hark back to the ancients, and yet another triumphal arch, stood at the base of the Torrazzo. Near them stood a bronze statue of a helmeted woman seated on a lion, to symbolize Cremona. She wore a gorgon's head on her breast, and at her feet, fluttering blue silk streamers represented the Po River.

Everyone watched the prince as he dismounted and stepped onto the platform, where he and the bishop greeted each other with a stiff embrace. The bishop then thanked God for Philip's safe arrival and for sending Cremona such an illustrious visitor. After an uncomfortable delay that caused the horses (and not a few Cremonesi) to stomp and snort with impatience, the head of the Cremona council took the stage. Relishing such a large audience, he made a florid welcoming speech, just long enough to dissipate more of the crowd's energy and enthusiasm and to cause a restless murmur. When an infant began to wail inconsolably, the murmur changed to laughter, and the councillor cut short his speech.

The procession regained its vigour when, along with most of Cremona, it surged out of the city to a field where for months, dozens of young men had been perfecting their jousting techniques, determined to claim the garland of victory.

Sofonisba and her family filed into the front row of the wooden stands. But before any thundering of hooves, tradition required the ritual hurling of flags. No outdoor display of bravado could begin without this show of civic pride. While horns blared and drummers drummed, the Anguissolas watched as young men in colourful, wide-sleeved shirts and stockings filed onto the field waving flags the size of bedsheets on long poles. Each flag bore the coat of arms for one district of the city. In an intricate, precisely regulated pattern, the men tossed the flags high over their heads in dizzying whirls. The spectators hooted and howled, each in support of their own district. Sofonisba noted that every time Philip clapped politely, his large group of travelling companions followed his lead.

She leaned forward when the joust was announced. The mounted and armoured competitors began with ring spearing. Each rider galloped around the edge of the field and tried to thread long lances through dangling bronze rings. A trumpet fanfare accompanied the winner as he removed his helmet, and with a dazzling smile, gallantly placed his collection of rings at Philip's feet.

Finally, one after another throughout the chilly afternoon, as horses snorted, lances were held poised, and the crowd reeled on edge, pairs of riders in armour took turns galloping toward each other in an effort to knock their opponents off their mounts. Various horsemen fell to defeat until the contest narrowed down to two. In a sudden unearthly silence, the two riders took their places at opposite ends of the field. A drumroll sounded. All eyes focused on the prince as he lifted a small Castilian flag. He pulled the flag down sharply, and the riders charged toward each other.

Sofonisba felt her heart pound along with the horses' hooves until *thwulk!* A decisive blow to the chest thrust one horseman backward to the muddy ground amid screams and cheers. The trumpets blasted their congratulations.

The winner, still mounted, circled back to confirm that his opponent was still alive. Satisfied, the victor removed his helmet and waved to the throng. He accepted a garland of carnations from a beautiful young woman and placed it around his neck. He rode up to where the prince sat applauding in the grandstand and bowed his head.

Then the horseman's eyes seemed to search the crowd. "Sofi, it's Ercules Vizconti, and he's coming this way!" Elena jumped up and down and grabbed her sister's arm.

Ercules trotted over to where the Anguissola family stood in the grandstand and nodded at Amilcare, who nodded back. Ercules then shifted his intense gaze to Sofonisba and smiled broadly. He removed his gloves and plucked a red carnation from his victory garland. "To the fairest lady in the crowd," he said, handing the carnation to Sofonisba. The horde, which had never stopped its cheering and clapping, intensified its clamour.

Sofonisba smiled back, took the carnation and said, "I am honoured, sir." Ercules paused a moment, then turned to acknowledge a mob of well-wishers that had surrounded him and his horse.

All the Anguissola sisters began to talk at once. "Oh, Sonia, how exciting! The winner of the joust chose you! It's *beyond* thrilling! What a handsome, gallant young man! Did you see that smile? How absolutely, fantastically *romantic!*"

Elena asked Sofonisba whether she was finally convinced that Ercules Vizconti had his eye on her.

"Yes, I suppose he does," Sofonisba said calmly, sniffing her carnation.

"Is that all you can say?"

"What else can I say? We don't know a thing about him."

"Oh yes, we do. The Vizconti family has been around for ages. Their nobility goes back much further than ours. Ercules stands to inherit pots of money." Elena ticked off the young man's other qualities on her fingers. "We know he's handsome, an excellent horseman, a brave competitor, and a gallant suitor. You could do far worse."

Sofonisba chuckled. "Well, this is a change. For once, you look at the romantic as well as the practical side of something."

"Ach, you're hopeless." Elena shook her head.

It fell to the nobility of Cremona to accommodate the prince's retinue, and the houseguest of the Anguissolas was the duke of Alba, the prince's closest adviser. Alba had served Philip's father as both diplomat and soldier, and in Spain he was the indispensable aide who supervised court ceremonies, appointments, and discipline.

Later that evening the Anguissola housekeeper announced, "Signore and signora, Fernando Álvarez de Toledo, His Grace the duke of Alba," and into the sitting room stepped a grim-faced man of about forty years. He held his back straight as a fencepost, a posture that gave him the appearance of looking down censoriously on all around him. He was dressed for the reception in short padded breeches of dark blue with gold embroidery and a matching jacket, and white silk hose. The family had hosted countesses, bishops, and other dukes before, but Sofonisba could not remember the last time a guest had been "announced" in this way. She looked around at the unconcealed curiosity in her sisters' faces.

Amilcare stepped forward. "Your Grace, good evening, I am Amilcare di Annibale Anguissola. It is a pleasure to see you again after our brief meeting this morning. Welcome to my home. I hope it suits you and your retinue. If there's anything at all you need, do come to me."

"You are most gracious, Signor Anguissola, and your home is more than adequate." Alba spoke with a certain reserve, but in perfect Italian, which impressed Sofonisba.

"I only regret that your visit must be so short," Amilcare said.

"Yes, we'll be leaving tomorrow, at dawn," Alba said with some relief, and clutched his fine leather gloves.

Amilcare introduced Bianca, then Lucia and Elena in turn, adding: "Along with her sister Elena, my eldest here, Sofonisba, is a painter."

"Indeed? Not one but two young women painters in the same household," Alba said. Sofonisba thought she could detect calculation and intrigue in his expression. She stored away in her memory his long moustachioed face and his beard that separated to form two points.

Before Sofonisba could say anything, Bianca announced: "Enough talk about painting. It is time to meet the prince."

Sofonisba and Elena gasped when they entered the normally plain stone reception hall of Palazzo Cittanova. Their eyes reflected the tall candles that blazed high along bunting-covered walls. Candelabra cast a shine on their best silks and made their jewellery sparkle at their throats and earlobes. Dozens of other noble ladies and gentlemen floated around in a regatta of finery: the men wore fresh feathers in their caps, and the women had entwined their uplifted hair with strings of pearls and gems. The Anguissola girls quickly noticed that everyone radiated with perfume.

Sofonisba felt the energy and cheer in the air, infused by the light melodies played by the prince's own minstrels, brought along on the journey to serve his ardent love of music.

While the guests began to form a line to meet the prince, Sofonisba told Elena, "Now remember what we talked about. Curtsy,
like we practiced, when you are introduced to the prince, do not
speak until he does, and don't chatter on. And stand up straight."

"In this new corset, what else can I do?" Elena said, and let loose
a fit of nervous giggling.

"I should take you home right now," Sofonisba said, but there was
no time, because the line was already moving toward Prince Philip.

"Your Royal Highness, this is my wife, Bianca Ponzone, daughter
of Count Ponzino Ponzone," Amilcare said. The three of them
exchanged pleasantries, each in their native languages. Alba hovered by the prince, filling in when a word did not quite leap the
gap. Then Sofonisba heard her father say, "And this is my eldest
child, Sofonisba."

Sofonisba curtsied and then stood tall, to take a good look at her
future sovereign. The promised monarch of Christendom wore a
high velvet hat over sandy blond hair. When he kissed her hand,
Sofonisba noticed his full lips, a typical Habsburg trait.

"Sofonisba," he said. "Were you named after an ancient Car-
thaginian heroine?"

"Indeed I was, Your Royal Highness. It means I must strive to
imitate her literary and musical knowledge, charm, and cleverness."
She was struck by the paleness of Philip's skin and the precise trim
of his short, pointed beard and moustache.

"Ah, and not her tragic end, one would dearly hope," Philip said.
Then he seemed quite at a loss for words, his dark grey eyes darting.
Sofonisba could hardly bear the awkward pause.

"My daughter is a painter," Amilcare interjected.

The prince's face brightened. "That's excellent, signorina!"

"Thank you, Your Royal Highness. Yes, I am studying painting."

"I, too, have been interested in painting, since childhood. When
I was thirteen, I had a book made with large sheets of blank paper,
so I could sketch and paint in it." He had a faraway look for a

moment. "The results were quite unremarkable, but I enjoyed it. Ah, so what is it that you paint, signorina?"

"Portraits, sir, and devotional canvases. I have an excellent teacher, Signor Bernardino Campi."

"And where will painting take a young woman, I pray?" Philip asked, wrinkling his broad forehead.

"I don't know, sir, but it is the thing I most love to do." She was afraid she had annoyed him by saying too much, but she relaxed when he smiled.

"It has been a distinct pleasure to meet you, Signorina Anguissola."

"The pleasure has been mine, Your Royal Highness."

Amilcare next introduced the prince to Elena, as the line advanced: "And my second daughter also paints…"

The sumptuous dinner was marred only by a chicken that escaped from the kitchen and ran, fluttering and squawking, nearly the whole length of the banquet hall, until a chef's apprentice managed to grab it. After a pageant for the prince's amusement, the daughters rode home in the family's carriage through dark and bolted streets. *It's like another world, this night world,* Sofonisba thought, one she had never experienced outside her family's palazzo.

Elena and Sofonisba sat on Sofonisba's bed.

"It was surely the grandest, loveliest thing that ever happened in Cremona. So many jewels in one place!" Elena sighed.

"The backdrops for the pageant — the ones we helped paint — they came out quite well," Sofonisba said. "But in all the excitement, I wonder if anyone noticed them. I do wish our teacher could have been there."

"I was so envious of the easy way you spoke to our handsome prince. I think he had much more that he wanted to say to you, but the line had to move on," Elena said. "And you looked so beautiful."

"Elena, you were by far the most beautiful woman in the room," Sofonisba said. "I was envious of *you!*" They laughed and talked until a knock sounded at the bedroom door. It was their mother, who had just returned.

"Sofonisba, go down to your father's study. He wants to talk to you — he says it can't wait until morning."

"I had a feeling you wouldn't be asleep yet," Amilcare said as Sofonisba entered his study. "I just had to tell you what an impression you made on Prince Philip! There, in the receiving line — you completely charmed him! I introduced him to many people tonight, and you're the only one he spoke warmly to. A *distinct pleasure* to meet you, he said." Amilcare undid the top button of his jacket. "You see, toward everyone else, the prince was withdrawn and guarded, almost cold. People complained about that in Milan. And in Genoa, they were happy when he left. But then he comes to Cremona, and it's my daughter who breaks through the royal barrier! It's *too* splendid! I've never been so proud!"

Suddenly the thrills of the long day caught up with Sofonisba, and fatigue washed over her. She could only smile weakly and say, "I'm glad, Papa."

"Now run off to bed, my dear."

Elena had waited for her. "Well? What did Papa want?"

"Oh, nothing, he just said I charmed the prince, or something like that. Really, it could have waited till morning."

"Just as I said. Well, good night." Elena started to leave the room.

"Wait. Remember when we were little, and we shared a room?" Sofonisba asked.

"Yes, and then in your ninth year or so, you insisted on having your own room, and threw me out."

"Let's share again, just for tonight."

"All right."

Bianca had waited outside Amilcare's study. "So what, pray, was so important that you had to keep our Sonia from her bed even later tonight?"

"I just had to tell her that the prince was so taken by her," Amilcare said. "It could bode well for her future. Philip will hold great power some day."

"Amilcare, honestly! Now you imagine our Sonia consorting with princes? What rubbish! And I still do not want my daughters to paint. Painting is work for ragged, uncouth..." She struggled for the words. "*Labourers!* Not for my noble daughters." She glared at her husband and folded her arms.

"But my dear, Bernardino Campi says that Sonia is extremely gifted. You know that she's clever and beautiful. You don't have to worry about our Sonia."

"But I *do*. And I despair."

"You've both learned so much," Signor Bernardino said to Sofonisba and Elena at the end of their lesson, as they put away their canvases, cleaned the brushes and palettes, and gathered up the scattered paint rags. "It's been three years now that I've been teaching you. And now I have something important to tell you."

Sofonisba and Elena, still in their smocks, stood before him with puzzled looks. Campi took a deep breath. "I've been called to Milan by the governor, Ferrante Gonzaga, to paint portraits of his family. I'll be leaving in a fortnight, and I expect to be there a long while."

The three held a stunned pause, like actors who had forgotten their lines. Then Sofonisba stuttered, "Signor Bernardino, I ... I..."

She suddenly remembered her manners. "Congratulations on this great honour, signore. To paint in the governor's household…well done!" She forced herself to smile.

"So you're leaving Cremona," Elena said, trying to grasp the news. "I too congratulate you, Signor Bernardino."

Campi said that he would suggest to their father that he hire Bernardino Gatti, the one they called *il Sojaro,* to continue their lessons. "He's an excellent painter — he did that *Ascension of Christ* on a vault in San Sigismondo."

"But we'll miss you," Sofonisba asserted, fearing the awkwardness of the words, but fearing more to leave them unsaid. "You were our first teacher, and have become our friend. I know Signor Gatti is very good, but still."

"This is difficult for me, too," Campi said. "Before I go, there's something I want you both to know." He picked up a paintbrush and rolled it absently between his hands. "I was, well, reluctant to teach you at first. I thought you two were flighty young noble-women, mere dabblers, and I certainly didn't need pupils like that in my studio. Your father made, shall we say, a strong argument, and he persuaded me. It took a while, and a push from Buonarroti, the Florentine, to wake me up to your abilities and serious minds. Now I am glad to have been your teacher."

"So that's why our first lessons were so, I don't know, so stiff and cold," Sofonisba said. "And you were so — pardon me for saying — distant. I've wondered about that."

Campi set down the paintbrush. "So now you know. Remember the first day we met, Sonia? I told you then that a painter must travel. Now I'm going away, and you, too, have many travels ahead of you. And so do you, Elena."

No one could think of anything more to say. Sofonisba and Elena hung up their smocks. "Well, we'd better be going along now," Sofonisba said. "Good day, Signor Bernardino. We will be back tomorrow." *But our tomorrows are numbered now,* she thought.

⌒

"Mama, Signor Bernardino is moving his household to Milan," Sofonisba said when they returned home.

"Oh, so will you have no more painting lessons?" Bianca asked. To Sofonisba's dismay, the question sounded much too hopeful.

"Well actually, Mama, he suggested that Papa hire another teacher. He would be another Signor Bernardino — Signor Gatti," Sofonisba said.

"Oh, I see," Bianca said in a low tone. Sofonisba felt helpless.

Then, in an excited rush Bianca asked, "But do you think you really should continue, I mean, do you both *want* to?"

Sofonisba dreaded the direction of the conversation. "Yes, Mama, at least *I* want to. On the first day I met Signor Bernardino, he said painting is the greatest thrill in the world, and although I still have a long way to go, I've come to agree with him."

Bianca looked tired. "Oh … well, what about you, Elena? Do you want to continue your painting lessons?"

"Yes, Mama, I do," she said.

"Well then." Bianca shifted in her chair, making a rustle of brocade. "Your father is determined, and you both seem to enjoy it." She sighed heavily. "So that's that, I suppose. Of course I'll have to meet this Signor Gatti before I send my daughters to his studio." She stood up. "And now I have to go see what the cook is doing with those skinned rabbits she bought." She left the sitting room.

"Elena, just now, your 'yes' sounded rather unenthused," Sofonisba said to her sister.

"I *do* want to continue my lessons," Elena said. "I just didn't want to confront Mama. You're braver than I am. Anyway, I can't let you traipse around painters' studios without me." She gave her sister a tiny smile.

"All right, dear sister."

⌒

Signor Gatti was older than Signor Campi by twenty-seven years — the Greybeard, Elena secretly called him, for his curly grey beard and the ring of grey hair around his baldness. His home was larger than Campi's and in a finer section of Cremona, and his studio was also bigger, befitting a more established painter. He impressed Sofonisba and Elena with his vast collection of brushes of all sizes and materials, arrayed in colourful ceramic jars in tidy rows, and samples of every pigment, even the treasured lapis lazuli.

With his professional manner and achievements, Gatti had pushed painting out of the realm of craft and made it more honourable and prestigious. No one would ever call Signor Gatti a mere tradesman.

"I began by studying Correggio of Parma's work, and that's where I'll start with you," he told Sofonisba and Elena. He showed them a series of drawings, among them women of unusual voluptuousness. "You can see the influence of Raphael of Urbino, and Leonardo, the great Florentine. Now, Leonardo invented a technique that he named *sfumato*, that is, it diminishes and seems to evaporate."

He led them to his easel to demonstrate. "*Sfumato* means to create transitions between light and dark that are imperceptible." He quickly painted a woman's head, then used his finger to blend the corners of her eyes into shadows, creating a softness. "Erase outlines, have no sharp separations of form or colour, no brushstrokes. Leonardo did this especially well with *La Gioconda* — the corners of her eyes and mouth are indistinct. Now you try it."

It was the first of many challenges that Signor Gatti posed for Sofonisba and Elena, leading them further into painting, expanding their range of techniques. He taught them to mix colours and shades they had never imagined. He also told them how to put a posing subject at ease, how to select the proper frame for a painting, and how to set a fair price for their work. He took them to obscure Cremona churches where they could copy frescoes and paintings in peace. Both sisters soon had much to distract them from the sadness of losing Signor Campi.

Every August brought intense sunlight of such a soporific quality that all of Cremona's commerce and traffic slowed considerably; indeed, anyone who could, fled to the cooler countryside. Merchants across the city opened only in the morning. Streets were nearly deserted from then until late evening, when people emerged from the shade to take a brief walk.

At mid-month the Cremonesi briefly abandoned this slower pace to celebrate Ferragosto, the feast of the Assumption of the Virgin. Sofonisba always wondered where the energy came from, after so many summer days of sunstruck indolence. Church bells reverently proclaimed the hour of six, then joyously rang again to announce the feast, and the Cremonesi formed a raucous river flowing toward the cathedral square to begin the annual procession.

At the head of the line, a young priest carried the Grand Cross, a treasure two arms long, made of gold and trimmed with silver plate. Next, following the bishop, men in white satin robes carried a Madonna statue on their shoulders. Priests and nuns followed, and then came the musicians wearing the colours of their city districts. The people of Cremona sang hymns to the Virgin, songs whose solemnity did not diminish the festive atmosphere. Some people were dressed as angels or saints, and some carried silk banners with devotional pictures. Trailing last were stilt walkers, jugglers, and other entertainers. The procession continued along the Po River until it reached a field where a feast of roasted wild boar would be prepared, and where the volume of red wine consumed would nearly rival the water volume of the Po.

As soon as the Anguissola family reached the field, Amilcare joined a group of men, Bianca chatted with some women friends, and Sofonisba accompanied her sisters and their maids to the part of the field where minstrels, jugglers, and puppeteers performed. Standing at the edge of the crowd with Rosa, laughing at the show, Sofonisba felt a sudden shadow behind her. She turned and faced Ercules Vizconti.

"Good evening, Signorina Anguissola," Ercules said. "I hope you are enjoying the feast."

In the second that she paused, Sofonisba took in his straight dark hair and deep brown eyes under a black velvet cap. *Portrait of a Young Man*, she thought. "Good evening to you, Signor Vizconti. Yes, Ferragosto is always a pleasure."

"It seems we only meet at times of celebration," Ercules said. "The last time was last January, at the joust during Prince Philip's visit."

"I remember. You extended a great honour to me," Sofonisba said. She was glad for Rosa's near yet unobtrusive presence.

Ercules just smiled. To the relief of both, the show reached its climax and the crowd let loose a roar of appreciation.

"And may we meet again sometime," Ercules yelled to Sofonisba over the din, as the revellers began to surround them.

"Maybe we shall," she yelled back. The hungry crowd stampeded toward the roasting boar, and Sofonisba and Ercules rejoined their respective clans.

As evening fell and everyone had eaten their fill, the crowd cleared a large space in the field and ringed it with torches. Any sign of Christian observance disappeared. Players presented stories from ancient Rome, Eros made an appearance dressed as a baby, and Bacchus sang obscenely. Then, with the circle cleared, the musicians began to play dance music, but no one stepped out.

"No one wants to take the lead. How silly," Sofonisba said.

"I'm glad you think so," said Ercules, again appearing out of nowhere. "Shall we?" He extended his hand.

Sofonisba smiled uncertainly and took his hand. They stepped to the middle of the circle and soon others joined them, gliding and leaping to the fife, lutes, and horns. Sofonisba noted that Ercules was a good dancer, but far behind her own accomplished pace.

Later, walking home with her family, Sofonisba looked above their drooping heads and felt elated to see a morning star rise at the thin edge of dawn.

CREMONA, TWO YEARS LATER

To everyone's surprise, it had been a difficult confinement. Bianca, after all, had given birth to six healthy daughters with no harm to her own health, and at thirty-seven, she still felt strong. But as she tried once again for a long-desired son, her body revolted and raged, and the family physician had ordered her to bed.

"If this offspring is not a son, then it does not please God to give you one," the physician told her and Amilcare. "Signora, your womb must not carry another child ever again."

It alarmed Sofonisba to see her usually vigorous mother propped up in bed, her face pale, her hair indifferently pulled back into a cap. *I don't care if I have a brother or not, but for Mama and Papa's sake, let it be a healthy boy,* she prayed to the Virgin. *And let Mama still be with us when it's all over.*

She and Elena returned from their painting lesson to find the household in an uproar.

"The signora is in the throes of birth, God protect her," a servant told them. "The midwife's been fetched. The signore is with your mother. Everyone else is in the sitting room."

To the sisters and their maids, Lucia was reading from the Psalms: "*I will praise thee, O Lord, with my whole heart; I will show forth all thy marvelous works. I will be glad and rejoice in thee: I will sing praise to thy name, O thou Most High.*"

Then they prayed the rosary, each of them furtively glancing toward the door, wishing someone would burst in and give them the hoped-for news, and dreading that the message would be of another sort.

"All right, Minerva, it's your turn to read," Lucia said when the last Hail Mary of the rosary ended. She handed her sister the family's weighty Bible.

"*When mine enemies are turned back, they shall fall and perish at thy presence,*" Minerva began, and Sofonisba could hear the anxiety in her voice.

Sofonisba stood up. "You'll all have to excuse me," she told their surprised faces. She went directly to the studio and lit a lamp and began to draw a fantastical landscape with a many-towered castle and trees and little streams with stone bridges. Later, as the bells of San Giorgio tolled five in the evening, Elena joined her.

"I just couldn't stand it any more," Sofonisba said. "I couldn't sit still for one more word of one more psalm. I have to *do* something, even if it's just sitting here drawing."

Elena sat down at the long table. Sofonisba was startled by her sister's dazed expression.

"I walked by Mama's room," Elena said, almost in a whisper, "and I heard Mama scream." Sofonisba put a hand on Elena's shoulder and after a moment, said, "Here —" handing Elena a piece of chalk and a scrap of paper. Elena began to draw, but her strokes were random and aimless.

Rosa soon brought them supper on a tray, and they found that hunger surpassed their fear. "Have you heard anything?" they quizzed Rosa, but she had nothing to tell them. "The other babies came quick," the maid recalled. "Elena, you came so fast, your mother hardly had a chance to get to bed first. The midwife said she had never seen nothing like it! Lucia and Minerva took just an hour or two, and by the time Europa and Anna Maria came along, your mother was so used to it, she hardly put down her reading long enough to have them!" Sofonisba and Elena smiled.

"But with this one..." Rosa shook her head. "It's quite different. My poor signora's had a very rough time these months, you know, and now ... Lord protect her. Well, I can only say it *has* to be a son — a daughter would never be so much trouble!"

They waited, talking about nothing, pausing once in a while to pray, through hours punctuated by the relentless bells of San Giorgio. No one mentioned sleeping. It was nearly midnight when an excited knock at the studio door made all three jump.

"It's a boy! A healthy boy, praise God!" a servant told them before dashing away. Sofonisba, Elena, and Rosa sank to their knees in grateful relief. "We thank you, Lord, for giving a son to the signora and signore," Rosa said excitedly, "and now if you'll excuse us, and forgive us for such a short prayer." Then the three stood and bounded to Bianca's room.

They stepped into the shadows cast by a single lamp to see an exhausted mother holding her red-faced son, attended by Amilcare and the midwife. The younger sisters had long since gone to bed.

"Mama, we were so worried!" Sofonisba said.

"Well God be thanked, I'm all right," Bianca reassured them in a weak voice.

The midwife was more voluble. "I haven't seen such a hard birth in many a day, I tell you. I delivered all your babies, Signora Anguissola, and none of them was this difficult. You was very brave, a heroine, you was!"

"What is he called?" Sofonisba asked her father.

"My son will be called Asdrubale," Amilcare announced, "after two noble Carthaginians who resisted the power of Rome."

"Asdrubale..." Sofonisba and Elena repeated.

The midwife placed the baby in its cradle. "And now, everyone out, the signora needs to rest, you can admire your new son and brother in the morning."

Elena dropped her paintbrush for the second time this lesson. Already that day she had removed a pot of oil too soon from the fire, and then nearly spilled it while putting it back. When the lesson ended, Elena said to her sister, "Sofi, you and Rosa go home without me. I have to talk to Signor Gatti. One of the maids here will walk me home later."

"Very well." Sofonisba hid her great surprise and curiosity. When Elena returned, Sofonisba met her in the upper hallway, and dropped all pretense of indifference. "Well, what is it? What did you have to talk to Signor Gatti about? Come on, tell me!" She followed Elena into Elena's bedroom and closed the door.

"Sofonisba…" Elena began, a bit too carefully, and Sofonisba froze. *She never calls me that — something must be terribly wrong.*

"I won't be taking painting lessons anymore. You see, I have decided to enter a convent and become a nun."

Sofonisba felt as if a horse had kicked her in the stomach. She gasped.

"*What?* A nun! How can you? You want to leave us? To leave *me?*"

"Sofi, please, Papa has six daughters. You know the family's money is uncertain. He can't give us all suitable dowries. I'm sixteen now, and I'm the second-born — it's traditional. And you always said I was the practical one."

"Well, I'm sure I don't care about tradition!" Sofonisba said, her shock giving way to anger. "Because of money, you want to lock yourself in some convent? What about your painting? You can make money that way."

"You're the great painter, Sofi, not me. That's something you'll always have. I'll never be good enough." She looked straight into Sofonisba's face and saw horror and disbelief. "I've thought about this a lot, really."

"Have you? And not a word to me all the time you were doing all this thinking? I thought we shared *everything.*"

"I had to sort it out for myself first, before I talked to anyone."

"And what about Mama and Papa?"

"I told them this morning."

"Oh, *Elena,*" Sofonisba said with a touch of disgust. She felt a bit dizzy, as if her world had been upended. "And you told Signor Gatti before you told me." Sofonisba crossed her arms tightly over her stomach. "*Oh, Elena.* First Signor Bernardino Campi, and now you."

"I knew you'd be upset, Sofi, but this is the best thing for me, for all of us. Pray try to see that." Elena reached out both arms to her sister, but Sofonisba drew back.

"And so, that's it? It's all settled, *fini?* Once you're gone, we'll never see each other again. This is *horrible.*"

Elena straightened. "Helping Mama and Papa, and giving my life to God, is not horrible."

Sofonisba bolted from the room before the tears began — angry, bitter tears of betrayal and loss. She wondered how she could have been unaware that her sister was weighing such a momentous decision. She skipped supper that evening to lie sobbing on her bed, and nursing a headache. Rosa, hearing the sobs through the door, knocked and entered.

"Oh honestly, Sonia, carrying on like this! Elena's showing great maturity. Why can't you?"

"Because it hurts too much."

"Ah, Sonia." Rosa sat on the edge of the bed. "You know, Elena doesn't *want* to leave you. Of course she'll miss you. But she feels she must do this. Try to understand."

"I understand that I'll be miserable. And she'll never paint again."

"Then you must paint for you both."

The sobs turned into sighs, and the world slowly started to right itself, though the pain remained.

"I will, but it won't be the same, not having her beside me as I paint. We've always done everything together."

Rosa took Sofonisba's hand between hers. "You know, you'll leave here too, someday. Your painting will take you far. I know you don't want to say it, so I will: You're a much better painter than Elena is."

Sofonisba did not argue.

"So, my Sonia, you know what you must do now," Rosa said, and left the room.

Sofonisba stood up and tidied her hair. She took a deep breath and let it out slowly as she walked to Elena's room. The door was ajar. She saw Elena sitting at her dressing table, observing herself in the mirror while she distractedly brushed her hair. Sofonisba walked in and closed the door.

Still looking in the mirror, Elena silently handed Sofonisba the hairbrush, and she took over the ritual with slow, careful strokes through the thick, dark-gold mane that Sofonisba had always envied. *The nuns will chop this off*, she thought bitterly.

She was grateful for Elena's silence as she made several runs of the brush. "You didn't tell me exactly where you're going," Sofonisba said finally, forcing an even tone.

"I'm going to the Convent of the Holy Virgins, at the church of San Vincenzo in Mantua. It's just a day's ride away — not quite the end of the earth," Elena said lightly.

"And when?" Sofonisba blinked back tears.

"Saturday next, after morning prayers." Sofonisba merely raised her eyebrows, but her heart screamed, *So soon!* She made more tender brushstrokes. Sofonisba looked at her sister in the mirror, especially at her huge, too-innocent brown eyes. Then Sofonisba sat down on the bed, the brush still in her hand. "Um, you must write often," Sofonisba said awkwardly.

"Sofi, I'll miss you awfully," Elena sighed, startled by her sister's puffy eyes. She had not expected tears. "I'll miss the garden, the lessons, our studio here, Papa's jokes, even Mama's warnings. And the way you always looked after me. But let's not be so gloomy in my last days here."

This time it was Sofonisba who reached out her arms, and the sisters hugged warmly. "I'm sorry I..."

"Never mind," Elena said. "Let's see, Lucia and Minerva will love having my dresses, and I want you to have this." She opened a silver box on the dressing table and took out a gold pendant with an engraved and enamelled image of the Virgin rising into heaven.

"Elena, I can't take this. It belonged to Papa's sister, who you were named after. It's your favourite!"

"I don't want anyone else to have it."

Sofonisba pressed the pendant between her hands. "In return, I promise this: Somehow, I'll come to the convent and paint your portrait."

"Oh Sofi, that's the best gift you could give me!"

"Now you look awfully tired, Elena. Get some rest. Good night."

"Good night, Sofi."

Evening had begun to engulf the room, and as she left, Sofonisba did not see the start of her sister's own, silent tears.

⌒⌒

In her prayers that night, Sofonisba begged the Virgin's care for Elena, and strength for herself. She cancelled her painting lessons for that week to spend time with Elena. Her father, though displeased, did not object.

On the night before Elena was to leave, maids moved a bathtub to her room, filled it, and scented the water with rose oil. Sofonisba laid out a fresh nightgown. She was surprised when, the tub ready, Elena dismissed the maids.

"But you stay, Sofi." Elena turned around so that Sofonisba could unlace the back of her bodice. Elena worked her way through the other layers, carefully laying them on a chair, but when she untied the front of her corset, she let it fall to the floor. She paused there in the lamplight, a sculpture in voluptuous white and pink, crowned with gold. "My most beautiful sister," Sofonisba whispered. Then, louder, "Now get in that tub before you catch your death."

"Always telling me what to do," Elena shook her head in mock disapproval as she stepped into the tub. "Remember those drawings we did a few years ago? You know the ones? My heart almost stopped when Mama knocked on the door," Elena said.

"I'll never forget!" Sofonisba said, and managed a smile.

The next morning, after prayers, a carriage pulled up in front of the palazzo. Each took a turn saying goodbye: the servants, Amilcare, Bianca, and the younger sisters. At last Elena faced Sofonisba.

"Sofi, I always wanted to do whatever you did. Now I've found my own way. I had to."

Sofonisba knew she would miss that steady practicality, but at that moment she could not stomach it. "You're the only one I ever let call me Sofi," she ventured.

"There is one more thing," Elena said. "And that is, be patient with Mama."

"I will try. God be with you."

They embraced with a painful intensity. Elena still looked at her sister as she gathered her skirts and stepped into the carriage, and for a moment they held hands through the window. Then the driver urged the horses along, and Sofonisba watched the carriage become a dot far down the street.

Sofonisba wiped her eyes on her handkerchief, then turned to Lucia and Minerva, who also stood there with woeful looks. Sofonisba saw that Lucia's rosy complexion was darker than usual, and Minerva's grey eyes suited that girl's mood. The big sister put one hand on Lucia's shoulder and the other on Minerva's. "Come along, you two. I've got something to show you." Lucia and Minerva let their sister guide them into the palazzo and up to the third floor. Sofonisba led them down the main corridor and turned down a narrower, side hall that led to only one place — the studio she had shared with Elena.

"You're letting us into the studio?" Lucia asked, unbelieving. "But what will…?" She then remembered, with a jolt, that their intrusion would not matter to Elena at all.

"Go on in," Sofonisba urged.

Lucia and Minerva stepped inside and looked around, their

curiosity greater than they had realized. Two easels, side by side, dominated the room. The sisters slowly took it all in: the jars of brushes, the glass cabinet that held the raw pigments, unfinished canvases against the wall, the stacks of drawing paper, some blank and some full of sketches. Sofonisba put on an apron and bustled around, sorting out the various tools that were scattered everywhere.

"We'll have to get a third easel. We seem to have enough of everything else. Here, put these on." She pulled two more aprons off the wall and handed them to Lucia and Minerva.

"Sonia, Papa forbids us to be here. He *always* has," Minerva said, her usually sharp eyes uneasy.

"Papa won't mind, not when I tell him I'm teaching you two to paint," Sofonisba replied. "You're almost twelve, Minerva, and Lucia, you're fourteen. It's high time you learned. We'll start with some drawings."

She sat them down at the long table, gave them each a sheet of paper and a piece of charcoal, and took her place between them.

"Look at this vase. Notice the curves, the shiny surface, the shadows and the bright areas. Try to draw what you see."

A few weeks later, Sofonisba sat alone in the studio, the day's lesson over. She could hear her sisters talking animatedly in the garden below. Before her stood a canvas by Signor Bernardino, one he had given to her and Elena when he left for Milan. It was a *Pietà*, and he had told them to copy it. He said they should remember the sketches they had seen of Buonarroti's marble *Pietà* and try to capture the same profound emotion.

They had tried, but had only completed a stack of unsatisfactory drawings before getting caught up in lessons with Signor Gatti. Sofonisba decided to try again, but no matter how she tried to duplicate the grief Signor Bernardino had placed in the Virgin's face, nothing worked.

There were too many distractions in the scene, she decided. Around the mournful Virgin, holding her dead son across her lap, Signor Bernardino had populated the canvas with onlookers: St. Catherine of Alexandria and three prophets. Sofonisba took a new sheet of paper and began again. This time she outlined only the Virgin and the lifeless Jesus against a rocky background, with a vague pathway leading back to a mountaintop at sunset. She rendered the scene at the end of the day, after the Roman soldiers had finished their murderous mission, leaving only a mother and her desperate, inconsolable grief.

Sofonisba spent several days carefully mixing and applying the colours — a shadowy blue for the Virgin's robe, green for its lining, a watery red for the sunset. The *sfumato* treatment she had learned from Gatti appeared in the faces and the landscape. When she was finished, she set her version and Signor Bernardino's side by side on the easel, and felt a surge of confidence. *Well, not bad. I may be grasping the notion of painting, finally.*

Sofonisba was delighted to receive from Elena a description of her convent days. Amid Elena's report of floor scrubbing, prayer, and meagre meals, Sofonisba particularly noted what Elena wore: "…a white linen habit with long, loose-fitting sleeves — I'm sure I could hide entire loaves of bread in them! A snug wimple encircles my face and covers my head and neck. On top of that I wear a broad white veil, which hangs past my shoulders."

Sofonisba folded the letter and brought it to the studio. She put on a smock, then lit the fire and built it up to a strong blaze. She placed a pot of water over the fire. While waiting for it to boil, she grabbed a piece of paper and began to sketch a young novice in her habit, with its deep sleeves, wimple, and veil. Wide brown eyes looked out from a face full of sweet innocence. The novice seemed to be in the middle of prayers — her unlined hands held a prayer book.

Sofonisba placed some sheep parchment in the boiling water and stirred it around, watching it break down into smaller pieces. She added powdered white chalk and stirred again, then took the pot off the fire. The liquid size gave off the dead-animal smell that had so repulsed her the first time she encountered it, in Signor Bernardino's kitchen. Now she hardly noticed it.

From a pile of canvases she had already stretched, she chose one that was medium-sized and applied the warm liquid sizing in thin layers. While waiting for the last layer to dry, she mixed the priming, taking her time to grind the white lead in a marble bowl, and adding the oil slowly. She applied the priming in a thick layer, taking extra care to make the surface perfectly smooth. It would have to dry overnight.

The next day she returned to the studio immediately after the noon meal, in the hour when the household always settled into a drowsy peace, and she would still have a few hours of November light through the studio windows. She began to mix white paint in a large bowl, knowing she would need plenty. Signor Bernardino had told them there were several shades of white: grey-white, beige-white, star-white, and more. She would need all of them now.

Over several intense days of work, an image emerged of her distant Elena, and the experience was both joyous and mournful. Sofonisba was especially satisfied with the face — the large eyes looked directly at the viewer with an expression of humility and intelligence. *I must not make her face too sad*, Sofonisba told herself. She felt a certain relief.

It took some concentration to get the right shades of white in the wimple and veil that shrouded Elena's dark-gold hair. The habit called for a greyish-pink shade of white, difficult for Sofonisba to mix and apply, but while wrapped up in that difficulty she did not dwell on the youthful body that the habit now hid.

It would be the first painting she had ever signed: *Sophonisba Angussola, Virgo, Pinxit.* MDLI.

⌒〰

The next morning Sofonisba took the painting of Elena when she went to Signor Gatti's studio for her lesson.

He set it on an easel and looked it over slowly and carefully. Sofonisba stood calmly to the side, next to Rosa in her customary seat.

"Well, you avoided painting your sister's habit in one shade of white. That would have been as tedious for the viewer as for you, the painter," Gatti began. "Instead, I see a variety of subtle whites, showing that you learned something from the Correggio paintings you've seen. The face shows a reverent but not overly pious young novice, someone with dignity and modesty, sweetness and shyness. So, in both technique and human insight, you've joined the Lombard tradition, and I must say you've excelled here, Sofonisba." He paused dramatically. "I don't think there's anything more I can teach you."

"Signor Gatti!" Sofonisba, her face alight with joy, turned to Rosa, who stood and hugged her. "Congratulations, Sonia!" Rosa said.

Sofonisba then turned toward Gatti. "I cannot thank you enough, signore."

"It was your own hard work, and Signor Campi's instruction, that brought you most of the way," Gatti said. "I merely took you the final distance."

"There is but one more thing I need from you," Sofonisba said. She took a deep breath. "I need you to get me into the guild of painters."

Sofonisba had anticipated Gatti's hesitant look. "The painter's guild?" he said. "But there has never been a woman member. I do not even know if it's possible."

"But you could try," Sofonisba implored. "Now that my lessons are over, I have no good way to study other paintings and drawings.

If I'm not in the guild, I'll always be on the outside. You know that isolation is deadly for a painter."

Gatti crossed his arms. "Still, such a group, for a young noblewoman? I just don't know. At meetings you would have to sit through endless talk about payments, commissions, all sorts of dull business matters." Gatti absently stroked his beard.

"But you also talk about technique and style at the meetings, and you study paintings and drawings, correct? And it might help me find work," Sofonisba said. "But most of all, signore, if I could join the guild, people would regard me more seriously as a painter. And I would *feel* more like a real painter."

"I see you've given this a lot of thought. Now I have to think this through. I will let you know," Gatti said, his concern still evident.

"Thank you."

"In the meantime, don't forget your painting!"

"Oh, how could I? Painting is my life now, it's everything to me, it's…"

"I just meant, don't forget your portrait of Elena," Gatti said, pointing toward the easel.

As Sofonisba and Rosa entered the family palazzo, Bianca appeared: "Pray what have you got there?" she asked, while Rosa slipped discreetly upstairs.

"I've been meaning to show you this, Mama," Sofonisba said. They went into the sitting room. When her mother was seated, the painter removed the portrait's linen wrapping.

Bianca gasped. "Oh, it's my Elena — " She put a hand to her face, and her eyes filled with tears. Sofonisba sat down beside her.

"Mama…" She did not know what to say. Her mother's tears spilled over, as the two women sat and looked at the painting for a while. Sofonisba realized that in her own grief over Elena's departure, she had never considered that her mother missed Elena too.

Sofonisba leaned toward her mother and put one arm around her shoulders. "I miss her terribly," Sofonisba said. "I'm so glad to have Lucia and Minerva with me in the studio."

"Well," Bianca said, her composure returned, "what did Signor Gatti say about this painting?"

"He said I have excelled, and that there's nothing more he can teach me."

"I see."

Sofonisba moved to a chair opposite her mother, her interlaced hands on her knees. "Mama. Tell me…" Her voice was firm, and her determination to air the conflict outstripped her dread.

"Tell you what, pray? That it is a good thing that you have chosen to be a painter? Sonia, I just *cannot*." Bianca ran the back of her hand across her dark brown eyes, then focused them steadily on her daughter. "You want it, I know, and more important, your Papa wants it. So there's no point in my asking you to stop." She lifted her hands, then dropped them. "But I see it, well, as just the wrong road for a woman. Working in a studio, grinding away on pigments, heating oil to that ghastly smell, then dealing with patrons, and haggling over money. Is that any life for a noblewoman? It makes you more like a tradesman."

Sofonisba looked at her mother with eyes full of misery. "I am so sorry to disappoint you, Mama," she said. Studying her mother's face sympathetically, she observed the proud, strong Ponzone features that she herself had inherited: the high forehead, the long nose, the elegantly curved ears. For the first time, Sofonisba saw something else — her mother's aging, apparent in the lines around her eyes, a slight sagging of the aristocratic jawline. It was a face that Bianca had never let her paint.

Sofonisba gestured toward her painting of Elena. "It's like this. Elena has found her place with the Dominicans, and with painting, maybe I have found mine. Yes, there is frustration and difficulty with painting sometimes, indeed." She drew her eyebrows together. "But preparing the paints, seeing that glorious colour emerge — even though it is smelly — then guiding the brush just so, and making the image take shape, well, it's the time when I feel a bit of joy." She paused, and her words hung there.

"'A bit of joy,'" Bianca said, not rudely. "Your painting of Elena, it just reminds me that she has left, and I dread the day that you will leave me, too."

Sofonisba froze at the echo of Campi's assertion, made years ago: "the painter must travel."

Bianca continued. "Do what you must, my dear. But Sonia, don't ask me for something I cannot give." She wrung her hands.

"No, Mama, I won't," Sofonisba said, not adding, *"and don't ask that of me, either."* In her bedroom, she asked herself why she had wanted to paint. Campi had said it was thrilling, and she, too, felt that, but it was harder than she let her mother know. The moments of joy were countered by struggle. She had just told Gatti that painting was her life, and it was true, but at such a high cost. *Oh Holy Virgin, why can't Mama just be proud of me?*

The painter's guild of Cremona, gathered around long tables one afternoon in a back room of Sant'Agata's church, had just finished a tiresome discussion about hiring carpenters to make picture frames, when Bernardino Gatti rose to address the group.

"I have a nephew, the son of my sister, clever and industrious, who has worked some years as a painter. He lives in Padua but will soon make his home in Cremona. Here is one of his paintings," and Gatti held up a canvas depicting the *Pietà*. The other painters leaned forward. "You will of course recognize this as a copy of a *Pietà* by Bernardino Campi. My nephew did this from a sketch of Campi's work." A murmur went through the room.

"So what do you think of this painting?" Gatti asked.

"That is exquisite." "The contrast of light and shadow is very well done." "A sensitive work." "This shows a highly capable painter."

"Gentlemen, I bring this to your attention, because of course, when my nephew arrives, he will want to join this guild."

The other painters assured Gatti that the painting showed sufficient skill to qualify this young man to join them.

"I want to be sure," Gatti said. "Are most of you of the opinion that the painter of this work shows sufficient mastery of our trade to join us?" Heads nodded all around the room, and voices gave their assent.

"We look forward to meeting him," one painter asserted.

"Ah yes," Gatti said. "You need not wait long. In fact you can meet 'him' right now."

"What? But you said he still lives in Padua."

While the buzz of confusion and bewilderment among the painters rose, Gatti moved over to a velvet curtain, pulled it back, and out stepped Sofonisba. "Here is the painter of that work," Gatti said, and smiled craftily at his peers. He barely got the words out before the room erupted.

"Jesus! Sofonisba Anguissola! You mean to say a *woman* painted that?"

"You tricked us, Gatti!"

"What *are* you playing at?"

Gatti raised his voice to be heard above the tumult. "Gentlemen, you said that the painter of this work showed enough ability to join our guild. Sofonisba Anguissola is that painter. Therefore I propose that her membership in the guild be approved at once."

Kruk, kruk, kruk — the head of the guild, Giuseppe Perri, a round-faced man of minimal painting ability but firm convictions, knocked his fist on the table, silencing the painters. Rosa stepped out from behind the curtain to stand beside Sofonisba, who lifted her chin defiantly as she scanned the room.

Perri could barely splutter out his words over his indignation. "Bernardino, a woman cannot join the guild."

"Why not?" Gatti demanded.

"I've never seen a woman member and I'd be pleased to keep it that way until I die. Because, as is well-known, a woman's mind is inferior to a man's, and leaves her incapable of excelling in the art of design." Perri sat back and folded his arms.

"'Well-known?' That's not 'well-known' to me," Gatti argued. "And worry about your own place in this group, Giuseppe, if we are to set requirements of intellect." He paused and an amused rumble flowed around the room. "Giuseppe, you were among those who praised this work. Now that you know it's by a woman, you say it's not good enough?"

"God has created a place for women, as the bearer and nurturer of babes and a helpmate to her spouse, not as a painter," Perri said.

"Are you saying I was wrong to teach her? Choose your words carefully, Giuseppe," Gatti glared.

"Oh, Bernardino, I mean you no criticism. You did the best you could with her."

Other opponents of Gatti's proposal said a woman who paints is a miracle, a bizarre and unnatural exception among her sex. One painter pointed out that as men, they had wives and children to support, and no woman had that burden. As a woman, Sofonisba would be an unnecessary and selfish competitor for commissions. At that, Sofonisba could stay silent no longer.

"I wish to speak now," she proclaimed, and Perri, mouth agape, merely nodded.

"I thank my esteemed teacher for proposing my membership. Now, I want you all to know that I too am helping my family with my painting," she said, breathing hard with anger. "I am one of five Anguissola daughters who will need dowries someday. And I am devoted to my work, as much as anyone. *That* is why I came here today." She paused and glanced around at blank or doubtful faces. "You all know my father, Amilcare Anguissola, and he has been a generous friend to many of you."

The rumble resumed, and Perri knocked again. "We will decide, but in private, signorina."

Gatti whispered to Sofonisba to wait for him at the church entrance. When Gatti approached a few minutes later, she could tell the result from his face.

"I'm sorry, Sofonisba."

She put a hand to her forehead. "Oh…"

Rosa said to Gatti, "Thank you for your efforts, signore. We will be going now."

"Wait," Gatti said. Sofonisba, tired and annoyed, forced herself to regard him politely.

"Sofonisba, whenever you need help or inspiration, come to my studio," Gatti said. "You will always be welcome."

"Thank you, signore," Sofonisba said woodenly. Rosa put one arm in Sofonisba's and steered her toward home.

Sofonisba's hands shook as she and Rosa walked, so she clenched them into fists of bitterness and snarled, *"Perri, Perri, Perri…"*

⌒⌒

Sofonisba met occasionally with Gatti, which cheered her and nearly but not quite wiped away her resentment. Other painters were often there — whether by chance or arrangement, she never knew. It gave her a bit of the camaraderie she longed for. When she had no commissions, a situation more frequent than she would have liked, she continued to paint her family. Amilcare advised her that she must never let it show how desperately she wanted a commission. "Hint that you are very busy, but will fit them in," he said.

"Ha! Papa, I can fit everyone in. I want all the experience I can get," Sofonisba told him.

"Yes, but don't let them know that."

Slowly, more and more patrons found their way to the palazzo in the San Giorgio. While a signore or signora posed for preliminary sketches, Amilcare would engage them in unrelated conversation, while Sofonisba took up chalk and paper.

"Perhaps you'd like a portrait something like this," she would say, handing over the paper. Sometimes the patron would say with pleasure, "Yes, that's exactly what I want!" Other times the patron would say, "Could you just add a book/a pair of gloves/strands of pearls/a sapphire ring/a feathered cap, or make me look younger/prettier/more vigorous/more commanding?" Sofonisba would alter the sketch as requested. "Yes, that's it," they would say, contented.

A painting she considered more important than any commission was the long-planned portrait of Signor Bernardino. She intended the painting to commemorate their friendship, and as a gift in return for all he had given her. The unusual and daring composition was a double portrait, showing Signor Bernardino painting a portrait of her. It was the largest painting she had ever done, nearly two arms square. In her portrait within the painting, she wore a bright red dress with elaborate gold embroidery. Sofonisba would never directly depict herself that way, but reasoned that she could fairly indulge in such luxury, because the portrait was not really her but Signor Bernardino painting her. She placed Signor Bernardino's right hand over her left, which was in turn over her heart. She used the *sfumato* technique in the faces, and felt quite satisfied with the result.

MARCH, 1552

Whenever her sisters were preoccupied and there were no patrons to satisfy, Sofonisba was her own most convenient and cooperative model. When she turned twenty she painted a self-portrait in which she wore a black velvet dress and a chemise with a lace-trimmed stand-up collar. Painted from her mirror image, she appeared in the portrait to hold a piece of parchment in her right hand and paintbrushes in her left. It did not enter her mind until later that the composition would make it look as though she were left-handed. She signed it with the traditional spelling of her name — Sophonisba — because she did the painting to mark her birthday, the day she got that name steeped in Roman lore.

FEBRUARY, 1554

A scholar-friend of Amilcare's, Marco Gerolamo Vida, wrote an essay listing Cremona's greatest painters of the age. Sofonisba was happily stunned when Amilcare showed her the list and her name was on it.

"Ah, I am glad to see that you blush," Amilcare said. "That shows a becoming modesty."

"Praise the Virgin," Sofonisba said. "Signor Vida honours me greatly."

"Now, there's another reason I asked to see you," her father said. "Remember your drawing of a boy being pinched by a crab? Maestro Buonarroti, the Florentine, had asked you to paint a crying boy. So I sent the drawing to him. He was so impressed that he has invited you to Rome."

Sofonisba was thankful that she was sitting down. "The Master has invited me to Rome?" she said, savouring the sound, the beauty, the glory of the words.

"That's right. You and Rosa will be leaving in mid-March. Daughter, I am so proud!"

4.

Rome

Women in every age are blessed by Nature
With highest gifts of judgment and of courage,
Nor are they born less apt, with zeal and study,
To equal men in wisdom and in daring.
                    —Moderata Fonte (1555-1592)

JANUARY, 1555

Sofonisba stood with Michelangelo, looking up at the ceiling of Pope Sixtus IV's chapel. As the Master described to her the experience of painting his magnificent frescoes, students with chalk and parchment gazed up at the works and reverently copied. They stopped their labours when they recognized him, and approached him in greeting. He answered their questions and gave them a few words of encouragement.

"I admire your patience with them," Sofonisba said.

"Oh, it's nothing. I have other concerns, of other worlds," the Master said. He looked back up at the ceiling.

"What do you mean, Maestro?"

"Oh, never mind about that." His face knotted up. "I'm an old man. Seeing these young painters, your contemporaries, reminds me of something very important that I must tell you: I know it's hard to avoid, but try not to put yourself in competition with others."

"I'll remember that, Maestro."

The organist began playing, and then from somewhere a choir joined in. The music, the voices, the frescoes, all combined to lift Sofonisba to a place of unearthly bliss.

"The Master is already in the studio," Tommaso said, standing stiffly in the doorway as he received Sofonisba and Rosa. An ordinary statement, but said in a deliberate and earnest way, and with a grave look. Not comprehending, they asked, "He's…?"

"He's waiting for you."

The Master was seated beside the fire. The studio held its usual air of creative energy, but something had changed. He gestured to two chairs opposite him.

"You'll forgive me for not standing. It's these gouty knees again. So, how long have you been coming here, signorina? An old man loses track of these things."

"About ten months, Maestro Buonarroti."

"Ah. And has it been worth your while?"

She wondered if he were joking, and paused to hear him laugh. But he kept silent, so she took his question as he posed it. "Maestro, it has been the most instructive, the most — *illuminating* time of my life."

"Ah well, you're young," the Master said. "I expect you'll have many more illuminating times. The trouble is," his expression looked regretful, "my health, and my other commitments, mean that our time must end now."

"Oh, I see," was all that Sofonisba could think of to say, in her sad surprise.

"And, well, it's not just my gout and my work," Michelangelo said, his eyebrows lifted. "Over many months, I've been having… doubts."

"Doubts, Maestro? About what?"

He shifted in his chair. "Signorina, this is hard to say, hard for me to face, but as I get old, I can deny it no longer. I have come to realize that sculpture and painting keep us focused on what we can see, on the surface of things. I now find that quite disturbing. As death approaches, I see my devotion to art as idol worship, and now it is time for me to turn to God, and God only."

Sofonisba needed a moment to take in his words.

"Maestro, I am so sorry to hear of your, uh, disturbance. Do you mean that I should stop painting?" She held her breath.

"Oh no, signorina, you are young, you must go on, and use and develop the great gifts that God gave you. My decision is for myself alone."

"But what about San Pietro? Will you finish your glorious dome?"

"Others will finish it for me. That is just as well."

Rosa saw that Sofonisba was overcome with sadness. The maid ventured, "Maestro Buonarroti, we appreciate all you've done. We will carry dear memories back to Cremona."

"Signora Marco, it was a pleasure to teach your mistress — someone so attentive, so receptive," the Master said.

"Maestro Buonarroti," Sofonisba said, "for all you've given me, 'thank you' does not seem adequate."

"Go out into the world, into your work, and push forward, always, challenge yourself, try difficult things, don't let anyone stop you." The Master was more impassioned than Sofonisba had ever seen him. "Don't be deterred by setbacks, no matter what," he said. "And do not dwell on my dark notions. Oh, and there's one more thing." He stroked his beard. "The first day we met, you asked me what 'Raven's Slaughterhouse' means. Now I can tell you." He turned in his chair and picked up a plaster cast of a hand that sat on a table nearby. He looked it over a moment and continued to hold it and turn it as he spoke. His timeworn face became grim.

"In the early days of the Church, when many Christians faced persecution, St. Lucy, a Roman widow, remained steadfast in her faith, and was condemned to death by beheading. She was taken for execution to the small piazza opposite this house. But Our Lord stepped in, and a miracle occurred: the executioner turned to stone, except for one hand, which remained flesh. That didn't save poor Lucy, however. Another executioner, unafraid of another miracle, was found, and with a swing of his axe he fulfilled her martyrdom and sent her on the road to sainthood. Anyway, the Roman dialect of those days for the words 'hand of flesh' became corrupted over the centuries to 'Raven's Slaughterhouse'."

Sofonisba looked at him uncomprehendingly. "Pray, why didn't you tell me this when I first asked?"

"We did not know each other yet. It did not seem appropriate to tell you then, because of the horribleness of the event — the bloody execution of a pious widow. My dear friend Vittoria Colonna was also a pious Roman widow. How could I tell a story so harsh, so heartbreaking, to a daughter of the nobility, whom I had just met?" He set down the plaster hand. "But then I showed you the naked *Risen Christ*, and the nude figures in the *Last Judgment*, which some have rejected as vulgar and lewd. You, however, didn't shrink with embarrassment or get the vapours. Then I knew it was all right to tell you the story of St. Lucy."

Sofonisba reflected a moment on what she had just heard. "What would you have done if I had shown myself too weak, Maestro?"

"Oh, I would have invented something," he waved a hand casually. "*Invenzione*, you know, is a painter's cleverest achievement."

Sofonisba took a long look around the studio. She appreciated the rare privilege of proximity to the Master, the brilliant force that lived within these walls. But it was time to leave.

Sitting up in his chair, the Master called, "Tommaso," and his friend helped him stand up. Sofonisba stood, too, and stepped toward the Master. He took her hand. "Farewell, Signorina Anguissola."

"The Lord truly blessed me when He sent me here," Sofonisba said. "Farewell, Maestro Buonarroti, and God bless you."

Rosa and the Master said goodbye, and Tommaso led the women to the door. As they stepped out they heard the usual street vendors' cries, but the January chill had subdued the frantic traffic they had known in April, and chased off most beggars and running children. Sofonisba recalled her initial fears, shook her head, and smiled.

"What, Sonia?" Rosa asked.

"Remember our first visit to the Master, how nervous I was? You pulled me through, or should I say, pushed me — right through the Master's front door. Now, looking back on all I learned from him, I have to say thank you, Rosa."

"You're very welcome, love."

The two women continued toward their lodgings, stepping around a pile of animal guts that a butcher had just thrown into the street.

CREMONA, MAY 1555

In the sitting room, Sofonisba finished a tune on the clavichord, then turned away from the instrument to look over at three of her sisters, who hovered around a chessboard. Lucia, a grown woman at eighteen, sat opposite Minerva, the scholarly Anguissola child. Europa, everyone's darling Little Bird, who had just turned thirteen, perched between them and watched the game with amusement. "It's your move," Minerva urged her sister.

"No! *Don't* move!" Sofonisba said, and hurried from the sitting room.

"What's that all about?" Bianca asked the room. Her lapdog, Cesare, twitched his white tail.

"Oh, she had that look again," Lucia said. "The one our Sonia gets whenever she has an idea for a painting. Maybe she's going to paint us at our chess game."

Sofonisba returned with parchment and chalk and sat down near the chessboard. Her right hand moved swiftly, sketching in Lucia to the left of the board, Minerva to the right, and Europa, in back, looking on. She drew in the board and some of the chess pieces and the patterned cloth covering the table.

"Pray tell, can I make my move now?" Lucia asked, with mock deference.

"Yes, go ahead."

"Check," Lucia announced. "Aaargh," Minerva replied, and Europa laughed her melodic trill.

"Ah, that's nearly perfect," Sofonisba said, adding more details to her drawing.

"You know, Sonia, if you want to paint our portraits, we'll pose for you, like we always have," Lucia said.

"No, I don't want the usual poses. I want something more natural. I want to capture a moment of everyday life," Sofonisba said.

Lucia glanced around at the others with one eyebrow arched and an "I told you so" look of triumph.

"…And the three of you around a chessboard shows education, a certain intellectual leaning," Sofonisba went on. "Anyway, single portraits aren't the challenge for me that they used to be. Oh, I can't wait to paint this!"

At dawn the next morning Sofonisba was in her studio, preparing a canvas. She decided that because the scene of the chess game showed her sisters in one of their natural elements, she would bring nature into the picture. She placed leafy oak trees behind Lucia and Europa and a hilly landscape in the distance behind Minerva. On the hills stood an imaginary town in a bluish *sfumato* haze, representing both Rome and Cremona. She gave her sisters the same gestures they had shown the night before: Lucia's right hand extended over the chessboard for her final move, and Minerva's raised right hand of surrender, while Europa looked at Minerva and laughed.

Sofonisba added an element unrelated to the actual chess game:

she placed Rosa peeking over Minerva's shoulder. It was an anomaly — a servant would never join the family in the sitting room — but Sofonisba did not care. She reasoned that she wanted to honour her companion and friend. She dressed her sisters lavishly in velvet and brocade, with lace trim on their collars and pearls and jewels on their headbands. Lucia wore a rich red gown with a green overskirt pulled to the back. Minerva's gown was a luscious black velvet with a high collar heavily embroidered in gold silk. A jewelled pendant hung from her pearl necklace, and along with a pearly headband, jewels were intertwined with her braids. Europa's chemise had gathered white linen embroidered in black, and she wore a short carnelian necklace.

Along the edge of the chessboard Sofonisba signed *Sephonisba Angussola. Virgo. Amilcaris Filia. Ex Vera Efigie Tres Suas Sorores. Et Ancillam Pinxit.* MDLV (Sofonisba Anguissola, Virgin. Amilcare's daughter. Painted this true likeness of three of her sisters and a servant, 1555).

More and more she described herself in her painting signatures as "Virgo" — not only denoting her impeccable morality, but also implying self-possession, even heroism, the sort of traits she most longed to have.

↷

She brought her sisters and Rosa to the studio to see it first. "Well, you're the ones in it, so why not?" She dramatically lifted a white veil, then joined her four subjects in a semicircle in front of the easel.

Europa immediately let out a shriek of surprise. "Is that me? I look ... ha! Ha! ... I look like a monkey!"

"I dare say I'm a better painter than that," Sofonisba said, and put a gentle hand on Europa's arm. "Little Bird, you look like the sweet girl that you are."

"And I look rather dignified in defeat," Minerva said. "Well done, Sonia!"

"I'm quite the noble lady, in that gorgeous gown," Lucia said. "Not what I usually wear to play chess."

"It's true that the naturalness of the scene does not extend to the clothes," Sofonisba said. "I couldn't resist putting my sisters in their best finery."

Rosa had not made a sound. While her sisters continued to energetically discuss their painted images, Sofonisba noted that Rosa had a troubled look.

"Rosa? What's wrong?"

"Oh, nothing, love," her maid said. "Silly me. It's just that you painted me so kindly, so, um, delicately…"

"So sensitively," Lucia offered.

"Yes, that's it," Rosa agreed. "Even made my grey hair shine. Who would think that a servant could get into a painting at all, and so beautifully?"

"You know you've always been more than a servant to me, Rosa," Sofonisba said. Rosa smiled at Sofonisba, then turned to the sisters. "Well, my loves, let's go, and let the painter carry on."

Lucia and Minerva sat down at their easels, used dull knives to place thick circles of paint on their palettes, and picked up their brushes made of boar hair. Sofonisba followed Bernardino Campi's good example as a teacher: to let a student work independently and not correct every false move at once. "Let's see what we have now," she said after a while. "Lucia, that's very good, how you added the shadow of the tree on the pond. Finish that. Minerva, you seem to have had a little trouble with —"

"Aaaagh! I can't do it!" Minerva flung her brush to the floor. "I just can't *do* this anymore!" She slumped in her chair and crossed her arms.

"Min*e*rva!" said a stunned and bewildered Sofonisba, but her sister only glared at her, obstinately. "Lucia, will you excuse us?"

Sofonisba said, and Lucia fled the studio, still wearing her apron.

"What in heaven's name is the matter?" Sofonisba asked.

"I'm no good at this, and I *don't like it,*" Minerva said testily, sitting up in her chair. "Remember all those lessons you gave me and Lucia, before you left for Rome? You know I was a rotten student. Lucia, she's brilliant, just like you, but I'm not, and I never will be."

"You weren't 'rotten.' Maybe you just need more time and attention," Sofonisba said. "I could teach you privately, without Lucia."

"No. I *don't want* to paint any more." She held her delicate features in a determined scowl. "I just don't see in it what you and Lucia see. It's too hard. I didn't do any painting while you were gone."

As Sofonisba tried to gather her thoughts, Minerva picked up the rejected paintbrush and set it down carefully on the easel.

"Well, pray what *do* you want to do, Minerva? Just wait around for a husband to find you?"

"I am in my sixteenth year, after all. Would it be so awful if I married? But no, I do not wait for that. I've … I've written many poems. I've kept them secret because I can't bear Papa's disappointment. He so much wants a whole flock of painting Anguissolas." Minerva had squirmed while she spoke, but then sat still and eyed her sister. "Can *you* understand me at all?"

"Yes, I think I can." *Those probing grey eyes!* "Don't worry, I'll talk to Papa. Now, would you tell Lucia to come back?" Minerva hung up her apron and walked out.

Irritation overtook Sofonisba in a prickly wave — not toward her sister, but toward herself. She realized that Minerva had hinted at her feelings many times before revealing them so bluntly that day. Minerva was often late for lessons, always seemed to be only half-listening, and often gave up on a painting when it just needed a bit more effort. But Sofonisba had ignored all that. She wondered whether, in her own way, she herself had been caught up in her father's dream of the painting Anguissola daughters.

Minerva was right about Lucia — as a painter, she was brilliant. There was no doubting her interest and enthusiasm. Sofonisba felt her annoyance dissolve at the moment her gifted sister re-entered the studio.

♈︎

It surprised Amilcare when Sofonisba told him she wanted to paint his portrait.

"Me? You have four beautiful sisters here, a sweet little brother, and your lovely mother, and you want to paint an old goat like me?"

"It was you who got me started, Papa, so it seems only right. And in my hands, you won't look like an old goat."

"Very well."

In her studio the next morning, Sofonisba saw that her father's reluctance to be painted was a bit of an imposture. Vanity had triumphed over modesty. Amilcare appeared dressed in his best brocade jacket, a dark red embroidered in gold, with slashes in the sleeves that allowed a bright blue silk layer to show through. Over that he wore a fur-lined vest that puffed out at the shoulders and extended just below the jacket. If the vagaries of the local economy did not always make him a successful Cremonese merchant, at least he could dress the part. Sofonisba had intended a portrait view from the shoulders up, but when she saw her father in his finery, she decided to make the portrait full-length.

She carefully sketched his receding grey hair, his moustache, and his full but well-trimmed beard that framed his square face, and his long nose. "May I see what you've done?" Amilcare asked.

"Not until it's finished. By the way, Papa, I've been talking to Minerva." She kept her eyes on her drawing board. "You know I was teaching her and Lucia to paint before I left for Rome. Lucia loves to paint, and she's very good, but Papa," she looked up at him, "Minerva has no heart for it. And she's so worried about displeasing you."

Amilcare let out a tiny sigh. "So another one steps out." He held his pose. "My fanciful idea, 'The Six Painting Anguissola Daughters,' ended some time ago, when Elena left for the convent. Our sweet Elena." Sofonisba saw his eyes mist over.

"Papa...?"

"Now Minerva, too, must follow her own heart," Amilcare said.

"She'll be glad you said that," Sofonisba said, and continued with a new piece of chalk. "Soon, I'll start to teach Europa. *If* she's willing, that is."

"Sonia dear, don't let this portrait interfere with the ones you do for paying patrons," Amilcare cautioned.

"I won't, Papa."

The posing and drawing went on in comfortable silence.

Many citizens of Cremona marvelled at Amilcare's ceaseless energy in the advancement of his eldest daughter's career. He visited and wrote to wealthy friends, encouraging them to have Sofonisba paint their portraits. He had merely to mention the magic name of "Buonarroti" to raise interest in Sofonisba's work. Many Cremonesi appreciated the fame she brought the city, because apart from its artists, Cremona had few weapons in its competition with the eternal rival, Milan.

But some Cremonesi clung to old, indelible beliefs. Sofonisba knew well that disdain for women painters was not limited to the painters' guild. Instead of discouraging her, that knowledge was like a growling in her gut that made her hungry to excel, to press on.

At least the Dominicans, a wealthy order, were good patrons. Sofonisba painted a Dominican astronomer pausing in his calculations to smile, his left hand on a small celestial globe. She remembered a sketch she had seen of a painting showing a monk holding astronomical instruments but wearing an improbably lavish fur-trimmed vest. Her monk wore the traditional Dominican habit, his hood raised against some invisible chill. She turned the painting upside down so she could sign it on the sheet of calculations the monk was writing.

One day a large parchment envelope arrived for Sofonisba from Rome.

"From Rome? Oh my, is it from Signor Buonarroti? It is!" She pulled a drawing from the envelope and showed it to her mother.

"Good heavens, who's that?" her mother said, looking over the Master's drawing of a woman with hair piled atop her head in an exotic confusion of curls and tendrils. One braid hung down and curved around her neck and bare left shoulder. Her expression was morose. "Aaagh, it must be Cleopatra, with a snake on her breast! How hideous!" Bianca exclaimed. "Why in the world did he send that here?"

Sofonisba read Michelangelo's note aloud. " 'You have depicted many virtuous women — yourself, your sisters, and your esteemed Mother. Now use this sketch to depict someone perhaps less virtuous...' "

" '*Perhaps less virtuous?*' I should say so!" Bianca said. "Cleopatra, who had Lord only knows how many lovers, and who then committed suicide, a sin against God! So he expects you to copy this?"

"Yes, Mama, he does. I need to try many different kinds of subjects," Sofonisba said.

"I don't see why," Bianca said.

Before Sofonisba could respond, Amilcare walked in. "What's all the fuss about?"

"My lord, that mad Florentine has sent our daughter a simply dreadful drawing," Bianca said. "Look at that."

Amilcare studied the drawing. "Cleopatra, eh? So how do you intend to paint her, Sonia?"

"Never mind *how* she intends to paint her," Bianca cut in. "I'm not sure I want my daughter to paint that ancient hussy at all."

"Mama, I have to! The great Maestro Buonarroti— "

"The great — Maestro — Buonarroti," Bianca repeated, in a plodding tone of exhaustion. The words fell down on Sofonisba like blows. The air in the room seemed thicker, harder to breathe.

Bianca added, "I'll thank the Lord and all the saints if I never hear that name again."

"Bianca," Amilcare said curtly.

"I know, I know," Bianca said, and sighed heavily.

"Sonia, take the drawing to your studio," Amilcare said. She winced at the sound of her parents arguing as she went up the stairs.

When Sofonisba painted Cleopatra, she gave the subject a long neck and face in the Cremonese tradition, and she made the eyes roll up, to depict the moment of Cleopatra's death. She did the work in her few private hours in the studio, without her sisters watching, and then she put it away and told no one about it.

JANUARY, 1556

Sofonisba, along with most of Cremona, became engrossed in the extraordinary news that the Holy Roman Emperor Charles V had abdicated, a tired old man by age fifty-six. Since the age of nineteen, he had, through inheritance, strategic marriages, and military conquest, been ruler of Spain and its dominions, including those in far-off America, as well as great chunks of Italy and the Habsburg lands in Germany, Austria, the Netherlands, Bohemia, and Hungary. Charles eventually retired to a monastery where, ill for some time with gout, he nevertheless ate like a starved wolf, the rumours said.

Charles turned part of the empire over to his brother Ferdinand

and made his eldest son, Prince Philip, the king of Spain and its lands in Italy and the Netherlands. The new monarch would be known as King Philip II.

In the Anguissola household, reactions varied from Asdrubale's utter indifference and immediate boredom to Sofonisba's intense intrigue.

Somewhere in-between was Amilcare's view that the change might have little importance for Cremona; at least, he and the rest of the city council hoped that Philip would let the city govern itself. Amilcare still intended to send the new king a hearty letter of congratulations, in the interests of business. There was also the possibility that Philip could end the war with France, which had been awful for business.

As Sofonisba turned the news over in her mind, her memory went back to a candlelit reception hall, radiant with jewels and excitement, and a receiving line, where the then-Prince Philip had held her hand and professed an interest in painting, seven years ago that month.

$\backsim$

Teaching Lucia and Europa to paint often astonished Sofonisba and brought her unexpected gratification. She was proud of their talents and revelled in the admiration that her sisters at least pretended to hold for her. Lucia, especially, showed prodigious ability, and Sofonisba wondered whether her sister would surpass her one day. Lucia's portrait of the Anguissola family physician, Dottor Pietro Maria, perfectly captured his good-natured personality. Showing great skill, Lucia made his eyes inquisitive and sharp.

But Sofonisba was dismayed by a self-portrait that Lucia had painted.

"Lucia, those hands, and that dress — that's not your style — it's mine! I told you never to copy anyone, and certainly not me! And you don't dress like that." Lucia had depicted herself seated and holding a book, in a dress and chemise of Sofonisba's preferred simple style and her hands in Sofonisba's angular fashion, although Lucia made her fingers plumper.

"Sonia, it's my homage to you, my thanks for all your patient instruction."

"Oh! Thank you."

Sofonisba also began to teach Anna Maria. The eleven-year-old reminded Sofonisba of herself when she first met Bernardino Campi — she was about the same age, and as eager and curious.

⌒

Sofonisba's father had a letter to show her from the Gonzaga court at Mantua. Amilcare had told the court about Sofonisba taking instruction from Michelangelo, and the duke and duchess were predictably impressed. They wanted Sofonisba to visit and paint some portraits.

"Mantua! That's where — Oh Papa, could we?" She held her breath.

"Yes, while we're there, we could visit Elena," Amilcare said.

"Oh, thank the Lord!" Sofonisba bounced in her seat. "I've missed her so much."

"Ah, that's my Sonia, more excited about seeing Elena than about painting portraits of one of the most powerful families in Italy. You see, making this connection could be useful for you."

"I don't know which is the greater good fortune, Papa."

Amilcare laughed. "And I have another letter, from the Farnese court at Parma. After hearing from me, they also want to meet you. Your fame is spreading, my dear. I could arrange for you to meet the miniaturist, Giorgio Giulio Clovio, while we're there. I've heard he's eager to meet the woman painter of Cremona."

"Giulio Clovio," Sofonisba said. "Oh yes, Signor Bernardino mentioned him. They both studied with another painter, I forget his name."

"Clovio has something else in common with your first teacher. Clovio also taught a woman — a Fleming, Levina Teerlinc. She's now the court painter to King Henry in England."

"She is? A lucky woman indeed."

They had crossed the flat, fertile plain of eastern Lombardy and into Virgil's beloved homeland, a countryside of soft, misty light. As they entered Mantua, Amilcare told a disappointed Sofonisba that they simply could not go to the convent right away. Propriety dictated that first they attend their hosts, the Gonzaga. Their journey finally ended at the Piazza Sordello, site of the ducal palace.

Sofonisba found herself going through the motions of good manners when she met the duke and his wife, and barely noticing the frescoed rooms and richly carved furniture. When their hosts suggested that they rest before supper, Amilcare saved her.

"My second daughter, Elena, is a nun at the Convent of the Holy Virgins, at the church of San Vincenzo here. She left the family home five years ago, and Sofonisba, especially, has been eager to see her. So with your permission, we'll do that next."

Amilcare escorted Sofonisba and Rosa to the carriage but did not get inside.

"You're not coming, Papa?"

"You and Elena have much to talk about. Sisterly things. I'd just be in the way. You go, and tell Elena I'll visit her tomorrow."

"Thank you, Papa."

Once the carriage was off, it rolled from the ducal palace into narrower streets, turning left, then right, then left again. Sofonisba quickly felt restless. *How far can it be? Mantua's no bigger than Cremona. Can't this thing go any faster?*

Finally the carriage stopped at the convent gate. A novice brought them into a sparsely furnished reception room.

"Elena!" "Sofi!" The sisters rushed together at first sight and hugged, laughing, and then they observed each other at arm's length.

"Look at you in your Dominican habit — Suor Monica. And still so beautiful!" Sofonisba said.

"And you, the travelling portrait painter!"

Then Elena greeted Rosa, and the three sat down and talked about their family, Cremona, the convent, Rome and Michelangelo, jumping back and forth among the topics in cheerful collision.

"I have a surprise for you," Elena announced. She stepped into the hallway and returned with a large leather-bound collection of the Gospels.

Elena pointed to the illustrations. Some, in the upper left corner of several of the pages, were tiny squares. Others extended across the margins at the top, sides and bottoms of the pages. "I did these," she said with a touch of pride. "I'm the convent's illuminator."

Sofonisba's eyes went wide. "Elena! So you have continued painting!" She examined the tiny blossoms, birds, fruits, leaves, crosses, swirls, and curlicues, and the scenes of lush gardens and riverbanks, in gold, silver and every brilliant colour. "These are *beautiful!*"

"I couldn't stand not painting at all," Elena said. "So when I saw other books here like this one, I asked Reverend Mother if I could do the next one, and to my surprise, she said yes!"

"Oh Elena, I was afraid you would never paint again." Sofonisba turned a few more pages, continuing to marvel over her sister's work. Then she carefully closed the book.

"Now, there's one more thing I must do today. Sit down there, in the light of that window."

"Still commanding people where to sit, I see," Elena joked.

Sofonisba took out the parchment and chalk that Rosa had obligingly carried, and sketched a half-length portrait of Elena in her black veil, white cowl and white habit.

"When I finish this, I'll bring it back here and show you. So, I'm finally keeping my promise!"

Over the course of the next few days Sofonisba painted the duke, his wife, their children, and various other Gonzaga relatives. She worked on Elena's portrait whenever she could spare the time. After several weeks, the painter and Rosa returned to the convent.

"So here it is. What do you think?"

Elena studied her portrait carefully. In her right hand, Sofonisba had placed three lilies, symbolizing the trinity, purity, and the Virgin Mary. In her left hand Elena held a crucifix piercing a red heart, to symbolize contrition and devotion.

"Oh Sofi, it's completely wondrous."

"The best compliment I ever had! And just what I need to take with me on the rest of my journey. You see, we are leaving tomorrow for Parma."

Neither sister dared to say that they would not see each other again for a long time, perhaps never. The image of Elena standing in her black and white garb, her hand on the convent gate, with those same chestnut eyes full of parting sadness, imprinted itself deeply in Sofonisba's mind.

The next morning, the carriage wheels rolled alternately through mud and dry road, jolting the passengers southwest toward Parma. The invitation had come from Margaret, the duchess of Habsburg. The duchess was the daughter of former emperor Charles V, the result of a dalliance before Charles' marriage, making her the half-sister of King Philip II of Spain. That last fact was something that Amilcare made sure Sofonisba understood.

"And like her brother, she's very interested in painting," he said.

Between painting portraits of the duke and duchess of Parma and their son, separately and together, Sofonisba went to see frescoes by Correggio in the cathedral and in the refectory of the Convent of St. Paul. One day, the duke's carriage conveyed Sofonisba and Rosa to a large stone house on a quiet street. "Welcome, do come in," Giorgio Giulio Clovio greeted them. "It is good to meet other woman who paints, like my former student, Levina Teerlinc."

Sofonisba needed a few seconds to decipher Clovio's words, buried under the accent of his native Croatia, unlike any accent she had ever heard.

"Um, good morning, Signor Clovio," she managed to cough out. "How kind of you to see me."

She was further befuddled when Clovio said, "Wait here!" and dashed off toward the back of the palazzo.

He returned a minute later. "Excuse me, ladies. I was in middle of rather complicated paint mixture, big mess, and if I left 'til later, oil would dry and I have bigger mess. Let's go into sitting room." "But surely you have assistants to do that sort of work for you," Sofonisba said as they sat down.

"Oh no. No assistants. Had one once — always cleaning up after him. Am better off alone. You have many assistants in your studio in Cremona?"

"Well, in a manner of speaking. They're my sisters!" They all laughed.

A servant-girl entered the room with a carafe of wine. She poured three cups, and everyone took a sip.

"Maybe you heard that I am known as *il Macedone*, because some here think I am from Macedonia," Clovio said. "Don't know how that got started. Am really from Croatia. But I now live in Italy long time, since my eighteenth year. Maybe you heard about my adventures during sack of Rome."

"No, Signor Clovio, I haven't. Tell us."

"Well, the attack dogs of Emperor Charles, under duke of Bourbon, were determined to capture pope, but he escape into Castel Sant'Angelo. I hid in wine cellar with my landlord and his wife. We could hear such awful sounds above us, pounding, thumping and screaming..." Clovio wiped one eye with his sleeve. "I will spare you ladies the horrible details. 'Constable' Bourbon's troops found us and took us prisoner. I was so scared, I vowed to God I would take religious life if he let me live. Our guards got roaring drunk one night and we escape, and I made my way to Mantua."

"*Holy terror! Holy terror! Aaach!*"

Sofonisba and Rosa jumped. It was an inhuman, croaking voice, more like a screech. They turned toward the sound, and in a far corner of the room a parrot perched inside a hanging cage, in feathers of flaming red, green and yellow.

"Pigo! Stop that! That's very rude!" Clovio called over to the bird, but it kept on. "*Santo Gesu! Aaach!*"

"Pigo!"

Muttering, Clovio stood and called down the hallway. "Antonio! Antonio, come here! Oh, that boy! So sorry, ladies! *Where* is that useless boy? Antonio!"

Sofonisba and Rosa looked at each other and traded smiles, while Pigo continued to squawk and Clovio called, "*Antonio!*"

A boy of about fourteen years appeared in the doorway. Clovio spoke excitedly to him and pointed toward Pigo. The boy carried the cage out of the room, Pigo shrieking all the way.

"Excuse, please. Now, pray, where was I?" Clovio said as he sat down again in the sudden calm.

"You had escaped to Mantua," Sofonisba said.

"Ah yes. I entered abbey of San Ruffino, to join Benedictines," Clovio continued. "But I was not, how you say, 'cut out' for that life, and I was released from vows. I still try to live simply, almost like monk."

Sofonisba looked around at the large, bright and tastefully decorated sitting room, where they sat on thickly cushioned chairs.

"Oh, now you think me fraud," Clovio said, and laughed. "'Like monk? In this comfort?' you're thinking. But all this luxury is from kindness of Her Grace, the duchess, Margaret of Habsburg, fine lady, you know. Even if it was her father's troops who devastated Rome. I did some illuminations and other work for her, and she rewarded me well. But, enough talk about me. Tell me about your work."

Sofonisba talked about her teachers and some of the portraits she had done. "But my best-known teacher by far was Michelangelo Buonarroti, whom I had the honour of meeting and studying under in Rome."

"Ah, Buonarroti the Florentine," Clovio said. "Indeed, the greatest. How fortunate for you."

In the pause, Sofonisba said, "Signor Clovio, I would really like to hear about Levina Teerlinc."

Clovio took a long sip of wine. "Sometime after I left clergy, Pope Alessandro Farnese, now called Paul III, writes to me and he says, 'Giorgio, come to Rome.' Now, you don't say 'no' to that, do you? Even though in all God's creation, Rome was last place I wanted to go. You understand. So, in Rome working for pope, that's where I met Levina, daughter of Simon Beninc, famous miniaturist. A big girl, blond. Levina was with husband George, on business. We met through painters' circle, around 1540, and I taught her six years. In that time, sent her works to all around Europe, kings, queens, cardinals, princes, hahaha!" He drank more wine. "It worked. Now she does portraits of Tudors in England. Some of the most important folks anywhere, yes indeed!"

"What is her painting like?"

"Hmm, yes." He set down his cup. "She has great talent for portraits. Carefully models people's features. You might even say, me-ti-cu-lous. A fine painter, my student, Levina." A wistful look came over him. He crossed the room and took a small oval-shaped object off a shelf and handed it to Sofonisba. "I paint this just before Levina left Rome." It was a miniature portrait of a blond woman.

"She was lovely as well as talented," Sofonisba said.

"Like you," Clovio said. "Maybe, also like Levina, a royal appointment 'waits you."

Sofonisba smiled obligingly. "Thank you for your generous compliments and your faith, Signor Clovio, but a royal appointment seems quite unlikely for me," she said.

"Why? Europe's full of courts, and in some of them, are rulers with sharp eye for painting." He leaned forward. "And, in all of them, is vanity and desire to see themselves and family painted. So, is possible."

Into the silence Sofonisba blurted, "Signor Clovio, I'd like to paint your portrait."

Clovio smiled. "Ah, child. Oh, do excuse me, you no child. It's just that, since I become old man, all young people seem like child to me." He sighed. "You do me vast honour, Signorina Anguissola, wanting to do portrait. Yes, you may."

Sofonisba had never had another painter pose for her, except for her sisters. She had done her portrait of Signor Bernardino from memory. She was quite proud of the portrait she painted of Clovio, believing that she had captured the warmth and humour behind the short beard and moustache. Clovio posed in his odd hat — a round, pleated one with a brim folded down his forehead — and a plain black jacket that he preferred. In his left hand he held his miniature of Levina Teerlinc.

"I received an urgent message from your mother today," Amilcare said to Sofonisba one evening. "Here, you read it."

> *Cremona*
> *March 23, 1556*
>
> My lord, my husband, my darling, I have missed you greatly these past weeks. Perhaps what I tell you here will hasten your return.
>
> Ercules Vizconti, whose father you know well, has asked about our daughter Sonia. The young man ap-

proached me as I was leaving San Giorgio and asked after Sonia's well-being and her current whereabouts. He was exceedingly polite and showed nothing but the most thoughtful concern. I told him that Sonia was visiting her sister Elena in Mantua and painting portraits of the ruling families there and in Parma. Young Vizconti appeared suitably impressed.

He did not reveal any depth of feeling for Sonia nor any intentions or wishes, as I suppose he would not, to me, her mother. But the nature of his interest in Sonia is clear. You know he has had an eye on her for several years. He is a fine young man, heir to a fortune, and he won't wait much longer. I realize there are complicated financial matters involved—there's the question of the dowry — but in any case I think that you and Sonia should return home now and settle this.

I send all my love and warm embraces, my lord, and I count the hours until I see you again. Give my love to Sonia.

Your loving wife, Bianca

"So what do you think, Sonia?"

Amilcare waited while Sofonisba rose and went to the window. She gazed down as if a revelation lay in the Farnese courtyard. Strands of longing, doubt, and ambition tangled into a knot that she hoped to somehow never have to untie.

"Of course, my marriage is not my decision, Papa, that's up to you," she said, trying to sound self-assured. "Mama is right. We should go back and settle this, one way or another. I have just the final touches left to do on the family portraits here."

As their carriage headed northwest a few days later, Amilcare noticed a contented, dreamy look on Sofonisba's face. *Ercules*, Amilcare thought, proud of his insight, unaware that the real reason for his daughter's pleasant reverie was the memory of Clovio's words, on quite another subject: *"Is possible."*

Later in the journey, Sofonisba's dreamy look vanished, and one of serious reflection replaced it. It was then that she was thinking of Ercules.

⌒⌒

Minerva, Europa, and Anna Maria, looking down from the third-floor balcony onto the street in front of the Anguissola palazzo, witnessed the arrival of an exquisite white carriage trimmed with gilt. Out stepped Amilcare's friend and fellow consigliere, Andrea Vizconti. The sisters raced to the stairs landing that overlooked the entrance hall. They watched as Amilcare greeted the visitor warmly, took him into the sitting room and closed the door. Word of the gentleman's arrival spread quickly through the house, and caused more excitement than the return of the travellers the evening before.

I'm glad that didn't take long, Bianca thought.

It could mean a new destiny for my Sonia, Rosa thought.

Will I lose my teacher? Lucia wondered.

How incredibly romantic! swooned Minerva, Europa, and Anna Maria.

The sisters burst into Sofonisba's room to tell her. "Sonia, he's here!"

"Who's here?"

"The father of Ercules Vizconti, that's who! He's talking to Papa in the sitting room right now!"

"Well, they're old friends, they're just talking," Sofonisba said, ignoring a flutter in her chest, forcing herself to speak and move calmly as she rearranged the objects on her dressing table.

"Sonia, you know what they're talking about," Minerva said. "Ercules Vizconti wants to marry you."

"Who's joining me in the studio today?" Sofonisba asked as she started to leave the room. "Europa, Anna Maria, come and show me what you did while I was away."

Sofonisba was preparing a canvas when Rosa knocked on the studio door and told her that her parents wanted to see her, in the sitting room. She felt her stomach tighten along with her jaw, and her feet felt like lead weights, but no matter how slowly she moved them, taking the longest route possible, she still reached the sitting room much too soon.

Her mother and father, seated at the small round table, both sat still and straight as the Torrazzo. "Sonia, Ercules Vizconti has asked for your hand in marriage," Amilcare began. "His father pleaded the young man's case well. He said he was intelligent, strong, of good humour, and has a significant inheritance. But I already knew all that."

Bianca spoke up. "Sonia, your fame as a painter is spreading. You know how I feel about that. You cannot live on fame — it comes and then it goes. As the wife of Ercules Vizconti, you'd never have to worry. Surely you would not, must not, allow your painting to get in the way of a good marriage."

Sofonisba inhaled and exhaled once, slowly. "Mama, I am worried about the exact opposite. I am worried that a husband could tell me to stop painting, and I would have to stop."

"Oh Sonia." It was the tone Sofonisba had heard her mother use so many times, the tone that said how much her eldest daughter exasperated her.

"Painting is not what I dreamed of for you, not at all," Bianca said. "You are a Ponzone, don't forget, just as much as you're an Anguissola. And the Ponzone nobility is long established and highly respected. For a Ponzone, especially a *daughter*, to be in a trade is just more than I can bear."

Sofonisba steeled herself, measuring her words. "And just what did you dream of for me, Mama?" she said evenly.

"I see you as a fine lady in coloured silks and brocades, gold-embroidered, not those serious black and brown dresses you insist on wearing. I see you married to a man of character, the mistress of a fine palazzo, with children. A respected and admired woman."

"Mama, that is *your* life," Sofonisba said.

"And is there anything wrong with that?" Bianca's voice grew testy. "It is a fine life, and I thank the Lord for it every day."

"Now, Bianca, Sonia didn't mean anything unkind," Amilcare said. "You say you want her to be respected and admired — well, she already is. You should have seen her in Mantua and Parma. She moved so well, so confidently, in such noble circles — charmed them personally and impressed them with her painting. And her work in those places was so inspired."

"I have not changed my mind," Bianca said slowly in a low, firm voice. "I still think of painting as something unbecoming a noble daughter. But my lord, and you know this is an old concern of mine, are you just thinking of the money that her painting brings in?"

"No, absolutely not. If I were, we wouldn't be sitting here talking about it — I'd simply forbid this marriage. But I want to know what my daughter wants. What does your heart say, Sonia?" Mother and father turned to her.

Holy Virgin, help me. "Ercules has shown me some kind attention. He's a fine young man from a fine family. Many women would gladly marry him. But I ... I feel differently."

"So, you do not wish to marry him?" Bianca looked at her.

She paused, then said, "No, Mama, I do not." Their eyes locked a moment. Sofonisba's head began to pound.

"My Sonia, are you *sure* you mean to reject him?" Bianca asked in her deliberate, almost rhythmic manner.

Sofonisba gripped the edge of the table. "I am as sure as I *can* be, although it's very hard. All the way home I was thinking about it and praying." She turned toward her father. "Papa, if you decide that I am to marry Ercules Vizconti, then I will, and I'll carry out all the duties of a wife, but with a heavy heart." Her mother also looked to Amilcare, holder of all power over Sofonisba's future, as surely as the bells of San Giorgio then struck the hour of four: *bong, bong, bong, bong.*

Amilcare glanced at Bianca and then at Sofonisba before he said, "I won't agree to the Vizcontis' proposal against your wishes."

Bianca put her face in her hands.

Sofonisba, afraid to speak, looked at her father gratefully, then turned to her mother. "Mama?"

"Oh, I'll be all right," Bianca said, folding her hands on the table, her face in a placid expression that Sofonisba could not be sure was real.

"Now please excuse us," her mother said to her gently, and patted her hand.

When Sofonisba opened the sitting room door, Minerva, Europa, and Anna Maria fell into the room at her feet. "Well, well, three little eavesdroppers," she said as she helped them up. "Come on, let's go."

⌒

"Well, what did Papa say? We didn't hear a thing, honest." Sofonisba's sisters hung on her as she made her way to her room. "Come on, Sonia, tell us!" They arranged themselves on her bed and various chairs. Lucia and Rosa came in.

"Yes, Ercules Vizconti wants to marry me," Sofonisba announced.

"Ooooh!" The younger girls shrieked and laughed. "I knew it! It's just *too* romantic!" Lucia and Rosa said nothing, but they smiled proudly.

"However, I have turned down his proposal."

"Huh? You turned him *down*? What? Sonia! Why?"

"Ercules Vizconti is an honourable man. It's just not time for me to marry right now, that's all."

"But Sonia! Why not, Sonia?" her sisters continued. Rosa caught Sofonisba's sudden look of fatigue.

"Now now, you heard your sister," Rosa said. "I happen to know that the cook just pulled a batch of jam tarts out of the oven. Everyone to the kitchen!"

Grateful for the solitude and sudden quiet of her room, Sofonisba took an inkwell, quill, and sheet of parchment from her dressing table drawer. She sharpened the quill and began to write a letter to Elena. She wrote that Elena's long-ago prediction had come true — that Ercules Vizconti had asked for her hand in marriage. Sofonisba explained as best she could her reasons for turning him down. Her greatest sadness in the whole affair was her mother's reaction: "Oh Elena," she wrote. "Mama is distraught. She fears that my refusal will ruin my life. Maybe she is right. It weighs heavily on me that I have further disappointed her."

In the sitting room, Amilcare pushed back from the table. "Well, that's that."

Bianca stared at him. "How can you be so casual about this?" she said.

"This just might be the best for her. Isn't that what you want, dear?"

Bianca looked away. "We have different ideas about what is best. Do you remember, my lord, when we first decided that our daughters should be thoroughly educated, beyond what is usual for girls of their station?"

"We wanted them to have the best of everything."

"The wish was that such education would make them better women. Now look what it's led to," Bianca moaned. "My daughter wants to ply a trade, more than anything in the world. I never thought I'd see such a dreadful day, when she would turn down a perfectly good marriage prospect. I simply cannot stand it."

Amilcare took Bianca's hand and held it in both of his. "I know you do not value her painting skills, that you even disparage them, but perhaps it is what she was put on this earth to do. Surely you would not have her enter into marriage unwillingly."

Bianca sighed. "Maybe it's silly, but when Sonia was born I already imagined her as a bride, arrayed in the finest silk. And at her wedding, we would all be so happy."

"Try not to despair, my love. We have four other daughters quite capable of giving you that happy wedding day," Amilcare said. "Lucia turns nineteen this year and Minerva seventeen, and the others will come of age all too soon. Let's leave it in Our Lord's hands. Will you join me in prayer?"

They folded their hands and bowed their heads. "Dear Lord, who has so much blessed this family, guide us to know Your divine will, and protect our children from all evil. Oh, and let Andrea Vizconti be understanding. We ask this in Your holy name and with all humility."

"Amen."

Sofonisba threw herself into her painting. She had never before felt more pressured to excel. In one portrait, she painted a monk in three-quarter length, young and beardless, his head bearing just a faint hint of brown stubble. With folded hands, he gazed off the canvas with a contemplative look.

Another portrait of a monk, this time a Dominican, was quite different. In that half-length view, the bearded subject was in his forties, his baldness making a tonsure immaterial. He looked straight at the viewer with a slight smile. Sofonisba took extra care with the black cape and the texture of the white surplice. No one posed more patiently or with greater stillness and silence than the monks; Sofonisba wondered whether they were lost in prayer the whole time.

She began yet another self-portrait. For the first time she painted herself at the easel, wearing a simple brownish-red dress with a round collar, the type she usually wore for painting, but she did not depict her apron. The high white collar and the cuffs of her chemise were edged in short ruffles. On the easel in the picture Sofonisba painted a *Madonna and Child*, with the Virgin leaning toward her son affectionately.

JUNE, 1557

A woman in her late twenties and a boy of nine years, both dressed all in black, appeared one day in the Anguissola sitting room.

"I am Isabella Rangoni, wife…" the woman gasped into a black handkerchief, her eyes welling up, "I mean, *widow*, of Ermete Stampa, the second marchese of Soncino. This is my son, Massimiliano."

"I'm so sorry about your husband, signora, and your father, Massimiliano," Sofonisba said. "Now tell me what I can do for you."

"My son is now the third marchese of Soncino, and I'd like you to paint his portrait, to mark this event."

Sofonisba gave Massimiliano a look of sympathy and compassion. *He's so young to bear such a lofty title and such responsibilities. He's only a few years older than Asdrubale.* "Of course. Were you thinking of a half-length portrait, or full-length, or something else?"

"I don't know." The woman looked at Sofonisba despairingly, and the painter knew she must not ask too many questions. "Let's all sit down." She picked up a sheet of parchment and a piece of chalk.

She quickly sketched the boy, noting his large brown eyes in a melancholy face that narrowed down to a cleft chin. In her drawing, he stood with one arm resting on a column's tall base and the other over a long sword hanging from his belt, a symbol of his new status.

"That's fine, except it needs something, something about his father," Rangoni forced the words out.

"Massimiliano, do you have a dog?" Sofonisba asked.

"Yes, signorina, I have a dog, a retriever."

"What does he look like?"

"He's mostly white, but he has a big, light brown spot on his right side, and he has a brown head and ears."

Sofonisba took back the sketch. She added a dog curled up and sleeping at the boy's feet, a symbol of a recent death.

"Oh, that's perfect!" Rangoni said, and nearly smiled.

"Massimiliano, what do you think?" Sofonisba asked.

"I like the dog best, signorina."

"Good. Signora Rangoni, I'll keep you both in my prayers as I complete this."

When Isabella Rangoni and Massimiliano Stampa returned a few weeks later to claim the finished portrait, they brought two girls, also dressed in black. Rangoni introduced them as Massimiliano's older sisters, Barbara and Victoria.

"Girls, this is Signorina Sofonisba Anguissola, the esteemed portrait painter."

"Good afternoon, signorina," the girls chimed, and giggled. With one look from their mother, they quieted down and straightened their backs.

"Pleased to meet you," Sofonisba said, charmed by the childish warmth that their mourning clothes could not diminish. "Signora Rangoni, you have such lovely children." She directed the girls to a settee and had Massimiliano stand between them.

"That's a wonderful scene, with their bright, youthful faces!" Sofonisba exclaimed. Bianca's dog, Cesare, as if sensing the presence of friendly visitors, scurried into the room. "Awwww," the children said.

"Pick him up, Massimiliano," Sofonisba said. "Now Barbara, turn a bit this way. Good. And Victoria, like this. That's it. Signora Rangoni, you must let me paint them, together like that."

"Oh, I don't know, Signorina Anguissola, the portrait of Massimiliano is all we really can — I mean, it's all we need." Sofonisba understood at once that Rangoni could not afford another portrait.

"Signora Rangoni, I will not charge you for it. It will be my pleasure," Sofonisba said.

"Very well, then," and the children took turns holding and petting the dog.

"One thing," Sofonisba said. "I realize they have just lost their father, may he rest in peace, and excuse me if what I'm asking is inappropriate, but I would like them to pose for their sittings in everyday dress, not mourning clothes. Would that be all right?"

Signora Rangoni put one hand to her mouth. "Well, all right."

The resulting painting glowed with the children's energy. It was hard for Sofonisba to see it wrapped up and carried off to Signora Rangoni.

While thoroughly charmed by the painting of the children, Amilcare regarded it with mixed feelings. "I hope you're not going to make that a habit, Sonia. Doing paintings for free, I mean," he told her.

"Papa, you've given away several of my self-portraits."

"That was to let others know of your ability, in the hope that they would spread your fame and seek their own portraits," Amilcare said.

"Maybe that portrait of the marchesa's children will do the same for me," Sofonisba said. "Who knows? I might have to open a studio in Soncino."

"That little speck of a town? Ha!"

"Papa, you think no city anywhere compares with Cremona."

"None does!"

CREMONA, 1558

The studio in the Anguissola palazzo crackled with creativity. Sofonisba and her sister-students poured forth an array of portraits and devotional panels. There had been many other families in which painting was the family business, but they all involved fathers, brothers, and male cousins. Only the Anguissolas could boast (but never did — that would be improper) of a household of young women painters.

The gifted Lucia had advanced to the point where she needed no more instruction. She painted a *Madonna and Child* that was so beautiful that it took Sofonisba's breath away. The tender look in the Virgin's face as she gazed at her Child was deeply moving, and the folds of her clothing were expertly done.

At sixteen, Europa had grown into a dark-haired beauty who returned the glances of young men as the family went to and from church. While not as formidable as Lucia in her painting abilities, she did produce an admirable depiction of St. Andrew in the moment he decided to follow the Lord. Anna Maria's *Holy Family with St. Francis* showed an exceptionally sweet-faced infant, and she and Sofonisba worked together to create an emotive *Holy Family with St. John*. With Europa and Anna Maria, Sofonisba was careful not to make the same mistake that she had made with Minerva — assuming that they wanted to paint and never asking them. Both sisters reassured her that their interest in painting was genuine.

An old friend of Amilcare's visited the family for several weeks. He was a dignified gentleman with a beard almost halfway down his chest, and an affable manner. He agreed to Sofonisba's request to paint his portrait. She dressed him in a black velvet robe with fur trim, in keeping with his "elder statesman" bearing, and seated him with his left hand on an open book and his cap beside it.

But Sofonisba's most important painting of those days was a group portrait of her father, Minerva, and Asdrubale. Even before she finished it, she knew it would be her best work ever. She set out to capture the pride and affection that Amilcare felt when he finally had a son, who was then in his seventh year. She placed

Amilcare in the centre, seated, with his left arm around Asdrubale's shoulders. Amilcare was dressed plainly, in black, with just a white collar and cuffs showing. Sofonisba made sure that his loving and caring nature showed clearly in his face. Asdrubale stood, looking up at his father, his face in profile, and his right hand resting on Amilcare's. The boy wore a reddish jacket and matching short pants and hose, and his beloved terrier sat loyally at his feet.

Minerva and Asdrubale had always been close. "An alliance of the Anguissola children who don't paint!" as Sofonisba put it. They played ball in the garden and chased the dog around, then when they tired of that, Minerva entertained Asdrubale with stories that she made up. Sofonisba placed her in the painting to the left, in a sumptuous blue silk dress with red undersleeves embroidered in gold. Her right hand held a bit of the dress fabric to show off its lustre, and in her left hand she held a small bouquet to her breast. A ring that Elena had given her was on her left little finger.

In the rear a red curtain was pulled back to reveal a mythic-looking town — Cremona as in a fantasy, with Roman-style ruins, which Sofonisba had sketched when she was there.

Although Sofonisba loved the hours she spent painting, a restlessness began to overtake her. So it seemed a timely blessing when Bernardino Campi and his wife invited her to visit them in Milan. Amilcare at once began to arrange for her to meet various noblemen of the city and government officials, in the hope that they would want their portraits painted. Sofonisba looked forward to presenting Campi with the double portrait she had painted years ago, of Campi painting her.

The night before the journey, Amilcare found Sofonisba on the sitting room balcony, looking out at the darkness of Cremona's streets. The rest of the palazzo was silent. "Sonia, you should be in bed now. It looks like a summer shower is coming, and you'll be travelling tomorrow."

"Papa, I couldn't sleep. I just wanted to take one last nighttime look at Cremona."

"You'll see it again, of course," Amilcare said.

"But maybe not for a long time," she replied.

They stood quietly looking out at the rough shapes of the other palazzi, the towers, the empty street below.

"So, you are excited about this prospect," Amilcare said.

"I am pleased, and filled with anticipation, but I would only be 'excited' if Mama approved."

Amilcare grimaced. "I know your mother's attitude makes it hard for you. But God has given you ability, and this chance, and you must use them both. I will do everything I can to ease your mother's mind."

Sofonisba turned to Amilcare and leaned against him. A wind gusted out of nowhere, and light rain began to fall.

"Come on, Sonia, let's go in."

5.

Milan

For virtue does not lie in strength of body,
But in soul's vigor and the force of genius
By which anything known can be possessed.
And I am certain that in such endeavors
Women are not in any way less worthy,
But often show a greater aptitude.
—Veronica Franco (1546-1591)

JULY, 1558

As Sofonisba hugged Asdrubale the seven-year-old stiffened, as if by resisting he could keep her from leaving for Milan. Outside the palazzo, in the cruelly mocking sunshine, she then said unsteady goodbyes to Anna Maria, Europa, Minerva, and Lucia in turn. Her father put on a brave face, but his eyes betrayed him. Finally, only her mother stood between her and the carriage.

"Mama, I know you do not favour this," Sofonisba said, meeting her mother's eyes.

"Oh, my daughter," Bianca said, grabbing Sofonisba into a vise-tight hug. Sofonisba closed her eyes and tried to imprint the embrace on her memory. "My love goes with you," Bianca said, and released her.

Sofonisba could only whisper, "Farewell, Mama." She stepped

into the carriage as if in a trance. Rosa, seated beside her, took her hand.

Milan, the momentous, loomed in her prospects — it was the seat of the Spanish influence in Italy, more important even than Rome, a place full of power, promise, and destiny.

After two days of bad roads, she and Rosa entered the city, passing through immense fortifications that had replaced the old Roman wall. Sofonisba raised the carriage window shade to get a look at the streets and saw the city bustling in its morning commerce. Vendors of flowers, fruit, and fish sang out for customers. Spanish soldiers of occupation stood everywhere. The carriage rolled through the dust raised by other carriages.

Sofonisba soon became aware of streams of people, all heading in the same direction and speaking in hushed tones if at all, unlike the usual babble of city streets. When the carriage arrived in a large piazza, a crowd blocked its progress. Sofonisba opened the window and stuck her head out. Above the heads of the crowd, she saw, on the gallows in the centre of the piazza, a bound and blindfolded man standing beside a priest, and she heard the crowd, finally aroused, roaring its horror and approval. "Rosa!" she screamed, as the prisoner plunged through the gallows' trapdoor.

She ducked back into the carriage and buried her head on Rosa's breast. *"Madre de Dio!"*

Rosa had also seen the execution. "Not a very warm welcome to Milan," the maid murmured. The carriage remained stuck for half an hour until the crowd dispersed.

Sofonisba was coming out of her shock when they arrived on Bernardino Campi's doorstep.

"Aren't you happy to see me?" Campi chided. "Wait — your carriage must have gone through the piazza of the executions." Sofonisba nodded.

"Oh, Sofonisba, I'm so sorry you saw that," Campi said. "Your father shielded you well from such public spectacles in Cremona. Ah, here's Anna." Sofonisba hugged Campi's wife.

"I'm afraid our visitor had a rude arrival," Campi told Anna.

"A glass of wine will calm you," Anna said.

Sofonisba relaxed in Campi's large, well-furnished sitting room, a glass of young red wine in her hand. "Thank you both for inviting me. I truly am eager to see Milan."

"Well, look at you!" Campi said. "You were only sixteen when I left Cremona. Now you're quite the mature, well-travelled, experienced painter."

"And still lovely," Anna added.

"You're both too kind," Sofonisba said. "I've missed you, these nine years. And everywhere I've been, I've been proud to say you were my first teacher, Signor Bernardino." She noticed that Campi and his wife were fashionably dressed, in an abundance of silk and lace that she had never seen in their lean Cremona years. And was that a band of tiny jewels on Anna's head?

"Recently, I was painting a portrait of an old friend of Papa's," Sofonisba continued. "I became so frustrated — I just couldn't get the left hand right. Then I saw how you painted St. Jerome's left hand in the cupola of San Sigismondo, and I knew exactly what to do." She and her former teacher smiled at each other.

"Well, now that we've gotten all that mutual admiration out of the way, we can really talk," Anna said. "How do your parents fare, and all the other Anguissolas?"

"Papa still trades in painters' supplies, books, herbs, and grain. Elena is now Suor Monica, and she is the illuminator at her convent in Mantua. So, your instruction of her still bears fruit. Lucia is a brilliant painter now, and I expect her to put me to shame some day." She paused to sip her wine. "Minerva has decided to write instead of paint. Europa and Anna Maria are coming along well as painters. As for Asdrubale, at only seven years, he already knows he's the crown prince, and he gets away with endless misdemeanours."

"Well, that's everyone except your mother," Campi said, not knowing.

Sofonisba looked down a moment. "Ah, Mama," she began. "You see, Mama regards painting as, shall we say, 'inappropriate' for a noblewoman." Unwilling to say more, she took a large sip of wine.

Campi and Anna looked confused, and Rosa stepped in. "Sonia, show Signor Campi that special portrait you brought."

Sofonisba sorted through a pile of rolled-up canvases and pulled one out. "This is for you." She stepped aside from the double portrait and intently watched Campi's reaction.

"Oh, Sofonisba!" He said her name almost in a whisper, then paused awkwardly, his eyebrows high. "It shows great *invenzione* and skill," he said. "This must be larger than anything you've ever done, and the figures in it are larger than life-size, which shows your confidence. To think I nearly … this is simply magnificent."

"It is extraordinary," Anna said, but Sofonisba noticed a reserve, a hesitation in her voice.

"Your right hand sits atop my left, showing how you guided me in teaching me to paint for so many years," Sofonisba explained. "Think of this as a tribute to our friendship."

"The vivid red of that dress is superb," Campi said. "Thank you, Sofonisba, for this tribute. As soon as I get it framed, I will display this prominently."

Anna suggested that the travellers must be tired, and surely would want to rest before dinner. A servant showed Sofonisba and Rosa to their room.

In the sitting room, Anna said to her husband, "Of course you can't leave it like that."

"Pray what do you mean?"

"Your hand over her hand, and her hand over her heart? It's quite improper for a teacher and his maiden student. You knew it too, the minute you saw it."

Baffled, Campi took a step back from his wife and looked at her intently. "Anna, it was envy of her abilities that caused me to hesitate. But there's nothing wrong with this painting. You know quite well there was never anything 'improper' between me and Sofonisba."

"Oh, Nardo, I know that. I'm not implying there was." Anna stepped closer to the painting. "But this painting makes it look as if you two were ... well, more than just teacher and pupil. If you intend to display it as prominently as you said, you will damage her reputation — not as a painter, but as a woman and a noble virgin daughter."

Campi looked again at the painting. "I think you're wrong. Would her parents have let her take an unseemly painting out of the studio?"

"She painted it for you. Maybe her parents never saw it."

Campi opened his mouth, paused, and stepped closer to the painting. He studied it intensely, then turned to his wife. "It's a splendid painting — perhaps worthy of Titian of Venice. I was too mild with my praise. As I paint her in the painting, so, she's saying, I 'created' her— the famous woman painter, Sofonisba Anguissola. Yet her figure is larger than mine. I have to admit, it's brilliant! In any case, the painting's finished. There's not much I can do."

"You'll have to alter it."

"*Alter* it?" Campi's jaw dropped. "That would be defilement." He groaned. "She honours me with this, and I thank her by changing it? Besides, she has surpassed me now. Even I can see that. If anything, *she* should be altering *my* paintings. I only hope she didn't notice my envy."

"Just repaint her left hand so that it's visible, instead of underneath yours," Anna said. "If you truly care about her and her future, you'll do it."

"Oh, Anna." Campi grunted and shook his head. "Well, I won't do anything until she leaves Milan. Until then I will keep it in storage, and we'll tell her that I am designing a special frame."

"All right."

⌒

Sofonisba, Rosa, and Campi made their way among the people in the streets of Milan, a people more colourful in appearance and confusion of languages than Sofonisba remembered in Rome. There were envoys to the Spanish Habsburg court, and merchants and bankers from across Europe and from Asia and North Africa. Some wore oddly twisted or pointed headpieces and flowing robes in startling colours that contrasted with their skin, which came in shades from ivory to midnight.

Maestro Buonarroti had spoken admiringly of Leonardo, an esteemed fellow Tuscan, and Sofonisba had asked Campi to show her a particular work by him. She had seen sketches of Leonardo's works, including one of his most highly praised creations: a *Last Supper* mural in the refectory of the Dominican monastery of Santa Maria delle Grazie.

"Are you sure you want to see it?" Campi had asked.

"Of course, why not?" Sofonisba had replied.

"I must warn you — the work is not as Leonardo intended it, for many reasons," Campi had said. "He was a genius, it's true, but his technique was experimental, and … well, all right, maybe you should just see it for yourself."

So on this day they went, and a monk led the group into the refectory. Campi handed him a gold coin, and he disappeared. "Oh my Lord," Sofonisba gasped in amazement when she first saw the grand sweep and boldness of Leonardo's creation. But stepping closer, and looking up at it carefully, she understood Campi's warning. Peeled, flaked-off paint distorted large areas of the work, and some places were so blurry that she could hardly make out the figures of the apostles.

"The fresco technique didn't suit Leonardo," Campi said. "Instead, he painted this in oil on a dry wall, because it allowed him to proceed slowly. The result is that the paint is not bonded to the wall. But try to look beyond the damage. You can still see how the eye is led to Jesus, and how the light surrounds him."

"I'm overwhelmed by the thought that went into this, indeed, the brilliance of it all," Sofonisba said.

"Yes, this work is a marvel, and at the same time, so sad to observe," Campi said. "The deterioration had already started during the great Leonardo's lifetime. And moisture in the walls is furthering the damage."

Even something created by the great Leonardo can just fade away, Sofonisba realized.

She continued to scan the mural. Soon her reflections on impermanence gave way to an undeniable resentment. "I'll never do anything as large and complicated as this," she said.

"Yes, you could, you have the skill," Campi said.

"Please, Signor Bernardino, you *know* the reason," she said. "It's not a matter of skill. It's because I'm a woman." Her painting hand formed a fist at her side. "Such a work is not considered suitable or proper for me. I've known this forever, but still, it rankles."

Rosa placed a hand reassuringly on her back. "Oh, Sonia, you've painted so many great things. Don't lose heart over this."

"It's true that some things are closed to you, as a woman," Campi admitted. "That is indeed regrettable."

Sofonisba closed her eyes a moment. *Lord, if my complaint is a sin, forgive me.* She opened her eyes and straightened her shoulders, and let her right hand go slack. "Yes, well, thank you for showing me this, Signor Bernardino. And now we'd better go before the monks want their refectory back."

They walked slowly back into the streets and to a shop that sold artists' supplies. "Bernardino, good to see you, and you must be the painter, Sofonisba Anguissola of Cremona," the proprietor said. "I'd be pleased to supply all the materials you need while you're in Milan." Campi bought several pigments and hog's hair for brushes.

"So, have you told everyone in Milan that I was coming?" Sofonisba asked him when they left.

"Everyone who matters, and some of them already knew," Campi said. "Your father did his usual good job of promoting you by announcing your visit. People were already aware of your work, of course. Nobles, courtiers, painters, they all want to meet the woman painter of Cremona who has achieved so much. Tonight they're all invited to a reception I'm holding in your honour."

∽

Rosa helped Sofonisba into her finest ink-blue silk gown, then entwined strings of pearls and jewels into her uplifted hair. Sofonisba looked down from her window and saw the earliest guests arriving.

"Well, hurry on down now, don't keep the people waiting," Rosa said.

The stone walls and flagstones turned from grey to gold as the sunlight waned in Campi's garden, where flowering vines crossed overhead and a quartet played beneath a white linen canopy.

"And this is Giovanni Battista Moroni, a brilliant portraitist who came all the way from Bergamo, just to meet you," Campi said, introducing a man several years older than Sofonisba.

"I'm flattered, Signor Moroni," Sofonisba said. "I've seen drawings of your portraits. Quite inspiring. And I hope to do more full-length portraits like yours."

"Ah, the famed Signorina Anguissola," Moroni said, taking her hand. "Thank you for the compliments. From what I've seen of your portraits, we have much in common. May I call on you while you're in Milan?"

"You may, signore."

Campi cut in. "Lovely. Now please excuse her, Gianbattista."

"Of course." Moroni let go of her hand and faded into the crowd.

"And here's another painter you must meet..." And so it went for about an hour until, having been introduced to most of the painters of Milan, a familiar figure in black and gold approached her.

"Ah, here's someone you absolutely must get to know," Campi said. "Sofonisba, this is Fernando Álvarez de Toledo, the third duke of Alba. Your Grace, may I present Signorina Sofonisba di Amilcare Anguissola, of Cremona."

"Signorina Anguissola. Perhaps you remember me," Alba said, his back as baton-straight as ever.

"Indeed I do, Your Grace." She smiled inwardly at his same strange double-pointed beard.

"You are acquainted?" Campi said.

"Yes, we have met," Sofonisba explained. "His Grace and his retinue stayed with my family when he accompanied the future His Majesty King Philip II to Cremona, in 1549."

"Of course. So I'll leave you two to reminisce," Campi said, and stepped away.

"You travel to many places, sir," Sofonisba said.

"I am now both viceroy of Naples and governor of Milan. I go where His Majesty needs me." He seemed to be looking Sofonisba over in the same calculating way that she remembered from their first meeting. "Pray, may I inquire of your mother and father, and the rest of the family?"

"They are well, thank you, sir. And I finally have a brother."

"I recall that you were a student of painting when we first met. Now you are the esteemed woman painter of Cremona," he said stiffly. "The world has come here to praise you." He waved a hand to indicate the garden, and Sofonisba noticed that the hand was devoid of rings. *Strange that a man of his wealth and status did not wear even one showy ring.*

She also thought she noted a certain chill, an insincerity beneath Alba's words that gave her an insecure feeling, as if she stood at a darkened crossroad and could not be sure which way to go.

She quickly gathered her thoughts. "Ah, thank you, sir," she said. "With this gathering, Signor Bernardino and his wife have paid me a great compliment. I can never repay all their kindness."

Alba surprised Sofonisba with a short laugh. "Don't be too sure you haven't repaid them already. I don't follow artists' gossip, but I understand that just as you benefited from Campi's instruction, so he has benefited from your fame. Many people want to hire the painter who first taught Sofonisba Anguissola."

At that moment a gong sounded, directing the guests to enter the dining room. "May I?" Alba said, and held out his arm, with its black sleeve expertly embroidered in silver.

"Certainly," Sofonisba replied, taking his arm and hoping that she sounded more confident than she felt.

Sofonisba, as the guest of honour, and Alba, as one of the most prominent residents of Milan, were seated together at the long banquet table. The pipers and violinists arranged themselves at one end of the dining room. The wine's unceasing flow began as the guests sampled sugared dates and almonds.

She decided to speak boldly. "You say you don't follow artists' gossip, sir. But I suspect you follow much of the talk around Milan, and are aware of nearly everything that goes on," Sofonisba said.

Alba's moustache twitched. "It is my duty to stay well-informed," he said with a casualness that struck Sofonisba as forced. "France and Spain have been at war for more than ten years, and in conflict for fifty years before that, each wanting to dominate this peninsula. Here in Milan, between northern and southern Europe, I might learn things that could be useful to His Majesty." He picked up a date and chewed it carefully. "Pope Carafa, that is, Paul IV, wants the Spanish out of Italy, so for me, these are demanding times."

"I see you are devoted to His Majesty," Sofonisba said.

"I am privileged to promote my country's interests, and I try to do that with wholehearted diligence and, as you say, devotion."

As the music continued, servants brought plates of olives and sharp cheese.

"So how fares His Majesty King Philip, sir?"

"His Majesty is quite well. Four years ago I had the pleasure of arranging his marriage to Queen Mary, of the House of Tudor, of England. Though she has not yet given him an heir, we are hopeful."

"But doesn't the king already have an heir — his son Don Carlos?" Sofonisba asked.

Alba's knife clanked against the side of his plate. Then, calmly, "You see, signorina, Don Carlos has always been ... sickly," he said, his eyes shifting. "His Majesty has been advised to sire more sons, in the unfortunate event that Don Carlos is unable to assume the throne."

"I see."

Alba said little for the rest of the meal. He did ask Sofonisba about political and economic conditions in Cremona. The two said nearly nothing over the roast partridge breast in a sweet-and-sour sauce, the slices of roast suckling pig dressed with walnuts and oranges, some boiled onions, the lettuce salad with olive oil and vinegar, and slices of quince.

When the guests had finished the last course — small but artfully arranged chestnut cakes with lemon sauce — Campi stood up, signalling the musicians to pause.

"Ladies and gentlemen, revered nobles, fellow painters, my friends, I am overjoyed to have you here. Tonight we honour an esteemed guest in my household. She was a girl of ten when I first met her, and fourteen when it was given to me to teach her to paint. She has taken my feeble instruction and become a painter of remarkable *invenzione* and well-deserved fame." He lifted his glass. "A toast to Sofonisba Anguissola!"

"To Sofonisba! Here, here! *Brava*, signorina!" The words repeated down the table and echoed off the stone walls and set the many candles flickering, and even the servants set down their trays and applauded, and the pipers saluted with a *toot-toot-toooooot*.

"You should stand, my dear." Against the din, the duke of Alba was whispering in her ear. So she stood, smiling broadly as she looked down one side of the table and up the other, soaking in the approbation. *O, Dio, grazie.*

Campi signalled the musicians to resume playing. The guests left the table and it was moved aside, and the dining room became a ballroom. The men and the women, except for Alba, formed sep-arate rows facing each other, and the dance began.

Soon a commotion could be heard bouncing off the walls of the entrance hall. "I must deliver this message to the duke of Alba!"

"But my master has forbidden any interruptions!"

Sofonisba saw Campi break from the row of dancing men and stride swiftly into the hall. "I'll deliver your message to the duke," he told the messenger, dusty from the road.

"No, sir. I have orders to place it directly in His Grace's hands."

Campi returned to Alba and, with profuse apologies, brought him into the hall where the messenger waited. Alba read the message, looked up at the ceiling and said, "Praise God! Signor Campi, I hate to interrupt the dance, but this is glorious news that I must share with everyone, at once!"

"You are my guest, sir," Campi said, gesturing back toward the ballroom.

Alba told the musicians to stop. Sofonisba and the other guests, their dance steps already uncertain from vague dread, broke from their lines and formed little whispering clusters.

"Ladies and gentlemen, I have just received news from the battlefield at Gravelines, near Calais," Alba announced, in an uncharacteristically buoyant tone. "The forces of His Majesty King Philip II of Spain have soundly defeated the enemy, France. The end of the war is in sight!" He raised both his arms.

The guests sent up whoops of delight and raucous applause. The musicians launched into a spirited galliard.

"Signorina?" Moroni held out his hand to Sofonisba. They moved through the kicks and leaps with a joyous energy, far into the night, pausing only to change partners, the music accelerating and slowing, then speeding up again before it stopped, and a breathless Sofonisba sank into the chair that Moroni offered.

"Signorina, you're a magnificent dancer," Moroni said.

She waited until she could speak with more ease, then managed to breathe out, "Thank you, sir."

The next morning, while her head still hummed from the glorious night, a message arrived: "Signorina Anguissola, I request that you paint my portrait as soon as possible…" It was signed, "Fernando Álvarez de Toledo, duke of Alba."

Milan
July 28, 1558

Dearest Mama,

I am overwhelmed by the warm hospitality I have experienced here in Milan. Signor Campi and his wife have made Rosa and me feel most welcome. On my second evening as their guest, to my great surprise and pleasure they held a reception in *my* honour — praise heaven! I was reacquainted with the duke of Alba, who stayed with us when His-Almost-Majesty Philip came to Cremona, you remember. Alba hasn't changed much, he still has that beard that we girls all found so amusing, except that he has risen in rank and power. He's now King Philip's leading military man in Milan and all-round envoy.

While Milan is fascinating and impressive with its power, I miss Cremona, and my sisters and brother, and Papa, and especially you. I beg you to try to understand and perhaps forgive me, Mama, and maybe find a bit of peace and comfort.

May the Lord protect us all until we meet again.

Your loving daughter,

Sonia

⌒⌒

Giovanni Battista Moroni came to call. Sofonisba and Rosa received him in Campi's studio. Sofonisba asked Moroni about his philosophy of painting.

"I try to see and to capture the human character, the individuality, in my subjects," Moroni said.

"So do I, signore. When I painted a group portrait of my father, brother, and one of my sisters, I tried to show Papa's warmth and tenderness, and the special bond between him and his son. I still have to finish that one. Then, in my painting of the third marchese of Soncino, who is just a boy, really, and his two sisters, I showed the girls with their secretive half-smiles, and the boy holding a small dog, to reveal their playfulness, even though they were posed formally — oh no, does that sound boastful?"

"Not at all," Moroni said, and smiled.

"But perhaps this does: through Papa's efforts, I was lucky enough to go to Rome and study under Maestro Michelangelo Buonarroti."

"The Florentine they call *il Divino!* Indeed, signorina, that was lucky. To meet him is every painter's dream. What was he like?"

They walked around the studio as they talked, with Moroni inspecting the brushes, palettes, knives and other tools.

"The Maestro was always intense, but kind and patient with me. He had a bit of — shall I say, melancholy. But I did not see any of his legendary *terribilità*. He taught me about perspective and human anatomy, and how to strengthen a work by balancing opposing characteristics in it."

Moroni looked at her with an envy that Sofonisba had come to recognize whenever she mentioned meeting the Maestro.

"Now, signore, tell me about your work. And please call me Sonia."

"And please call me Giovan. Well, I've painted nobility, and some utterly unknown people, just because there was something interesting about their looks," Giovan said.

Sofonisba nodded. "I have wanted to paint someone who's not rich or prominent, but whose face has some feature that catches the eye. But," she cast her eyes down a moment, "I can't paint every scullery maid or butcher, because they can't pay me for it, and I have to earn money to help Papa."

"There's no shame in that, Sonia, none whatsoever," Giovan said. "What's the difference between you painting to help your Papa, and anyone else who paints to support himself and his family?"

Sofonisba looked into Giovan's black eyes and smiled. *He understands!* She silently celebrated. *He does not dismiss a woman painter as a dilettante.*

She decided to ask an untoward question, but one that had been nagging at her. "Giovan, as a man, you could paint frescoes, and leave your mark forever on vast walls, as the Florentine Leonardo did here. Yet you haven't. I'm curious — why not?"

He considered the question carefully. "It's because the demands of fresco painting don't allow the deep human revelation that portrait painting allows. Moving quickly to act before the plaster dries, there's no time to consider that other dimension. At least, my skill won't allow it! Many men desire that bit of immortality that you describe, but I don't."

In parting, Giovan asked whether he could call on Sofonisba again. She said yes, and Giovan said he would have a surprise for her.

The duke of Alba sat before her in the studio like a soldier, awaiting her orders. He wore a plain, high-necked black jacket buttoned over a white shirt with a ruffled collar and cuffs, and matching short black pants and hose. His eyes darted almost constantly around the studio.

"Your Grace, maybe you have heard the story about the Florentine ambassador in Rome who heard strolling musicians playing loudly on the street outside his palazzo. The man asked the musicians to move on, because his mother had died. Later, gentlemen called on the Florentine to console him, and they asked him when his mother had died. 'Over forty years ago,' the Florentine replied."

Alba chuckled. "If I seem preoccupied, signorina, it's because of the weighty political matters that I face," Alba said.

"Pray, can you tell me about these matters?"

"Oh no, that would be most imprudent, and anyway I would never want to burden you with them."

She had loosened him up just enough, shattering the pane of glass that had stood between them and allowing him to expose a tiny bit of himself. Added to what Sofonisba already knew about him, she had all she needed to make a detailed and sympathetic drawing of a man with a faraway look, in ordinary dress but with uncommon concerns, symbolized by the sword that hung from his belt.

"I know you're a busy man, sir, so I won't insist on repeated sittings," Sofonisba said as she put down her parchment and chalk. "I'll send word when the painting is ready."

Giovan stood in the sunshine in front of Campi's palazzo, holding the reins of three horses.

"Riding! Ah ha! So that's the surprise!" Sofonisba said. "How did you know I love to ride?"

"Oh, I have my ways of knowing things," Giovan said.

Giovan, Sofonisba, and Rosa mounted the horses, and Giovan led the group through a maze of streets and out a busy city gate. Down a dusty country road they stepped up to a canter, then turned to cross a blooming, buzzing meadow. Sofonisba revelled in the horse's vigorous gait; horse and rider created a breeze that refreshed her amid the summer's heat. Giovan led her and Rosa past somnolent fields of hay and barley, mulberry bushes, chestnuts and poplars. She felt herself nearly floating in the long-forgotten joy she had always found in riding, with its hint of freedom. Giovan then slowed to a leisurely trot and Sofonisba pulled up beside him.

"Oh, this is wonderful! I haven't ridden in a long time. Thank you so much, Giovan!"

"I'm glad you're enjoying it. It's quite beautiful out here, and Milan can be oppressive in summer." They continued in silence a while.

"There's a good place to stop." They dismounted, and Giovan spread a silk cloth on the grass for Sofonisba and Rosa. Then he pulled a bottle of red wine and three short cups out of a saddlebag.

After a few sips, and a bit of chatter about the landscape, Rosa stood, a bit abruptly. "I must have a bouquet of those primroses right over there," she said. "I won't be long." She stepped out of earshot.

Sofonisba and Giovan sat in awkward silence. She could not think of a thing to say. *Rosa! she called out in her head.*

Finally, Giovan broke the silence. "So, Sonia, esteemed lady painter, I wonder — what do you do when you have a problem with a painting? Or does that never happen to you?"

"Rarely!" She chuckled. "First, I look through my stacks of drawings for ideas. If I'm in Cremona, I also look at the works of my teachers in the various churches. Or I'll ask Lucia, Europa, and Anna Maria for advice."

"The teacher asks the students?"

"Well yes, why not? I shouldn't let pride and arrogance keep me from finding an answer. And if my sisters come up with a good idea, I get some credit, too, for teaching them to think like painters," she said.

"Sonia — that's quite impressive."

"Well, thank you, and then if I still need help, I go to see Signor Bernardino Gatti. Sometimes I pray to St. Luke. As the patron saint of painters, sometimes I feel him guiding me. And what about you, Giovan?"

"I also consult others, and pray, and then I go to my local tavern, where they let me run up a considerable tab."

"Actually, you've helped me, too," Sofonisba said. "I said I was inspired by your style and composition. I saw drawings of yours that made the rounds in Cremona. Two years ago I was struggling with a portrait of myself at the clavichord. Seeing your drawings helped me make shadows to soften the harshness, and to make a more ambitious composition."

"I revel in your praise," he said with mock solemnity. They both took lingering sips of wine. "Now, Sonia, stop me if this is a rude question, but is there no young man in Cremona who ever captured your heart?"

Sofonisba looked at him sharply. She waved away a persistent fly and glanced over at the horses, languidly grazing. She saw that Rosa had stopped picking flowers and was resting in the shade of a willow.

"I am sorry. I should not have asked," Giovan said.

"No, I don't mind," Sofonisba said. "In fact, there was a young man who wanted to marry me, but my father left the decision to me, and I turned him down. It wasn't easy — I can see the pleasures of family life, like any woman. But I love my painting. I can't devote myself to a husband. At least, not yet."

"Your father is to be commended." Giovan refilled her wine cup.

"And your family, in Bergamo?" Sofonisba asked, feeling awkward.

Giovan said that his young wife had died a few years before of consumption, leaving him with two children.

Suddenly restless, Sofonisba pointed out a line of poplars in the distance. "See those trees? Let's race." They mounted the startled horses. "Start us off, Rosa," Sofonisba called out. "Go!"

Sofonisba's horse took off across the meadow, deftly jumping a shallow stream as she leaned forward. She felt the old surge of competitiveness, the desire to outdo. Her horse drummed past the poplars a neck's length ahead of Giovan's. Sofonisba felt thrilled and exhilarated, but concealed her joy.

"Sonia! You have put me to shame," Giovan said, panting. "You're an excellent horsewoman."

"This is an excellent horse," she said modestly. They returned to the clearing, where Rosa waited. "Thank you again for this afternoon. It's been perfectly splendid."

MILAN, 1558

The flaming skies of August curbed the pace of life in Milan, and the city had barely revived itself in September's coolness when word arrived of the death of Holy Roman Emperor Charles V. The city draped itself in black crepe and sank into quiet mourning. Alba ordered all shops closed and all other business suspended for three days. The tolling of the cathedral's bells called all Milanesi to a requiem Mass.

Of interest to Campi and Sofonisba was the fact that Charles died while staring at Titian's *La Gloria*, a panel crowded with saints praising the Trinity.

Charles' death left his son, King Philip II, free to rule as he pleased.

Sofonisba poured extra diligence and time into her portrait of the duke of Alba. She was determined to capture his combination of devotion to duty, reserve, and his cunning mind. She had not yet finished when the duke, through his secretary, commissioned three more paintings from her, portraits of local noblemen of his acquaintance.

In November, word reached Milan that Queen Mary, wife of King Philip, had died in England. She had never given Philip a son.

Two months later, in late January of 1559, Sofonisba informed Alba that his portrait was finished. She was "invited" to the duke's quarters and instructed to bring the portrait.

"Such presumption! Such arrogance! He does not *ask* me to bring him the portrait, he simply commands it and assumes that I will! He does not know that my patrons come to *me*! Rosa, what should I do?"

"You'll bring it to him, of course. Eh, he's boorish, to be sure, but sometimes, love, you must overlook that. Alba is a man who could do you some good."

"Everyone keeps saying that, but I don't know what it means."

"It simply means that he is powerful, and a good man to have on your side."

In the palazzo that the Spanish rulers occupied, Sofonisba and Rosa climbed a massive, curving stone staircase past colourful tapestries. Down one hallway and another they walked, with one Spanish servant leading them and another following, carrying the duke's portrait. At last they reached the duke's study.

The long room was dim except for a lamp on Alba's desk and meagre daylight through the many-paned windows.

"Good morning, Signorina Anguissola," the duke said, and stood up. He told the servant to stand the painting on a table.

"Good morning, Your Grace," Sofonisba said.

"So, let's see what we have here," Alba said, pointing to the portrait and picking up the lamp. Sofonisba removed the linen wrapping.

"Ah ha, yes, very good," Alba said.

That's all he has to say? "Very good?" After all I put into it?

"You know, signorina, a painter as skilled as you could have many opportunities." He folded the linen cloth, absently.

"I do have many commissions, thanks partly to you, sir."

"I don't mean the usual commissions, I mean … let's sit down."

When they were all seated, Alba continued: "Pray tell me, signorina, do you have any ambitions?"

"Ambitions?" *The man is an unending puzzle*, she thought. "I don't
understand, sir."

"Well, you … ah, never mind. I'll be leaving Milan tomorrow,
on a mission for His Majesty."

"You must be pleased that His Majesty has such faith in you,
Your Grace," Sofonisba said.

"Oh I am, signorina." His smile teased. "My secretary will settle
the account for this painting, according to our agreement. Good
day, signorina, and, ah, enjoy the rest of your stay in Milan."

"Good day, sir, and safe journey."

～

She was glad to get back into the carriage.

"'Very good,' indeed! Rosa, that's all he said about one of my
best portraits ever!"

"The man's stiff as an oak door, that's for certain, but don't forget,
he also mentioned 'opportunities,' Sonia."

"Yes, he did." She stared off and thought a moment. "But he is
so reserved, so mysterious. What did he mean?"

"Don't trouble yourself about it, love," Rosa said. "Let things
unfold as God wills them."

～

Alba's great diplomatic skills did indeed bring about a treaty favourable to Spain. France was forced to finally stop interfering with
Spanish control over Milan, Naples, Sicily, and Sardinia. Italians
looked forward to renewed trade and the lucrative free travel of
pilgrims, at last unhindered by war. The accord also called for strategic marriages: the king of France's sister would marry the duke of
Savoy, and the king's daughter, Elisabeth of Valois, was betrothed
to King Philip himself. She would be Philip's third wife, charged

above all with providing her husband with a male heir. The two alliances would more closely intertwine Spain, Italy and France, and shift each country's focus away from England.

Campi said he regretted that the treaty's terms had not loosened Spanish rule over Milan and Cremona. "We cannot claim to be oppressed, it is true, but still, if only we could be independent, like Venice…"

Sofonisba dwelled mainly on King Philip, remembering the thrill and tension of meeting him, then a prince, during that long-ago visit that so aroused Cremona. But she forgot about the fortunes of royalty when she entered her studio and continued work on her *St. Catherine of Siena* painting. Two portraits and a *Holy Family* also awaited her attention.

～

Alba journeyed to Paris to prepare the proxy wedding ceremony of King Philip and Princess Elisabeth. Over the spring and summer, news of the wedding trickled into Milan from Paris, carried by merchants and pilgrims on their way to Rome, and other travellers who, because of the peace agreement, could now move about more freely. Milan remembered Philip's visit of 1549, his blond, decidedly un-Spanish looks and his withdrawn, coolly polite manner. His match with Elisabeth caught the city's imagination.

"It's so romantic — our king and the French princess! It's like a fairy tale!"

"Romantic? Not him. He was so guarded, so aloof, remember? We could hardly get a decent conversation out of him."

"Still, a woman so young and sweet might bring out quite a different side of him. She should have a warming, softening effect."

"She'd better, if they are to create heirs! And let's face it, that's the only reason for this match. The peace treaty is just a convenient excuse."

A few days after news of the joyous wedding, however, celebratory banners on the French envoy's palazzo in Milan were exchanged for black mourning cloth. Breathless messengers from Paris brought tidings of tragedy: King Henry II, Elisabeth's father, had been killed in a joust held in her honour, one of the many wedding celebrations and tournaments. Sofonisba prayed for the young bride-queen.

"That poor girl! One day, happily dressed in gold and jewels, and the next, all in black!" she said to Rosa.

AUGUST, 1559

Sofonisba took her time, balancing each wooden stick a moment in the crook of her right hand, one by one, savouring their smoothness and weight, and then lining them up on the table in order from thinnest to thickest. She sorted carefully through a pile of hog's hair, separated the strands into small bundles of varying sizes, and then combed each bundle to align every hair. She tied a bundle to the end of each wooden stick to make paintbrushes.

She sat back and surveyed the new brushes with satisfaction. There was something inspiring about a new paintbrush — from handle to bristle tip, each one held possibility, foretold beauty, strength and drama.

She built up the fire and began to prepare oil for mixing paints. The *Holy Family* altarpiece still needed some final touches on the Virgin's robes and the background foliage. Absorbed in her painting, hearing little gossip, Sofonisba was not aware that Alba had returned to Milan until she received a note from him, summoning her to his office.

Alba startled Sofonisba and Rosa with an uncharacteristically effusive greeting.

Sofonisba silently resolved to be cautious. *Whatever he wants, don't say yes, at least, not now.*

"Good morning, Your Grace. Congratulations on the successful peace talks. We were all thrilled to hear about the royal wedding, then saddened over King Henry's death."

"Yes, it was horribly grievous. I called in Vesalius, the great physician, he's been serving King Philip for years, but there was nothing even he could do, the injury to King Henry was too great. The funeral rituals went on as long as the wedding festivities had." He sat up in his chair. "I'm afraid it was particularly wrenching for the young queen, Elisabeth, and that's why I wanted to see you, signorina."

Despite deep confusion, Sofonisba kept her dispassionate expression.

"She's only thirteen, still a child, really. In the course of a few weeks she has become a bride and a queen, and then lost her dear father. Now, for the first time in her life, she faces separation from her mother and everyone else she knows in Paris, when she travels to Spain to take her place as King Philip's queen."

Sofonisba's mind raced to comprehend what all this had to do with her.

"She's a well-trained, dutiful young woman, and she loves drawing and painting. Signorina Anguissola, I have suggested something to King Philip, and he has agreed." Alba paused dramatically, and looked at her with even more than his usual seriousness. "The king wants you to join Elisabeth's household in Spain as a lady-in-waiting, her special companion."

"Sir!" Sofonisba thought she heard a gong sounding somewhere. *King Philip is calling on me!* She looked for reassurance to Rosa, who smiled proudly.

"Now, I realize this is a lot to take in," Alba said. "Elisabeth, with her youth and inexperience, will need a close companion at court, someone older than her but still young — a big sister, shall we say, and that's a relationship you know well. And with your skill as a painter, you can portray the queen and other members of the royal household."

It was Rosa who responded first. "Sir, this is quite an honour."

"Indeed, Your Grace, I am honoured beyond all words," Sofonisba said.

"Words are not needed now, signorina. Of course, you must give this some thought. Spain is something of a distant land." He sat back in this chair and folded his hands. "While you consider it, may I write to your father and ask his permission?"

Sofonisba sensed his urgency, but she was determined to enjoy the moment. To Spain, as companion to the queen! She turned the words over in her head and found them surprisingly unfearsome, even tantalizing.

"Yes, sir, you may write to my father," she said, pleased with her self-possession. "And thank you. I'm overwhelmed by your confidence in me. Now, please tell me more about Elisabeth, and King Philip's court."

∾

Sofonisba stood on the deck of a boat that pulled inexorably from an already-distant shoreline. Standing on the shore and looking at her were Papa, Mama, Lucia, Minerva, Europa, Anna Maria, and Asdrubale, all standing together, and Rosa, standing alone. They watched her silently, in a line that appeared to shift up and down with the boat's movement. No one waved. And as the boat propelled farther away, they shrank into tiny dolls.

Then she awakened, in her room in Campi's palazzo in Milan, stuffy from the August heat. She went to the window and opened the shutters, breathed the heavy air, and looked across the rooftops of the dark city.

"Sonia." Rosa had awakened and spoken her name softly, to avoid startling her.

"Rosa, I dreamed that I travelled far from my family…"

"Ah, if you go to Spain, you will be far from them indeed."

"…and from you. Pray, is that part also true?"

"Sonia, I'm afraid it is." She put one hand on Sofonisba's shoulder, and they sat down on the bed.

"It's like this, love. I'm a servant, from poor Cremona stock. I have no place in the court of His Majesty King Philip, the ruler of Christendom and half the world, no less." She rubbed her eyes. "You'll have other companions, new responsibilities. It's time for you to move on, without me."

"But I'll miss you terribly," Sofonisba said, a sob escaping.

"And I'll miss you, lovey, every day," Rosa said, pushing back a lock of Sofonisba's hair. "You've become like a daughter to me, like...." Her voice caught. "Now you are old enough to know, if you don't already."

"Know what?"

Rosa looked away for a moment. "Do you remember going to the cemetery at Sant'Agostino's, one day when you were in your tenth year?"

Sofonisba's heart seized in pain. "Yes, I do," she said weakly.

"You saw the grave of my beloved, Federico Mariano, and maybe you noticed the baby's grave next to it."

"Oh, Rosa, the memory still burns me with shame, for having gone where you had forbidden me," Sofonisba said. "I did see that tiny grave, but I didn't know then what it meant. Perhaps, over the years, I came to understand, but shame pushed the matter deep into my mind, and I tried so hard to forget the whole encounter."

"Now you are old enough to know." There was a long pause. "Yes, that was our baby, Federico's and mine. The poor little thing died the day he was born, just barely baptized, he was." In the dark, Sofonisba could not see that Rosa's eyes had welled up and her long pointy nose had reddened. "Sonia, you are to me like the child I never knew." They embraced.

"Maybe I shouldn't go to Spain."

"Oh Sonia, you *must* go. It is your destiny, it is *fortuna*."

"Thank you," Sofonisba breathed softly and with great relief, for Rosa's forgiveness and permission, for confirming what she already knew.

They sat together a while, watching the sky begin to lighten.

"Aye, the summer dawn comes too early, lovey," Rosa said. "Lie back and get some more rest."

Cremona lost no time in claiming credit for the honour that the Spanish king had bestowed on Sofonisba, even proposing that the city's longstanding favour toward artists had finally been duly rewarded. The summary rejection of Sofonisba by the painter's guild was conveniently forgotten. Everywhere he went, Amilcare heard: "We're all so proud! Sofonisba brings Cremona great glory and fame!" It particularly gratified Amilcare to hear such sentiments from people who once told him that women should not be taught to paint.

He went to Milan, and father and daughter reunited along with Campi in the family's sitting room. "Who would have thought, Bernardino, when I asked you to teach my daughter to paint, that things would come to this?" Amilcare asked.

"I am exceedingly proud of my former student," Campi said.

Sofonisba gulped before asking a question that had troubled her. "Now Papa, pray tell me plainly. What did Mama say about all of this?"

"Ah, well, I am afraid that she has not changed her beliefs about your painting. She said that your going to Spain was a painful thing for her. Then she said that it must be God's will, and she would just have to bear it. She has spent more time in private prayer lately, and more time at San Giorgio, lighting candles. I told her that you had received a great honour, and she did not argue."

"I see," Sofonisba said, her face lengthening. She shifted in her chair. *Poor Mama!*

After the awkward pause, Amilcare said, "I have something to show both of you."

He reached inside a leather pouch hanging from his belt and pulled out a velvet bundle. He untied it to reveal a small red silk packet, and then slowly pulled out a bronze medallion. He handed it to Sofonisba.

It was about the size of her palm. She was depicted on it in profile, and around the edge it read, *Sophonisba Anguissola, Amilcare's daughter.*

At first, she admired the exquisite work, detailed enough to show a braid wrapped around her head, the lace of her collar, even the ties of her chemise. Then she began to realize the meaning of the object.

"Papa." She handed the medallion to Campi. "Oh, Papa, it's so beautiful, thank you," she said. Tears began to well up.

"Now, now, none of that," Amilcare said. "This commemorates the great honour you have received, and forever records your many achievements."

"It's splendid, Amilcare," Campi said, handing back the medallion. "Just the proper gesture." He excused himself.

Sofonisba put the medallion back in its silk case. Father and daughter were happy with the chance to speak in private.

"So, my dear, you've had much to think about during the past few weeks," Amilcare said. "Ach, I'm such an old man now. I've got to stretch after that long carriage ride."

He rose and paced around the room, taking in the fine tapestries, the rugs, and the silver goblet in his hand. "I see Bernardino's done quite well for himself. But not as well as you've done, ha ha!" He sat down again. "I knew when you met King Philip all those years ago in Cremona, that you were destined for something grand."

Sofonisba furrowed her forehead. "Rosa said something like that. I was worried at first about leaving you all, but Rosa said I must go, that it's my destiny."

"And she's right. The family will be fine. Business has picked up in Cremona, so we are in a good situation. You've served the family well with your painting. Now go and serve your king, and take from this all the adventure and glory you can!"

"I will try, Papa, but I cannot forget that Mama is suffering be-cause of me."

"Hmm. No, of course, you cannot just forget," Amilcare said. "That is the thorn in this rose of triumph. But you must have faith, my Sonia, that your mother will find her strength."

Milan
September 27, 1559

Dear Mama,

In writing this, I humbly ask your understanding as I go on this journey, which our king has requested and which gives the family great honour.

I do not deny my eagerness to paint the royal family and to see something of the world beyond Italy, but I undertake this enterprise with humility and gratitude. God, through King Philip, has seen fit to grant me this opportunity. My eagerness is tinged with displeasure because of your reservations, and the long distance this will put between us.

May God strengthen us to endure the days of separa-tion. Pray for me, Mama, and be assured that wherever I go I will think of you, and the wise lessons you always taught me, and the love in which you raised me.

Your loving daughter,
Sonia

Sofonisba's travels could not wait until spring, when the roads would be in better condition, because she needed to arrive in Spain around the same time that Elisabeth would arrive. So one morning in mid-October, an unusual line formed outside Campi's palazzo: at its head was a horseman armed with pistols. Next came a carriage in which Sofonisba's two companions waited, and third came another carriage carrying six servants. Finally, at the tail end, was another armed horseman. The door of the companions' carriage hung open.

She had already said goodbye to Campi and his family ("A palace is just the setting your work deserves!" her former teacher had said). Then, speechless with sorrow, she hugged Rosa as if she would never let go.

"I'll always be with you in spirit, my dear Sonia," Rosa said, then fled back into the palazzo.

"Papa, give this letter to Mama," Sofonisba said, handing Amilcare a sealed parchment.

"I will. You have a fine day for travel, cool, and with this autumn sun," Amilcare said as he tucked the letter away. "Now, don't forget the Anguissola motto."

"The lone snake is victorious."

"That's right. Not a pretty image, perhaps, but *respectable*." Each of them looked into the other's blue-green eyes before they embraced.

"Oh Papa, will I ever see you again?"

"You *must* come back to Cremona. You still have to finish that portrait of Minerva, Asdrubale and me, remember?" Amilcare smiled.

"Oh yes, of course." Her father pressed both her hands in his, and Sofonisba stepped into the carriage and closed the door.

The line of horsemen and carriages began to move. When it had disappeared down the street, Campi stood beside Amilcare and put a hand on his shoulder.

"Is this what the rest of my life is to be — watching my daughters roll away in carriages?" Amilcare asked, and then he could not speak any more for the tightness in his throat.

6.

The Centre of Christendom

And therefore do not cease, gifted women,
To launch your ships of talent on the ocean!
— Laura Bacio Terracina (1519-1577)

LATE AUTUMN, 1559

Outside Milan's wall, the coaches and their guards entered a fertile plain where mulberry bushes, grapevines, olives, and rice normally grew. But it was late fall, so the plain was covered with spindly brown stalks. Scattered scarecrows pathetically insisted on their needless posturing over the dormant countryside.

Despite the barrenness, Sofonisba saw flashes of strange beauty: gaunt poplar branches cast jagged reflections on the surface of a pond in the light of late afternoon. Low dark clouds hung over a field like a blanket about to descend for the winter, to protect the earth and ensure a fruitful spring. She considered each view a painting, if she could only stop long enough to paint them.

Crossing the Po River, she thought longingly of Cremona, but pushed the thought away and focused on the adventure, trying to let it engulf her.

She turned to her travelling companions — Aurelia Poldi and Beatrice Bessano, daughters of friends of Alba's, and close to her age. The three told each other about themselves and their families.

Then, when Aurelia let slip a few words of Spanish and Beatrice responded in the same way, Sofonisba suggested they speak nothing but Spanish for the rest of the trip, so that she could learn. In turn, she would sketch their portraits. She smiled at the thought of impressing King Philip by speaking to him in his mother tongue.

Beyond the Lombard plain, the group entered the mountains of Liguria and their deep, narrow valleys. In an isolated village, they stopped in the main square at noon while the horsemen changed mounts. Sofonisba and her companions joined a crowd that had gathered, all eyes on a travelling preacher as he stood above the villagers and harangued them about the evils of this world and the pains they would suffer in the next if they did not avoid sin. He showed them a bridle and claimed it had been worn by the donkey of St. John of Capistrano. A young man in the crowd, a stranger to the village, began to shout at the preacher, "Liar! Devil! Liar!" Then he howled and fell to the ground, writhing in agony as if struck by lightning. The black-robed preacher stepped down into the crowd, holding his hands to his breast, and when he reached the tortured young man he said, "Begone, Satan! Despicable one, return to your fiery depths!" The young man stopped shaking and writhing, then stood up slowly, his legs wobbly, his eyes raised heavenward. The preacher grabbed the man's hand and raised it high. "Praise the Lord, he is freed from the Devil's grip!" The crowd gasped, and many shouted and sang to give the Lord praise. "And now, dear ones, please help me, help me only to live as I carry the Lord's work to other places far more blighted than your village, blighted with souls gone astray," the preacher said as he carried a cap among the crowd. Many gave a coin or two, and no one noticed that the young man had disappeared. Sofonisba turned to Aurelia and Beatrice and started to whisper ridicule aimed at the credulous villagers, but stopped herself when she saw her companions' rapt faces. "What, Sofonisba? Were you about to say something?" they asked, distractedly.

"Ah, no, nothing important, I only said I hoped we get on our way soon."

⌀

In a cell in the convent of Sant'Agnese, by a sputtering candle, Sofonisba wrote in her journal.

December 17, 1559

Through the Lord's good grace and protection, we have finally reached Genoa. The sisters of Sant'Agnese took us at once to evening vespers and then shared with us their meal of bread, vegetable soup, figs and wine.

After more than seventy miles across Lombardy and Liguria, it will be a welcome change to leave the carriage behind and transfer to a galley, because the bouncing, rocking motion of the carriage, I fear, is forever imprinted in my limbs. It was not my first carriage journey and not at all my longest, yet I felt it more deeply, both in body and mind.

⌀

The women stood on the dock at the port of Genoa, watching dark-skinned men load their trunks onto a ship. *The bad dream of leave-taking becomes real,* Sofonisba thought. Even so, she found it exasperating to wait while all the cargo and supplies were loaded first — only then could the passengers finally board. *Oh Holy Virgin, watch over me,* she prayed as she stepped off her native land and onto a ship for the first time. As the ship headed out, she refused to look toward the shore.

Buoyed by the ship's motion, Sofonisba felt almost weightless as she relished her freedom from the carriage's jolts. She spent most of her time in her cabin, reading and sketching, and the ship's steward brought her meals to her there. Aurelia and Beatrice came daily for long talks in Spanish. Despite their good company, one day the confinement became unbearable.

"I'm going up on deck. Come with me," Sofonisba commanded.

"We can't! The captain said it's unsafe for women to be on the deck!"

"He meant that it's unseemly. Sailors are superstitious about women. I want to breathe a little sea air, and take a look around." She almost laughed at their stricken faces. "If we all go together, and don't stay long, it'll be all right. Come on!" She stepped out of the cabin. Aurelia and Beatrice looked at each other with alarm, and followed her.

It took some lifting of skirts and careful stepping to get up the steep, narrow ladder. Once above, they lined up along the rail and looked out toward the shore, watched the fishing boats, and took deep breaths of the Ligurian Sea's chilly breezes.

They heard a voice behind them. "Good afternoon, my ladies," said the captain, and they all jumped. "I hope you are not too chilled up here."

"Good afternoon, captain," Sofonisba replied. "I know you advised us to stay below, but my curiosity got the better of me, as this is my first sea voyage. And after six days down below, I needed some fresh air, and my companions were kind enough to indulge me."

"I see," the captain said. Sofonisba noticed him suppressing a smile. "Now that you've had a look around, perhaps you're wondering why we travel so close to the coast. That's because of the danger of pirates."

The women shivered with cold and fear. "We'll be going below now. Do excuse us," Sofonisba said.

"Of course, my ladies. By the way, if the wind stays favourable, we should arrive in Barcelona the day after tomorrow."

"Christmas Day," Sofonisba said. *Surely it would be a good sign to arrive in Spain on the feast of Our Lord's birth.*

They did indeed step off the ship on the day the captain had predicted. Sofonisba and her companions huddled together and said a prayer of thanks for a safe sea voyage. A military escort, sent by King Philip, waited to take them across the perilous countryside. "Commandante Calderón, señora, at your service," said her burly guardian. "To protect you from bandits, wild animals, tricksters, desperate types of every persuasion, señora!" He let out a belch. "Oh my, a *thousand* pardons, señora. But have no fear, no fear at all, King Philip says to get you to Guadalajara safely, and by God, that's what we'll do! By the way, *feliz Navidad!*" He cackled with laughter as he turned his horse around. The women boarded their carriage, and they were off.

They would travel almost three hundred miles to Guadalajara, where King Philip's court awaited Elisabeth's arrival. By Calderón's order, the women stayed in the carriage through Catalonia: "Bandits, my ladies. They're common in these parts, supported by French Protestants, who are sworn enemies of King Philip."

In Aragón, Calderón scared and enlightened his charges with tales of rioting just a year before. King Philip had raised taxes, and food was scarce because of floods one year and droughts the next. "Anger and hunger make a dangerous combination."

JANUARY, 1560

On the Sunday after the feast of the Epiphany, the women found themselves in the town of Zaragoza. Commandante Calderón wanted to leave right after Mass, but an agitated crowd gathering then in the cathedral square made him pause. In a foreboding tone, he told the women that something was about to happen that they had to see.

"A trial of heretics, ladies, a cleansing of their evil from the community. It's called an *auto-da-fé*. A deed of faith. You've heard of the Holy Inquisition, no?" He arranged for the women to stand on a wide raised porch at one end of the square, giving them a good view. Clouds blocked the late-morning sun.

The crowd soon filled the square and every balcony overlooking it. Six prisoners were led in, three women and three men, all appearing exhausted and in pain, some walking in a stiff-legged tread, others hunched. Each prisoner wore a yellow tunic and carried a cross painted green. The crowd jeered and shouted words of hatred; guards had to restrain the onlookers from beating the prisoners.

Calderón explained that the prisoners were the *sambenitos*, the accused. They would be tried, convicted unless they repented, and sentenced. Sofonisba, Aurelia and Beatrice pulled their woolen capes tighter. The bishop stood and signalled for the trumpeters and drummers to stop.

"Oh most holy God, we humbly carry out your vital work here today, ridding your people, your land, of the scourge of blasphemers, non-believers, idolators, and heretics." The crowd called out "Praise the Lord!"

The crowd then roared in fury after hearing each charge against each *sambenito*, then roared again when each of the accused was loudly proclaimed guilty. The official then approached each *sambenito*, one by one, and asked, "Do you renounce and repent your evil deeds and all your sins against God?"

The first *sambenito* sneered at the official and grunted. The second paused, took a deep breath and shouted, "Yes! I repent! Jesus save my soul! Lord have mercy! Lord have mercy!" and the crowd cheered hysterically.

The third, fourth and fifth *sambenitos* did not look at the official or say anything, and the crowd shifted back to pouring forth invective. The sixth, upon hearing the question, straightened his bent back, looked straight at the Inquisitor, and spit in his eye.

The mob exploded into a frenzy, shaking their fists at the *sambenito* and screaming, "God save us! Oh, Blessed Jesus! He must die!" Guards barely stopped the people from mounting the stage. Commandante Calderón joined in the calls for God's protection and urged Sofonisba, Aurelia, and Beatrice to do the same. When they gave him doubtful looks, he said, "You have to! If you do not, you may be accused of being non-believers yourselves," he said. "At least just fold your hands and act like you're praying."

They obeyed. Sofonisba's hands shook as she pressed them together. "What will happen to them?" Sofonisba asked as the *sambenitos* were led away.

"The one who repented will be put back in prison, and if her penitence is deemed to be real, she may even be released," Calderón said. "The others will be taken outside the city today and executed."

There was a strained pause. "Will they be burned?"

"Oh, señora…"

"Please! I want to know," Sofonisba persisted.

"Yes, señora, they will be burned."

As the group continued its travels across Aragón, Sofonisba noticed that one village after another seemed full of no one but Moriscos. She recognized them by their clothing because despite their conversion to Christianity, these Moors kept their distinctive garb. The women wore colourful loose pants and long tunics; white veils covered all but their eyes. The men wore long flowing robes and turbans. They kept their customs, too. Sofonisba saw a group step out of their shoes and wash their hands before entering a church. She was fascinated, especially by the women, and longed to paint their portraits.

"Now the Moors are good at working the land, clever about irrigation, so they are dear to the landed nobility. These here in Aragón are good Moriscos, you see, not like the bandits of Valencia. Those make the Gypsies look like choirboys!" Calderón said and laughed.

"Gypsies? Here?" Sofonisba asked.

"Yes, lots of them. Don't you have them in Italy?"

"I've heard about them, but I've never seen any."

"Then, señora, you'll no doubt see your first Gypsies here in

Spain, perhaps once we pass into Castile."

The land became more rugged over the Castilian border, and to Sofonisba's delight, the women left the carriage and mounted horses. Sometimes Sofonisba thought she sensed curious eyes watching as the group moved through forests and across streams, but later dismissed her "visions" as anxiety planted by Calderón's tales.

But one day, through the pines she saw a wagon, some shaggy horses and a group of women sitting in a circle around a fire, talking and sewing and feeding babies. The women wore knitted shawls in indigo, scarlet, gold, and purple — the same array of bold colours as in the designs painted on the wagons and the horses' bridles. The vivid flashes against the dull grey and black of the trees struck Sofonisba's painterly eye. She maneuvered her horse until she was alongside the commandante. "Are they Gypsies?" she asked.

"Yes. They move constantly from one area to the next, staying out of cities. It's their way. They're also thieves and swindlers, and given half a chance," he looked at her with wide eyes, his beard twitching, *"they kidnap children."*

"You're joking."

"I am not, señora." Commandante Calderón glanced back protectively over the group. "You want nothing to do with Gypsies, señora. Believe me. But, as I said when we started, have no fear!"

"Why don't I see any men among them?" Sofonisba asked.

"Some of them must have seen us coming. When the men realized that a military contingent was on this road, they no doubt disappeared even deeper into the wild. You see, all male Gypsies must serve on the royal galleys for six years — if we catch them. And catching them is quite difficult."

They rode on in silence.

At last, on a dreary day in January, the commandante stopped his horse at the edge of a ridge. "There she lies — our destination — Guadalajara!"

Sofonisba looked down a long slope and suppressed a feeling of disappointment. The first place in Spain where she would stay for more than one night was an unimpressive cluster of stone buildings and slate roofs in a low valley. Only one building stood out for its size. "Pray, what is that building — the long white stone box?" she asked the commandante, pointing.

"That's where I'm taking you, señora. You see, the house of Mendoza controls Guadalajara, and that building, well, that's the house of Mendoza *house!* Ah, ha ha ha ha!" He had to wipe his eyes with a handkerchief. "There, you'll be joining King Philip's court, señora. Ha ha ha, house of the house." He shook his head in wonder at his own wit.

On seeing the palace up close, Sofonisba forgot her unpromising first view. No one looking at the palace could doubt the family's wealth and power. Indeed, Cardinal Mendoza was one of the highest-ranking members of Philip's court. It was the cardinal who kindly — and shrewdly for his career prospects — offered his house for the court's accommodation while it waited for Elisabeth. Sofonisba was drawn to things like the palace's centrepiece: a rectangular courtyard with a gallery on each of the two floors, formed by spiral columns supporting oddly pointed arches. This Court of the Lions got its name from the creatures carved in high relief above every arch.

The palace struck Sofonisba as the perfect setting for the fairy-tale wedding ceremony that Philip and Elisabeth would act out in the palace chapel. No one seemed to care that officially, they were already married.

Sofonisba longed to make a calm and quiet review of the palace's architectural wonders, but the atmosphere was a roiling fever of excitement: "Elisabeth arrives tomorrow!" Some servants were busy preparing the queen's room; others made sure there were enough provisions for a grand wedding banquet; and others bustled about cleaning and decorating the palace chapel and banquet hall.

When word reached the palace that Elisabeth's carriage was a mere five miles away, rows of the curious began to line the streets along the route from Guadalajara's northern gate to the palace's main gate. They waved and cheered as the carriage passed, but the queen stayed hidden behind its leather-shaded windows. Sofonisba joined a crowd of courtiers that had formed in the palace courtyard and that surrounded Elisabeth's carriage as it approached the main door. A hush fell over the courtyard as the duke of Alba opened the carriage door and extended his hand.

The cheering started again, this time louder, when the young French bride stepped out, turned to the crowd, smiled and waved. Alba whisked her inside, where lines of servants and courtiers bowed and curtsied as Elisabeth went by. Alba escorted Elisabeth to her chamber, and over some time the palace excitement dissipated as everyone slowly returned to their duties. It took the rest of the day for the carriages and laden mules of Elisabeth's entourage to roll in and be unloaded.

Two days later, a knock sounded on the door of the ladies' room. "Her Majesty will meet you now, Señora Anguissola," said a young member of the royal guard. "I will escort you."

"Oooh, how exciting!" Aurelia and Beatrice said, their glee reminding Sofonisba of her sisters. "Let me put this jewelled clip over your braids!"

Philip had arrived in Guadalajara the previous week, and by his order, the room reserved for the new queen was the largest bed-chamber in the Mendoza palace, much bigger than the king's own room and filling almost an entire floor. Rumours suggested it was the best room in the palace, and as she looked around, Sofonisba had to agree. Her trained eye knew at a glance that the murals were expertly painted. She noticed the elaborate coffered ceiling and stepped gingerly on the colourfully tiled floor, afraid of leaving a mark. A group of courtiers practiced dance steps, seamstresses added extra pearls to the queen's wedding gown, and attendants planned the seating arrangement for the wedding banquet. Even with all the varied activity, the room was large enough for the queen to have a quiet space by the fire to receive visitors.

"Your Majesty, may I present Señora Sofonisba Anguissola, the painter from Cremona in Italy, sent here as your lady-in-waiting by the duke of Alba," the guard said, and stepped away.

Sofonisba saw a girl of fourteen, a high starched ruff framing a face not beautiful, but pleasing enough. She curtsied low. "*Votre Majesté, c'est un honneur de répondre à vos.*"

The queen gasped with delight. "You speak French!"

"*Oui, Votre Majesté*, I thank my parents for giving me a classical education."

Sofonisba was instantly touched by the queen's youthful appearance, but why such sadness in those hazel eyes? Then Sofonisba remembered — *Of course! Her father!* "Your Majesty, please accept my condolences on the death of your most eminent father."

Elisabeth's voice caught. "Thank you." She looked down and placed one hand on her high forehead. After a moment she looked again at Sofonisba and said, "Señora, please sit down," and Sofonisba saw that her eyes were dry, the young face composed.

"It is hard to be far from home, Your Majesty. We have that in common," Sofonisba said as she sat down on an intricately carved chair beside the queen.

"Yes, it is hard." Another pause, then the queen sat back in her chair and ran her hand over her dark brown hair. The queen seemed to remember something. "Señora, the duke told me practically nothing about you, that's his way, always so busy with affairs of state … I only know that you're a painter from Cremona, very famous, very accomplished. First, um, if it's not an impertinent question, how old are you?"

"I am twenty-seven, Your Majesty."

"Oh, then I must seem like quite a child to you," the queen said.

Sofonisba wanted to choose just the right words. "Your Majesty, I have a sister your age. If I treated her as a child, I would never hear the end of it. And so, I would never regard you that way, either. His Grace saw me as close enough to your age to be a good companion. And that is my intention."

Elisabeth smiled, and Sofonisba noticed her dimpled chin. "Let me tell you what happened yesterday, when I met my husband — *my* that word sounds odd — anyway, when I met him for the first time," Elisabeth said, suddenly energized, and leaning toward Sofonisba conspiratorially. "I didn't know what to say at first, and he said, 'Pray, why are you looking at me like that? Are you inspecting me for grey hairs?'"

Sofonisba laughed. "Perhaps His Majesty is a bit overly aware of the fact that he's eighteen years your senior."

"And you, señora, tell me about your family."

She named her parents and siblings and said a few words about each. "...Two of my favourite, and if I may say, best, paintings are of them: one showing three of my sisters around a chessboard, and the other of Minerva, my father, and Asdrubale. I still have to finish that one." Her father's reminder when they parted came back to her, bringing a painful twinge, and she was glad when Elisabeth chattered on.

"I grew up around great art, you know, in various royal palaces, and I *love* it," Elisabeth was saying. "Paintings, sculpture, tapestries. I love to draw, but I've had no training. Please, señora, if you taught your sisters to paint, then could you teach me? I mean, would you?" The young eyes pleaded.

"Your Majesty, of course I will teach you. It would be my privilege," Sofonisba said, taken by surprise.

"*Merci*, señora." They smiled at each other. "Now señora, you are here as one of my ladies-in-waiting, and not as a court painter, at least not officially, despite your fame. Is that disappointing to you?" the queen asked.

Not a child, indeed! Sofonisba thought.

"Your Majesty, it is a high honour for me to serve you. I could not be disappointed. With your permission, I will paint your portrait, and if other members of your family agree, I'll paint theirs, too, as long as the work does not interfere with my service to you." She stopped, and when the queen only nodded, she went on: "So perhaps my role here at court is, shall we say, flexible."

"I'm glad to hear all that, señora. It's been a great pleasure to meet you."

Sofonisba stood and curtsied. "Your Majesty."

She stepped out of the chamber and was met immediately by a woman in black with a chillingly serious, almost grave expression.

"Good morning, Señora Anguissola. You are wondering how I know you. I make a point of knowing everyone who comes near the queen. That is my duty."

She means to frighten me, but she will not, Sofonisba thought to herself determinedly as the woman looked her up and down. "Madam, may I know your name, please?"

"I am the duchess of Alba. My husband brought you here." Her nose had a downturned tip like a hawk's, and her dark hair was pulled back tightly and covered with a short black veil.

"And I am grateful to him for that, Your Grace," Sofonisba said.

"You are ultimately under the king's authority, of course, but we do not bother him with matters concerning the queen's ladies-in-waiting. Those matters are my responsibility. I am the *guarda mayor de damas*," the duchess said.

"I see," Sofonisba said. The duchess' dress was plain, buttoned to the neck, and her white chemise showed no lace at the neck or cuffs.

"Come with me," the duchess commanded, and led her to a

small antechamber. She sat down at the table and pointed to the other chair.

"It's only fair that I let you know what is expected of you here. You were brought here because of your success as a painter, of course. Your family's nobility is of too low a rank to be the reason."

"Madam, I'm sure —"

"But *I* don't care a whit how many paintbrushes you have or how well you paint. Here, your first and most important duty is to the queen." The duchess pressed her palms onto the table. Sofonisba noticed her bulging knuckles. "Never forget that for a moment. Above all, you must behave *chastely* and *decorously* at all times. Your reputation must remain immaculate, because the reputation of every lady-in-waiting is unfailingly linked to the *queen's honour*." As she paused, her face seemed to Sofonisba to reflect a certain satisfaction.

"Your Grace has made herself quite clear," Sofonisba said.

"And do not think you will get away with anything. I am watching you, and all the ladies-in-waiting, always," the duchess said, almost allowing her thin lips to form a smile. *Ah, the eyes of a hawk, too.*

"The ladies-in-waiting receive no visitors until I have met them and given my approval. You will have only one personal servant. You will share a room with the other ladies-in-waiting, and all of you will eat all your meals together. You will accompany the queen everywhere and will always put her needs, comforts and desires before your own. Now, Señora Anguissola," she said, folding her hands. "Do you have any questions?"

"None, madam."

"Then you may go."

JANUARY 29, 1560

Cardinal Mendoza stood at the altar of the Mendoza chapel beside King Philip, a bridegroom resplendent in white stockings and a gold-embroidered vest of white silk over a white and gold shirt. Sofonisba, as a painter of portraits, took particular interest in the royal raiment. From Philip's shoulders hung a short purple velvet cape of French design, trimmed with jewels, and he wore a black hat with white feathers. His apparel was a significant departure from his usual sombre black, and he cut a stunning figure. As the chapel organ heaved, Elisabeth, on the arm of the duke of Alba, moved down the aisle arrayed in a wide skirt of silver brocade trimmed with fur, and a cape of black velvet adorned with pearls and jewels. The train of her dress extended more than halfway down the chapel aisle and was held up by a dozen pages, scrupulously rehearsed.

As Philip and Elisabeth walked down the aisle together after speaking the words of the marriage service, an irrepressible cry arose from the crowd, inappropriate for the chapel, but no one could hold back: *"Isabel de la Paz! Isabel de la Paz!"* The royal couple moved to a balcony overlooking a large field, and the crowd that had waited there took up the chant: *Isabel de la Paz!* Everyone believed that "Elisabeth of the peace" had brought Spain into a new, shining age, brimming with hope.

"I was intrigued when I heard that you would be coming to Spain," said the tall young man seated beside Sofonisba at the banquet table. He was Riccardo Velleti, the envoy from Lucca.

"How did you know I —? Wait —"

At the same time that she said "Papa," Velleti said, "Your father."

"Ah, Papa," Sofonisba sighed, "my ardent promoter." They delved into the first courses: sausages, caviar on white bread, and anchovies.

"Your father sent word some weeks ago that you would be arriving, even before the duke of Alba officially announced it," Velleti said. "The news travelled quickly around the court that an Italian woman painter would be a lady-in-waiting to Elisabeth. For myself, I am happy to have someone else to speak to in my native tongue."

"So am I, señor," Sofonisba said. She guessed that Velleti was about her age. She admired his curly, light brown hair.

Then she had to pause to hum with pleasure at the taste of the salmon baked in meltingly buttery pastry, a dish she had not eaten since Cremona, and rarely then. Velleti saw her rapt expression.

"It *is* delightful, this food, and this meal has barely begun!" Then he gestured toward the table laden with the best china, crystal, silver, and linens.

"So, Señora Anguissola, what do you think of all this?" Velleti spooned up some lemon sorbet.

"Sometimes I cannot quite believe that I am here," Sofonisba replied. "I remember that it was eleven years ago this very month that I met the king for the first time. And señor, if we are to be foreigners in a foreign land together, please call me Sonia."

"All right, and here in Spain I am called Rico," her companion said. "Now anything that you want to know about the royal court, just ask me. I know many of its secrets, its sordid past and present, and what may fall out of its closets in the future."

Sofonisba enjoyed small portions of the smoked meats, the roast veal, and the roast suckling pig, each heavily seasoned. *If the stays of my corset do not burst, I will thank the Virgin for having performed a miracle,* she thought. Despite her satiety, she could not resist when the servants brought in large platters of fruit, and finally, the sweets. Placing a crisp sweet fritter in her mouth, she let its warm honey coating form a pool on her tongue. Next, she savoured the tenderness of the candied chestnuts and marzipan. She thought it fitting that the last of the seventeen courses was rice pudding, because nothing could surpass its sensuous creaminess.

After the dinner and many toasts to the happiness and fertility of the king and queen, the guests began to move toward the ballroom, but Rico suggested, "The dancing won't start for a while. Let's go up to the gallery."

Sofonisba sighed at the view below them of the gorgeously candlelit ballroom, a properly magical, lyrical, otherworldly setting for the fairy-tale day. Her feet itched to dance on the gleaming wooden floor where men in feathered hats and women in shimmering gowns milled around sedately while the musicians tuned their instruments. Even up in the gallery she caught the scent of orange blossoms: as a gift to Philip and Elisabeth, the Mendoza family had ordered several orange trees to be brought hundreds of miles from southern Spain and somehow coaxed into unseasonable blossom. The singing of colourful caged birds in the corners of the ballroom added to the springlike atmosphere.

"The French delegation will go home with grand, effusive tales of this splendour," Rico said. "And for the king, that is the whole point."

"Who is that man over there, the one with the short black beard and moustache?" Sofonisba asked. "The one with the intense expression, who looks like he'd rather be someplace else."

"He's one of your fellow painters — Alonso Sánchez Coello, court painter to the king."

"Really? What do you know about —?"

"The music's starting! Let's dance!"

The music seemed to unleash a joyous energy, untypical for the sober Spanish court. The courtiers and wedding guests formed lines and began to step briskly through the traditional rhythms. Sofonisba found herself relaxing, moving with confidence and ease, not at all minding the increasing number of eyes on her, including the king's.

Excitement riffled through the throng when it was announced that the king wished to dance a galliard. "Light the torch!" Philip proclaimed.

The king took the torch and handed it to his queen, signalling that they would have the first round of the lively dance. The queen handed the torch to a guard and took the king's arm, and as they stepped to the middle of the floor, the entire room went silent for the only time that night. Even the songbirds paused. Everyone focused on the king and his young bride in their splendid silver and gold. In the hush, for a long moment, they locked eyes. Then the spritely music began. The royal couple moved gamely through the dance's quick steps and leaps, and when it was over, flushed and smiling, Elisabeth took the torch back and handed it to her cousin, Prince de la Roche, who asked Sofonisba to dance. She accepted gladly, and their performance won them approving glances.

Then it was Sofonisba's turn to choose a partner. Feeling emboldened, and having heard that her host, the duke of Mendoza, was an excellent dancer, she approached him and handed him the torch. The crowd began a fitful, uncertain humming at this daring move. The music began.

One, two, three, turn, four, five, leap! Her leaps were nearly as high as those of the much-taller duke. She felt transported, afloat on exhilaration, and she was sure she had never danced better.

"She's the best dancer here! She's Italian, you say? From Cremona? She's enchanting!"

As the crowd burst into applause and cheers, Sofonisba made one final whirl — and found herself directly in front of His Majesty, King Philip.

Struggling to catch her breath, she curtsied. To her astonishment and that of those around her, the king bowed deeply.

"Señora Anguissola," the king said.

"Your Majesty." Sofonisba dared to try her Spanish. "I am so pleased that Your Majesty remembers me," she said stiffly.

"You have learned Spanish. How clever," Philip said. "That evening in Cremona was a highlight of my long continental journey." He took her hand and looked at her probingly with those dark grey eyes, just as he had years before. "You have charmed my court tonight, señora. Welcome."

"Thank you, sir."

"Do continue dancing, please."

She curtsied again. "Your Majesty." He turned his attentions back to the queen, and Sofonisba turned to Rico, suddenly at her side. He led her away from the dance floor.

"Sonia! The king bowed to you in front of everyone!" She basked in his frank admiration. "His Majesty has paid you the highest compliment possible — your place in this court is secure!"

She smiled. "I hope you're right."

"Oh, I am. I've been here long enough to know what these gestures mean."

The celebration continued the day after the wedding with a bullfight and a joust, and the following day, a hunt. Sofonisba felt herself swept along as if in a windstorm. After some time to recover from those exertions, the court began preparations to leave Guadalajara. Philip had decreed that the empire needed a new, permanent capital: "The French, the English, even the godless *Ottomans* — " he made a gagging sound when he said that word — "they all have permanent, settled capitals." He chose Madrid, in Castile, because it had no strong local lords or clerics to make trouble, and he hoped that if he lived there and wielded power directly, there would be no more of the tax rebellions that had ripped through Castile in the past few years. Until the new royal palace in Madrid could be readied, the court would stay in Toledo, the former capital and a bustling commercial town.

In the Mendoza palace courtyard and on the street outside, a long train of pack mules, carts, and coaches formed, each loaded with trunks containing clothes, linens, jewels, books, candles, religious articles, bolts of cloth, barrels of grain — the spectre of famine was always nearby — and finally, the courtiers and royals themselves. The travellers would stop in the university town of Alcalá de Henares and then in Madrid before continuing southwest to Toledo.

The students and scholars of Alcalá de Henares greeted the royals with lavish triumphal arches decorated to depict ancient wisdom.

Cheering crowds who braved the chilly weather got a glimpse of their new queen and poured out their love for her, endlessly calling out, *Isabel de la Paz!* On the day the entourage was to pass through Madrid on its way to Toledo, the queen declared herself tired of huddling in the royal coach and instead mounted a horse. She rode into the city under a fringed gold canopy, followed by coaches carrying her French ladies-in-waiting and Sofonisba. Crowds along the road to Toledo cheered and waved, and the city, not wishing to be outdone by Alcalá de Henares or Madrid, steeped itself in pomp. Arches, fountains, and monuments were scrubbed clean and embellished with figures of saints and angels. A grand reception for the royals lasted all night. In the days that followed, the king and queen saw theatrical performances, the running of the bulls, and a procession of guild members, key civic figures, and religious leaders, all to show the city's loyalty to the crown.

"It seems like all I've done since arriving in Spain is eat and be entertained," Elisabeth said to Sofonisba as they sat on the terrace of the old palace of Toledo. They wore lynx-lined hooded capes against the chill.

"You've done more than that," Sofonisba said. "You've given the people of Spain something to grasp on to, the possibility of a peaceful future after so many years of war."

"I suppose," the queen said doubtfully. "But the real reason I'm here is to give the king sons, and — " she sank deeper into her hood, "well, that won't happen soon."

Sofonisba understood, as did all the court, why the king and queen had retired to their separate bedchambers after the wedding celebration, instead of trying to create an heir to the throne — Elisabeth was still too young for Philip to take to his bed.

"But it will happen," Sofonisba reassured the queen. "You and Philip will have many sons."

"And this *town*," Elisabeth moaned. "It's controlled by the clergy.

There was all that fanfare when we first arrived, but now? Now the clergy frowns on parties, dances, theatricals. They seem to have banned the very idea of merriment. Philip says I must not plan anything cheery."

Sofonisba longed to comfort her, and suggested that they begin Elisabeth's drawing and painting lessons. In a corner of Elisabeth's chamber, below a window, Sofonisba set out her drawing tools. "Here's some parchment, some pieces of chalk, and a knife to sharpen them. Hold the chalk like this."

The queen insisted on daily lessons, and it was the time of day when she seemed happiest. She impressed Sofonisba with her enthusiasm and diligence. It was clear that she would never be an accomplished painter, but Sofonisba considered Elisabeth's work respectable for her efforts. Sofonisba flashed back many years and miles to her old studio in Cremona, and the days of teaching her sisters, and to her pleasant surprise, the memories filled her not with painful longing, but with pride.

⌒⌒

Her Majesty sat at the clavichord in the afternoon, playing a familiar tune. She had had the instrument shipped from France, at great expense. Her ladies were arrayed around her in the large drawing room in an attentive, doting way, some humming along, all impressed with her musical skill, or pretending to be. Young courtiers stood or sat around the room, chatting or playing cards. In a far corner, a violinist played for some courtiers who practiced their dance steps.

"It's your turn now," Elisabeth said to Sofonisba. "Play something. Anything." She stood up from the clavichord and Sofonisba took her place.

Sofonisba played "something," then accepted the queen's compliments on her talent.

"Sonia, you seem distracted," Elisabeth said. "What is it?"

"My queen, you are quite perceptive," Sofonisba said. "But I will not burden you."

"I pray you tell me," Elisabeth said, firmly. *She is beginning to sound like a queen*, Sofonisba thought. "I had understood that I must wait to set up a studio until the court moved to Madrid," Sofonisba said. "But now the spring has turned to summer, and there is still no sign of the move. I suppose I am growing restless, here in Toledo."

"Then begin," Elisabeth said, and smiled. "I'll have someone find you a room for a studio."

Sofonisba had barely set up her painting tools when a parade of courtiers began to file in and out, all seeking portraits, which she fit in between the queen's lessons and her other duties.

Her most unforgettable portrait subject was Don Carlos, the king's only child and the son of his first wife, Maria Manuela of Portugal, who died shortly after Carlos was born.

Sofonisba met Carlos while walking in the garden with the queen and the other ladies. He approached them boldly, with determined but oddly off-kilter steps, and Sofonisba moved closer to the queen's side.

"Ah, dear mother!" Carlos said to Elisabeth, removing his cap and bowing theatrically. The queen forced a small laugh.

"Sofonisba, may I introduce His Royal Highness Don Carlos, the king's son," the queen said. "He's quite a joker, you see, I am actually his stepmother. Don Carlos and I are the same age. Carlos, this is Sofonisba Anguissola of Cremona."

"Sofonisba Anguissola of Cremona," Carlos repeated. "I see." He smiled a wide, disturbing grin with his full Habsburg lips, the lower one jutting forward.

"Your Royal Highness," Sofonisba said, meeting his eyes.

"Señora Anguissola is a painter," Elisabeth said. In the awkward silence Sofonisba noted Carlos' unusually high, round forehead.

"A *painter*, really!" Carlos said mockingly. "Will you paint *my* portrait?" He turned sideways and struck a profile pose that outlined his slightly misshapen spine. "How's this? Ha haha *ha!*"

"I'll gladly paint your portrait, if it is Her Majesty's wish, sir," Sofonisba replied.

Carlos turned toward the queen, his mouth comically open. "We-eh-ell, is it your wish, dear stepmama?"

"Perhaps, if Señora Anguissola has the time."

Elisabeth crossed her arms, and Sofonisba saw the fingers of one hand drumming against the opposite arm. She cut in before Carlos could respond.

"We'll continue our walk now. Good day to you, sir." She took the queen's elbow and steered her past Carlos, and the other ladies followed.

"Oh, thank you, Sonia," the queen said when they were farther down the path. "Philip has ordered me to be kind to Carlos, but — well, it's difficult. When I think that I might have ended up married to him…" She shook her head. "It had been suggested, you know. Still, I pity him."

Sofonisba heard much court gossip about the prince's odd personality, especially his ferocious temper — he had thrown a page he disliked out a window; he had attacked Philip's ministers with knives; and he brutally mistreated his horses. But as long as the king tolerated his son, the court was forced to do the same.

So one day, Sofonisba found herself sketching the prince as he stood in her studio, with two of the duchess of Alba's assistants and a guard in attendance. Another guard stood at attention just outside the door.

"So, you're a painter, and a lady-in-waiting to my stepmother," the prince said as he stood in the studio in a gold jacket, short pants and hose, a short black cape lined with lynx fur, and a black velvet cap with one red and one white feather. His left leg started to jiggle. "Hmm, hmm … I could have been a painter, too, you know."

"No, sir, I did not know," Sofonisba said hesitantly, not wanting to begin a conversation with him. She had not noticed when they met that his eyes were the same grey as his father's, only small and heavy-lidded.

"That's right, I could have been, if it weren't for … oh, those bloody little … agggh, yecch…" He stared past Sofonisba, rubbed his face, shook his head in rapid little twitches, then started scratching all over his chest. "JesusMaryandJoseph," he muttered, his blasphemy halting Sofonisba's hand. "Your Royal Highness?" the guard asked Carlos.

"Perhaps Your Royal Highness would like to stop for now," Sofonisba said, seeing the frightened looks on the faces of the duchess' ladies. "We can finish later."

The prince threw off the cape and stormed toward the door. "I'll get those bloody little…" he called out, to no one, as he disappeared.

Sofonisba painted Don Carlos' eyes a little larger than they normally appeared, and did not let his mouth gape open. She hid his uneven shoulders and slightly malformed back by draping the cape over his shoulders. She placed his hands on his hips, so that the cape spread widely. He wore his sword by his side. In a background window, Sofonisba painted an eagle in flight, holding a column, to symbolize the Habsburgs. Both Don Carlos and the queen were pleased with the painting, and rewarded Sofonisba with a sapphire.

SUMMER, 1560

Queen Elisabeth had emerged from the shyness that had held her back when she first arrived at court. Now she resisted the court's sombre nature, and planned carnivals (to mark the holy days), long horseback rides, theatricals, musical performances, and dances. She developed a passion for gambling, and often had to borrow from administrators and pawn some of her jewels to cover her gambling debts. Philip opposed gambling but he never tried to stop her, indeed, he would never deny Elisabeth anything.

So when the summer ended with weeks of rain, and the court

drew in off the terraces and out of the gardens, Elisabeth was happy to pass the time with the usual entertainment, banquets, and games. She and Sofonisba spent hours drawing and painting together, until one day.

"Elisabeth, you don't look well."

The queen set down her chalk with a shaky hand. Her face was flushed. "Oooohh, Sonia…"

Sofonisba jumped to the queen's side, and ordered two ladies to help her get the queen to her chamber. She told two others to find the duchess and tell her to bring a physician to the queen at once.

Sofonisba helped Elisabeth undress and get into bed. She had barely laid down when she said, "Oooohh, I'm going to…" and leaned over the side of the bed. Sofonisba whisked a chamber pot into place just in time and held the queen's head. The other ladies-in-waiting, who had filed in as word had spread around the palace, froze in dismay.

"All right, everyone out," the physician Andreas Vesalius of Brussels demanded as he strode into the room.

"I want Sonia to stay!" the queen wailed. Everyone left except Vesalius, the duchess, and Sofonisba.

The queen spent the next few days miserably alternating between fever, chills, headaches, and nausea. Sofonisba held the queen's hand, put damp towels on her forehead and adjusted the covers.

On the fourth day, a rash spread across Elisabeth's body. After a week the rash turned to raised spots. "It's the pox," Vesalius intoned.

Sofonisba's eyes grew wide. Over many decades, periodic waves of the pox had killed scores of people in Cremona. Horrified, Sofonisba asked the physician, "Can't you do anything?"

"Señora, the pox must be allowed to run its course. I saw it enough times to know, years ago when I attended the household of His Majesty's father, the Emperor Charles," Vesalius said. "Now the Spanish doctors here may disagree, but they are simply jealous that the queen has been put in my care. And you, señora, must not stay with her any longer, or you could catch it, too."

Sofonisba agonized for two weeks, praying for Elisabeth and trying to concentrate on painting. It became clear to Sofonisba that she had come to love Elisabeth almost as a sister. The queen was kind and intelligent, and quickly learning the ways of the court. It touched Sofonisba to see everyone's regard for Elisabeth, from the doting of those most intimate with her, on down to the peasants and labourers who pushed to get a glimpse of her in royal processions. And Elisabeth returned that love — she waved to the people her carriage passed, and sometimes even moved among them, chatting and admiring their babies. The queen also frequently asked about the well-being of her ladies and their families.

So Sofonisba felt great relief when Vesalius told her that the danger had passed, and that she could see Elisabeth.

"Sonia," the queen said softly.

"My lady!" Sofonisba grasped the queen's hand. "Oh, I am so happy to hear you speak. How are you feeling?"

The queen wrinkled her brow, as if she had to concentrate to form words. "Aw-ful. I ache all o-ver."

"You shouldn't try to talk now. Just rest."

Elisabeth looked directly into Sofonisba's eyes. "Sonia, am I going to — die now?"

Sofonisba fought off the urge to sob. "No, you're not going to die, my lady. You're getting better. Vesalius is quite confident. Now, would you like me to fetch a book and read to you?"

"Yes."

Sofonisba went quickly to her room and back. "This is a tale of knights and dragons and lovers."

"Just right." The Queen smiled weakly.

Elisabeth's spots turned to scabs, and when the last one fell off, four weeks after she fell ill, Vesalius declared her cured.

"And I have hardly any scars!" she said to Sofonisba.

Sofonisba returned to the palace chapel, where she had prayed daily for the queen's recovery. Kneeling and giving thanks, she suddenly felt exhausted. She went to her room, anticipating a rest.

She was surprised to see all the other ladies there, reading or sewing.

"The queen has recovered," she announced. "She's resting now."

"Praise the Lord." "Thank the Virgin." "St. Elizabeth watched over her."

"So what is everyone doing here in the middle of the day?" Sofonisba asked. "I should think you'd be out riding or something."

"We were too worried about the queen for that," said Veronique, one of the ladies Elisabeth had brought from France. "We care about her, *too*, you know."

"What do you mean?" Sofonisba said, instantly suspicious despite her tiredness.

"Just because you're the queen's favourite doesn't mean you're the only one who cares about her," Veronique pouted.

"I never thought I was the only one who cared. What are you getting at, Veronique?"

Veronique glanced at herself admiringly in a mirror, then looked back at Sofonisba.

"Of all of us, the queen wanted only you around when she was sick. You sit beside her at royal banquets. You call her 'Elisabeth,' we call her 'Your Majesty' or 'My lady.' The queen spends hours and hours with you, drawing and painting. Where does that leave the rest of us?"

"First of all, the queen asked me to call her Elisabeth —"

"Exactly. She asked you, but not us."

"...and more important, we are here to serve the queen, not the other way around," Sofonisba said. "Do the rest of you feel slighted?" About half the ladies nodded.

"Her preferences are what matter, that's all," Sofonisba said. "What you or I feel about them is unimportant."

"It's not fair," Veronique said, fingering her gold necklace. "All those hours you two spend in the studio together when you teach her to paint, and you being of low nobility, from the *merchant* class, after all."

"That does it, Veronique." Sofonisba planted herself in front of her. "You really are a … a …" She lifted her arms and let them drop in resignation. "I need to rest now." She lay down on her bed and closed her eyes. Soon she was too deeply asleep to care how the others spent the afternoon, or what they thought of her.

The next day Sofonisba had an idea.

"You seem to resent that I teach the queen to paint," she said to Veronique as they returned to their room after morning prayers. "So, do *you* want to learn to paint, Veronique? Just as I teach Her Majesty?" Sofonisba said, sure that would put an end to the exasperating conflict.

But Veronique said petulantly, "Yes, I do."

"Come on, then." Sofonisba grabbed Veronique by the upper arm. "Let's go."

"What? Now? Let go of me."

"You say you want to learn to paint, so why not right now?" Sofonisba opened the door and stepped out. "Come *on* Veronique."

The others goaded her: "You asked for it, Veronique."

"Yeah, let's see you paint something!"

"Bonne chance!"

Veronique sneered at them and stepped out behind Sofonisba, who walked at a furious pace down the corridor. They stopped only when they turned a corner and found themselves face to face with the duchess of Alba, in all her black augustness.

"I thought I heard the sound of galloping down the corridor, like a couple of wild colts. It must have been you two. Is everything all right, ladies?"

"Everything is *quite* all right, madam," Sofonisba said. "I'm taking Veronique to the studio to teach her to paint."

"Very well, since you have little to do for Her Majesty until she fully recovers. Now slow down and remember how a lady is supposed to behave here."

"Yes, madam," Sofonisba and Veronique said in unison.

"Off you go now."

They stepped into the studio. Sofonisba told Veronique to close the door, and tossed her an apron.

"You expect me to wear this ragged, stained thing?" Veronique said, wrinkling her tiny nose.

"Would you rather get oil and paint on your fine silks?" Sofonisba said as she lit the fire to cook some oil. "Now, get that big jug of oil off that shelf and bring it here. Pour some of the oil into this pot."

"Ugh. It smells," Veronique said.

"Now stir it well and set it on the fire." Veronique did as she was told, then stepped back from the fireplace.

"Well you have to keep stirring it, of course," Sofonisba said. "Go on." Veronique picked up the spoon. Sofonisba fetched some cinnabar.

"All right, just leave that for now," she commanded. "Take this stone and grind these pieces of cinnabar. I need paint in a vermilion hue."

"Grind this with my bare hands? Are you daft?"

"No, Veronique, I'm not daft, I'm a painter, and this is what a painter does, and you said you wanted to learn to paint."

"Well, I won't do it." Veronique struggled to untie her smock. "I'm leaving."

"But we've barely started! Don't you want to stay and mix up some sizing, to prime a canvas? For that we'll boil up some dried rabbit skin. You'll *love* that smell," Sofonisba smiled.

Veronique threw down the apron and ran out. "And next time, hang up your apron!" Sofonisba called gaily down the corridor, confident in the unlikelihood of a next time. She removed the oil from the fire and began to grind the cinnabar.

FEBRUARY, 1561

Here we are, all the queen's twelve ladies, in our Sunday finery, in our usual pew, waiting for Mass to begin, Sofonisba mused as she looked around the chapel. *Soon this chapel will be packed with courtiers. It was never intended to serve such a large court.*

We had a lovely Christmastide — a torchlight procession through the palace courtyards and nearby streets before the candlelit midnight Mass, then a masked ball on the octave feast, and a banquet and dance on the Epiphany. Now that's all over. It's February, and it's always either overcast or raining. Everyone is restless, waiting for spring and the move to Madrid. I can sense it even from how they squirm in these pews.

Now we all stand, because Elisabeth and Philip are coming in. Now, they're sitting down in their red velvet chairs at the side of the altar. She's wearing yet another new piece of jewellery: a filigreed silver broach. The organist is playing some solemn chords. Soon I'll smell the incense — ah, there it is.

"Dominus vobiscum."

"Et cum spiritu tuo."

It occurs to me that I've been here in Spain a year now. I've sat through many of these palace Masses. When Elisabeth reappeared in this chapel after the pox, everyone called out, "Isabel de la Paz!"

But this is a quite ordinary Mass. The priest is wearing a mundane green and the flowers on the altar look a bit wilted from here.

"A reading from the prophet Isaiah: And as the bridegroom rejoiceth over the bride, so shall thy God rejoice over thee..."

It may be that Philip rejoices over Elisabeth, but in his own reserved way. He treats her not so much with affection but with care and gallantry. Beside her at the weekly court dinner, he ignores his own plate and glass while making sure that she is satisfied and comfortable.

There's Ruy Gómez da Silva, Philip's friend for many years. As chamberlain, he's the one in control of Philip's household. He can even enter the king's bedchamber. Even Elisabeth can't do that. A very

powerful man, but modest and humble, they say. He and the duke of
Alba — what a pair! Ruy Gómez is circumspect and tactful, while
Alba is ambitious and arrogant, and disdainful of Ruy Gómez's humble beginnings. No wonder they clash so often at the Council of State
while debating foreign affairs and advising the king on them. Rico told
me that each man fancies himself Philip's favourite, but Philip resists
having one — he believes that having a favourite would lower his royal
prestige. There are twelve councils, needed to organize the government
of a huge empire, but His Majesty's habit is to make the final decision
on most issues alone, instead of assigning things to others. He insists
that all orders bear his signature.

"...Now there are diversities of gifts, but the same Spirit. And there
are differences of administrations, but the same Lord..."

On the councils, Rico says, personalities conflict, and each council
defends its own area. Anyway, Philip prefers to avoid formal meetings,
and to see small groups or individuals. And there are papers coming
into the palace every day that he keeps from the councilors, leading to
confusion and contradiction. Rico must be here someplace...

Just across the aisle from us sits Princess Juana, King Philip's sister,
the most influential woman at court, after the queen. Her husband, John
Manuel, prince of Portugal, died just months after their wedding. They
say she abandoned her son Sebastian when he was only three months old.
Philip made her his regent while he was in England with his first wife,
Queen Mary. Plays both the viol and the vihuela very well. She also
knows Latin, loves poetry and art. And she's three years younger than me!

"The Gospel according to John. This beginning of miracles did Jesus
in Cana of Galilee, and manifested forth his glory; and his disciples
believed on him..."

But Juana is nowhere as intimidating as the woman sitting with
Alba: his wife and duchess, the guarda mayor de damas, the formidable woman now in firm control of my days. She decides when the
windows in the queen's part of the palace can be open or shut, and
how many candles burn in the hallway outside our room. We cannot

leave the palace grounds without her permission. *She is, perhaps, the only person at court without a trace of vanity. Not likely she will ever ask me for a portrait.*

"Ite, Missa est."

"Deo gratias."

SPRING, 1561

Soon the enormous royal congregation, nearly a city in itself, would move, with miles of carriages and heavy-laden mules, to Madrid, into a new royal palace, freshly swept and scrubbed. The move dominated every conversation, every meal, even the games. Courtiers could hardly sit down to a table for cards without servants trying to pull the table out from under them to pack it away. Everyone was relieved to know that it would be the last move. The court was simply too big to continue its peregrinations to the many palaces: El Pardo, Aranjuez, Casa del Campo, Valsaín…

Sofonisba wondered how many wagons would be needed just to carry Elisabeth's gowns, headpieces, jewellery, shoes, and all the other finery that the queen possessed.

King Philip wanted the new palace to rival in magnificence those of the French and the English. The court would reflect his claim to be the king not just of Spain and its empire, but of all Christendom. He had been planning the new palace for years — he had sent architects and gardeners to France, Italy, and the Netherlands to get ideas. It was so like him to get involved personally in so many details, such as choosing furniture, tapestries, rugs, lamps, even candlesticks.

For Sofonisba, the most exciting aspect of the move was the ample space that the new palace would have to hold King Philip's burgeoning art collection. She looked forward to seeing it.

"So, how do you like your new studio?" Elisabeth was arrayed in a splendid gown — or as splendid as the restrained Spanish court allowed. It was black brocade with wide bands of gold embroidery down the front and around the high collar. Above the collar was the usual starched lace ruff, and below it a snug, short necklace of jewels and pearls that ended in a cross of rubies. Sofonisba planned a bust-length portrait for this, her first likeness of the queen; later, she would build her confidence about this all-important subject by painting a half-length portrait, and finally, she would paint a full-length view.

"It is suitable," Sofonisba said diplomatically as she sketched the seated queen. "Enough room, enough light. I hope to be swamped with work. And how do you like Madrid, my lady?"

"Philip gave me the largest chamber, and the gardens here are beautiful."

Sofonisba sketched the face she had studied so often: the large ears, the straight yet wide nose, the barely existent upper lip, the full lower one. "There. I've got it. Did I tell you that Pope Pius has asked for a portrait of you? I will send him this one, and of course I'll do others. It's best if I don't keep the pope waiting."

There was a knock at the studio door. "Begging your pardon, señora, but as this is from your people in Cremona, the duchess thought it best to pass it right along." A servant handed Sofonisba a letter, curtsied to the queen and left the studio.

The letter was from Sofonisba's mother, telling her that her beloved Rosa had come down with the sweating sickness and died, in her fifty-fifth year: *"Just before she died she said that you had been a special light in her life, and that she loved you like a daughter."*

"Aaaaah!" Sofonisba let out one long moan of utmost pain. "My maid — and dear friend — Rosa Marco — is *dead!*" she told the queen between sobs.

"Oh, Sonia, I'm so sorry," Elisabeth said. "You've told me so much about her, how close you were. Veronique, fetch a glass of water."

When she was calmer, Sofonisba said, "I want to go to the chapel and light a candle. And have a Mass said for her."

"I'll go with you," Elisabeth said.

She dealt with the heartbreak by hiding in her studio. Elisabeth understood.

She thought about the hours Rosa had spent standing around or sitting on hard chairs in drafty churches while Sofonisba watched painters at work. She almost smiled over the memory of a spilled wine cup at the table of Maestro Buonarroti. She dwelled especially on Rosa's gift of dreams, her suggestion that Sofonisba's dream to be a painter was not to be discounted. In doing that, she had shared with Sofonisba her own lost dream. Sofonisba had held and treasured that confidence always.

She decided to remember Rosa in the best way she could. She included Rosa's image in a portrait she had already started, of herself playing the clavichord. That way, the portrait would show Sofonisba's love of music, and for Rosa.

While she worked, Riccardo Velleti came into the studio.

"I see from this portrait what Rosa meant to you," he said. "There's great warmth in her figure. And in your figure, the eyes are haunted and sad."

"That's just as it should be."

Sofonisba had a Mass said for Rosa, and lit a candle in the palace chapel daily for a month. She sent money to the sexton at Sant'Agostino in Cremona with instructions to put flowers on Rosa's grave, and Federico Mariano's grave, and the infant's grave beside it.

Demands for royal portraits kept her busy. One subject, Alessandro Farnese, was the young son of the king's half-sister Margaret, duchess of Parma. Sofonisba remembered painting him before, when he was a sullen boy of eleven, with light brown eyes that never looked at anything for long. Now he was fifteen, and *a bit too self-assured*, Sofonisba thought, but willing enough to pose, although she suspected that the portrait was his mother's idea. He had a handsome, boyish face with a cleft chin. To capture his youthful bravado, she placed a bright gold brocade jacket over his shoulders, and painted him pulling on a leather glove, as if he were about to head out for a ride or to hunt. She took great care with the rich embroidery on the jacket, painting it in extreme detail. Alessandro's expression, looking right at the viewer, showed his awareness of the impressive figure he presented.

Then there was Don Juan of Austria, the king's half-brother and uncle to Alessandro, although he was two years younger. The two young men had a close friendship, often going for long rides and hunts, playing dice games and cards, and accompanying Queen Elisabeth and her ladies to various types of entertainment. Sofonisba had heard the gossip — that Alessandro had turned Don Juan into quite an adventurer with women. But because he was royalty, she painted Don Juan with a serious facial expression in a fixed gaze. Unlike the family portraits she used to do, in which she tried to depict warmth and love, court portraits had to suggest vigour and strength.

◦◦◦

"Sonia, I woke up this morning, and I was bleeding." The queen had dismissed from her bedchamber the ladies who had helped her dress and fixed her hair.

"Do the other ladies know?"

"Oh yes. I swore them to secrecy, but you know how it is with secrets at court. Not that I care," Elisabeth said.

"Are you in any pain?"

"No. I feel ... I don't know, a certain relief. Because now, I can finally start to feel like a real wife. And soon, God willing, a mother." She giggled.

The duchess of Alba swept into the room. "I have informed His Majesty," she said. "He said to tell you that he will visit you here, in the evening, in ten days."

"Hmm. My husband is indeed eager for a male heir," the queen said, and she and Sofonisba laughed. The duchess hid a smile behind one hand.

"Come with me to the studio," Sofonisba said. "I want to sketch you and plan my next portrait of you while you're in this happy mood."

⌒〜

On the day of the king's choosing, the queen's ladies-in-waiting bustled about her chamber as the sun began to set. The duchess of Alba gave them instructions: "Remove those bed linens and replace them with these fresh ones. Sprinkle a little of this rose water on them — that's it. Tie back the bed curtains. Light this candle and put it there. Now stoke up the fire."

The queen entered. Her ladies helped her undress and put on a short white silk chemise. Sofonisba unpinned Elisabeth's hair and brushed it until it hung like a smooth dark brown veil that shone in the candlelight.

No one spoke until the queen said, "I am indebted to you all. Now you may go."

Sofonisba, the last to leave, felt she should offer words of encouragement, but none came to mind. The queen smiled charmingly, and as Sofonisba walked out, she wondered who was encouraging whom.

⌒〜

The queen was not alone for long. The king moved slowly, almost thoughtfully as he removed his jacket and shirt. He took off his short breeches and undid the tie at the top of his long silk hose. He kissed the silver cross on a chain around his neck, set it on the bedside table, and cautiously slid in beside Elisabeth. She turned toward him and let him kiss her face, her neck, her shoulders, while an aching swelled between her legs. She let him between her thighs, breathing harder, drawing into his rhythm, curling her face up toward his. The encounter ended when Philip, with a final stab, called out, "*O, Dios!*" and fell alongside her, but only for a moment.

Then he stood, replaced the silver chain and cross around his neck, and fumbled back into his clothes.

"Did I displease you, my lord?" Elisabeth asked.

The king cleared his throat. "Not at all, my dearest, not at all. Good night."

"Good night." The king left the room.

Elisabeth relaxed, then leaned over to blow out the candle. Sleep overtook her as she prayed to God to give her a son.

⌒

Sofonisba looked out into the corridor the next morning in time to see the duchess of Alba hurry into the queen's chamber to awaken her. Apologizing for the disturbance but maintaining her always-cool manner, the duchess removed a bloody linen sheet from Elisabeth's bed, and then sent the ladies in to help the queen dress. The duchess carried the bundled sheet carefully, and showed its stains to the duke of Alba, to the chamberlain Ruy Gómez da Silva, and to King Philip's secretary, Gonzalo Pérez, who made the appropriate notation in the court records.

⌒

"The Princess Juana will meet you now." It was one of those commands disguised as an announcement that the well-trained guards and servants of the court stated so resolutely. Sofonisba removed her apron and wiped her hands. With three of her ladies, Princess Juana, sister of the king, entered the studio in a plain black dress, severe even for the somber court. A cameo depicting her father, Emperor Charles V, hung from a filmy white scarf around her neck. That and the requisite starched white ruff were her only adornments.

"Señora Anguissola." The princess' eyes showed no emotion.

"Your Royal Highness," Sofonisba said as she curtsied. "It is an honour to meet you. Please sit down," Sofonisba said, and when the princess was seated, she sat down herself, at a respectful distance.

"I've received a letter from Pope Pius," the princess began. "He's heard that I've founded a Clarissan convent here, and he wants a portrait of me to commemorate that event. I want you to do it."

"Of course, Your Royal Highness, it would be my privilege. Now, portraits of women of this court are usually full-length or three-quarters, and the figures hold gloves, or prayer books, or fans. In the background there could be a window, columns, drapes…"

"My portrait will be full-length, I will wear what you see me wearing now, I will hold my gloves and a closed fan, and there will be a window in the background," Juana said, looking directly at Sofonisba with dark grey eyes like the king's. She pronounced each choice slowly, as if she were instructing the cook about a banquet menu, and was determined that not one olive or grape be forgotten. "And there will be a young girl of five or six years, to symbolize a future nun."

Sofonisba paused, careful not to interrupt. "And what would you want to appear in the window?"

"Nothing." The thin lips, so unlike a Habsburg, spoke with great certainty.

"I see. Would Your Royal Highness be willing to sit right now for a sketch?"

"Very well."

Sofonisba fetched a drawing board, a sheet of parchment, and several pieces of chalk. She started with the princess' modest, close-fitting white cap that revealed most of her light brown hair.

The high, broad forehead and sharp straight nose were like Philip's. She then realized that the princess had said "my gloves," as if she had only one pair.

"We're finished for now," Sofonisba said, and the princess stood and left before Sofonisba could finish saying "Good day, Your Royal Highness."

Riccardo Velleti walked in. "Was that the Princess Juana I just saw leaving here?"

"It was. I can see now why Philip trusted her to be his regent while he was in the Netherlands. So serious, so self-assured. Even, I must say, cold."

"Oh yes, that's her. They say the only thing she cares about now is that convent she founded. No feminine frills for her."

"Maybe she and Philip are trying to outdo each other in piety," Sofonisba said.

"Maybe. So, have you heard about Don Carlos?" Rico asked. "This morning he attacked a cardinal with a dagger, said the man gave him the evil eye. So the king finally has had enough of his behaviour, and plans to bundle him off to the University at Alcalá de Henares to attend lectures. He'll make an unlikely student."

AUTUMN, 1561

Sofonisba needed more canvas, for the large portrait of Juana. She walked distractedly, carrying a lamp, toward the big windowless storeroom where canvas and a multitude of other things were kept, lamenting to herself that Juana's instructions for the portrait had left little room to invent.

At once upon opening the door Sofonisba heard from a corner a soft thump and a rustling sound. *Mice*, she thought, as she stepped further inside and lifted the lamp. She jumped back in surprise when the lamp's rays bounced off two faces: one she knew well from having painted it — Alessandro Farnese — and the other,

her back against a wall and her skirt raised — Veronique.

"Veronique!" Sofonisba said in a whisper-scream. Alessandro nearly knocked Sofonisba over as he bolted from the room, one hand holding up his breeches.

"Sonia, wait!" Veronique called out, but Sofonisba, too, had run out of the room, gasping with confusion and disbelief. Barely breaking stride, she set down the lamp and put it out, then rushed for the stairs, down two flights and out to the garden. Walking as swiftly as her corset allowed, she passed strolling courtiers, ministers, and gardeners enjoying the sunshine, all of whom shot her curious looks.

"Sonia!" With her ash-blond hair flying loose about her face, Veronique ran from the palace in pursuit of Sofonisba, who ducked into a geometric maze of neatly clipped hedges twice her height, an amusement Philip had designed. She turned this way and that, hoping to lose herself, and Veronique. After a while, she left the maze on the side farthest from the palace, and sat down on a stone bench to rest.

"Sonia?" She jumped. It was Veronique.

"How did you get here so fast?" Sofonisba asked.

"I just waited here while you were running around in that maze." She sat down.

"Aaagh." Sofonisba rubbed her eyes, as if to remove the memory of what she had seen in the storeroom. "Veronique, *tu es folle!* In the storeroom, where anyone, including the duchess, could walk in at any minute!"

"No, she couldn't, at least not today. She's sick in bed with the catarrh."

"What about others? Oh, never mind. And with Alessandro Farnese, yet. The king's nephew. That arrogant fool. So it's true what I've heard about him."

"If you've heard that he's very loving, and charming…"

Sofonisba regarded the vain Veronique, her perfect oval face, her arrogant lips usually so quick to sneer, her blue eyes now feigning innocence.

"Veronique, do you realize what you've done? You are a lady-in-waiting to the queen of Spain. You should be with her right now, serving her needs, not your own desires. I could turn you over to the duchess, to the court magistrates…" She gave up when she saw that her words caused not remorse or regret, but only fear.

"Please, Sonia, you won't tell anyone, will you?" Veronique begged. "I can't be sent back to France, not like this. Oh, the shame! My parents would lock me in a nunnery."

"Stop."

"I'll do anything," Veronique writhed, "if you will just keep this secret."

"Anything? Hmm," Sofonisba considered. "If I have you clean my shoes and empty my chamber pot," she said, savouring Veronique's groan, "then my maid will be suspicious. So, something else." She leaned back on the bench, looked up at the sky through the chestnut trees.

"You know, Veronique, you have very beautiful hair," Sofonisba mused. "That rich colour of grey-blond. Perhaps the loveliest hair of all of us ladies."

"So?" Veronique asked fearfully, pulling back and repinning her fallen locks.

"Her Majesty gives alms to an orphanage in town. She would be quite pleased if you made a large donation."

"What's that got to do with my — ? Aaaagh! No! You want me to cut off my hair, sell it, and donate the money to the orphanage?!"

"Maybe you're not as dim as I've always thought," Sofonisba said sweetly.

"Oh, Sonia!" Veronique held the sides of her head.

The next day, when the duchess was well, Sofonisba and Veronique went to her, explaining that Veronique wanted the duchess to cut off her hair, then grant Sofonisba and Veronique permission to go to a local wigmaker, who would pay a high price for such thick, excellently coloured and well-kept hair. They would then take the money at once to St. Mary's Home for Lost Babies and Children.

"While this act is highly commendable, I must know why, Veronique," the duchess asked.

"It is to honour my dear mother, madam. The orphanage is named for St. Mary, and my mother is named Marie," Veronique said, repeating the response she and Sofonisba had rehearsed.

"Very well. You know, Sofonisba, you and the other ladies could learn from this example."

"Indeed, madam," Sofonisba replied with false gravity.

Elisabeth, hearing of Veronique's act, remarked to Sofonisba: "What generosity! Somehow I never would have expected that from Veronique. Normally I want all my ladies to look as beautiful as possible, but for what Veronique's done, I don't mind that she'll be wearing a long veil for a few months."

In the following months Sofonisba suppressed a laugh every time she looked at Veronique and reflected on how much the veil made the young Frenchwoman look like a nun.

Sofonisba was concentrating on the portrait of Juana when a knock sounded at the studio door. "Señora Anguissola, the king's painter, Alonso Sanchez Coello, will meet you now," a guard said.

She barely had time to remove her apron before Coello entered the studio with two of Elisabeth's ladies, there to serve as chaperones and spies.

"Good day, Señor Coello, I've been hoping we could meet," Sofonisba said, setting aside her annoyance at the interruption.

"Señora Anguissola."

He said nothing more, and in the awkward silence, Sofonisba

had a feeling of having seen him somewhere before — the intense gaze, the night-black moustache and short beard… "Señor Coello, I've been wanting to talk to you about your work, there's so much —" His cold expression stopped her.

"Señora Anguissola, I won't waste your time or mine. I came here today because my curiosity finally got the better of me." He was dressed all in black, having been with the court a long time. "Of course I've heard all about you — the famous woman painter of Cremona, known throughout Europe, and so on," Coello said. "You know that you are not here because of your nobility, don't you?" Puzzled, Sofonisba decided that Coello was not seeking an answer.

"Señor, what is your concern? I am here because His Majesty asked me to serve the queen."

"You are a favourite of both Their Majesties, a lady-in-waiting who also paints. I could live with that; in fact, up until now, your presence at court meant nothing to me."

"And what is different now, señor?"

"Now you've been asked to paint a portrait of Princess Juana. A portrait requested by the pope. But years ago, it was Princess Juana who recommended *me* to the king, who secured *my* place here." He was tapping one foot. "*I* should have been asked to paint this portrait, Señora Anguissola, not you. I finally had to meet the woman who stole this work from me."

Sofonisba's eyes widened. "Stole, señor? That's a harsh word. Princess Juana asked me to do her portrait. Could I refuse?" She grabbed at a hunch. "Surely you've painted her portrait already."

"Yes, I have, and I won much praise for it. Well-deserved praise." He began to walk around the studio. "Yet when the *pope* requested a portrait of her …" He shook his head. "And you have only painted family portraits."

"Señor, that is not true! I have painted princes, dukes, scholars — I've painted the duke of Alba himself."

"Aacck…" Coello said dismissively. "You're not ready for court portraiture."

"I beg your —"

"So, is this it?" Coello stopped his tour of the studio where the unfinished portrait of Juana rested on an easel.

"Yes." Sofonisba stood beside the portrait.

"Full-length, yet! And why, pray, have you included this child? The princess has no daughter."

"The princess has founded a convent. The girl symbolizes a future novice. She holds three roses, for poverty, obedience and chastity."

Coello smirked. "Señora, you're still stuck on all those sister portraits you did. But court portraiture is different."

"I *know* court portraiture is different." Sofonisba said the words with calm deliberation, fighting the urge to scream them. "This is what the princess requested, and that's all that matters." Something else Coello had said stuck with her. "You complain that I'm a 'favourite' of Their Majesties. Yet you have a three-story house here within the palace walls, with a large workshop, and I hear the king visits you there regularly. Look around you, señor. This humble studio is all I have. The king's never once set foot in it. And I share a room with eleven ladies-in-waiting."

Coello remained impassive. "You *are* a lady-in-waiting."

"And I am a painter." She took one step away from the painting, keeping her eye on Coello. "Señor, do you disapprove of women painters?"

Coello sighed heavily. "You and I are competitors for commissions and royal favour. It is simply *not proper* for a woman to compete with a man in that way."

Sofonisba regarded him with contempt and gritted her teeth. She knew that Coello's belief was all too widely held, yet to hear it stated in her own studio was more than she could tolerate.

"Señor, I just do not know what to say. And I suppose that nothing I say will change your mind." Sofonisba let a pause draw out and took another step toward the door, so that the two painters stood facing each other but far apart, in space and attitude. "There will be many commissions, and enough royal favour to go around, I should think. You and I each want the best for ourselves, that's natural, but señor, that need not make us enemies." Inspiration dawned: "In fact, when I met Maestro Michelangelo Buonarroti…"

"Buonarroti? The Florentine? You've met him?" Coello asked, and Sofonisba smiled when he flashed an awestruck look, even though he squelched it just as quickly.

"I have, and he told me to never put myself into competition with others. I plan to follow his advice."

"Bah!"

"And now I remember where I've seen you. It was at the royal wedding reception. You were the only one in the room who looked miserable."

"Such fancy goings-on are not for me. I stick to myself, to my work."

"Señor." Sofonisba exhaled with exasperation. "I see I was mistaken. We have nothing to talk about, after all."

Coello lifted his chin, turned and left the studio, the two ladies trailing in a shuffle of silk.

"Holy Virgin, give me strength," Sofonisba said, too riled to focus on the princess' portrait. Instead, she decided to grind pigments into new colours that she would soon need. She put her apron back on, took the pigments from the cabinet, and picked up a grinding stone.

"That man" — *grind* — "the arrogance" — *grind* — "positively odious" — *grind* — "trying to tell me" — *grind* — "I who have met Buonarroti" — *grind* —

The new focus of gossip that echoed in the palace corridors did not take long to get back to Sofonisba: "He insulted her family."

"She talked to him like he's a servant."

"He told her she couldn't do court portraiture."

"And then she practically threw him out of her studio!"

LATE NOVEMBER, 1561

Elisabeth urged Sofonisba to do a self-portrait. The painter had just turned twenty-nine. Sofonisba called it her *Spanish Portrait*, because in it she was wearing a black velvet gown, as was the custom for the cooler months in Madrid. It was decorated with silver embroidery, also in the Spanish style. The neckline was edged with ermine — something she never would have worn in Cremona, but Elisabeth, as Queen of Spain, would not have her ladies plainly dressed. It was an attitude the Queen had brought from France. Sofonisba's hair, just beginning to sprout bits of grey, was in its usual braided crown, and when Elisabeth saw that, she insisted that the painter add jewels entwined into it. Elisabeth also lent Sofonisba a double-strand gold necklace.

In the portrait, as in her life, Sofonisba saw herself as confident and serene, basking in the approbation of the royals, and wrapped warmly in a cloak of good fortune and joy.

MARCH, 1562

The pre-dawn darkness clung like a dark fog over the city and palace, until giving way in the eastern sky to a pink, then golden bloom. The light crossed the palace walls at the stables first. As the chapel bells struck seven, the royal equerry — the man of the horses — strode in the intensifying light from the palace to the stables to awaken the grooms, who lay motionless on mounds of straw in the loft.

The grooms stretched and scratched, shared the night pot, slipped into their clothes and descended the loft ladder. They tore off pieces of brown bread from the loaves the equerry offered. "Now you've eaten, boys, get a move on. Those stalls won't muck themselves out!"

Nearby, in the courtyard, the loud *kree-eee-irrk* of the main gate's

hinges sounded as the gatekeeper admitted a parade of vendors —
robust men and women carrying handbaskets filled with grapes,
oranges, carrots, parsley, other fruits and vegetables, and eggs and
meat. Trailing after them came the maids and other palace workers
who lived outside, beyond the palace walls.

On the third floor, in a warm, bread-fragrant corner of the large
kitchen, the court baker told an apprentice to draw the last fresh
loaf out of the brick oven, using a long paddle. Then the baker
wiped his hands on a towel and sat down on a stool. He had begun
his work even before the dawn, punching down the bread dough
that had risen overnight, forming it into loaves, and sliding them
into the oven — white bread for the royal family and its intimates,
and brown bread for everyone else. While the bread baked, he and
his apprentice had begun making meat pies and jam tarts, but now
he took some time to rest before finishing them.

King Philip's tiny bedchamber in the centre of the palace, reached
only by a well-guarded maze of corridors, allowed no natural light,
yet he always awoke between seven and eight. He remained in
bed about an hour, reading official papers. Next the king rose and
stepped behind a curtain to use his personal chamber pot, which
was set inside a velvet-padded wooden box. An office holder known
as the groom of the stole would empty it later, but before he did,
the king's personal attendant, Pablo de Sevilla, would check the
pot to see what he might glean from its contents about the king's
health. For now, de Sevilla entered the bedchamber along with
a barber. "Good morning, Your Majesty." De Sevilla laid out the
king's clothing for that day while the barber tended to Philip's
beard and moustache according to the king's precise instructions,
and shaved the pale skin around the trim hairs. De Sevilla helped
Philip to dress. The silk stockings, all one piece, tied at the waist.
Over them went puffed-out short breeches and a white silk shirt
with ruffled collar and cuffs, the only thing Philip wore that was
not black. De Sevilla then guided the king into a snug-fitting

jacket and carefully fastened its dozen gold buttons.

Next Philip attended his daily private Mass in the palace chapel. He would not eat until lunch in the late morning.

Shortly after Philip left the chapel, Elisabeth and her ladies filed in for morning prayers. A priest read to them from the scripture, then left the women to their private meditations. Sofonisba prayed for her family and for Elisabeth and Philip. Elisabeth prayed for the same things she always did: for the health and long life of her husband, his family, and hers back in France; for the prosperity of Spain and its empire; and, most ardently, that her husband would come back to her bed and she would conceive a son.

Elisabeth then returned to her chamber and sat down to write a letter to her mother. Around her, the ladies embroidered or read or merrily chatted. Carmela strummed her lute.

Sofonisba excused herself after a while to go to her studio. On the way she passed courtiers, clerks, servants, priests, and buffoons, talking and gossiping and trading poems, or placing bets on how much longer the current pope would live, when the king would impregnate his bride, and which of two drops of water would slide down a particular window first. *And my sisters think that court life is a constant whirlwind of excitement*, Sofonisba thought wryly.

The duchess of Alba sat in her anteroom and reviewed the ladies' accounts: the number of candles for their room and for the corridor outside, what they ate, the upkeep of their horses, their servants' pay, and so on. She carefully noted every escudo in leather-bound ledgers embossed with the royal crest.

The king went from the chapel to a meeting with the Council of State, and after sitting at the head of the long table for a while, he considered running from the room in despair. But before he could stand, the image of his father, the Emperor Charles V, came to his mind unbidden, and he realized how unthinkable it was that his father would ever take that course. He forced his attention back to the subject at hand.

"Alba, we've been talking about the Turkish threat for thirty minutes now. How long have we been at war with them?" the king asked.

"Since 1551, Your Majesty."

"Eleven years. Too much time to fight, and too much time to talk about it." The king leaned on one arm of his chair. "The Ottoman Turks," he said bitterly. "My father, the emperor, may his soul rest, made peace with them, then six years later they attacked our bases in North Africa. The emperor sent one hundred and fifty thousand troops — a *multitude* — all in vain." He flipped one hand in the air at the futility of it all. "I think it was his frustration with the Turks that drove my father to abdicate."

There was a long silence; the advisers as still as if in a group portrait. Then the king addressed Alba again.

"You said that the Turks still hold Tripoli, which they wrested from the Knights of Malta. What should we do about it?" the king asked.

"When we can, Your Majesty, we should form an expedition to retake the city."

The king withheld a groan. "We tried that last year. Have you forgotten already? It was a disaster — twenty-seven galleys lost and ten thousand men captured! So, we won't be able to try that again soon. Unless any of you has another suggestion, I declare this meeting closed."

No one spoke. "Then good day, gentlemen," the king said with a trace of anger.

In the afternoon the queen and her ladies went riding. After slow rounds through the woods and meadows, Elisabeth challenged them to races. Sofonisba won the first race and could have won the rest, but she subtly held back and let the others win. The group rested briefly after returning to the palace, then rehearsed the theatricals they planned to perform soon for the court.

That evening, in the palace's large central room, Elisabeth could be found with her ladies and other women of the court, along with Don Juan, Alessandro Farnese, Riccardo Velleti, and at least a dozen other young men. Sofonisba looked around and saw some gentlemen and ladies dancing, some wagering away at cards, and others conversing about philosophy, history, literature, and painting. She noted their wit, elegance, and nonchalance as they told jokes and shared anecdotes, pleasantries, and puns. Nearby, the bells on a buffoon's slippers jangled as he amused a small but appreciative group by walking on his hands. The violinist and the piper never stopped.

Finally Sofonisba's gaze rested on Elisabeth, seated in one of the two large chairs always reserved for her and the king. To no one's surprise, the king's chair was empty. "Elisabeth, don't you want to dance? This is one of your favourite tunes," Sofonisba suggested.

"Not right now." The queen signalled to a guard. "Please bring a chair for Señora Anguissola."

"Is anything wrong, my lady?"

The queen looked around before responding. "Sonia, my husband hasn't been to my chamber in weeks." Her lower lip trembled. "I lie there, waiting … I pray. His second wife, God rest her soul, she complained about the same neglect."

"Elisabeth, you must be patient, that's all." Sofonisba squeezed the queen's hand.

"He works far into the night, de Sevilla says, reading stacks and stacks of endless reports."

"He will come to you again soon, I'm sure," Sofonisba said.

"Oh, enough about him," Elisabeth said, and stood up. "I'm going to join that card game."

"Elisabeth, remember what happened the last time? You had to borrow from Alba to repay…" Sofonisba said.

"Well, I feel like my luck's about to change."

The card players stood ceremoniously and made room for the queen at their large round table. She wagered recklessly and bluffed unconvincingly but laughed the whole time, and the other gamblers obliged her by laughing along. And she gave them good reason to laugh — in a short while she had amassed a large debt. Still, she played on.

"Numerus 30."

"Ten escudos."

"Primero 50 at 20 escudos." Around and around the bids rotated. Elisabeth grew restless whenever she, or the other players, had to declare modest hands such as numerus and primero. *Two or three of the same suit, or one card of each suit. How dull. Doesn't anyone have a chorus?* she wondered. *I'd love to see that — four of a kind! Then this game would get interesting.*

Many of the courtiers had drifted from the room when the queen finally pushed back from the table.

"Ladies and gentlemen, thank you for the amusement," Elisabeth said. "Now you'll have to excuse me."

Her ladies gathered around her. "I'll go to my room now. All that card playing has made me tired." She showed not the slightest distress about her losses.

Her ladies helped her dress for bed and left the room. Elisabeth was just about to put out the candle when the king entered her chamber. *I was right — my luck is about to change*, she thought, and her heart began to race.

JUNE, 1562

The royal convoy of women in carriages and men on horseback made its way labouriously north from Madrid to the king's country house, El Bosque, at Segovia. The king believed that the woods there would be cooler and healthier than the June swelter of Madrid. Philip and Elisabeth led a fairly small group — only de Sevilla, to serve the king; Sofonisba and five other ladies-in-waiting to serve the queen; cooks and grooms to feed the humans and the horses, and a few of the ever-requisite musicians and jesters.

"Ah, it's a fine day, and what a clever idea of my husband's to move to El Bosque for a while," Elisabeth said to the ladies sharing her carriage. She raised the silk window shade to reveal tidy rows of grapevines, their fruit still the light green of summer. Elisabeth waved to group of vineyard workers, who waved back. Soon the convoy would cross a row of mountains to El Bosque, just beyond.

"My lady, you seem especially pleased about this trip," Sofonisba said.

"That's because…" Elisabeth glanced down shyly, then looked around at them to announce: "It looks like I am with child." She smiled proudly.

"Oh, my lady!"

"That's wonderful!"

"Your prayers were answered!"

"Praise the Lord!" They laughed and sang all the rest of the way to Segovia.

On arrival, Philip and Elisabeth went straight to the cool and dim monastery chapel and lit a candle, his rugged hand lovingly over her pale one as she held the long match.

The royal couple went hunting together every day for weeks. They chatted, laughed, shared meals, danced, and celebrated more than ever before in their married life.

At least, until the dawn when a scream from Elisabeth's chamber announced that her hope had been false, and the party packed up and left for Madrid in a procession back over the mountains and past the vineyards, as dejected as the ride out had been festive.

Sofonisba was desperate to cheer or at least to distract the queen. "Elisabeth, come with me to the studio," she said when the carriage pulled into the palace courtyard.

The queen's young face, usually so alive, was long and inanimate. In the carriage on the way home she had not said a word or glanced even once out the window. She merely pretended to be reading.

"What for?"

"I used to take my sisters into the studio when melancholy over-came them. They would paint or draw, or just sit and pose for me. Sometimes it helped."

"All right." Elisabeth sighed heavily, but let Sofonisba lead her to the studio.

"It's time I started another portrait of you," Sofonisba said. "Sit right there."

Elisabeth's sad face was heartbreaking. Sofonisba looked beyond the sadness and saw a maturity, a seriousness, an aspect of wom-anhood that had not been there when the queen had posed for her before.

Sofonisba sketched her pulled-back dark hair, her eyes that were thoughtful but not grim, and her tight mouth that, while unsmiling, refused to give in to despair. She took her time, wanting to get each part just right. Elisabeth did not shift or squirm at all. Still, Sofonisba was mindful of the queen's low spirits.

"That's enough for now. Now let's walk in the garden."

♁

Soon after the return from Segovia, a breathless messenger galloped to the palace with horrible news: the crown prince Don Carlos had fallen down a flight of stairs at the University of Alcalá and broken his skull.

Under Vesalius' care, Don Carlos slowly recovered, to the regret of many courtiers. "That staircase in Alcalá knocked a devil into him," they said. He treated his horses even worse than before, running them into exhaustion. Late some nights, he would pay a dwarf in bottles of wine and gold coins if she would let him whip her. While most of the court tried to avoid him, the king kept a loose hand on his wayward son, rejecting all criticism. "He'll never be king, you know," Elisabeth told Sofonisba. "Philip told me. He knows Carlos is too erratic, unpredictable and foolish, and Philip cares too much about the monarchy to entrust it to anyone like that. It must have been hard for my husband, to realize that his own son cannot succeed him."

"Indeed, it must have been," Sofonisba said.

"So you see, that makes it all the more important that I — oh, Sonia, I *must* give the king an heir!" Elisabeth said.

"And I'm sure you will," Sofonisba said soothingly.

AUGUST, 1562

The two guards had held their mouths firmly when Sofonisba passed, as if trying hard not to smirk or giggle. And were they not whispering to each other as she approached? And why, while on her way to the studio that morning, did she have a sense of conversations ending when she entered a room or turned a corner and encountered the usual courtiers, clerics, and servants?

Sofonisba tried to paint but was too preoccupied by the decidedly disconcerting atmosphere in the palace. As she gave up the effort, Rico knocked on the door.

"It's been the strangest morning, I get the feeling everybody's … Rico, what in the world is going on?" His worried face made her heart sink.

"Sonia, there's a rumour, uh, making the rounds of the palace, about, about you," he said, looking stricken.

"Me? What about me?"

"Now you know how these things are here, everybody just likes to talk…" He avoided her eyes.

"Rico! Tell me *now*!"

"Sonia, they are saying that during the night someone saw you go to the stables, and climb up to the loft."

Her jaw dropped. "The loft ... where the ... " She sat down, took a deep breath. "What a vile, slanderous lie! And *how* could I do that, with the duchess' hawk eyes always on us?"

"They say you slipped out in the wee hours this morning, after the duchess' last check on the ladies' bedchamber."

Sofonisba felt dizzy with confusion. Then anger returned, and she dashed out of the studio. Charging into the bedchamber she shared with the other ladies, she grabbed Veronique by her thin blue-silked shoulders and shook her, screaming "Why? Why have you spread this evil story about me?"

Veronique pushed Sofonisba away and screamed back. "Let go of me! *Mai non!* I never! *Tu es folle italienne!*"

"You petty, conniving, cunning little..."

Then all the ladies were screaming: "Think you're so superior ... you French whore!"

"Leave her alone ... Italian harlot!"

"I did *not!* ... Spanish trollop!"

"Wait!" Sofonisba yelled over the chaos. "Stop! I know now who did it!"

At that moment the duchess of Alba thundered into the room. "What in heaven's name is going on here? A guard fetched me, worried that the ceiling was falling!"

All the ladies started talking to the duchess at once. She raised her right hand, gave a look of doom, and silence instantly reigned. "Señora Anguissola, come with me."

Sofonisba, head held high, followed her to her study.

"Madam, I apologize for the noise. I know now who invented and spread such a wicked tale about me. It was — "

"I don't care who it was," the duchess cut her off. "A lady's reputation is everything, especially for the ladies who serve the queen."

Sofonisba sensed a certain perverse — what was it? — *enjoyment* in the duchess' manner.

"There is only one person who can save you now."

Sofonisba felt a distinct chill. "Elisabeth," she said. "Then I will go to her at once."

"You will not. You are to stay away from all members of the royal family, for the time being. I suggest you spend this afternoon in quiet contemplation and prayer." The duchess pursed her lips.

"But I'm taking Elisabeth to see the new garden at Casa de Campo."

"The other ladies will accompany her."

Sofonisba walked in a slow daze to her studio. She sat down, unable to work, not even wanting to move. *Coello*, she thought bitterly. *So this is how he tries to drive me out.*

The duchess had been right about a lady's reputation. The king's sister, Princess Juana, once fell from her horse, and the king was horrified at the mere *thought* that a man *might* have helped her to remount, even though no man had come near her.

What if I have to leave Madrid? I've been here barely three years. Elisabeth still needs me, she is still so young. To have to go back to Cremona in shame, to the city whose painters' guild had rejected her — *what would I do? And to face Mama and Papa like this?* She leaned forward and covered her face with her hands. *Holy Virgin, help me.*

If only she could speak to Mama and Papa now, to hold them in hand. She knew they would comfort her, understand that she had done nothing wrong, had neither betrayed her queen nor sullied the Anguissola honour. Her feeling of homesickness had never been stronger. It made her throat tighten and her hands and feet turn cold.

She stood up and paced the room. Why had she come here? To paint? She could have done that in Cremona, in fact was doing it, even without the guild's anointing. Had she come for adventure, and to serve the king and queen? Her motives seemed so vain and frivolous now.

Despite the prospect of returning there a ruined woman, she could not stop thinking about Cremona, her room in the family palazzo, the garden, her lost and loyal Rosa. She squinched her eyes tight, refusing to cry.

Surely there will be some word from Elisabeth soon. She waited and prayed, listening for a servant's knock, looking for a note slipped under the door. She heard only the chapel bells chime unerringly, hour after hour, and saw only the shift in sunlight through the studio windows. She sank back into the chair, her head aflame.

Just after the bells struck the hour for the evening meal she heard another sound, the one she had longed for: a gentle knock. She flung the door open to find a guard, then shrank from him with a gasp of horror.

"Señora Anguissola, I am to escort you to the evening meal."

"What!" she exclaimed. For a moment, she felt relieved that she was not to confront a harsher fate. She had forgotten that it was the day of the weekly dinner with Philip and Elisabeth. "You mean, with Their Majesties? Oooh, I can't."

"Señora." The guard gestured for her to step into the hall.

My humiliation is to continue — in front of all those courtiers. Her knees wobbled as she walked.

In the dining hall, she tried to slip unnoticed to a place at the table beside the other ladies, but they saw her, set their faces grimly, and studiously ignored her.

Everyone stood and went silent, as usual, when Philip and Elisabeth glided into the room and took their places at the head table. Sofonisba could not look at them.

But out of the corner of her eye Sofonisba saw the queen move away from the head table and come toward the table where Sofonisba stood, until she was standing opposite her. Sofonisba started to panic as the silence became more oppressive. Flustered, she nearly forgot the protocol, but then, awkwardly, she curtsied.

"Sonia, please come and sit beside me," Elisabeth said.

Sofonisba was not quite sure she had heard the queen correctly. She had to repeat the sentence to herself, then, still uncertain, she forced herself to follow the queen's command. When Elisabeth and Sofonisba reached the head table, Sofonisba was astonished, even wary, when she saw the king smiling at her. Then Philip and Elisabeth sat down, the cue for everyone else to sit and for conversation to resume.

"Sonia, I hope you appreciate what a friend you have in the envoy from Lucca," Elisabeth said.

"Rico?" *What could he have to do with this?*

"He spoke to me most eloquently on your behalf," Elisabeth said. "Waited for hours to see me." A servant filled the queen's wine cup, and she picked it up. "Now, should I wear the yellow silk tomorrow? And what jewels would complement it best? I think I have nothing that's quite right for that dress. You'll have to help me design something new…"

The first dish was slices of pickle, something Sofonisba had eaten many times, but this time she truly savoured the way the spices tingled on her tongue.

DECEMBER, 1562

Always at the back of Sofonisba's mind lurked the realization that Coello would strike again.

She retreated to the studio. She was determined to excel, to surpass all her previous achievements, with the three-quarter-length portrait of Elisabeth. It was one of the most complex paintings she had ever done, and she lavished attention and care on it. To portray the queen's stature as a Spanish sovereign and her firm establishment as Philip's consort, Sofonisba had her pose in a fitted bodice and bell-shaped skirt of black, the colour so unmistakably linked with Philip's sombre court. Yet the painter pushed against the sombreness, in keeping with Elisabeth's youthful spirit and her Parisian taste, by painting the undersleeves in red with gold embroidery. On the black velvet outer sleeves and down the middle of the skirt, Sofonisba painted red satin bows trimmed with bits of gilded silver — decoration on decoration — a uniquely Spanish touch. Against the black velvet the queen wore a belt of gold with alternating settings of rubies, sapphires, and pearls, matching the chain around her neck. Three columns of rubies and sapphires ran down the front of the bodice to her waist. Sofonisba also draped two long strands of pearls around the queen's neck.

Short red and white feathers topped the queen's black velvet cap, which bore diagonal rows of pearls. She rested her right hand almost casually on a brocade-covered chair, a symbol of the throne, in keeping with her regal status. In making the work shine with relentless ostentation, Sofonisba set out to exalt and promote the royal house, and to place it on a level of glory at least as high as that of France or England.

When she had completed the portrait, in February 1563, Sofonisba covered it with a white silk veil. Exhausted yet exhilarated, she went alone to the chapel. *Dear Lord, this new portrait of the queen is the greatest it has been my pleasure to create. Your loving hand guided me, and I commend to You any glory I may receive for it.*

She arranged a private unveiling for Philip and Elisabeth, in Philip's study.

Elisabeth gasped at once. "Oh Sonia, *c'est magnifique!*"

The king sat wide-eyed. "My dear señora," he finally said. "I have many paintings of many members of my family, but there is none, by God, as well executed as this one." He stood up and moved closer. "You made my queen's face and hands just glow, and those red lips! You've also captured her charm and spirit. Well done!"

Sofonisba and Elisabeth discussed the jewellery, the lace ruff trimmed in gold thread, and the faithful reproduction of Elisabeth's dark brown hair.

The king cut in. "I was, shall we say, uncertain about having a woman painter at court. Many questioned my judgment. Sofonisba, you are not as well known here as you are in Italy. Besides, it seemed unwise for my wife's closest companion to also be busy with painting. But now that I see this, I know that I made the right decision in bringing you here."

"Thank you, Your Majesty," Sofonisba said.

Courtiers came to see the painting when it was hung among the most treasured works of the royal collection. Sofonisba hid behind a velvet curtain and listened.

"That clever little Cremonese! Now look what she has done!"

"It's a splendid likeness of the queen!"

"Elisabeth's warmth and virtue are apparent."

She also heard a remark that nearly caused her to burst out of her hiding place with indignation: "Sofonisba's quite talented for a lady-in-waiting."

Sofonisba was pleasantly surprised to learn that one of the French ladies-in-waiting extolled the painting in a letter to Catherine of France, Elisabeth's mother, who then told Sofonisba that a copy would please her greatly. The papal nuncio in Spain sent word of the painting's marvels to the pope, who also wrote to Sofonisba to request a copy — the highest honour of all.

Elisabeth rewarded Sofonisba with a length of silver brocade — "for a dress to wear on feast days." It was then that Sofonisba knew she had truly regained her place in the queen's eyes.

$\sim$

She was in the studio early one morning, hoping to work in the favourable light of dawn. A panicked knocking annoyed her.

It was José San Martín, the young assistant to Coello.

"Help me, help me," he flustered, rushing in. "The master is in a terrible state."

Sofonisba wanted to spit at the designation of "master" for Coello. "The state of your dear 'master' is no concern of mine."

"No, no, you don't understand," San Martín said. "He doesn't know I'm here, he doesn't know anything right now, because he's passed out cold on the divan in his studio."

His divan, Sofonisba thought scornfully. *A comfortable item that would not fit in this cramped studio.*

"He went gambling and drinking last night, far into the night," San Martín continued, but Sofonisba interrupted.

"I really do not care about Señor Coello's poor handling of liquor." The whole court knew how Coello behaved when his wife and children were away, and that at that moment they were visiting her sister in Zaragoza.

"Please, señora. Let me explain. The master went to sleep it off in the studio, and when I tried to rouse him this morning, he only grunted and rolled over, went back to sleep. But the envoy from Naples is leaving for home today. The king commissioned a portrait from the master, and it is to be presented to the envoy this afternoon." His words came faster and more desperately. "But the portrait is not finished, and my master is in no condition to finish it in time. And if he does not, for him it could be — " He made a slashing motion across his throat. "I humbly ask you to come and finish the painting for him."

Sofonisba regarded San Martín coldly, at a loss for where to start in rejecting the request, then she looked away and folded her arms. Of course Coello would not lose his life. But he could lose his position, and be cast out and disgraced. At least she would let San Martín squirm a while. *How absurd that Coello needs me. If he were in my position, he'd let me fail. Rejoice in it, even.* "Please, señora, you're the only one in the whole palace who can help him," San Martín implored. "There isn't much time. The painting only needs the final touches."

"Ha! And why should I help him? Señor, you do not know what you are asking."

"Oh yes I do, señora," San Martín said, looking into her eyes. "I know what the master did to you. Still I ask you, because I believe you to be a fine lady. I understand that your heart is bitter toward Señor Coello, but please consider this: it would also be a great embarrassment for the king if he cannot present this portrait to the envoy."

Sofonisba tried to collect her thoughts. Her shoulders sagged when she realized that indeed, she could not let the king suffer for Coello's irresponsibility. It was a nasty circumstance that in protecting the king, she would be rescuing her enemy. Then a thought occurred to her, shining like that dawn: Coello's dilemma could mean the end of hers.

"For the sake of the king, all right, let's go," she said. On the way to Coello's studio she and San Martín met Teresa, a Spanish lady-in-waiting whom Sofonisba considered a friend. "Come with us, Teresa," Sofonisba said. *It would be just like that snake to try to frame me by spreading rumours about me being alone with a young, handsome man in his studio.* Teresa joined them, without asking any questions.

In Coello's bright and spacious studio, nearly twice as big as her own, Sofonisba buried her envy as she regarded the portrait.

"It will take me one hour to mix and apply the final glazes," she said. "Then the portrait will need four hours to dry."

"That is very well, señora," San Martín said. "That will leave just enough time to deliver the portrait to the king."

She concentrated, not wanting to make a mistake that would keep her in the studio a minute longer than needed. She and Teresa both laughed when, from across the room, they heard steady snoring from the rumpled figure on the divan.

"Now when Señor Coello recovers, you be sure to tell him what happened, and who it was who saved his hide," Sofonisba said to San Martín as she set down a brush and wiped her hands.

"Oh, I will, señora, and God bless you."

During the night Sofonisba tossed and turned with uncertainty.

Coello might ignore the favour and continue his campaign against her. Had she been foolish to believe that he would feel indebted enough to leave her be? The catastrophe of an ejection from the palace, instigated by him, would pain her all the more if it came after she had helped him. *Holy Virgin, don't let me regret what I did today.*

MARCH, 1563

Sofonisba was walking in the garden in a rare interval of solitude while the queen rested and nothing was pressing in the studio. She turned down an alley of tall shrubs and hesitated when she saw Coello walking toward her beside a stranger. It was too late for her to disappear. Her heart thudded as the pair approached.

"Señora, good afternoon," Coello said to her with a joviality strange for him. Was he mocking her?

"Good afternoon." She kept her inflection cool and her face frozen.

"A warm day for early spring, no?" Coello said.

Will he insult me by not introducing his friend? The other man was older, dignified, and dressed more brightly than most courtiers. Clearly he had not been at court long enough to adopt its solemn palette.

Coello seemed in no hurry to walk on. "Señora Anguissola, perhaps you have heard that the previous envoy from Naples has returned home?" he said casually.

Sofonisba held back a gasp and wished that she could punch Coello. *Does he not know?* "Ah, yes, I did hear something like that," she said mechanically.

"Well then, allow me to present the new envoy from Naples, Bartolomeo di Giovanni de Aversa. Señor, I present to you Señora Sofonisba Anguissola, from Cremona."

"How do you do, signore," Sofonisba said, using her native language.

"A pleasure to meet you, señora," the envoy replied.

Coello then addressed the envoy: "Now, Señora Anguissola is a…" and then he looked right into Sofonisba's eyes, "painter, in the queen's household."

"Indeed! A woman painter," the envoy said, and prattled on with, "I had heard that Philip had a good eye for artistic talent…" while Coello nodded slowly to Sofonisba. She relaxed her expression.

"Welcome to Madrid, Signor de Aversa," Sofonisba said as soon as the envoy paused. "Good day, gentlemen," and she continued her walk with a proudly determined, unhesitant stride.

7.

A New Pinnacle

Loosen your golden tresses, lovely Venus,
And crown your head with myrtle and with laurel,
So may these loves, hallowed by holy vows,
Make harmony with you in peaceful sojourn.
                    —Veronica Gàmbara (1485-1550)

APRIL, 1563

With the planets in propitious alignment — Philip never would
have allowed such a momentous beginning otherwise — grunting,
swearing, gesticulating men manipulated thick ropes to drag and
shove great blocks of grey granite into place, while Sofonisba, Elisabeth and the other ladies looked on through the feeble sunlight.

The women stood on a plateau on the southern slopes of the
Guadarrama Mountains, about a half-day's carriage ride northwest
of Madrid, as a new palace took shape.

It was April, during a gap in the frequent spring rains that washed
the land of its winter pallor. Philip had ordered a new home for the
royal family. Ostensibly, he wanted to commemorate the victory
of his troops over the French at Saint-Quentin six years earlier,
but his true motive was to advance his efforts to promote himself
as the greatest leader in Christendom.

Sofonisba heard the court clamour over the ambition of Philip's plans. The palace complex would be a home, yes, but with a large church, because anywhere Philip lived, a church had to be at hand. And there had to be a monastery, and a seminary to supply the monastery. There also had to be a library for the books, the maps, the antiquities that Philip could never resist. A vast garden was required. And, in a new feature, Philip ordered a royal mausoleum.

The victory at Saint-Quentin had taken place on St. Lawrence's Day, so the new palace would be called San Lorenzo del Escorial, which everyone quickly shortened to El Escorial. "Place of the slag heap," from the grey stones of the area, struck Sofonisba as an unlikely name for something that Philip hoped would be as grand as the temple of Solomon.

FEBRUARY, 1564

Sofonisba dreamed one night of being back in her old studio in the family palazzo in Cremona. She was finishing the portrait of Amilcare, Minerva, and Asdrubale when the bells of San Giorgio began to toll, a relentless, hideous funereal tolling, and a black shadow spread across the painting, and no matter how furiously she stroked at it with her brush she could not stop its shrouding effect.

"Papa!" she called out as she sat up in bed.

"Sonia, are you all right?" Teresa asked from her bed. Sofonisba began to cry.

"There, there, you just had a bad dream," said Teresa, holding an arm around Sofonisba's shoulders until she relaxed and laid down again.

Sofonisba was painting with Elisabeth in the studio the next morning when the duchess of Alba entered. At once she saw the letter in the duchess' hand. "Ohhhh, Papa — " She froze and her heart pounded.

"Well yes, this letter is from your father, but how did you know that?" the duchess asked.

"Huh?" Confused, Sofonisba opened the letter.

"…Your beloved sister Minerva passed on to the next life on 12 January. She had the spotted fever … not yet twenty-five years in this life… my precious daughter, try to keep well…"

Minerva! Sofonisba dropped the letter and grabbed at the tightening in her chest. She could barely breathe, let alone cry. Elisabeth picked up the letter. "Oh Sonia, I'm so sorry." Her own eyes filled with tears.

"My deepest condolences, señora," the duchess said, and left the room.

Sofonisba sighed painfully. "She didn't want to paint. I tried to teach her, but … maybe she thought she'd disappointed me."

"No, I'm sure she didn't," Elisabeth reassured.

"Her poetry, all her writing … that's what she was born for."

In the chapel, as Sofonisba lit a candle, out of some corner a voice rose up: "*I don't want to paint any more.*" She covered her ears.

God of Heaven, open the gates for Minerva, well-named for the goddess of wisdom, the scholar among us.

A packet arrived some weeks later from her sister Lucia, full of Lucia's last drawings of Minerva. Sofonisba used them to paint a memorial portrait of her sister, decked in lace, velvet, and fur, the eyes intelligent and keen, and on a gold medallion on a chain around her neck, the figure of the goddess Minerva.

Death had more to say. Soon after she finished the painting of Minerva, Sofonisba heard through the papal envoy about the death of Michelangelo Buonarroti in Rome. He was eighty-nine years old. She remembered his torment, his feelings that art was an unworthy vocation. But Sofonisba saw his art as praise to God; she could not look at his *Pietà* without a sense of the divine — *il Divino*. Her memories of him remained like a glowing hearth on a chill day.

MAY, 1564

"Your Majesty, the French ambassador, Jean d'Ebrard, seigneur de Saint-Sulpice, wishes to see you."

Buried in reports, his hand cramped from writing decrees and instructions, Philip hated the interruption but leaned back in his chair with resignation. He could not easily refuse the representative of his wife's homeland. "Send him in."

"Your Majesty."

"Seigneur. Please sit down."

"*Merci.*" Saint-Sulpice settled his considerable bulk. "I bring tidings from your esteemed mother-in-law, Queen Regent of France Catherine de Medici, widow of His Majesty Henry II, may he rest in peace, and mother of Her Majesty Elisabeth —"

"Yes, I know who Catherine is," Philip cut in. "Now, what does the dear woman want to tell me?"

"First, she sends her great affection, and she notes that you have been a fine husband to her daughter, indeed a kind and exemplary spouse," Saint-Sulpice continued. "However, the Queen Regent feels compelled to raise an issue that is, shall we say, somewhat delicate."

"And that issue would be…?"

"Queen Catherine has instructed me to remind you of her desire to see some grandchildren. She said this would support her opinion of you as a good husband."

The king burst into laughter. "Ah, dear Catherine," he said between chuckles. "Seigneur de Saint-Sulpice, assure her that I will take special care to preserve her good judgment of me."

Philip took his wife to the royal palace at Aranjuez, nearly a day's ride south of Madrid. They spent several idyllic days together. Elisabeth was enchanted by the vast gardens of blooms. She gasped with delight when she saw their bedchamber, where Philip had ordered that the bed be covered with a fragrant layer of red rose petals. A few weeks later, Philip sat at the queen's bedside in Madrid as a doctor examined her. "Well, is it true, what my wife suspects?"

The doctor straightened. "Congratulations, Your Majesties. Her Majesty is with child."

At once Philip ordered public celebrations. Canons fired repeatedly in the palace courtyard, and when the canons were stilled, musicians played, and the crowds who had gathered in Elisabeth's honour danced in the July sunshine.

"I've never been so happy," the queen told Sofonisba when the celebration was over and all was quiet. "My husband! You should have seen him at Aranjuez."

Sofonisba smiled. "I'm happy for you, my lady. And now you should rest."

The queen spent her time drawing, writing letters, and playing the clavichord. Despite her care, she complained of weakness and stayed in bed on August fifth. On the ninth, her nose began to bleed profusely.

The Spanish physicians exhausted Elisabeth further with bloodletting, purges, and enemas. Sofonisba, by her lady's side, despaired when Elisabeth lapsed into a delirium. While the queen held a sweaty grip on Sofonisba's arm and pressed it against her chest, her womb expelled the baby.

Elisabeth swayed between life and death. After three days, the physicians filed solemnly out of her chambers, staring straight ahead, right past her twelve anguished ladies-in-waiting. Sofonisba confronted the doctors.

"Señores, we would know Her Majesty's condition now."

"Please, señora." The doctors kept walking.

"Pray tell us!" Sofonisba insisted, pursuing them down the corridor.

"Just say prayers for her, ladies."

Exasperated, Sofonisba turned to the others. "Let's go in."

They filed into the room and saw Elisabeth lying there, white-faced and speechless, her eyes closed. "They've given her up," the king said, raising teary eyes to the ladies but not seeing them.

Only his friend and chamberlain, Ruy Gómez da Silva, accompanied him. "Let's all pray." They knelt. Several of the ladies began to silently weep. *No, God, please, not her…*

Word of the doctors' surrender spread to the crowd gathered below Elisabeth's window. The news made many wail and sob. Even the brutish clown Don Carlos was subdued. Some said he, too, was moved to tears.

The brilliant Vesalius was no longer at the court to help the queen. Weary of the scorn and envy thrown at him by the Spanish doctors, he had asked for royal permission to undertake a pilgrimage to Jerusalem. Vesalius left Madrid in April 1564, and in the same year, on his way back from Jerusalem, he fell ill and died.

"Enough of those treatments," Philip scowled, looking over the queen's scars from tourniquets and incisions. "It's time to give her only nourishment and rest."

"Your Majesty — is that wise?" da Silva asked.

"Well if the doctors are so wise, why is she in this state? What have they done for her?" Philip thundered. "And Vesalius, damn him, running off on a pilgrimage! *I* will look after my wife now!"

Elisabeth began to stir. The king leaned in close to her face. "The roses at Aranjuez…" she murmured.

JANUARY, 1565

By the time the winter drizzled in, the queen had recovered well enough to amuse herself by planning a masque, to be presented on January 6, the feast of the Epiphany. This type of drama, performed by masked actors and rich with allegory, was still unknown in Spain. Elisabeth had loved masques while growing up in France, and Princess Juana, who had known such entertainment in Portugal, agreed to help her.

Philip surprised everyone by taking his place beside Elisabeth to watch this performance, and delighted in trying to figure out the drama's "Eleven Chivalric Riddles."

"You and Juana have done well," Philip said.

"Thank you, my lord," Elisabeth replied, wondering briefly whether her husband would be so complimentary, or even whether he would have attended, if she had not nearly died the year before. His next words erased her doubt.

"I have a mission for you, my dear. I want you to represent me, along with Alba, at a meeting in Bayonne, about the Protestant scourge."

"Bayonne! Then I'll be able to see my mother!" Elisabeth's face lit up.

"That's right."

"And my brother, who's now the king! Oh, Philip, that will be a great joy! It's been … six years! When will we leave?"

"In early April. It will be a long trip, across the Pyrenees. Now don't forget, this is not a social call, there are serious issues to be dealt with," Philip said, but his wife's happiness pleased him. "You are to tell your mother, in firm tones, that she must take a stronger position against the Huguenots. Those *Protestants*" — he snarled out the word, "must be fought. It's our sacred duty, blessed by God. Alba will travel there ahead of you."

"Yes, yes, you'll have to tell me all about that, what I should say and do," Elisabeth said. "But to be in France again! Praise St. Elizabeth and the Virgin! I will need new gowns, new headpieces, new jewellery…"

Philip's concern about the Huguenots was well-founded. They wanted to destroy him, and the Church. And they were not content to work against him only in France. They also stirred up the Catalonian bandits, and the Moriscos in Valencia. That group of converts from Islam had the outward appearance of observant, pious Christians, but Philip was convinced it was only an appearance.

Worst of all for Spain, the Huguenots supported the rebellious Protestants in the Netherlands.

"You see," Philip told Elisabeth, "if troubles worsen in the Netherlands, and our hold on the area weakens, I won't be able to focus on our biggest menace."

"Of course," Elisabeth said, "the Ottoman Turks." Spanish soldiers had barely driven off the Turks at Oran in Algeria two years before, and they were certain to attack again.

"So I'm counting on you and Alba, my dear, to ease this dreadful Huguenot scourge," Philip said.

"I will try, my lord."

Philip ordered Sofonisba to begin a new painting of Elisabeth to commemorate the Bayonne venture.

Elisabeth was no longer a mere dutiful girl-wife but a mature queen, and the painter was determined to portray her that way. Standing beside a column — a symbol of power — her expression was more knowing, more serene, and more confident than in other portraits. Sofonisba ordered the royal seamstresses to create a truly regal gown just for the portrait, with wide sleeves split open to show gold-embroidered white silk undersleeves, and long "wings" below the arms that nearly touched the floor. To show her role as her husband's representative, the queen held in her right hand a medallion with a portrait of Philip.

BAYONNE, FRANCE, JUNE 14, 1565

Elisabeth, too excited to be tired from the long journey, stepped out of her carriage and directly into her mother's arms. There in the courtyard of the bishop's palace they held each other in a joyous clutch. Then Elisabeth reached out for her brother Charles, now almost fifteen, and brother-king and sister-queen hugged and laughed once again like children. Sofonisba joined in the applause of the welcoming crowd of court officials, clerics, guards, and courtiers.

That evening, two thousand lords and ladies attended a banquet with twenty-five courses, given in honour of the visitors from Spain. The French hosts believed that the roasted squab with tart cherries, the almond pudding, the lakes of wine and all the rest of the feast, eaten to the spritely tunes of a string quartet, would somehow smooth the way toward a productive meeting.

A theatrical performance followed the dinner. At its climax, a child representing Benevolence and wearing only a gilded laurel wreath burst through the rays of a paper sun.

The musicians broke into dance music. Sofonisba, who had danced rarely since Philip and Elisabeth's wedding, gaily poured forth her old grace and energy.

Elisabeth wrote to Philip about her fears that she and Alba were not accomplishing much. The Huguenots were too distrustful of both France and Spain to make an effective agreement. For Sofonisba, on the other hand, the visit was a lark. At the end of the meeting she took part in a staged "combat" between Love and Virtue. She was awarded a gold medallion for her virtue, beauty, and kindness, and for her expert dancing.

Her time to bask in glory was brief. When Sofonisba returned to Madrid, she learned that her sister Lucia had died of the pox, in her twenty-eighth year. In a letter, her mother said that Lucia never quite recovered from the loss of Minerva, and that maybe she could not fight the pox because of a broken heart.

Sofonisba recalled Lucia's companionship in the studio after Elena had left. In the good-natured rivalry among the painter-sisters, Lucia had been a stronger competitor than Elena. A self-portrait Lucia had painted seven or eight years before came back to haunt Sofonisba — there was something unfathomable in Lucia's expression. Sofonisba decided it must have been a sadness, and a feeling of inferiority. *Perhaps she felt cursed to have me as a sister, always overshadowing her. Given time, she would have surpassed me … given time…*

The pleasures of Bayonne then felt distant to Sofonisba, and even a bit silly. Perhaps she would recall them later and give them their due place in her memory, but for now, there was only the memory of Lucia.

JANUARY, 1566

Elisabeth, Philip, and the new court physician, Jorge de Maldonado, were gathered in the queen's chamber. "Your Majesties, I congratulate you," the physician said. "Her Majesty is once again with child. The baby will come in August, God willing."

Philip took his wife's hand in both of his. "Praise God," he said.

"But I warn you," Maldonado continued. "It won't be an easy time. I have been told of the difficulties the queen has had with previous confinements."

The warning did not prevent the announcement of Elisabeth's condition from adding further merriment to the time of feasting just before Ash Wednesday, a three-day celebration known as Carnestolandas. There were fireworks, bonfires, and masked dancers in the palace courtyards and the streets of Madrid. Teams of twenty-two horsemen performed at a special tournament. Sofonisba and the other ladies kept Elisabeth company as she watched from a balcony, where Philip had ordered her to remain. The new French ambassador wrote to Queen Catherine that Philip seemed more in love with Elisabeth than ever before.

In May, 1566, Sofonisba received a particularly welcome letter from her father. He told her in happy words about an extraordinary houseguest of the Anguissolas — Giorgio Vasari, a painter and writer from Arezzo, in Tuscany. Amilcare had known him for years, and Sofonisba recalled that Vasari had arranged for her introduction to Michelangelo. When Vasari heard about a remarkable family of sisters who painted, he was determined to meet them. He regretted putting off the visit as long as he had, so long that Europa and Anna Maria were the only painting daughters still living there. Even so, he was greatly pleased to see Sofonisba's painting of her sisters playing chess. Amilcare wrote that Vasari said the figures all seemed so alive that he nearly expected to hear them speak.

In the early summer, Philip and Elisabeth moved to the El Bosque country house at Segovia in its setting of extensive woodlands, a place cooler and quieter than Madrid, and in Philip's long-held opinion, healthier. Philip was determined to protect his wife during her confinement.

Elisabeth took her whole retinue of ladies-in-waiting. One day she summoned Sofonisba to her chamber.

"The day is not far off now," the queen said. The grim tone of her voice disturbed the painter. Elisabeth sat a bit slumped in a well-cushioned chair, her hands on either side of her expanded belly.

"Not far at all, my lady, and — I must say, you look a bit upset."

Elisabeth shook her head and sat up straighter. "Please sit down there." She motioned toward a writing table by the window.

"Oh, that's just right," the queen said. "With this sunlight, you don't even need a candle. Now take this down: Segovia, 27 June, in the year of Our Lord 1566. I, Elisabeth of Valois, queen of Spain, wife of His Majesty Philip II, being of sound mind, do solemnly declare this my last will and testament."

"Elisabeth!" Sofonisba gasped.

"It has to be done," Elisabeth said briskly. "You know well what could happen. I almost died the last time. Please, I pray you, just help me."

"All right." Sofonisba, chilled despite the sunlight, carefully dipped a quill pen and wrote what the queen had dictated.

Elisabeth reeled off a list of relatives, leaving them jewellery, paintings, gold candlesticks, and other possessions. To each lady-in-waiting she left money for their dowries, and instructed Philip to look after them. She mentioned Sofonisba last. "And I leave to my Sonia," she waited while Sofonisba caught up with the writing, "the dearest to me of all my ladies-in-waiting ... the sum of 3,000 ducats and a bolt of brocade ... for her matrimonial bed."

Sofonisba's hand stopped and she looked up. "Oh, my lady," she said through a tightened throat. She was deeply touched, but her stomach twisted with fear.

She then fetched two ladies-in-waiting to be witnesses. Everyone signed the will, and Sofonisba closed it with Elisabeth's seal.

Elisabeth's confinement passed uneventfully until the first day of August.

Sofonisba awoke to hear Elisabeth screaming "Aaaagghh, this is it!" She ran into the queen's chamber and saw her breathing like a fireplace bellows. But it was not yet time. For the next eleven days Elisabeth swung between fever and chills.

Then, when the pains of birth tormented her once again, Philip gave her a special potion meant to ease the pain, prepared from instructions her mother had sent. Despite it, the queen's screams racked the country house, and Sofonisba thought back to the tension and fear of waiting while her mother gave birth in Cremona.

She had to grit her teeth and will herself not to faint as she wiped the sweat from Elisabeth's forehead. The queen's screaming unnerved her. *St. Elizabeth, protect your namesake!* Sofonisba prayed. The queen sat up. The physician Maldonado yelled out his orders:

"*Push*, Your Majesty!" From Elisabeth came a monstrous grunt and a rush of blood that caused Sofonisba to cover her mouth. A baby's cries replaced the queen's, and both women fell back with relief. It was just after dawn.

"A daughter."

Philip, seated beside his wife's bed, said the word deliberately, thoughtfully, and as Maldonado handed him the washed and well-wrapped infant, it was not clear exactly what the king meant by his inflection. There was no denying that he looked pleased and proud.

"With such a difficult delivery, I was worried, but she's the healthiest newborn I've ever seen," the physician said. "What will you call her, Your Majesty?"

"Isabel Clara Eugenia, after my mother, may her soul rest," Philip said. "But my wife? How is she?" The queen lay with her eyes half closed and her hair black with sweat.

"I have something here to help her sleep, Your Majesty," Maldonado said.

"It's not a boy," the queen moaned to Philip, but he reassured her: "Just live, my love." The queen slept, but her ordeal was not over. Sofonisba tended Elisabeth as she lay sick with fever for weeks, at times hovering close to death.

⌒

Standing in the chapel with the rest of the ladies and the few courtiers at Segovia, Sofonisba watched the strangest baptism she had ever attended. First, it did not take place until the infanta was almost two weeks old — for the sake of the child's soul, an uncommon and dangerously long wait. *The physician must have been very certain she would survive*, Sofonisba thought.

Then, a cardinal presided over the ceremony — perhaps not unusual for a princess, but this cardinal was the nuncio of Pope Pius V. *Undoubtedly the first time any minion of the pope's has ever set foot in humble Segovia.*

But the strangest thing about the baptism was Philip's absence, after waiting seven years for a child. *Is he staying away out of disappointment that the child is not a boy?* Sofonisba wondered, and the possibility filled her with disdain.

Then, as the cardinal poured holy water over the baby's head, Sofonisba noticed a movement at a window. Philip! He *was* watching the ceremony — furtively, from outside the chapel. Sofonisba felt both cheered and dismayed.

The king left for Madrid a few days after his daughter's baptism. On the way, he felt a flush of fever, and could hardly stay on his horse. While he burned in his chamber in Madrid, word arrived that plague had broken out in the village of Segovia, and the king felt terror for the queen and their child, and worry that his fever was a precursor to his own death. He brought a priest into his chamber to pray with him, and he recovered. Meanwhile, before anyone could be stricken, the royal household fled the country house, even though Elisabeth was still feverish. Upon arriving in Madrid, the duke of Alba also was stricken with serious fever, and also recovered.

MARCH, 1567

Sofonisba and the other ladies arrayed themselves on either side of the queen in curved lines of chairs so that each of them could admire the seven-month-old infanta, sitting with her mother on the long balcony outside her chamber. Sofonisba joined in as they all proclaimed the baby's great beauty. "Everyone adores my beautiful child," Elisabeth said. "She has her father's grey eyes and golden hair." Approving noises stopped when Elisabeth said, "And everyone will adore the next one just as much."

"The next one, my lady? Are you again with child? So soon?" The ladies tossed their questions in a polite volley, but with intense interest.

"The child will come in October," the queen said, smiling briefly. It was early spring. A moment of fearful silence followed.

Sofonisba remembered the perils the queen had suffered bearing the bright-eyed child now seated beside her, under her protective arm. Then Sofonisba remembered her duty as a lady-in-waiting. "Congratulations, my lady," she said. "I am sure the king is pleased." The other ladies expressed their good wishes.

"And may it please God to give me a boy this time," Elisabeth said.

Her second daughter was born in October, just fourteen months after her first. As healthy as her sister, the baby was baptized Catalina Micaela, after Elisabeth's mother. This time Philip left alone for Aranjuez a few days after the child's birth, and did not return for her baptism. The ceremony was performed only nine days after the birth. *Better, but still!* Sofonisba thought.

Sofonisba knew the king was obsessed with troubles in the Netherlands, a prosperous territory his father had bequeathed to him and that was much too independent-minded for Philip's taste. Worse, the land leaned toward Protestantism, especially Anabaptism and Calvinism in the northern part known as Holland. When anti-Spanish unrest broke out in 1567, Philip sent the duke of Alba and 10,000 troops to put it down.

FEBRUARY, 1568

Riots in the Netherlands, the birth of another princess, and the queen's ill health — she drifted in and out of fever once again — would have served as more than enough fodder for every court conversation, but there was also Don Carlos, whose weak mind had become increasingly unhinged. Throughout the autumn, he stashed away money, and made no secret of it. Just after the new year, Philip learned through his half-brother Don Juan that Don Carlos had planned to flee to the Netherlands. There he intended to aid the rebels and be their figurehead. Such a treasonous move would inflame the already unstable situation in the territory.

When Philip later learned that Don Carlos had bragged that he intended to kill a man, the king had to act. As the channels of court gossip roiled and shuddered, Philip himself led a group of guards toward Don Carlos' chamber. The noise of their feet on the stone floors and their agitated voices echoed ever louder off the walls. Word of the impending arrest soon led various courtiers and the curious, including Elisabeth and Sofonisba, to join the group.

Don Carlos had heard the commotion coming his way, but it was too late. He jumped up from the table where he had been emptying a bottle of wine and ran toward the fireplace, just as a guard broke open the door and charged in. The guard barely stopped Carlos from lunging into the flames. "Aaaaaaghhh!" Carlos screamed and struggled. Several other guards grabbed him. The crowd filled the room, and everyone was yelling.

"Don't hurt him!" Elisabeth screamed, but her words were lost in the storm. In the same way, no one heard the duke of Alba pronounce Don Carlos under arrest for treason.

"Just kill me now! Just kill me now!" the writhing Carlos begged his father, over and over.

Sofonisba and Elisabeth pushed their way to Philip's side. The king roared when he saw them: "Señora Anguissola, get out of here, and take my wife with you!"

Don Carlos was taken in the dead of night to the tower of a castle to the northwest. Sofonisba was disgusted with the court bookmakers, who took wagers on how long the prince would last.

In July the news reached Madrid that Don Carlos had died, of "fever." The oblivion that began after his arrest was complete.

AUGUST, 1568

Sofonisba started a new portrait of Elisabeth, to be sent to the queen's mother. Because of the torpor they both felt from the summer heat, and the queen's frequent need to rest, the posing sessions were rare and brief.

The two-year-old Infanta Isabel delighted everyone, and Philip provided her with a companion, a dwarf named Magdalena Ruiz. Magdalena laughed too loud and did somersaults and cartwheels down the palace corridors, all of which fascinated little Isabel.

From her sister Europa, Sofonisba received a letter that excitedly described her wedding to Carlo Schinchinelli, a distant cousin who had been courting Europa for three years. "The Little Bird has flown the nest," Sofonisba told Elisabeth. "Maybe soon I'll have a niece or nephew."

⌒

In mid-September, Elisabeth and her ladies were walking in the garden when the queen grabbed her side and collapsed. "The child in her womb," everyone thought, but Maldonado said otherwise: "Her means of passing water is disturbed." The pain spread to her back, her face turned puffy, and her ankles swelled. She lost her appetite and slept poorly. The doctors applied ointments, but the pain remained. She fainted repeatedly and had trembling fits.

Sofonisba and the other ladies were hopeful for five days late in the month when Elisabeth seemed better, until a cruel breeze blew in from France. A letter from her mother said that her brother, King Charles, was very ill. Elisabeth cried for hours.

Her ladies could do little more than talk with her and read to her and massage her temples during her frequent headaches. When they were not in her chamber, they held a prayer vigil in the chapel. Philip carried on the business of the empire each morning as long as he could concentrate, then spent hours with his wife, talking about his plans for the gardens and courtyards of El Escorial.

"It will be splendid, my dear, you'll love it," he told her.

Sofonisba stayed with the queen constantly, sleeping each night on a divan beside her.

"I have tried, haven't I?" the queen asked Sofonisba one day when Philip was not in the room. It was a question out of nowhere. "I mean, I tried to be a good wife, even to reconcile France and Spain."

Sofonisba forced her voice to stay even. "Please don't talk like that, my lady. You've been ill before, and you recovered. You still have much more to do."

Elisabeth smiled faintly at her. Sofonisba could not tell whether the queen believed her. Elisabeth reached out a pale hand, and Sofonisba held it.

"You have been my dearest friend. I thank you," Elisabeth said.

"My lady…" Sofonisba felt a sob rise in her throat. She thought the silence in the room would pummel her to pieces. *Oh Holy Virgin, give me the strength to be there for her.*

A dreadful stillness replaced all dancing, music, card playing and chatter inside the palace, while a woeful crowd gathered in the courtyard below Elisabeth's room. Philip gave up any attempt to rule and spent all his time at his wife's bedside. The hourly tolling of the palace chapel bell went on relentlessly, obliviously.

The king took Elisabeth's hand.

"What is that I hear, Philip?"

"That's the crowd in the courtyard below, my love, they're singing a hymn. For you."

"Oh, what lovely people. Philip, my lord?"

"Yes, my dear?"

"I'm sorry I never gave you a — a — aaaaaggghh!" Throwing back her sweaty head, Elisabeth's scream ripped the air and caused everyone to jump. Her loins convulsed hideously, and when Maldonado tore away the black-and-red stained bedsheet, balled it up and handed it to a maid, Sofonisba knew it contained the doomed baby, the heir not-to-be. Sofonisba, at her lady's side opposite Philip, leaned closer and grasped the queen's hand. "Elisabeth. Elisabeth. *Elisabeth!*" she urged desperately. The other ladies flowed silent tears. A priest waved a crucifix above the queen's head in blessing. The chapel bells tolled the hour of noon.

The physician gently closed the mute hazel eyes. "Oh, my love, oh dear *God!*" Philip wailed. After a moment, everyone filed out of the room to let Philip mourn in peace.

Sofonisba, in a daze, heard anguished sobbing from the courtyard. At first she drifted with the other ladies toward their chamber, then she veered away from them to her studio.

She slammed the door shut, then leaned back against it, panting. She covered her face with her hands and began to howl in grief. "*Elisabeth!*" she raged. "Oh God, why *Elisabeth?*" She felt a madness overtake her. She swung her arm across the top of a work table, knocking jars of brushes and pigments to the floor. Stacks of sketches flew upward. She moved on to the other work tables and did the same, shrieking and crying. She lifted plaster models of heads and hands high in the air and smashed them against the walls and floor. As she picked up a knife, Rico burst in.

"What in heaven's name — ?" Holding the knife high, Sofonisba staggered toward her easel, where her unfinished portrait of Elisabeth stood. Rico grabbed her.

"Let go of me! Let me destroy it!" She struggled and kicked against him.

"Sonia! Stop it!" He seized her arm and twisted the knife out of her hand. Sofonisba sank to the floor, sobbing.

"Rico, I don't want to *live* any more."

Elisabeth lay in an open casket in the palace chapel, surrounded by candles, for one day. After filing past with the other ladies, Sofonisba sat in the chapel, tired and inconsolable, even indifferent about prayer. She watched as other members of the court arrived, many softly crying.

The next day, four noblemen carried the casket slowly through the streets full of black crepe to a convent where the body would rest until a tomb could be prepared for it at El Escorial. People reached out to touch the casket and to place flowers on it as it passed.

Philip withdrew to a monastery to grieve alone. It was said that, quite against his nature, he wept openly when he attended services for Elisabeth, twice a day.

Autumn turned at once to winter, if not in the sky over the palace and city, then at least in the stillness, the long mournful pause that drew out like a pained sigh of despair.

MARCH, 1569

"So, you said in your note you had some news," Sofonisba said as she met Rico by the fountain of Neptune in the royal garden on the first warm, rainless day of the spring. They began a stroll down an alley of cypresses.

"I'm going home to Lucca to be married," Rico said. A flock of sparrows shuddered past.

"What?" Sofonisba stopped walking and turned to face him. "You're leaving Spain?"

"Yes, on Monday next. To get married. Such a look you give me, Sonia! You don't seem happy for me."

"Oh, well, it's … Sorry, Rico, of course I'm happy for you, congratulations," Sofonisba said, willing the disappointment out of her face. "It's just that you've been such a good friend to me here. I can't quite grasp the notion of your leaving." They walked on. "So who is your fortunate bride?"

"She's a Lucchese woman I've known since childhood, from a fine family. In fact, our two families arranged this. I'm thirty-six now, Sonia. It's high time I married. I want an Italian home, and children."

"Oh. Well, of course I understand."

"Court life has its great troubles, great anxieties, as you well know, and yet, in a strange way, I will miss it. And I will miss you deeply," Rico said.

"The same for me. You have been such a steadfast friend," Sofonisba said. "You *saved* me, you know."

Rico smiled. "Perhaps the noblest thing I've ever done. And what about you? Do you ever plan to marry?"

Sofonisba's mind ranged back over the years through a thick fog. "I haven't given it any thought since I turned down an offer of marriage, years ago in Cremona." She told him about Ercules Vizconti.

"What ever happened to him?" Rico asked.

"I don't know," Sofonisba said. A momentary panic set in. *Did I choose the wrong way?*

A group of young courtiers, chattering and laughing, passed them on the path.

"You see, I am really rather adrift right now," Sofonisba continued. "Elisabeth's other ladies-in-waiting have all gone home. The king has not pressed me to decide my next step. I may stay here a while." They stopped by a statue of St. Francis. "The infantas have been such a comfort. To play with little Isabel — though no one could take her mother's place — it begins to fill the void, just a bit."

"Have courage, Sonia, and trust in the Lord. I'm sure you'll find your way," Rico said.

"I'll be there to see you off. Dear Rico," she sighed and reached out to him, and they embraced briefly, as friends do.

After Rico's departure from Spain, Sofonisba wrote in her journal.

Madrid, April 21, 1569

It has now been four weeks since Riccardo Velleti left here to return to Lucca to be married. He was my dear friend, my advocate and my mainstay, a fellow Italian who stood by me and cheered me so much.

Rico's departure stirred something in me that I had not known I would ever feel, and I have been dwelling on this feeling and turning it over in my mind ever since. Years ago, when I turned down Ercules Vizconti's offer of marriage, it was because I could not bear to risk the end of my painting, something I loved and had worked on so hard and that had just received the blessing of the greatest artist of all, Maestro Buonarroti. I know of one woman who continued to paint after marriage — Levina Teerlinc — but I could not be sure I would have her same good fortune. I still feel certain that I made the correct decision. I will always be glad I came to Madrid, the center of Christendom, the court of the most powerful sovereign of Europe, perhaps the world. With God's help, I pour into my paintings all the skill and passion I possess, and I dare say I have done work of great invention, the best work of my life. There can be no higher appointment for me as a painter, no greater honour in my lifetime than the one I have enjoyed here in Madrid these nine years.

That means that I am free now — free and eager to embrace the married life, the affection and companionship of a husband and the happiness of a home, if God sees fit to provide them. I still enjoy painting and will continue to do it. As a young wife I could not have been sure of that, but I am older now and under His Majesty's protection, so that I am in a stronger position. And perhaps — do I dare wish it? — when I am married, Mama and I will find the harmony that has eluded us since I began to paint.

I feel calm and strong in this decision, and I resolve to move my life in this new direction at once.

The king, seated behind his large desk, set down his quill.

"Your Majesty, thank you for seeing me," Sofonisba began, noticing newly etched lines of grief on the king's face. "I have come to an important realization, after much thought and prayer, and now I am certain." She paused for a moment. "I want a husband. I want to get married."

Philip looked surprised, but only briefly. "Well, I knew this day had to come sooner or later. Actually, I didn't think you'd wait this long." He sat back and folded his hands over his chest. "I will have my secretary make a list of Spanish noblemen who would be lucky indeed to have you as a wife, and to join you here at court. Fine men, of course, with any of them you'd never lack for anything…"

"Ah, there is something I should make clear, Your Majesty." Sofonisba knotted her fingers. "I have lived at your court nine years. I have been blessed here in many ways, but the truth is that I'm homesick. I want to marry an Italian man and live in Italy again."

Philip leaned across his desk toward her. The bells of San Lorenzo intoned five o'clock.

"Sofonisba," he said. "You know you've been like a daughter to me all these years, and not just because I was your guardian by law, but because, well, for many things." She nodded.

"I would hate to see you go, but for all that you meant to my dear Elisabeth," pain flashed across his face, "I will carry out your wishes. Is there anyone in particular you have in mind?"

"There is someone — a Cremonese man I knew years ago — Ercules Vizconti."

"I'll have my secretary ask him on your behalf."

"Thank you, Your Majesty. Oh, and there is one more thing. Your secretary, your agents, should tell any prospective husband that I intend to continue painting as long as the Lord provides me with a keen eye and a steady hand."

"That is a wise condition," Philip agreed. "Once a suitable husband is found, we'll see about a pension for you, and a dowry."

"Thank you, Your Majesty."

"Now, you understand, this process will take some time," Philip said. "While you are still here, there's something I want you to do. My daughter Isabel is two and a half years old. I want you to be her special companion. I've seen you with her, and she seems to like you, almost as much as she likes that dwarf I gave her."

Sofonisba smiled. "And I like her, even love her. She's a dear."

"You have experience with young girls, having all those sisters," the king said. "Before too long she'll be ready for tutoring. But for now, just be like a big sister to her. And Catalina, too."

"Of course, Your Majesty."

"Oh, and I should tell you," the king said, "I received a letter from my late wife's mother, Catherine de Medici. She asked me to pass on to you her thanks for the portrait of Elisabeth you recently sent her. She said it has been a comfort in this awful time."

"Oh!" *Thank you, Holy Virgin, for not letting me destroy it.* "It is a lift to my spirits to hear that. Your Majesty, it was the hardest painting I ever did."

⌒⌒

"Guard," the king called when Sofonisba had left his study. "Get Enrique in here."

"Our Sofonisba wants to marry an Italian," Philip told the secretary, Enrique Lopez. "She suggested a Cremonese man she once knew — one Ercules Vizconti. See whether he's available. It seems doubtful, as it was long ago, but if he is available, and he's interested, make sure he's an honest, respectable man of gentility and intelligence. You know, people can change after many years. Also, he must appreciate painting, and agree that Sofonisba will continue with her work."

"As you wish, Your Majesty," Lopez said.

Very soon, the court bookmakers had something else to take bets on.

JULY, 1569

It took three months for Philip's envoy to make the first inquiries on Sofonisba's behalf, and for word of the results of his search to arrive in Madrid.

"Your Majesty, Señora Anguissola's first choice, Ercules Vizconti of Cremona, is not interested, I'm afraid," Enrique Lopez began. "It's unfortunate, because the Vizconti are influential and the man has a fortune, but he simply says that while he was once interested, marriage is now out of the question."

"Hmm. And whom else have you asked?"

"Cesare Casato of Novara, also of noble and powerful descent. He said he would marry Sofonisba if given the governance of Novara. Our envoy rightly refused."

"So who does that leave?"

"At the moment, Your Majesty, that leaves, well, no one."

Sofonisba confronted Lopez in his office. "Señor, I have not wanted to bother you, but rumours are running rampant around the court, and I must know. What was Ercules Vizconti's answer?" She looked right into his eyes with impatient determination.

"It is no bother at all," Lopez said. "I am so sorry, but the fact is that Ercules Vizconti is not available, señora."

"Not available?" She gripped her chair's armrests. "You mean, he is already married?"

"No, I'm afraid he … oh, I realize this is hard to bear," Lopez slowed his words, "but he simply is not interested in marrying at this time. I am sorry."

It is me whom he simply is not interested in marrying, Sofonisba thought, and she felt deflated. *How foolish I was to think his offer might still hold.* "And have you found anyone else?"

"Not yet, señora. You must be patient."

AUGUST, 1570

Sofonisba had resigned herself to a long wait for a husband, so she filled her days with the infantas. This day, she and the four-year-old Isabel had zigzagged all over the palace gardens, chasing each other down the paths and around the shrubs, sneaking up on a goldfinch, slowing down to sniff the gardenias, mums, and roses. Finally, holding Isabel's hand, she stopped at the edge of the lawn.

"Come on over here, lovey!" The dwarf, Magdalena Ruiz, standing in the sun in the middle of the lawn, called to Isabel, who looked up at Sofonisba inquiringly with her big grey eyes.

"*Allez-y.*" Isabel ran over to Magdalena and the two began galloping around the lawn.

Sofonisba sat down on a stone bench nearby. *Isabel is a joy, a delight, and I thank you, God, for her, but she does tire me out.*

A nurse appeared with Isabel's younger sister, Catalina Micaela, nearly three years old and the image of her late mother, with the same hazel eyes and dark brown hair. Isabel and Magdalena ran over to her and the three held hands, danced in a circle, then fell down, laughing. Watching them, Sofonisba did not notice the approach of Princess Juana, Philip's sister. Sofonisba stood up hastily.

"Your Royal Highness," she addressed the princess, and curtsied.

"Señora Anguissola, may I join you?" Juana said.

"Of course, madam," Sofonisba said. The princess settled herself, and Sofonisba sat down again. They had spoken little since the day the princess had posed for her portrait, nine years before. With Juana absorbed in establishing her convent, their paths rarely crossed.

"And how is Your Royal Highness faring now? I have heard there was illness," Sofonisba asked.

"I'm rather well, thank you. And you must be busy with your paintings."

"Yes, I am. I will soon begin a double portrait of the infantas."

"And, I suspect, soon one of Anne, the Austrian princess and our future queen," Juana said.

"Anne of Austria? What do you mean, madam?" Sofonisba asked.

"Oh dear, I may be speaking out of turn," Juana said. "Philip called me to the palace today to tell me that he intends to marry Anne. She's our niece, you know, and the negotiations have been going on for some time. Philip still needs an heir, after all. Everyone will know soon enough."

In the coming weeks the palace slipped into the bustle of preparing to welcome a new queen and planning a royal wedding, set for early November. For Sofonisba and other courtiers who remembered the last royal wedding, an edge of sadness intruded on an otherwise happy prospect. Philip told both Sofonisba and Alonso Sánchez Coello to paint portraits of him to commemorate his fourth marriage.

Princess Anne, aged twenty-one, arrived from Austria to a sumptuous Madrid welcome, passing through triumphal arches that depicted events glorifying the monarchy. Officials of the city and ordinary citizens lined her route to the palace, waving and cheering. Jousts and mock battles entertained the court and the people all day. When she could slip away, the queen-to-be went to the chapel to give thanks for a safe journey.

The day before the wedding, Sofonisba was called to Enrique Lopez's tiny office, just outside Philip's study. Her insides began to shake. *Has he found…*

But Lopez's first words were, "The king wants you to paint a portrait of Anne, right away."

She shrank into her chair. "Oh," was all she managed to say.

"Is there some difficulty with doing this portrait?" Lopez asked. "The king regrets that he did not order it sooner."

"Oh no, señor, it's just that — that I thought you had brought me here for some other reason."

Lopez furrowed his forehead. "Ah, of course. You thought perhaps I had found you a husband. Unfortunately, I have nothing to tell you about that, señora, but be assured, our agents are working on it. I am sorry it is taking so long."

"Thank you, señor." She sat up straighter. "Now, about a portrait of Princess Anne. The king wants *me* to paint it? When I heard nothing about a wedding portrait of her, I assumed that Señor Coello had been asked to paint it."

"Strange. I saw him today, and he said he thought *you* had received the commission," Lopez said.

"But what about the portrait of the king I'm doing now?" Sofonisba asked. "I've only finished the face and the armour."

"Oh yes, His Majesty has said that you must stop work on that. Coello will finish it, and you are to start right away on Anne's portrait."

Sofonisba looked doubtful. "What is it, señora?"

"I don't mind someone else finishing the king's portrait, señor, but I believe Señor Coello will mind it very much."

"It is the king's command. Do not worry about Coello, señora."

NOVEMBER, 1570

The entire court packed up to travel to El Bosque in Segovia for the candlelit wedding. Both bride and groom wore dark grey silk, for a ceremony that was brief and perfunctory. Philip and Anne's faces expressed not so much happiness as satisfaction in an obligation well-performed.

But at the wedding banquet, an appropriate air of celebration grew steadily over the twenty courses and sailed on the sea of wine. In the ballroom, the light of candles, scent of perfume, and lilt of music combined splendidly. For just long enough, the sorrows of the past, while not entirely driven out, at least receded into the shadows.

Sofonisba, waiting with the other guests at the edge of the dance floor for the king and the new queen to make their grand appearance, hid her dismay when she noticed Coello standing beside her.

"I just want you to know how much I hate being assigned what you have left undone," he said.

"Good evening, Señor Coello." She continued to scan the dance floor, watching for Philip and Anne to lead the first dance.

"Did you hear what I said?" Coello pressed. "What do you have to say about the king's portrait?"

"Nothing at all, señor. I do not question the king's commands." She felt proud of her calm, her fearlessness. Things were so different now; so much had happened.

"At least you don't have to look so cheerful," Coello snarled.

"This is a wedding celebration. What did you call them? 'Fancy goings-on'? It is not appropriate to wear a glum face at a happy event like this."

He glared at her, and Sofonisba turned her eyes back to the dance floor. More conversation was impossible, because of the sudden cheering and applause of the crowd as King Philip and Queen Anne began to dance. The courtiers quickly paired off and joined them. The envoy from Urbino took Sofonisba's hand. Coello drifted off, and the steps, leaps, and turns of the dance drove him from her mind.

Queen Anne fulfilled her duty with Philip later that night, and the court bookmakers took bets on when the first royal progeny would arrive.

A month later, Sofonisba completed the painting of the infantas, working from quick sketches of their faces. She had servants bring to the studio the infantas' formal black and gold dresses, placed on wire models and held out with wide farthingales. At four and three years of age, she could not make the girls pose for long. Sofonisba captured exactly the soft peach tones of their faces, which looked directly out from the canvas. She included a parrot — a gift from Isabel's father — perched on Isabel's left hand; as the elder, she held this hint of Spain's empire and the adult world that awaited the sisters. Catalina rested her right hand on the paw of their beloved spaniel as it lay curled up on a small table between them. The dog served as a symbol of their childishness, but also of their youthful liveliness and curiosity — traits that Sofonisba could not let the royal children themselves display in the portrait.

To include a reference to the infantas' mother, Sofonisba crowned Isabel's jewelled headband with three gold lilies. The painter recalled that Philip had ordered a plot of white lilies, symbols of France, planted years ago in Elisabeth's honour. In painting the infantas' portraits, Sofonisba regained the interest in painting that she had lost when Elisabeth died.

A letter from Sofonisba's mother told her about another Anguissola sister's wedding. Anna Maria, the youngest of Sofonisba's sisters, had married Jacopo Sommi, a Cremonese nobleman. Sofonisba thought long and wistfully of her former student and especially of Anna Maria's completely charming painting, *Holy Family with St. Francis*, and how the sisters had worked together to paint *Virgin with the Christ Child and St. John*. The thought that Anna Maria was no longer the family's baby girl but a married woman of twenty-six made Sofonisba wonder when her own day at the altar would come. *Holy Virgin, grant me patience.*

In the studio, Queen Anne sat for the portrait the king had ordered. Sofonisba was struck by the deep blue shade of her eyes and her pale skin.

"I know I am plain of face, so do not flatter me here," Anne insisted.

"Your Majesty, you are not — " Sofonisba began to protest, but Anne held up a hand to cut her off.

"Please, señora."

"As Your Majesty wishes." Sofonisba finished the drawing. Anne approved of it after a few minutes' careful study and then left the studio.

While working on the portrait, Sofonisba let her mind roam over the changes she had seen at the court in her eleven years there. The court seemed more sedate than when she had arrived. That was largely because of Queen Anne — a down-to-earth, pious soul who made a good match for Philip. Her hands had never held playing cards or thrown dice, and she did not share Elisabeth's love of parties, dancing, and theatricals, so such events were rare. Sofonisba missed the old gaiety. Anne also dressed in a more austere manner and never bought new jewellery — the few pieces she had brought from Austria would suffice. Elisabeth, in contrast, had frequently delighted in all kinds of new silver and gold trinkets and jewels. It was whispered that her household was deeply in debt when she died. Sofonisba supposed that financial matters would surely improve under the thrifty and dutiful Queen Anne.

For Sofonisba, the happiest change was that she was no longer under the control of the formidable duchess of Alba, because she was no longer a lady-in-waiting. She was busy with her painting, and teaching the infantas. She spoke to Isabel and Catalina in French, while teaching them arithmetic and a bit of geography. She also introduced them to music, knowing it was one of the king's great loves. She would play the clavichord for them and they would sing along, usually off-key.

It always touched Sofonisba to see the king and his daughters together, on long walks in the garden or on rides in the countryside.

In keeping with Anne's wish that her portrait contain no falsehood, Sofonisba depicted the queen's long nose and full Habsburg lips. The painting showed Anne in a black velvet gown heavily embroidered with silver on the bell-shaped sleeves and down the front. The requisite starched white ruff stood over a neckband of gold jewels. Over her center-parted blond hair, her black velvet hat was trimmed with pearls, gold, jewels, and two short white ostrich plumes. Anne declared her satisfaction with the result, and invited Sofonisba to sit with her and Philip at a mock naval battle the next day at Casa del Campo.

APRIL, 1571

The gardens of the royal park, a short ride from the palace, were resplendent with spring flowers: red, pale orange, and yellow roses, bluebells, and carnations of all hues. Philip had also ordered several lakes constructed at Casa del Campo as part of his determination to display at least as much splendour as the other courts of Europe. Sofonisba sat with the king and queen on shaded wooden tiers, and the crowd of spectators encircled the lake.

A team of young men wearing the Habsburg colours performed the requisite ceremony of the hurling of flags. After the bishop pronounced a blessing, the galleys standing in for the Ottoman Turkish navy, each flying a red flag with a white crescent, were wheeled down a ramp and launched into the lake with raucous cheers from their "crews." After a blare of trumpets, galleys playing the part of His Majesty's navy followed.

Sofonisba found herself caught up in the excitement of watching the Turkish ships try to ram His Majesty's. Predictably, after some clever fakery, the Turkish fleet was destroyed and its "crews" captured and paraded before the royal couple. Philip shot up to his feet to applaud and raise his fists. Sofonisba knew the drama reflected an outcome that Philip desperately wanted to see in real life: the recapture of Tunis, which the Turks had taken the year before. The royal party returned to the palace in a buoyant mood.

"I shall go mad if I think about the blighted Turks one more minute today," the king said to Enrique Lopez. "And I have a message here from Alba. The campaign in the Netherlands is going horribly." He tossed the parchment onto the unruly stack of papers demanding attention on his desk — a stack thicker than his hand. "So tell me about something completely different. Have you found a husband for our Sofonisba?"

"Not yet, Your Majesty, and so we have started to look a bit further afield," Lopez said. "Señora Anguissola wants an Italian husband, but after having no success on the peninsula, we are now looking in Sicily. Our agent there is actually quite hopeful."

OCTOBER, 1571

The evening Mass was nearly over. Sofonisba stood in her pew along with a few dozen other courtiers and King Philip in the barely completed chapel at El Escorial. She was as horrified as the others when an excited messenger rushed in. "Your Majesty!" the young man called out. "Your fleet has won a spectacular victory against the infidel Ottoman Turks! It happened at Lepanto, off the coast of Greece!"

Everyone broke into cheers: "Bless the fleet!" "Bless His Majesty!" "Praise Our Lord God!" Everyone, that is, but Philip. "The priest must complete his final prayers," Philip commanded, and at his stern look around the chapel, decorum was restored, but barely. "Go on, padre."

The priest and the people tore through the final words at an alarming pace, then the priest cried out with joy: *"Gloria in excelsis Deo!"*

Only then did Philip allow himself to celebrate Christendom's biggest victory ever against the Turks. He ordered fireworks and stood on a balcony at El Escorial to watch them, and took part briefly in the spontaneous, exuberant dancing that followed. He firmly believed that God had smiled down and placed His benevolent approval and blessing on Spain's endeavours. *And Don Juan, that rascal, has triumphed,* Philip thought. Philip had appointed Don Juan commander of the combined Christian fleet, a reward for his discretion regarding Don Carlos.

Philip regretted only that his queen was not able to celebrate with him. Anne was back in Madrid, and would soon provide him with even more cause for rejoicing.

"A son! Praise God! Oh, my love!" Philip exulted in early December when Anne gave birth to their first child. "We will call him Ferdinand, after my father's brother," he told her.

With the rest of the court, Sofonisba enjoyed the celebration not only for the newborn son, but for some treasure-laden ships that had just arrived safely from the New World. In a gesture of thanks, Philip freed some prisoners, and was seen to wear silver-coloured velvet pants and hose and a fur-trimmed cloak — the sort of luxurious frills he allowed himself only in times of great elation.

 ᜕

A few days later the king called Sofonisba into his study. In the group of sketches spread across his desk, she easily recognized the style of Alonso Sánchez Coello.

"Tell me what you think of these," Philip said. "I have commissioned Titian of Venice to paint a commemorative panel to mark the victory at Lepanto and the birth of my son. I asked Coello to do some preparatory sketches. I need another opinion."

Though it was not the king's intention, his words were like relentless, piercing pellets thrown at Sofonisba's soul. Suppressing a growl, she coolly said, "I see."

"Titian painted a massive panel to commemorate my father's victory at Mühlberg, long ago. I want this one to be just as big. Not just for my own glory, of course, that would be wrong, but so that generations hence will know to thank Our Lord for our great victory … Sofonisba?"

She had remained in a stiff posture, looking at Philip instead of the drawings.

"What's wrong?" the king asked.

She took a deep breath. "Your Majesty, I accept that you asked the great Venetian to paint such a large, complex work," she said, struggling to keep her tone even and uncomplaining, but resolute. "But I must tell Your Majesty, and pray understand, it gives me some sorrow to know that you asked Señor Coello, and not me, to do the sketches in preparation for the painting."

"Ah. I think I understand," Philip said. "A bit of professional jealousy, then."

"Something like that, Your Majesty. I am not proud of it, but I cannot deny it, either."

Philip looked back down at the sketches, and then again at the painter. "I asked Coello to do these sketches because it seemed that military matters, battles, all of that, were masculine themes."

Again, she responded with a cool, "I see."

The king regarded her sympathetically. "You know that Coello did a double portrait of the infantas, more than a year after yours," the king said. "For what it's worth, I consider yours the superior of the two. Coello made the figures rather stiff, almost lifeless, not like real children at all. He made the portrait formal, as court portraiture has to be, but he took it too far. But in your version, my daughters have that spark of childhood, there's such warmth in their faces. You have them looking out at the viewer, and in his, they do not even look at each other. So you see, Sofonisba, I have the highest respect and admiration for your work."

She judged the praise to be sincere, although her disappointment remained. "I thank you for those sentiments, Your Majesty," she said with a touch of frost.

"Now about these designs," Philip said. "Yes, I asked Coello to do them, but I have asked you to do something even more important — to grant final approval, or rejection, of these designs."

She grudgingly admired his quick thinking, the smoothness with which he tried to extricate himself. As a loyal subject, she would pretend to believe he had reserved the higher honour for her, to convince him that his words had had their intended mollifying effect. Inwardly, she scoffed: *As if anyone but Philip himself would have the final say over every last detail of the painting.*

"Let's have a look, then." She moved closer to the desk, considered each sketch carefully, and rearranged them. It did not take her long to see what was needed. "Your Majesty, your gratitude and pride over the victory at Lepanto and the birth of your son are too momentous to be combined into one painting. And, the events should be depicted in different ways. This will require two paintings." She was pleased to have the king's rapt attention.

"In the first, the spiritual aspect of the military victory is emphasized; the fact that with God's help, your fleet preserved Christianity in Europe from the Turkish threat. This figure represents Spain." She pointed to a sketch of a robust woman, standing and holding in one hand a shield bearing Philip's coat of arms and in the other, a flag of victory. "This other female figure represents Religion. In the background is a seascape with a Turkish galley."

"And in the second painting?"

"It will be a prayer of thanks for Ferdinand's healthy arrival. In that one, Your Majesty holds up the newborn heir as if offering him to heaven. Your Majesty is pledging that this boy will replace you as the king and defender of Christendom. An angel, like this one here, descends from heaven toward you and Ferdinand and holds out a palm leaf with a message written on it. For just a hint of the victory at Lepanto, and to remind future generations of the vanquished threat, as you specified, a Turkish prisoner should appear in the foreground, with his turban removed."

Philip looked at her, his face alight with admiration. "That's it.

That's exactly how it should be. You've captured my intentions perfectly, and I thank you. But what should the message be that the angel carries?"

"That is only for you to say, Your Majesty."

The king stepped away and gazed off.

"I've got it," Philip said, turning back. "It will say, *'Maiora Tibi'* — 'Greater Triumphs Await You.'"

JANUARY, 1572

Shortly after the Epiphany celebrations of the new year, Queen Anne asked Sofonisba to do a portrait of one of the ladies she had brought with her from Austria. The lady's name there had been Charlotte, but in Spain she was Carlotta. Anne considered Carlotta's right profile striking, and said that the portrait must be posed to display it. The order meant a new challenge for Sofonisba, who preferred full or three-quarter faces, so she needed an unusual amount of modelling time. She also took the opportunity to experiment with some details from nature by including two roses and a pink carnation in a vase that Carlotta held before her. The painter took great care to depict the flowers as they appeared in nature.

Carlotta's dark auburn hair was braided and twisted into a knot above her right ear. The knot was set with pearls and sapphires, and one pearl hung down, to match her earring and necklace. Anne chose for her a black velvet gown covered with raised gold embroidery. Sofonisba was constantly amazed by the court embroiderers. She considered the skill of these women close to that of any painter. The intricacy of the embroidery on this gown exceeded all she had ever seen. She learned that the embroiderers pounded solid gold into thin layers, then cut it into thin strips, and worked it into the embroidery, with fabric scraps underneath the strips to make the gold stand out.

Queen Anne was pleased with the portrait, and when Carlotta saw it, she forgave Sofonisba for the tedium of the extended modelling sessions.

Princess Juana then asked for a portrait of her son, Don Sebastian, king of Portugal, which for the present he ruled from Madrid. Now that he had reached his eighteenth year, his mother wanted a coming-of-age portrait. Sofonisba regarded Sebastian as a complicated young man — usually well-mannered and sincere, but surly and mercurial sometimes, like his unlucky cousin, Don Carlos.

Sofonisba created a full-length portrait that placed him next to a column, a symbol favoured by the Habsburgs because they saw in it strength and stability. In an odd conversation they had while he posed, Sebastian told Sofonisba that he saw himself as a warrior. So he posed in black armour with gold engraving. He disdained the usual plumed helmet, letting his short red hair show. In painting his face, Sofonisba was struck by how much he resembled his uncle, King Philip, with the same prominent chin and full lips.

In her evening prayers, Sofonisba thanked the Holy Virgin every day for the companionship of Queen Anne, young Isabel and Catalina, and for her work, all of which saved her from loneliness. Nevertheless, she was quite convinced that if one more person urged her to have patience, she would go mad.

APRIL, 1572

"I believe I have found you a husband," Enrique Lopez said.

They were the words she had longed for, prayed for, stopped hoping for because hope was too exhausting. "Praise God! Señor, you don't know how much I've wanted to hear you say that."

Lopez smiled. "After so much waiting, Señora Anguissola, I'm so happy to give you this news. The man is Don Fabrizio de Moncada, a Sicilian, but his family has a Spanish nobility that goes back three hundred years — they're one of the most eminent families in Sicily.

He is forty years old, like you. He's been widowed for many years."
"Don Fabrizio de Moncada," Sofonisba repeated softly.

"He is, by all accounts, the honest, respectable and decent man
that His Majesty ordered me to find for you. His Majesty has given
his approval of the match, and he has decreed that you be given
a lifelong pension of 1,000 ducats, so that you're financially independent. You will also have a dowry, of course, made up of cash,
jewellery, brocades, and furniture. You said you wished to return
to Italy, but you should know that you and your husband may live
in any of the royal estates here in Spain."

Sofonisba's eyes began to well up.

"Señora Anguissola, surely it's a time for joy."

She smiled broadly. "And I am, truly, full of joy, señor, and I
thank you for your efforts on my behalf."

"You are most welcome. I'll have our notary draw up the marriage contract, and then we'll talk in more detail about wedding
arrangements."

"A wedding at last. I am truly blessed." She did not realize how
much tension she had been carrying until that moment, when it
all drained away.

In the corridor, the infantas, holding a pet turtle, ran up to Sofonisba. "Thereyouare! Señoralookwhatwehave!"

"Quelle merveille!" she said, relishing their breathless chatter,
already knowing she would miss it. "Let's take him into the garden."

"It's a *her*, señora," Isabel said, and both girls looked curiously
at Sofonisba's face.

"Señora, you're all, all smiley and excite-y," Catalina said.

"That's because I have wonderful news," Sofonisba said, her smile
wide. "Come on, I'll tell you."

AUGUST, 1572

Her days took on a vividness that sprang from her desire to absorb deeply the colors, scents, scenery, and music of her life at court, to store it all securely in her memory, now that her days there were numbered.

She was barely aware of the talk around the court that the duke of Alba had been recalled from the Netherlands. His harsh measures against the rebels had not only failed, but had stirred further resentment. The situation remained turbulent and a source of deep anguish for Philip.

Sofonisba painted small, separate portraits of the infantas in the hope that they would remember her. The one of Isabel presented her as more of a lady than her six years would suggest, and in Catalina's, the girl held her pet monkey, to illustrate her playfulness.

Queen Anne gave Sofonisba one of her gowns to be married in. "I'll have no use for it for several months," Anne said, patting her expanded belly, "now that I'm about to give Philip another heir. Your wedding will be just before my time."

Lopez alerted the bishop, a choir practiced daily, and ladies of the court ordered new gowns for the happy event. Most importantly, Lopez promised to tell Sofonisba as soon as he knew when Don Fabrizio would arrive in Madrid.

Then, an event far away threatened to crush her joyful anticipation.

"What do you mean, Fabrizio won't be able to come?" She thought she had not heard Lopez correctly.

"As always, it pains me to bear such bad news, señora. His older brother, Cesare, has just died. As a second son, your betrothed must take over the family responsibilities. He now becomes the *governatore* of Paternò, a rather important Sicilian town. With all the arrangements he has to make and the work he must do, he won't be able to come here for the wedding."

Her look told Lopez that she wanted to crawl away and cry.

"I am so sorry," he said. "Don Fabrizio has said that the wedding should proceed. A distant cousin of his, Don Ferrante de Moncada, will arrive here in a few weeks. He is authorized to sign the marriage agreement, and to be Fabrizio's proxy at the wedding. So just continue with the plans."

"All right." She had been floating among the clouds, and now she felt herself dumped rudely at the bottom of a muddy ditch.

LATE MAY, 1573

Don Ferrante, stand-in for Sofonisba's intended, arrived in Madrid, bearing a letter from Fabrizio. Fabrizio asked for Sofonisba's understanding about not being able to come to Madrid. He said that his cousin Don Ferrante would be a worthy proxy, and was as respectable and good-humoured a man as ever lived. Fabrizio looked forward to a happy life with Sofonisba, asked the Lord to protect them both, and referred to Sofonisba as "my betrothed."

"*My betrothed.*" She gave herself a moment to rejoice in the words, then refolded the note and sent a servant to fetch Don Ferrante.

He kissed her hand. "First, I thank you for coming from Sicily to handle this affair," Sofonisba said. "Now, pray tell me about my future husband."

"My cousin and I grew up together," Ferrante began. "When I was orphaned, his parents took me in. Fabrizio inherited all their compassion and generosity." A maid entered and set down a tray with a carafe of sweet wine. Sofonisba poured two cups and handed one to Ferrante.

"Do go on."

"Fabrizio is honest, considerate, rarely prone to moodiness or airs. He loves nature. Once when we were boys, walking in the woods, we came across a dazed bird, lying on the ground. It must have crashed into a tree. Fabrizio picked it up, brought it home and sheltered it until it could fly off."

Sofonisba took a sip of wine. "As a painter, and not just as a woman, you understand, I must know: what does Fabrizio look like?"

"Ah, of course." Ferrante ran his hand through thinning hair. "He is a bit shorter than me, and somewhere between thin and stocky. As far as his face, I don't really know how to describe it. It is, well, ordinary. He has brown eyes, a short beard and moustache."

"I have one more question," Sofonisba said, glancing aside. She put down her wine cup, then leaned forward, clasping her hands over her knees. "I must know. Why has your cousin Fabrizio agreed to marry me?"

"Ah. A fair question." Ferrante sat back and touched his moustache thoughtfully. "Signora, you know that Fabrizio was married before."

"Yes."

"His wife died of fever eleven years ago. They had only been married a year. A very sad thing. Fabrizio withdrew from the world for a long time. He told me then that all the young women he knew seemed silly to him, and that he had no interest in remarrying. Then, I don't know what happened exactly, maybe the Lord took his hand, and he seemed to reawaken, you might say. He told me he did not want to live the rest of his life alone."

Ferrante paused and set down his wine cup. "King Philip's agent came to Sicily late last winter to visit the viceroy, to discuss military matters. Sicily could be important to King Philip's campaign against the Turks. Anyway, the king's man mentioned your situation to the viceroy, who is a good friend of Fabrizio's. A woman his own age, a renowned painter who served at Philip's court — Fabrizio said he would be proud to be married to such a woman, that she would bring intelligence and glamour to his life." He paused to let the words sink in. "I was so happy for him."

Sofonisba glanced out the window, thinking through what Ferrante had said. "And did Fabrizio say anything else?" she asked.

"Anything else? I don't know what you mean, signora," Ferrante said.

Sofonisba took another careful sip. "Don Ferrante, Fabrizio must know that I will bring a substantial pension into the marriage," she said. "It will go to me, not to my husband, but still, it would be an attractive situation to many men. Did Fabrizio say anything about that?"

"I understand your concern, signora, and I assure you, he did not," Ferrante said, his eyes widening a little.

"Thank you again, Don Ferrante. For everything."

On a glorious morning in late June, Sofonisba's maid and two of Queen Anne's ladies awakened her with a tray of raisin bread, almond milk, and oranges. "It's the Spanish tradition for a bride on the morning of her wedding," they said.

"You know, it is just a proxy wedding. I won't be with my husband tonight," Sofonisba told them.

"Doesn't matter!" they all laughed. They prepared a bath for her, then helped her into her corset, farthingale and gown of ivory brocade embroidered with tiny pearls, and a long silk train. They bedecked her with a double-stranded gold necklace that had once belonged to Elisabeth. They brushed her auburn hair, its grey threads unmissable, then pinned it up in elaborate curls and twists, and crowned her with a circle of white roses.

As the ladies walked her to the palace chapel, she thought: *I'm too old to be excited and to blush like a young bride, but I don't care. This is what I prayed for, and praise be to the Virgin that this day has come to pass.*

The sky-blue train hanging from Sofonisba's shoulders draped many lengths behind her as Ferrante escorted her down the chapel aisle. The room was as radiant with tall candles as Sofonisba's face was with an overwhelming joy.

The day after the wedding, Queen Anne, sweating and suffering in the last days of her confinement, decided she could stand the summer heat of Madrid no longer. She and her household moved to El Bosque, in the cool woods and mountains near Segovia. Sofonisba was among those at Anne's side when the baby, another son, was born. He was named Carlos Lorenzo, "after Philip's poor, lost Carlos." After helping Anne settle for the night, Sofonisba went to her own room, but even lying in the cool comfort of the country palace, she could not sleep. Her mind seemed overstimulated, perplexed, stuck somewhere between joy and fear. Just a few days before, she had pledged herself, body and soul, to a man she had never met. She wondered whether Fabrizio ever lay awake at night, thinking of her. Would her family embrace him? Would Mama? Would *Papa?*

She bolted straight up in bed as if yanked by a chain. She got up and went to the window. A white eyelash of moon hung over the fountains, flower beds, long hedges and stone paths of the gardens and the woods beyond. As she watched, a wind arose, making the chestnut trees sigh and whisper to each other. Although the setting was different from the San Giorgio in Cremona, something, perhaps the wind, reminded Sofonisba of her last night in her family's palazzo. So she was not at all surprised when she turned back toward the room and saw her father standing there in the shadows.

"Papa," she said calmly.

"My dearest Sonia." Neither moved.

"So, I do see you again, Papa."

"Daughter, remember the motto," Amilcare said, and then vanished.

The bright light of the next morning seemed grotesque, even tyrannical. A messenger knocked at her door as the San Lorenzo bells tolled eight. The words of her sister Europa's letters blurred on the page: "In Papa's last moments, he repeated what he had told us so often, that he was always immensely proud of you."

She took out the bronze medallion Amilcare had given her and held it as she prayed. When she had no more tears or prayer, she lit a candle in the chapel of San Lorenzo, then joined Queen Anne and her ladies on the terrace of the queen's chamber, where Her Majesty sat to take a bit of sun.

"I am so sorry," the queen said. "How heartbreaking."

"Papa came to me, last night," Sofonisba said, and the queen looked alarmed. "Yes, he did, and I was not afraid. Again he reminded me of the Anguissola motto, 'The lone snake is victorious.' Well, I feel quite alone now."

"You are not alone." Anne reached out and put one hand on Sofonisba's. The painter looked at the queen in gratitude.

"Papa was my most faithful advocate. He made me a painter. I would have achieved nothing without him," Sofonisba told her. "Before last night, I had not seen him in fourteen years." She paused to wipe her eyes. "Oh God help me, I must get home!"

"You will, soon," the queen said.

⁂

In mid-August, Anne and Sofonisba returned to Madrid, where they found Philip engrossed in planning solemn ceremonies to mark the transfer of the coffins of his beloved Queen Elisabeth and son Don Carlos to the new royal burial chambers at El Escorial.

Sofonisba sought out Don Ferrante. "I would leave Madrid with you at once, but I must stay for these memorial rites. Especially those for my lady Elisabeth, may she rest in peace."

"Of course, I understand," Ferrante said. "Whenever you're ready to leave, we'll go."

"There's one thing I need your help with," Sofonisba said. They went to her studio, where she picked up a parchment sheet and chalk.

"You said my husband Fabrizio has an 'ordinary' face," she said. "What is the shape of that face, would you say? Oval, round, square?"

"Hmm, I would say he had a round face, signora," Ferrante said.

Sofonisba began to draw. "And his eyes — brown, you said, but close or wide-set?"

"Wide-set."

"And his hair — short, long, straight, curly?"

"Well, Fabrizio's hair is straight, very short, in fact, cropped closely to his scalp, and he has a high forehead," Ferrante said.

She continued to intently draw. "Now, about the nose — long, short, or somewhere in-between?"

"Somewhere in-between."

She finished the face, then added the moustache and beard.

"So, would you say this resembles Fabrizio?" she said, handing the sheet to Ferrante.

"My God, that's uncanny!" Ferrante said. "Yes, that's him."

Sofonisba smiled. "In the brief time until the reburial ceremony, I'll be painting a double portrait of myself and Fabrizio. Most of my things are already packed. So, the day after the ceremony, we will leave Madrid."

꒰꒱

Sitting in Philip's study in the first dawn light, Sofonisba saw in him the strain of more than seventeen years of rule. His hair had receded and long since paled even further to grey, and the lines on his face recorded his burdens and his losses. The king was now in his forty-sixth year.

"Sofonisba. So the day has finally come for you to leave us. How will you travel?" the king asked.

"I will meet my husband," the words still sounded strange to her, "in Genoa, and then we'll go to Cremona to see my family, before we set out for Sicily."

"In all your preoccupation with the arrangements, Sofonisba, I'm sure you didn't notice that Titian's latest canvases have arrived — the ones commemorating the battle of Lepanto. Would you like to see them?"

"No, Your Majesty, I would rather not," she said as gently as she could, admiring her own resolution.

"Perhaps it is better that way," the king sighed. She saw a troubled look cross Philip's face. "When I showed you Coello's drawings for those paintings, you said it pained you that I asked him to do them, and not you. Then when I saw Titian's finished work, I realized he must have had his assistants do most of it," he said, pressing his lips together momentarily. "I should have let *you* — "

"Your Majesty, you don't have to — "

"Yes, I do, it must be said. I should have had you do the drawings — and maybe the painting, too."

"Oh, Your Majesty." Anxiety drained away and warm satisfaction overtook her. "You've just given me a tremendous gift."

"I hope you'll accept one more," the king said, holding out a small, flat wooden box.

Sofonisba's eyes welled up at the sight of the exquisite double-stranded gold necklace that had belonged to Elisabeth, and that the queen had insisted Sofonisba include in a self-portrait — how many years ago, she could not remember — and that Sofonisba had worn on her wedding day.

"Thank you, Your Majesty," was all she could choke out.

A guard appeared at the study door. "Your Majesty, the coach is ready, and the driver is eager to set off."

"Dear Sofonisba, God protect you on your journey, and remember that you have a home here always, if you ever need it."

"God bless and keep you, Your Majesty, and farewell."

8.

Sicily

I nourished in my heart a lively hope
Gathered in a happy, noble land,
Which promised crops of sweet and pleasant fruit.
                    —Vittoria Colonna (1492-1547)

AUGUST, 1573

The blue? No, the yellow. Or the pale green. No, the lavender. Wait.
She would wear the blue silk gown after all.

In a cabin aboard the galley hurtling Sofonisba toward Genoa
with what seemed to her like frightening haste, the maid struggled
to coax Sofonisba's jittery limbs into her clothes. To arrange her
mistress' hair into a fashionably twisted braid on the crown of her
head, the maid had to work during the brief intervals when Sofonisba could hold still long enough. The chore required all of the
maid's patience and more than one muttered curse. Once dressed,
Sofonisba at first wanted to pace the small floor, then she wanted
to sit; she thought she would read her prayer book, then a moment
later she tossed it across the cabin with an exasperated, "*Aakkhh!*"

She had twisted and moaned in her berth throughout the previous
night. *What if he's a bore, or dumb as a stump, or puts on haughty airs?*
The many possibilities for misery multiplied in her mind.

In the late afternoon it came time to climb up to the deck. The other passengers scanned the shore, the same Genoan shore that Sofonisba had refused to look toward when the ship taking her to Spain embarked fourteen years before. *Do I refuse to look again, now that I'm sailing back in?* she wondered. Struck by a sense of absurdity, she laughed.

Don Ferrante approached. "Signora, I see you're in a happy mood."

She was glad that he did not know her doubts. "Ah, yes, and what a lovely calm sea we have today." She suppressed another laugh.

A large crowd waited on the dock. Sofonisba searched desperately for a man with a round face and wide-set eyes like the man in the portrait she had just finished, now stowed below the deck with her other baggage. Then Ferrante was waving and calling out "Fabrizio!" and a man was moving toward them as they walked down the gangplank to the pier.

Ferrante hugged the man while Sofonisba stood aside. Then, oblivious to the barks of the stevedores, the babble of passengers, and the squawking of gulls, Sofonisba and Fabrizio stood at arm's length, each searching the face that they had dreamed about.

"Signora, may I present Fabrizio di Francesco de Moncada," Ferrante was saying. "Fabrizio, Sofonisba di Amilcare Anguissola."

"Sofonisba, I am honoured," Fabrizio said, bowing slightly. "Welcome back to Italy."

"Fabrizio. At last," she said, noticing his Sicilian accent. *Smile, you fool!* she told herself, and extended her hand.

Ferrante said something about the baggage, and discreetly slipped away.

"Pray, how was your journey, Sofonisba?" Fabrizio asked.

"It was …" she paused, terrified of sounding silly. "It must have been uneventful, because I can't remember anything about it!"

To her relief, Fabrizio laughed. He offered his arm. They left the busy dock area and walked slowly into Genoa's confusion of street life. Fabrizio steered Sofonisba around the puddles and garbage and away from the more strident street hawkers. *He looks just as Ferrante described him*, Sofonisba thought, as she tried to look at him without appearing to look. *But Ferrante forgot to mention the warmth in those brown eyes.* On a quiet side street, they stepped inside an inn.

The proprietor showed them into a small room where high windows on one side cast evening light on a table set abundantly for two: roast beef, bread, an array of vegetables, oranges, a clay pitcher of red wine, and in the corner, a lemon cake.

They began the conversation with an exchange of condolences over the deaths of Fabrizio's brother and Sofonisba's father. Fabrizio served Sofonisba, pouring the wine, slicing the beef, peeling oranges, asking how everything tasted as they ate and drank heartily. When the meal was done they moved into the inn's garden, where they sat and conversed and listened to bird song for another hour, until darkness began to fall. After a pause in their talk, Fabrizio said, casually, "We should go inside now."

He took her hand and led her up three flights of stairs to a solitary room on the inn's highest floor. A single lamp and a candle revealed that Ferrante had sent up the *cassone*, the trunk he knew contained Sofonisba's elaborate trousseau. There was fresh water in a basin, red carnations offering their perfume, and a large, high bed with its brocade spread turned back.

"I'll tell your maid to come up," Fabrizio said, closing the door as he left.

Sofonisba opened the *cassone*, pulled out a white silk chemise and laid it on the bed. She took off her earrings and matching silver neck chain. Her maid arrived and helped her out of her gown, then started to undo Sofonisba's front-laced corset. But Sofonisba stopped her and said, "Thank you. I'll be fine now," and the maid left.

Sofonisba unlaced the corset and folded it. She dipped her hands into the basin of water and splashed it on her face and neck. Cupping more water, she poured it over her breasts, sliding her hands slowly over and around them, lifting them, pleased with their smooth, full pinkness.

After putting on the chemise, she knelt beside the bed to pray.

Holy Virgin, the journey to this moment was so long. I rejoice in my good fortune. Stay beside me. Let me give myself fully to Fabrizio, body, soul, and heart.

When she stood and turned around, she heard a tap at the door. "My dear," Fabrizio said, looking her up and down. He began to undress calmly, deliberately. When he wore nothing but an unbuttoned shirt, Sofonisba pulled the pins out of her long hair and let it fall.

They stood with their bodies pressed together, their lips joined in a long, deep, simmering kiss.

Sofonisba gasped when they finally let go, wanting all the more his lips on hers, his hot organs against her belly. Fabrizio swept her into the bed and ran his hands and tongue hungrily beneath the chemise, over her aroused breasts. His touch led her to a cliff of passion and pushed her off, into bliss. His first entry made her call out and he wanted to stop but she would not let him, so he pressed on until, with a grunt, he sank on top of her.

She pulled her burning legs together, felt her blood and his fluid between her thighs. She put her arms around Fabrizio and stroked his hair. She wanted this feeling of oneness, of mutual warming, to last far into the night, on into time. He seemed to know this, or perhaps he had the same wish, for it was some time before he turned over onto his back and pulled the linen sheet up. Then, to her surprise and consternation, he rose from the bed.

She watched his shadowy form move to the window opposite the bed and open the drapes and the shutters. Looking out the window, she understood.

"All those stars, just for us," he said, returning to the bed, and they laid in each other's arms, gazing at the shining heavens.

While repacking her *cassone* late the next morning, Sofonisba noticed a large flat package behind it. She recognized it at once as the wedding portrait — the last painting she did in Spain.

That sly Ferrante! Having this painting, and no other, brought up here! "Fabrizio, I have something to show you." She unwrapped the painting.

"It's us! And you had not yet seen me!" Fabrizio said.

"Ferrante described you well."

"I am flattered by all the tenderness you attribute to me," Fabrizio said. "One hand gently on your arm, the other on your shoulder."

"And I have indeed found such tenderness," Sofonisba said.

Fabrizio continued to examine the painting. "I see that you are holding a piece of fruit. Does that mean you hope to be fruitful and multiply?"

"It would be a foolish hope, at my age. We'll leave that to God. One more thing…" She placed a hand on his cheek. "Please call me Sonia."

The next day at noon, the newlyweds shouted their goodbyes to Ferrante out the window of a carriage headed toward Genoa's northern gate, and on toward Cremona. The sense of exploration, of gifts newly opened, of entering into a new life, filled them as they rode and talked. She was reminded of the sensation she had felt while walking to Bernardino Campi's studio for the first time with Elena and Rosa, when the streets of Cremona seemed to her so startling in their freshness. Now her painter's eye took in the same sea-foam clouds over Lombardy that she remembered from her youth, but rarely before had she felt her spirit soar among them. The ride was as jolting as any carriage ride she had ever taken, but with Fabrizio she noticed it less. In the spare accommodations of country inns, convents, or monasteries each evening, she and Fabrizio entered a vivid, encompassing private world that soothed the travails of the road.

When they emerged from the mountains north of Genoa and

turned east into the Po Valley, Sofonisba felt a surge of excitement. "Now it's not far to Cremona at all, and the road will be much smoother," she told Fabrizio. Soon after, she smiled when she spotted, through a haze, the beckoning Torrazzo.

Her homecoming was even sweeter than Sofonisba had dared imagine. Bianca, despite having reached fifty-nine years, hugged her daughter so hard that Sofonisba thought her own bones would break. Their wordless gaze into each other's tearful eyes was enough to put all the old tensions and conflicts to rest. As for Asdrubale, Sofonisba felt as if she were meeting her little brother for the first time. He had been a scamp of only seven years when she last saw him. Now, a tall and lean man of twenty-two years stood before her, wearing a crown of wavy dark brown hair. She suspected that his smile had melted the heart of more than one young Cremonese woman. She learned that Asdrubale occupied himself by running their father's old shop, which made their mother proud, but he had gambling tables in the back room, to their mother's dismay.

The happiness of reuniting with Europa and Anna Maria and meeting their husbands was dimmed only by their father's absence. The Little Bird had lost her first child just after its birth two years before, but now she had a new nestling — a daughter named Bianca, nearly one year old. Sofonisba was very proud to have a niece.

"Everyone loves Fabrizio," Europa told her sister as they sat in the garden with the baby snuggled between them.

"Oh, I was praying for that," Sofonisba said. "Especially that Mama would understand. You see, I fell in love with him on our first night together," an admission that made Europa giggle.

"No, not just for that!" Sofonisba said. "It was because of his caring, his concern for my happiness and comfort."

"Yes, of course it was," Europa said, and laughed.

The newlyweds' visit became a round of parties and dances in their honour. Everyone wanted to hear about Sofonisba's experiences at King Philip's court. As she stepped into the cheery social whirl, the last jagged edge of fear about her life's new direction dropped away.

❧

Sofonisba and Fabrizio stood alone at Lucia's grave in the family plot at the San Giorgio cemetery. "Oh, how I miss Lucia. A fine partner in the studio, a virtuous painter. She just didn't have my good fortune to be the first-born, and — " Her voice caught and she couldn't go on.

"And it pleased Our Lord to take her so early." Fabrizio gently finished the thought.

"Minerva," Sofonisba said, turning toward another grave nearby, with its inscription: *Virtuous, and Wise in Letters*. "Oh, that's perfect for her. She was a Latin scholar and poet who had the good sense not to paint."

Sofonisba saw Amilcare's tombstone last.

"Papa," she said, and tears filled her eyes. "Oh, Papa, I never finished that painting for you," and the tears splashed down. Fabrizio put one arm around her shoulders.

"Well, we'd better get back," Sofonisba said, wiping her eyes with Fabrizio's handkerchief. "Asdrubale must be ready to take you hunting now."

❧

It was well after midnight that night when a fierce wind began to rattle the shutters and awakened her. As her body awoke, so did a memory of another long ago late-summer wind followed by rain. She sat up in bed. *Papa, I'm coming*, she thought. As she got up, Fabrizio awoke.

~ 267 ~

"Sonia, what — ?"

"It's Papa. I have to go."

"Go? Go where?" But she was already in the dark hallway, wearing only a loose chemise, and heading for the stairs. Fabrizio, in his nightshirt, ran after her.

"You're not going out at this hour," he said. There was the slightest grind of thunder.

"No, not out, just to the balcony." She went down two flights of stairs to the sitting room, crossed it and stepped out onto the balcony, overlooking the San Giorgio. "Feel that wind? It'll start raining soon," she said, her eyes wide. "There was wind and rain just like that when I stood on this balcony with Papa, the night before I left for Madrid." She had to raise her voice against the tortured wind. "Now Papa's calling me."

"You just had a bad dream. Come back to bed," Fabrizio said, but she ignored him, leaning over the balcony. The wind pelted them with stinging beads of rain while thunder muttered above them.

"Papa!" she called, as lightning lit the street. She sobbed raucously, her tears mixing with the rain streaking down her face. As clearly and vividly as the lightning zigzagged around them, she realized all she had lost.

Fabrizio waited. At last, as the storm moved on, Sofonisba reached out to her husband. Soaked and barefoot, they stepped back inside. In their room, they peeled off their wet nightclothes and fell into bed.

"Didn't you mourn your father's death months ago, when you first heard of it?" Fabrizio asked her the next morning.

"Oh yes, I cried, I prayed, I lit candles, I had a Mass said for him. All the things one normally does. But..." She looked down and fiddled with the lace of her cuff. "Being back here, seeing this house again, set off something in me. All my memories returned. Now," she took in a deep breath and let it out slowly, "I feel at peace."

They broke their fast, then stepped out into the calm sunlit streets. Morning had healed the night. "That is Sant'Agata, where I met Bernardino Campi, my first teacher," Sofonisba said as they entered the piazza. "I used to go there to watch him paint frescoes for hours. He was very kind, took me up on the scaffolding, and I suppose he was flattered, too."

"Over there is Palazzo Cittanova, where Papa used to go for civic meetings. He was a *consigliere* for years. In the reception hall in there is where I first met King Philip, when he was still a prince."

"And this is the way that Elena and Rosa and I walked to Campi's studio for our lessons."

They continued through the puddled streets, past churches and shops and across piazzas that Sofonisba knew. They found themselves eventually at the city's main piazza. "Ah, now this is all truly home to me," Sofonisba said. "The cathedral, the baptistery, and the Palazzo del Comune. And the Torrazzo. Tallest bell tower in Italy. At least, that's what we always believed."

Fabrizio whistled his appreciation. "Have you ever been to the top?"

"Of course. Every Cremonese has, at least once. Papa used to take us. We sisters loved scampering up the stairs ahead of him. He'd try to scare us with the story of the evil ruler Gabrino Fondulo, who took Emperor Sigismund and Pope Gregory XIII up there, oh, well over a hundred and fifty years ago. Papa told us Fondulo tried to push the other two off."

"Let's go up. I want to see the view," Fabrizio said.

"Uh, it's almost 500 steps, dear," Sofonisba said. "When I was able to scamper up them, I was much younger."

"So we'll take it slowly," Fabrizio said. "Come on."

The climb was not as difficult as Sofonisba feared. At the top, they gazed out over tiled roofs in orange and brown and beyond the city's walls to the mosaic of the farm fields and meadows.

"More beautiful than I remember," Sofonisba murmured.

"It is indeed beautiful," Fabrizio agreed. When he had thoroughly taken in the view from all four sides, he turned his gaze to his wife, and put an arm around her waist.

"Sonia."

The low tone of his voice sent a tingle buzzing through her, a sensation that intensified when he leaned over and kissed her. His fingers traced her neck along the edge of her lace collar. Sofonisba felt her knees weaken.

They descended the tower and walked back to the Anguissola palazzo, wordless the entire way, their strides more urgent than when they had set out. Bianca, in the sitting room, saw them reach the stairs landing, and called out to them.

"There you are! Where have you two been, pray tell?"

"Ah, Mama, I've had a bit too much sun," Sofonisba said apologetically. "I need to lie down."

"All right."

Husband and wife continued up to their room, thankful that they did not pass anyone on the way. Once inside, they locked the door, closed the shutters, and raced to undress. They made a storm of love, as on their first night but with greater trust, and therefore, greater abandon.

The early afternoon heat and their exertions left them sweating, then drowsy, and finally they lapsed into a happy sleep.

Alone in the sitting room below, Bianca smiled and rested her embroidery needle. *Now my daughter knows a happiness I feared she would never find. Heaven be praised!*

"There is just one more thing I have to do before we leave," Sofonisba told Fabrizio, and made her way to her old studio.

It was not at all as she remembered it. Someone had cleaned and straightened the room thoroughly. All the paintbrushes stood in ceramic jars lined up in a precise, regimented row on the table. All the folded-up easels rested against one wall, and all the aprons hung neatly on hooks. Even the fireplace, where Sofonisba and her sisters had heated the oil for paints, had been swept bare. But it was the smell of the studio that disoriented her the most — the distinctive smoky smell of heated linseed or walnut oil was gone, replaced by an overwhelming mustiness.

In the silence, from out of the blank walls, came voices:

"I look — like a monkey!"

"Who would think that a servant could get into a painting?"

"Elena, you must have the loveliest breasts in Cremona."

"I don't want to paint any more!"

Rattled, she sat down. Then she noticed a tidy stack of drawings in Lucia's skilled hand, showing her meticulous attention to detail. Sofonisba was startled, then deeply moved, to see that all the faces looking back at her were her own. Lucia had drawn her sister-teacher's face over and over, at several angles, along with some half-length views and even a full-length one, showing a young Sofonisba in her old black dress.

She picked up the sketches and left the studio. She found her mother sitting in the garden.

"Mama, in the studio, I found these. They're by Lucia."

"Oh! My Lucia," Bianca murmured as she leafed through the pile. She looked over each drawing, her expression turning from pride to sadness. "I remember now. She was planning a full-length portrait of you when she … she…"

Sofonisba put one hand over her mother's, where it rested on the pile of drawings in her lap. They both looked up as a goldfinch intoned crazily above them.

Sofonisba and Fabrizio travelled on horseback to Mantua to visit Elena. Sofonisba was filled with renewed pride as she inspected

Elena's latest illuminations. They held each other tightly when they said farewell, each aware that another huge distance would soon lie between them.

⌒⌒

"Elena is special to you, I can see that," Fabrizio said as they rode back to Cremona.

"It broke my heart when she decided to join the convent. I cried and screamed, it was awful. I was closer to her than to any of the others — bread and jam, Papa called us." She gazed off. "We trained as painters together. And of the six Anguissola sisters, she is the most beautiful."

SEPTEMBER 29, 1573

The galley from Genoa to Palermo made swift time. At the dock, Fabrizio hired a carriage to take them first to the palazzo that had belonged to his brother Cesare, whose widow, Luisa de Luna, veiled in black, greeted them in few words, with a stiff extension of the hand.

She's still in mourning, Sofonisba told herself, trying to be compassionate. Luisa led them into her sitting room, lit only by two small lamps.

"How was your journey, Fabrizio?"

"We had favourable winds and calm water, thank the Lord."

"And so, Signora de Moncada," Luisa turned to Sofonisba. "How are your people faring? You're from Cremona, correct?"

"Yes, I am, and they're all well, signora."

"How nice." Luisa turned back to Fabrizio, and spoke in a flat voice. "I have an announcement to make. You were far away for some time, dear brother, and there wasn't time to write. It is this: I have become engaged to Antonio de Aragón."

Sofonisba stopped herself from congratulating the bride-to-be when she saw Fabrizio's jaw drop.

"Aragón," Fabrizio said stiffly, in a low tone that Sofonisba had not yet heard him use. "You have certainly chosen an important family."

Luisa looked at Fabrizio with an expression Sofonisba could not fathom — was it triumph? Then their hostess dismissed them: "You must be tired after your journey. I'll have someone show you to your room, and supper will be brought up to you."

"Thank you," Fabrizio said, with a snarl for the widow that shocked Sofonisba.

"So pray tell me what's going on here," Sofonisba said when they were alone in their big, drafty room. "I've never been treated so coldly. 'You're from Cremona, correct?' she said. She knows very well where I am from."

Fabrizio groaned. "I didn't think family difficulties would start so soon," he said. "When my brother died, I was made governor of Paternò, the Moncada ancestral home. It is far to the east of here, below Mount Etna. The position comes with an annual stipend of 400 ducats. But Luisa's family, the de Lunas, controls the position — I am dependent on them." He paused to let in a servant carrying a tray of food and waited until the servant lit the fire and left.

"If Luisa remarries — and I have no doubt that she will — I will become the legal guardian of her son, Francesco. He is my brother's only child. So in that, she is dependent on me. But Luisa is cunning. She must have something planned to make it all work out in her favour."

Sofonisba sliced off a piece of bread and handed it to Fabrizio.

"I'm not sure I understand all this," Sofonisba said. "How could Luisa's family control a position in the Moncada ancestral home?" She served them both some of the roast chicken.

"The land has changed hands many times. I suppose it's hard

for anyone who's not Sicilian to understand. The legalities are complicated," Fabrizio said, and poured two cups of red wine.

"How old is Francesco?"

"Let's see, he must be twelve years old now."

"Do you know this Antonio de Aragón?" Sofonisba asked.

"Oh yes. An imposing man. The Aragón are one of the most prominent Spanish-Italian families. I'm worried that a de Luna-Aragón alliance will somehow cheat Francesco, and me, out of our Moncada inheritance."

Sofonisba gave up trying to sort out the conflict. "Maybe Luisa won't do anything for some time. You know that engagements among the nobility can last a long time." She tasted the wine and winced. "I hope all the wines of Sicily are not this rough! Luisa must be saving the good libations for another occasion. Now, it could be that she only mentioned her engagement to Aragón to annoy you."

For the rest of the fall and through the winter, they stayed in Palermo in a rented house with room for a studio. Palermo's nobility, including the viceroy, entertained them with banquets and dances, and many Palermitani commissioned Sofonisba to paint their portraits. The city was fascinated by this Cremonese woman painter who had lived in their sovereign's household in Madrid, attended to his third wife as she died, and taught his children. They could not get enough of Sofonisba's tales of court life. Amid the parties, concerts, pageants, and hunting expeditions, neither Sofonisba nor Fabrizio gave much thought to Luisa de Luna.

In fact, it was something much more hideous and fearsome than Luisa that brought their paradise crashing down, something all the more terrible because it came with the blooming of the bougainvillea — the plague.

Overnight, ebullience disappeared; every ballroom and banquet hall lay shuttered and dark. In the streets, bonfires burned continuously to destroy the contaminated possessions of the dead. Corpses piled up in graveyards and were buried one after another, without ceremony. Those who could fled to the countryside or to the docks, to get a boat to — anyplace. Sofonisba and Fabrizio decided to go to Paternò, in the hope that the town's isolation had protected it from the plague.

Fighting panicked crowds at the dock, they managed to board a galley that travelled along Sicily's northern coast. Standing on the deck, watching a flock of gulls swoop above them, Sofonisba thought she saw a vulture.

They disembarked at the village of Piráino, and upon learning that Paternò was free from plague, proceeded south on horseback. The black summit of Mount Etna loomed in the distance, spewing trails of smoke.

"That volcano is like Janus," Fabrizio said as they started across the plain. "Its lava is deadly and it can sweep whole villages away, yet it makes the surrounding area so fertile. The orange and lemon trees you see here? We also grow them in Paternò, along with olive trees, and the grapes of our vineyards yield the best wine on the island. And this is the best time of year — it's all in bloom." He took a deep breath of the scented spring air.

As Sofonisba and Fabrizio crossed the Nébrodi Mountains, the fruit trees, with their blossoms and scent, gave way to forests of oak and ash. Then the travellers shifted southwest to skirt Mount Etna.

"There — there it is!" Fabrizio said, pointing to a block-shaped stone structure, barely visible in the distance. "That's the Moncada castle. Or at least, it was."

"What? A castle?" Sofonisba was jolted upright on her horse with surprise, straining to see. "You never mentioned a Moncada castle. And what do you mean, 'it was'?"

"About a hundred years ago, the family came on hard times, and sold it to the town. It's been used as a prison ever since."

"Oh," Sofonisba said. "Good thing I've already lived in a royal residence." She smiled at Fabrizio.

"My family's current home might not compare with the king's palace in Madrid, but I think you'll find it adequate," Fabrizio said.

They continued riding down the muddy road. Sofonisba inhaled once again the revitalizing scent of orange and lemon trees. She closed her eyes to better feel the intensifying April sun, and when she opened them, she noted newly awakened olive groves and vineyards. Larks and finches heralded the couple's approach to Paternò.

JUNE, 1574

Sofonisba and Fabrizio had been married for a year. The couple lived in a splendid palazzo near the heart of Paternò. Sofonisba rejoiced when she saw a clavichord. She played it every day, a pleasure that brought her back to happy times growing up in Cremona, and to when she played alongside Queen Elisabeth in Madrid.

Mount Etna was the constant brooding presence over their lives, strong and threatening. Often, wisps of smoke rose from the peak, and for several months a year the peak was surrounded by snow. Sofonisba and Fabrizio occasionally rode mules to the top — or at least, as close as they could safely go. It was cold up there even in the hottest months. It occurred to Sofonisba that hell must resemble that volcano. At the edge of the crater they looked down into a roiling, churning mass of glowing red lava and black ash that made a constant crackling and dull roaring sound. It thrilled and horrified them at once. In their daily prayers they never forgot to appeal to St. Barbara, the patron saint of Paternò, who protected the town from the ravages of Etna. On St. Barbara's feast day, December 4, young men in white tunics and caps carried her statue in a long procession around the town. Sofonisba and Fabrizio joined the rest of the faithful, following with torches, singing hymns and reciting prayers, and ending up at the main square, where St. Barbara presided over a festival of food and dance that lasted all night.

Sofonisba soon was busy painting portraits of nobles and their families. She also painted a *Madonna and Child* for the family's parish church, Santa Maria dell'Alto. She still revelled in the pleasure of painting, and thanked God that she could do it, even after so many years. She also thanked God for her husband, the greatest source of her contentment, her heart and soul, her comforter and confidant.

FEBRUARY, 1575

Sofonisba was glad to receive a letter from Isabel Clara Eugenia, oldest daughter of King Philip and Queen Elisabeth. The girl was not yet nine years old, but the letter showed an already intelligent mind. Isabel mentioned that the eldest daughter of Alonso Sánchez Coello, the court painter Sofonisba remembered all too well, had herself become a painter. That part of the letter set off in Sofonisba such hysterical laughter that Fabrizio thought at first she had quite lost her mind.

Soon after, Sofonisba learned that the second son of King Philip and Queen Anne, Carlos Lorenzo, a child of only two years, had died in Madrid. Sofonisba remembered attending to Queen Anne at the child's birth.

In the following year, more sadness intruded. Sofonisba heard through visitors from Cremona that Signor Bernardino Gatti, her second teacher, had died while painting an altarpiece for Cremona's cathedral. She would never forget his encouragement, and her joy when he said that there was nothing more he could teach her. Gatti had died in advanced years after a highly accomplished life as a painter — Sofonisba thought one could do far worse in this life.

Then in January 1577, Sofonisba received the first letter Asdrubale had ever sent her, and her hands shook as she opened it. *Mama...* "Our beloved sister Europa has died of consumption. The Little Bird will sing no more..."

Once again, she lit candles, attended another requiem Mass, and felt pain and loss, which never became routine.

JUNE, 1577

They were sitting on the terrace, overlooking peonies, lilies, and roses that showed off their springtime finery, when another message arrived, this time for Fabrizio. As he read it, his face drained white. "Luisa de Luna has married off my nephew Francesco to a daughter of Antonio de Aragón," he said. "It is despicable. The nerve…" He grimaced.

"Francesco? But he's only — "

"That's right, he turns only sixteen this year, not yet of age. And the girl is only fourteen. I told you Luisa would find a way. And she and Aragón will marry next week."

"What will happen, pray?"

"As Francesco's stepfather and father-in-law, Aragón can easily win guardianship," Fabrizio said. "That will put Francesco's inheritance, and mine, in doubt."

"So Aragón will have control over Francesco, but I don't see how that affects *your* inheritance," Sofonisba said.

"It's the law," Fabrizio said, shrugging.

Sofonisba crossed her arms. "A strange law. This would never happen in Lombardy."

"We're not in Lombardy, my dear, we're in Sicily, and things are different here."

"Isn't there any authority here who can help you? Or is that different in Sicily, too?" Sofonisba asked.

Fabrizio looked at her sideways with an expression Sofonisba could not read. Perhaps it was impatience. "It wouldn't help to appeal to the authorities here. Aragón would just bribe them."

"Hmm." Sofonisba racked her brain, trying to understand, trying to find the way to a resolution. She wished the birds would stop their lunatic chirping, a sound that normally pleased her.

"Write to King Philip. He still regards me highly," she suggested. "I just had a letter from Princess Isabel, and she said he still talks warmly about me. He will help us."

"Oh, my dear," Fabrizio moaned. "I would feel, well, debased, as if I have failed you, if I asked for the king's help."

"Nonsense," Sofonisba said. "I don't see it that way at all. It's just circumstances. I am sure that Philip will understand our pressing need, and your reputation will not suffer."

"All right." Fabrizio instructed a servant to bring him parchment, a writing quill, and ink. In his best handwriting, he wrote: "June 21, 1577, Paternò, Sicily, To the Most Excellent Catholic King, His Majesty, the King of Spain and its Dominions, Philip II...."

The summer ended, and autumn bloomed in with gold and red. Then the drizzle and chill of winter arrived, and still Fabrizio and Sofonisba heard nothing from the king. They did receive needling, vaguely threatening letters from Luisa, signed prominently with her married name. In April 1578, Aragón sent a covenant for Fabrizio to sign that would turn over all Moncada properties and funds to Luisa.

"Aragón is asking me to betray my family for an insulting sum of money," Fabrizio said.

"Let's not wait any longer," Sofonisba said. "If you appeal to the king in person, he will settle everything for us, I know it."

Two days later they stood in the courtyard of their home, Fabrizio's readied horse impatiently snorting.

"My dearest." Fabrizio had no more words.

"Here is a letter for His Majesty. And take this with you," Sofonisba said, and she pressed a gold St. Barbara medal into his hand. "For protection."

The summer

Fabrizio's galley, the *Capitana Palermo*, escorted by the *Sant' Angelo*, left Palermo April 25, setting a northerly course toward Naples, where the ships would take on more passengers and cargo before sailing west toward Barcelona. A more direct westward route might have been faster, but that would have brought the ships much too close to the Barbary Coast and its ravaging pirates.

In his quarters on the first night, the captain of the *Capitana Palermo*, Don Carlos de Aragón y Taviglia, looked over the passenger list by candlelight.

"Fabrizio de Moncada," he read. *Now where have I heard that name? Oh yes — he's the one my Aragón kin have been quarreling with over an inheritance, or something. Hmmm. An awful lot can happen at sea...*

The *Capitana Palermo* was fifty miles from Capri, off the Neapolitan coast, when land barely came into view. Soon after, when the *Capitana* was quite near to Capri, the waves shifted higher, clouds blotted out the sun and a mist rose, distracting the crew: no one saw a third ship until it was only five miles downwind.

"Ay, it's the devil's own! They're taking the *Sant'Angelo!*" screamed a crewman of the *Capitana*. The pirates sprang onto the escort ship *Sant'Angelo*, brandishing swords and dragging its crew and passengers onto their ship, and a glance of that horror caused enough panic and chaos on the *Capitana* to induce the oarsmen to jump overboard.

The loss of oarsmen left the *Capitana* helpless, so, desperate to avoid capture, the noblemen and other passengers aboard the *Capitana*, including Fabrizio, jumped over the rail and into the sea.

Fabrizio saw the captain, Aragón y Taviglia, floating a short distance away on a gangplank. "Help!" Fabrizio screamed, but the captain did not look his way. "Help! *Help!*" Was the shore near enough? He could not tell — the wind flung him into the now-towering waves. There was nothing to do but keep swimming...

The housekeeper stepped into the sitting room and said there was a messenger from Palermo, but that he would not give her the message, saying he had to give it to the signora personally.

That horrid Luisa, will she never stop harassing us — the arrogance of that woman, Sofonisba thought. "All right, send him in," she said.

Marques de Mondejar
Viceroy of Naples
April 28, 1578

Signora Sofonisba Anguissola de Moncada, it is with deep sorrow and regret that I inform you of the tragic drowning death of your husband, Fabrizio de Francesco de Moncada, on the 27th of April, in this, the year of Our Lord 1578…

There was more but Sofonisba's hands shook so much that she dropped the note. Then her whole body shook, and her scream, a howl filled with pure terror, brought the housekeeper running back into the room.

She sank into a time of perpetual night. She ordered the shutters kept closed against the heedless Sicilian sun, and laid in bed until late each morning. Between condolence calls from friends who offered phrases of sympathy to which she could barely reply, she moved from room to room, crying, imagining Fabrizio there. The cook brought trays of food that she hardly touched. When she guessed it was nightfall, she laid in bed wide-eyed, staring into the darkness.

Still in uncomprehending shock, she gazed at the funeral service through a black lace veil that obscured her red eyes, her devastated face. She was only dimly aware of the prayers, the hymns, the many candles, the large crowd.

The Aragón-de Luna clan immediately cut off payment of Fabrizio's stipend to Sofonisba. She could not live on her pension, because Fabrizio had borrowed against it to pay for his journey. Instead, she had to borrow money, at high interest. One day, wearing a thick veil and a pall of shame, she brought some of her jewellery to a pawnbroker.

The next day, as Sofonisba sat on the well-shaded terrace, an inexplicable warmth settled over her torso and head, nearly causing her to panic. Breathing heavily and sweating, she loosened the ties on her chemise and pushed it down to her nipples. As she implored the Virgin for relief, the wave passed, but it returned every few days. She had seen forty-six years and had long ago resigned herself to the end of her youth, but in this trial of fire she thought she could hear a cruelly demonic taunt: *"Now you're just an old, childless widow!"*

On one of her lone wanderings in the garden, Sofonisba tried to imagine Fabrizio's last moments, the cold, the rising of the killer water and wind that overtook him. *How did it happen? And why?*

When Sofonisba finally heard from King Philip, he said nothing about her problems with Fabrizio's family. Instead he invited her back to his court, to reopen her studio there and live once again under his protection. She was tempted, but in the end could not bring herself to return. The court, with the beauty of its palaces and gardens, and its intrigues, tragedies and excesses, seemed to Sofonisba like a strange, unfathomable world now. Besides, she wanted to join her mother in Cremona. The thought that she might receive word of her mother's death before seeing her again was more than she could bear.

While she floundered in grief, Sofonisba did receive a certain letter from Cremona, but it did not contain the news she dreaded. It was from Asdrubale. He went on at great length to express his sympathy over Fabrizio's death. Then he said that he would arrive in Paternò in the next few weeks to help Sofonisba deal with the many legal and financial matters that she surely faced. "I know you are strong, but you need someone from your own family with you now," her brother wrote.

JULY, 1578

She embraced her brother through her tears, and told him the long story of her financial woes, the battle with Fabrizio's relatives, all the details that she had spared her family.

"What about your pension, from Spain?" Asdrubale asked.

"I haven't received it in two years. Finances are often spotty at the court. Besides, it is owed for Fabrizio's passage."

"How have you been living, then?"

"Friends have been very kind, and I — " Sofonisba looked away. "I pawned some jewellery." That thought, and the whole ordeal, strangled her voice into a whisper.

"Oh, sister, you are in a state," Asdrubale said softly. "I'm so sorry." He handed her his handkerchief. "Things will be better now, I promise."

"How can you promise that?"

"Because I'm here now. First, you'll take no more charity — the Anguissolas do not depend on charity. I will redeem the jewellery you pawned. You see, Sonia, I had a very profitable voyage from Genoa. The ship's crew loved to gamble, but they sure weren't good at it. I, however, am quite good at it. Cards, dice, you name it — I almost felt sorry for them."

Sofonisba smiled a bit, for the first time in months.

"Second, there must be some income from the Moncada vine-yards," Asdrubale said, "and the olive groves, and the orange and lemon trees."

"Yes, but Fabrizio handled all that."

"I'll handle it now."

Sofonisba looked into Asdrubale's big brown eyes, so much like Mama's. "Asdru, I can't ask you to do that."

"You didn't ask. It was my idea."

"My little brother is quite a man now."

Asdrubale was as good as his word. Over the course of several months, he paid off Sofonisba's debts and bought back her jewellery.

Then he asked her when she planned to come home.

Home, she reflected. *And where is that?* It had once been Cremona, then Madrid, now it was here in Paternò. Soon it would be Cremona again.

"I've asked King Philip again for help with my dispute with the Aragón, and I am still waiting to hear from him. There's a great deal of money at stake. I'm afraid that if I leave, I'll never see any of it."

Asdrubale searched for a way to distract her. "When was the last time you painted?" he asked.

"Oh, not a bit since … I just haven't had the will to do it."

"Well, it's high time. Show me your studio."

"I still don't think I can paint, Asdru."

"Of course you can." He stood up. "Come on."

They went to her studio on the third floor, opening the shutters for the first time in nearly a year.

"So, to start a new portrait, what's the first thing you would do?" Asdrubale asked.

Sofonisba shrugged, "I'd have the subject pose for a drawing."

"All right." Asdrubale dusted off a chair. "Sit here. Then what?"

"Hmm, I suppose I would take a piece of parchment, a drawing board, and a bit of black chalk."

"Like these here?" He picked up some objects from a table covered with drawing and painting tools, dusted them off with a paint rag, and handed them to her.

"Here you go. Now what?"

"Well, now I just need a model."

"Fine. I'll be your model." Asdrubale sat down on a stool opposite her, threw back his broad shoulders and straightened his spine. "How's this?"

The first strokes required intense effort, as if she were learning to draw all over again. Then, slowly, the memory of her skills returned, and her hand moved over the parchment with confidence. She found herself unexpectedly absorbed, sketching her brother's thick hair, his clean-shaven face, and his cleft chin.

"Now I'm remembering that it was a drawing of you and Minerva that greatly impressed Michelangelo Buonarroti, may they both rest in peace," she said. "I did it when you were only three years old. And the last time I painted you was when I did that portrait with Papa, bless him, and Minerva." She had to pause to let the lump in her throat pass. "And you could hardly stand still. You were excited because Papa let you wear a sword at your waist. I must say, as a model you are much more cooperative now."

Sofonisba finished the portrait and a few devotional ones, but could not stand to look at her grief-distorted face long enough to paint a self-portrait.

Still no word arrived from Philip. It was a deep and bewildering disappointment. Sofonisba did not know that the royal family was suffering its own tragedies in 1578, the same year she had lost Fabrizio and Europa. Two of Philip's nephews died: one was a son of his sister Maria, and the other was King Sebastian of Portugal, whom Sofonisba had painted six years before in Madrid. Sebastian, only twenty-four years old, was killed while playing the warrior he had always dreamed of being, in a losing battle against the Moors in Morocco. Nearly eight hundred Spaniards were taken prisoner. Philip had mounted the North African crusade only reluctantly, at the urging of Sebastian and the duke of Alba, so when Philip learned of the disaster, he locked himself away in bitter regret over his decision. He soon became mired in the question of who would succeed Sebastian on the Portuguese throne, and at the same time he struggled to put down a rebellion in the Netherlands.

But Philip's greatest loss that year was his beloved son and heir, Ferdinand, in the boy's seventh year. Queen Anne gave birth that April to another son, named after his father, but that little Philip was in poor health.

Giving up on ever getting help from the king, Sofonisba and Asdrubale went to a notary to file suit against Fabrizio's family. "For all the good that will do," Asdrubale sighed. He arranged to close the palazzo, gave generous final payments to the servants, and packed up his sister's things. Only one task remained, and Sofonisba had to do it herself.

We didn't have much time together, Fabrizio, not when you think of a lifetime. She stood beside his memorial, a simple marble cross with Fabrizio's name that she and Asdrubale had placed in the cemetery of Santa Maria dell'Alto. His body had never been returned to her. *But it was so sweet. In you I found comfort, a companion, and a lover, beyond any dream or wish of mine. It took so long to find you. You opened up a new world to me, one of passion and romantic love, and I miss it terribly. I came to tell you that I am leaving now, to go back to Cremona. Family calls me, and besides, there is nothing here for me now, without you. This was your land, and I loved being here with you, but now it is time to go. You will always have a hold on my heart — my lover, my husband, my dear Fabrizio.*

DECEMBER, 1579

As brother and sister guided their horses into the Nébrodi Mountains, she turned in her saddle to take a last look at Paternò. "Don't look back, Sonia," Asdrubale said.

"If you mean, don't think any more about my dead husband, that's not possible," Sofonisba said.

"I know," Asdrubale said, sympathetically.

Then she did turn to face the mountains ahead, and away from the thin black plume that rose languidly from Mount Etna.

They sat eating supper in her cabin, a cramped space in a large Genoese galley.

"Asdru, when do we pass Capri?" She pulled the question abruptly out of the silence, from the pain that was never far away.

"Sonia, don't," Asdrubale said.

"I have to. I have to see the spot where Fabrizio … died."

Asdrubale concentrated on his food. "I don't know when we pass Capri, it depends on the wind, on the current…"

"Oof, never mind," Sofonisba said, and they finished the meal without speaking again.

She was out on the deck the next morning, well-wrapped against the December wind and damp, standing at the rail, looking toward the dull early rays of the rising sun. Only one other person was there, a tall man with an air of authority.

"Signora, it is awfully cold and dreary out here," the man said to her. "Excuse me, I am Orazio Lomellini, the captain." He removed his black velvet cap.

"Captain…" she said in a tired voice. She simply could not manage the usual social niceties. "I am Sofonisba Anguissola de Moncada, and can you please tell me when we will pass Capri?"

"Look there, signora," Lomellini pointed, "you can just make out the castle of Capri."

Sofonisba peered out across the water, raising her hood as the wind shifted and intensified. She reached out one black brocaded arm, as if she could pluck something from the sea air. Then she took two carnations, one white and one red, from inside her cloak and tossed them into the water. She watched them float as she pulled the cloak tighter and whispered, "God, open the gates of heaven for my dear Fabrizio."

The captain replaced his cap and waited. The oarsmen's strokes kept a steady rhythm below them: *pllisssssssh, pllisssssssh.*

"Signora de Moncada," he said. "Of course. You are the widow of Fabrizio de Moncada, who died in these waters in April last year. We all heard about that. Signora, you have my deepest sympathy. May your husband rest in peace."

She glanced into Lomellini's green eyes. "Thank you, sir. You are very kind."

She wanted to speak more but was unable. They stood at the rail in an easy silence a few more minutes, just looking out to sea.

"The pirates are godless thugs," the captain said. "All of us who sail this sea know we could be next." He removed his cap again to scratch his head. "Now signora, I don't mean to pry, but I saw you boarding the galley with a man, is he your…"

"He is my brother, Asdrubale," Sofonisba said, noting in Lomellini's face a fleeting look of relief. "He came to Sicily to help me."

"That was good of him. And do you and your brother find your cabins here adequate?"

"Yes, we do, thank you, captain." She was struck by his concern, his warmth.

"Signora, I am afraid that duty calls me now, but perhaps we shall have a chance to speak again soon," Lomellini said.

"Perhaps we shall, captain."

⌒

"Who was that you were talking to?" Asdrubale asked as he joined her at the rail.

"That was the captain, Orazio Lomellini," she said.

"I hope he wasn't pestering you."

"Oh no, he was very kind, in fact." After a few moments of

looking out at the water, Sofonisba said, "You know, Asdru, it's been twenty months since I lost Fabrizio."

"So? What brings you to mention that, pray?"

"Oh, nothing."

◦◡―

She returned to the same spot at the rail that afternoon. It was not long before Lomellini joined her.

"Good afternoon, Signora de Moncada."

"Good afternoon, captain." Had she noticed before that his face was nearly unlined?

"That shift of the wind this morning has slowed us down, but not too much. We should arrive in Livorno by late tomorrow afternoon," Lomellini said as the wind caught short strands of his black hair below his cap.

"How long have you been sailing the Mediterranean, captain?"

"Eight years. I sail this Genoese Republic galley between Corsica, Nice, Livorno, Naples and Sicily. I carry goods for the Genoese merchants in Palermo who trade with the Orient and Spain," he said, self-consciously fingering his neatly trimmed short black beard. "And you, Signora, I know now that you are the great woman painter from Cremona who has served His Majesty King Philip."

"You are generous in your praise, sir, I will only say that I did have the honour and pleasure of serving the royal family in Madrid."

Lomellini gave her a smile that intrigued her and raised her curiosity. "And now, are you returning to Cremona?" he asked.

"Yes, my mother is widowed six years now, and I want to be with her. Pray tell me of your family." It was only polite to ask.

"My father, Niccolò, still lives in Genoa, and my mother, who was a Spinola, one of Genoa's oldest families, she is dead these twenty years, may her soul rest." They watched idly as shore birds rode the wind.

"Captain, you remind me of another ship's captain, the one on a galley that took me from Genoa to Barcelona, many years ago," Sofonisba said. "He told me and my companions that ladies should not be on the deck, but once we did it, he never complained."

"He just didn't want his crew distracted by lovely women," Lomellini said.

She smiled a tiny, brief smile and looked back out to sea. *Lovely, ha. He's a flatterer, but harmless.*

"Signora, forgive my boldness, but what, pray, will you do in Cremona?" Lomellini asked.

It *was* a bold question, but Sofonisba sensed concern, not intrusion. "My mother and I will be old widows together," she said, shrugging. "I haven't given it much thought."

"Will you continue to paint?"

"I don't know. I started painting again recently after a long pause, but I will have to weigh my feelings when I get to Cremona."

"It would be a tragedy, indeed, if you did not continue to paint," Lomellini said, his brow furrowed.

"Again, you are most kind, sir. I am pleasantly surprised that a sea captain gives painting any importance at all."

"We Lomellini have many interests. We were innkeepers when we first came to Genoa. And some of us have been senators, while others have been members of the clergy, from parish priest on up to cardinal. Then, there are those who have been administrators of charities, other things."

"Like ship captains."

"Yes, in Genoa it's quite unavoidable. There's such a strong legacy — Signor Cristoforo Colombo bravely sailed west in the last century, and Signor Andrea Doria, the great admiral, sailed this very sea even as an old man. And the city is rich — it controls the silver from the Americas." He gave her that smile again, but Sofonisba was taken aback when it faded into a look of determination.

"Signora, instead of boring you with the history of my family and of Genoa, I should say…" He took a step closer to her, drew a deep breath, and locked onto her eyes. Sofonisba regarded him with bafflement.

"...that we arrive in Livorno tomorrow, and you will disembark, and disappear. Unless..."

"Unless what?" She barely breathed. *Pllisssssh, pllisssssssh* went the oars just below.

"Unless you become my wife, and live with me in Genoa."

Her heart began to pound. *So I have not imagined his interest,* she thought. "You want to marry me? Captain, this is all so fast." Sofonisba broke from his gaze and looked at the waves below without seeing them.

"You do not have to answer now," she heard him say.

Sofonisba turned back to him. "Sir, I must know something. How old are you?"

"I turned thirty-five in October, signora."

"Then you are twelve years my junior!" she gasped.

"Signora, that doesn't matter. God placed you on my ship, and in my life."

"You hardly know me," Sofonisba protested.

"I know enough. You are a justly renowned and warm, gracious lady, and one who has suffered a great loss."

"Ah, then could your feelings for me be mere pity?" Sofonisba asked.

"No, I am as sure as a man can be that they are not. Signora, I have wanted a wife for so long. I need someone beside me at my home in Genoa. Then when I am away at sea, I will look out at the colour of the blue Mediterranean and be reminded of your eyes." He placed his hand on the railing.

So he fancies himself a poet, Sofonisba laughed to herself.

A group of passengers strolled along the deck. "Good afternoon, captain," they said. "Good afternoon," Lomellini replied, nodding and smiling. "Yes, the wind is fairly brisk. That's right, we should arrive in Livorno tomorrow," he said, and the passengers walked on.

The pause gave Sofonisba time to realize that she could not deny her attraction to him, his engaging manner and intelligence. She felt both relentlessly practical: *While he's at sea thinking of my eyes, I'd have time to paint, undisturbed,* and full of longing: *Oh, to love, and be loved, again. And I did come deliberately to this railing at this moment…*

"There isn't much time," she began, thoughtfully. "Not on this sea voyage, and not in a lifetime. I had a great love, and I lost him."

"But can you love another?" Lomellini pressed, sliding his hand along the rail, closer to her.

Sofonisba looked down at the oars gliding out their steady rhythm. "Maybe there *is* room for more than one love," she said. "But there's something about me that may not have occurred to you. And that is, I could never give you children."

"I have all the nieces and nephews a man could want. And…" The captain paused. "I already have a son, who is three years old, in Palermo. When he was born I asked his mother to marry me, but she refused. She will not leave Palermo, and my home is in Genoa." His expression was serious and candid.

Sofonisba's racing heart had steadied. *To have an Italian home once more.* She placed a hand over Lomellini's on the railing and looked into his eyes again. "If you look at me and see more than an 'old widow,' well … then, I will marry you —"

"Ah!" Lomellini rejoiced.

"…on one condition."

"Name it, signora."

"That we go to Cremona together soon after landing, and have a long visit with my mother before we settle in Genoa," Sofonisba said.

Lomellini did not need to think. "Agreed."

She returned his broad smile. "And captain, please call me Sonia."

"If you will call me Orazio."

"Orazio it is."

Looking into her eyes, he lifted her hand and kissed it, then placed it back on the railing before walking away, slowly. Sofonisba threw her head back and smiled up at the white sky.

She waited until she and Asdrubale had nearly finished their evening meal. "Asdru, I have something to tell you."

"Huh?" With his teeth, he ripped the roasted flesh off a chicken leg.

"I am going to marry Captain Lomellini."

Asdrubale violently coughed the piece of chicken back onto his plate. "What?"

"He asked me to marry him, and I have agreed. We will visit Mama in Cremona, and then I will live with him in Genoa."

"Oh no you won't! A man you just met? I absolutely forbid it!" Asdrubale spluttered.

"You cannot forbid it! I've already decided!"

"You're crazy! A ship's captain? He's beneath you!"

"He is not. He's a nobleman, just like Papa, who was a merchant. What's the difference?"

Asdrubale *harrumphed*, and shook his head. "Sonia, you're just lonely. This voyage, passing Capri … you don't know what you're doing. Besides, isn't this Captain Lomellino much younger than you?"

"Lomelli*ni*. And his age doesn't matter. He is kind and gallant, and he respects my work."

"Paaaah! A man will say anything to win a woman. I should know." Asdrubale greedily finished off the chicken, then let out a belch. "What about Mama? She expects you to be her companion now." He took a gluttonous swig of wine.

"We'll be visiting her right away, for several months, and I will see that she has companionship after I leave. Besides, Anna Maria is still in Cremona."

"Is it possible that this man is only after your pension?" Asdrubale asked.

"My irregular, unreliable pension, which he doesn't even know

I have? No, it's not possible."

"Sonia." Asdrubale spoke calmly, but with determination. "In the morning you will feel different. You don't know a thing about him."

"Ha!" Sofonisba sat back and laughed. "I remember saying the same thing, long ago, to Elena, when she thought I should pay attention to Ercules Vizconti."

"Who?"

"Never mind." She drained the last of her wine. "And stop treating me like a child. You're the baby brother, don't forget. I never said anything when you went out late at night in Paternò. Don't you think I knew where you were going?"

"To the tavern — so what?"

"Are you going to deny visiting bordellos, too?"

"So what if I did? I'm a man. You said so yourself."

"Oh, Asdru." She sighed. "I am grateful that you came to Sicily, and for all the help you gave me, but now I need something else. Some*one* else. Orazio chose me, when he could have any number of younger, prettier women."

"And he probably *will*."

"Aaaagh! Now you're just being disgusting!" Sofonisba yelled. She threw her napkin down on the table and stood up, unsteady with anger.

"And don't you need King Philip's permission to do this?" Asdrubale asked, his face brightening fiendishly.

"No! I don't need his permission, and I don't need yours."

Asdrubale's glower returned. He went off to gamble with the crew.

Lying in her tiny berth that night, Sofonisba dared to imagine contentment, to dwell on the prospect of it, after having long forgotten what it felt like. *To shape my life to my own ends, by myself, for once. Thank you, Lord*, and she let the galley's motion lull her into a peaceful sleep.

Brother and sister spoke only in necessary monosyllables during the bustle of disembarking in Livorno. Orazio made arrangements for Sofonisba to travel by carriage to the Convent of San Matteo in Pisa, saying he would meet her there in two days, after completing some business in Livorno. Sofonisba told Asdrubale where she was going and he grunted a curt goodbye, and then headed for a sailors' inn.

Sofonisba and Orazio married in the convent chapel on Christmas Eve in a simple candlelit ceremony perfumed by incense. Asdrubale's willful absence disappointed Sofonisba, but only briefly. She beamed when Orazio placed a wide gold ring on her finger. "Getting that was my 'business' in Livorno," he explained. When they kissed for the first time, in their bedchamber, she felt long-buried urges awaken, and when Orazio undressed her and let down her hair, she reached for him without hesitation, letting his youthful energy carry her along to the pleasure of a newly served feast.

"When we met on the deck of your ship that morning — that was not just happenstance, was it?" Sofonisba asked Orazio.

"I did just happen to see a lovely woman standing alone at the rail, looking as if her heart were broken. How could I not approach you?" They were sitting before the fire at midday, after the convent's long Christmas Mass. "I thank you for standing firm in the face of your brother's objections."

"How did you know that Asdrubale objected to our marriage? I never told you," Sofonisba said.

"You didn't have to. The looks he gave me as you two disembarked told me enough. Now, do you know Genoa?" Orazio asked.

Sofonisba's two nights there with Fabrizio seemed to have happened a lifetime ago. "No, not well at all."

"My home is a grand palazzo on one of the city's best streets. In the

Genoese dialect the street name means 'Street of Gold,' " he said.

"'Street of Gold,'" Sofonisba chuckled.

"You'll want to set up your studio on the top floor, the fourth, because that's where the most light comes in," Orazio continued.

Sheltered there within the convent's walls, it was as though they had stepped out of a world of anger, raging seas, and the pain of loss, and into one of orderly peace, quiet, and warmth, a world that lulled them into mutual comfort and trust, and washed away the strangeness of their beginning.

Soon the convent bells summoned them to the nuns' refectory.

9.

Genoa

Hail, my belovèd fatherland, most happy
Prosperous country, dearly loved by heaven,
Which, as a gracious spirit, phoenix-like
Displays its valor clearly in the open.
　　　　　　　　　　—Veronica Gàmbara (1485-1550)

GENOA, 1580

Sofonisba marvelled at the great good fortune that made her the
lady of a grand Genoese palazzo. She had thought Orazio was
teasing when he said his palazzo was on the "Street of Gold," but
it was true, and she considered the name appropriate in multiple
ways. For her the palazzo was a bit of golden heaven. She had the
biggest studio she had ever had, on the top floor, where there was
also a gallery that let her look out over Genoa, toward the harbour,
so she could watch for Orazio's ship to return.

After all she had suffered when she lost Fabrizio, she would have
settled for a merely placid life, growing old in Cremona. But she
thanked the Lord every day for setting her on a different course.

She once again found great pleasure in teaching, this time to an
eager circle of young painters. Commissions also kept her active.
She finished three religious works: *Lot with his Daughters*, *St. John
the Baptist in the Desert*, and *St. Francis*. Her new Lomellini relations

and others asked her to paint their portraits. Among those was a soldier she painted in black armour with gold embossing, and a wide, lace-edged white collar — she found the contrast between those materials irresistible.

One day, a nobleman who was widowed in the previous year came to Sofonisba with his son, a boy of about ten years, seeking their portrait. The father wanted a small memento, so she painted the two on a copper oval a little more than a hand's length. To show familial warmth, she placed the image of the boy's head and shoulders on his father's left side, close to his heart. The father wore a fashionably wide and pleated ruff, an accessory that seemed to be growing broader every year. Sofonisba wondered whether it would stop when it reached the outer edge of the shoulders.

She established a salon every Wednesday afternoon. Many, but not all, of the visitors were painters. At first, Orazio had not understood.

"You want to entertain guests every Wednesday? A painters' salon?" His eyebrows shot up.

"It's not so unusual, Orazio. We painters need to share ideas and give advice, and … and just enjoy ourselves."

"Some of my relations would never have a painter in the house, except to decorate the walls and ceilings."

"And some of mine would feel the same. In fact, Mama would be entirely aghast at the idea. But I thought the Lomellini had many interests."

"We do, but some Lomellini are more broad-minded than others. Sonia, to me it just seems a bit forward, even gauche."

"It's nothing of the sort. Let's just try it once, I pray."

Orazio came to enjoy the salons, and was pleased with the attention and regard that the painters of Genoa bestowed on his wife.

Sofonisba's greatest gift was Orazio himself, whom she loved with a warm, encompassing passion, and indeed, her only anxiety came when he was at sea. She could not help but think then about what happened to poor Fabrizio … but at those times she coped by losing herself in her painting.

Genoa served as a crossroad. When King Philip summoned Italian painters to decorate his beloved El Escorial, they would depart for Spain from Genoa, but not until they had visited that city's greatest painter, seeking her blessing of their journey. Their service in Spain done, they would return through Genoa, and none would think of leaving the city without stopping at Sofonisba's home and telling her all about their experiences.

Genoa also linked Spain with its lands in the Netherlands and with the Austrian branch of the Habsburgs. Sofonisba watched with growing impatience while the city's noble circles raved over the Empress Maria, King Philip's sister, who travelled through Genoa in 1581. *"Look at those horses!"* the curious said when Maria's carriage entered the city. *"Better dressed than any of us! And it's said they have solid gold bits in their mouths!"* By the time Empress Maria's carriage arrived at the bishop's palazzo, where she and her entourage would stay, people had lined the street and crowded around the bishop's gate, hoping for a glimpse of her, speculating about the fortune in jewels she was said to be carrying, and wondering who would get to meet her.

Grief dogged the empress every mile of her journey. Maria's husband, Maximilian II, had died in 1576, after twelve years as Holy Roman Emperor. Maria had planned to stay in Germany after Maximilian's death, but in 1580 she was devastated by the news that her daughter Queen Anne, King Philip's fourth wife, had died in Madrid of a severe malady of her lungs, at age thirty-one. The loss drove Maria toward the solace of her Spanish homeland.

"Oh, the endless chatter! Hasn't royalty ever passed through Genoa before?" Sofonisba asked Orazio.

"Of course in Madrid you hobnobbed with royalty every day," Orazio said. "That's why *you're* not interested."

"I'm going to meet her."

"What?" Orazio shrieked. "I thought you didn't care!"

"Well I don't intend to fawn over her, as half of Genoa seems determined to do," Sofonisba said. "Maybe I'm the only one in this city who can give the poor woman what she really needs."

"Signora Sofonisba Anguissola de Lomellini," the empress' lady announced, and then gestured for Sofonisba to enter the imperial presence.

"Your Imperial Highness," Sofonisba said, curtsying deeply. "My condolences on losing your husband and daughter. May they rest in peace."

Sadness seemed etched into Maria's face. "Thank you, signora," the empress said. Over silver hair she wore a black lace veil that draped onto her shoulders. Sofonisba guessed that the empress was a few years her senior.

"Your daughter, Her Majesty Queen Anne, was a lovely young woman, and a good friend to me in Madrid," Sofonisba said. "It was horrible to hear of her death."

"She is safe now in God's embrace," the empress said with an odd air of distraction, as if she were reciting required words that she did not truly believe.

"I was a portrait painter in your brother's household, madam. When I did your daughter's portrait, she insisted that I not flatter her. She was utterly without pretense, without vanity," Sofonisba said.

"Ah, that is good to hear," Maria said. "Do sit down." Sofonisba moved into a chair beside her.

Sofonisba launched into a story about Queen Anne travelling to Segovia for her wedding. On the way, a group of villagers offered her linens, plates, cups, other things that any bride might need for a new household, according to the local custom.

"Her Majesty was so cheered by this gesture, and received these humble gifts with warmth and grace, and she personally thanked the people. They loved her for it," Sofonisba said.

The cloud over Maria's face lifted slightly.

"I was there when she gave birth to Ferdinand and Carlos Lorenzo, may they rest in peace, the poor babies."

Maria clutched the gold cross on a chain around her neck.

The quiet began to unnerve Sofonisba. *But I did come here to comfort her, after all, not to be entertained.* "Her Majesty Queen Anne, like her husband, was very pious, and so they were well-matched," Sofonisba said. "She was a good and dutiful wife. And I will never forget that your daughter lent me one of her gowns to be married in." Sofonisba paused, not wanting to natter on. "And she was very comforting to me when my father died, God rest his soul."

"The poor babies," the empress said. Sofonisba wondered whether those were the only words that the empress had heard. Then Maria added, "May one of Anne's surviving sons live long enough to succeed their father."

"May God so will it," Sofonisba agreed.

After another pause, the empress said, casually, "Anne finally gave birth to a daughter, this year. Named her after me. Do you have any children, signora?"

"No, madam."

"Yet you've said the sort of things a grieving mother needs to hear." *So my ramblings did get through.*

The empress sat back and fixed her brown eyes on Sofonisba. "You have brought me some comfort, signora. Pray tell me, what can I do for you in return?"

"Your Imperial Highness is most considerate," Sofonisba said, a bit startled by the offer. "But I am merely acting as a loyal subject of your brother, the king." She squirmed in her chair. "I felt especially able to sympathize because I knew your daughter well. I am sure that there is no one else in Genoa who knew her better. Perhaps many people try to gain your favour, but believe me, madam, that was not my reason for coming here today."

"I believe you," Empress Maria said. "Still, I would like to do something."

Sofonisba paused to consider. "I would like your brother King Philip's blessing on my marriage," she said. "I served His Majesty for many years, but I did not get his permission when I married for the second time. You see, events moved so quickly. Perhaps when you see him in Madrid, you could ask him to give his blessing now."

"I will do that," the empress said. "God bless you, and I thank you for coming here today."

Sofonisba wished the empress a safe journey back to Spain.

❦

"So, did the visit go well?" Orazio asked when she arrived home.

"Oh, Orazio," she sighed heavily. "It was a litany of the dead."

❦

A Decree from His Majesty
the Most Sovereign Catholic King of Spain
    and its Possessions,
Philip II of the Most Noble House of Habsburg.
16 January, in the year of Our Lord 1583

Be it known by all, that His Majesty, the Most Sovereign Catholic King of Spain and its Possessions, Philip II of Habsburg, does hereby and henceforth proclaim his royal recognition, assent, approval, and blessing on the marriage of the renowned painter from Cremona in Italy, Sofonisba Anguissola, daughter of the late and most honourable Amilcare Anguissola, to Orazio de Niccolò Lomellini, a sea captain of Genoa, which marriage took place in the year of Our Lord 1579 in the city of Pisa.

When he saw the king's red seal on the document, Orazio declared that it should be framed and hung in the sitting room, to impress all visitors. Sofonisba objected, saying that the document was highly personal, that it was about Philip's respect for her, and that it was not proper to show it off, like just any possession.

"There's another note enclosed. What does it say?" Orazio asked.

Sofonisba began to read. "Oh, Orazio! Philip is giving me 500 ducats as 'assistance,' to help me deal with Fabrizio's death. Don't give me that scornful expression, dear. Better a late kindness than none at all."

"Yes, a 'kindness' that's *five years* late," Orazio said. "You certainly could have used the money at the time."

"In the royal court, funds were often lacking." She went back to the note. "You'll like this part, my dear. It also says that my pension has been increased, from 1,000 ducats to 1,300."

"*When* it comes. You know how irregular those payments are," Orazio said. "Will you have to wait five years for that, too?"

SAVONA, JUNE, 1585

The receiving line moved with agonizing leisureliness. Sofonisba had last seen the infanta Catalina Micaela, second daughter of King Philip and Queen Elisabeth, when she was only six years old. Now the princess was eighteen years old and recently married to Charles Emmanuel, duke of Savoy. "Lina," as Sofonisba called her, stopped in Savona on her way to Turin, where her husband had his estate. Sofonisba was part of a group of Genoese who went to Savona on Orazio's galley to greet her.

Sofonisba was worried that Catalina would not remember her.

But Catalina shrieked with joy and threw her arms breathlessly around Sofonisba's neck.

"Señora!"

"Oh Lina, you do remember," Sofonisba said. She had to concentrate to recall her long-lost words of Spanish.

"I could never forget my Señora Sofonisba! And all our time together in Madrid. You were my first teacher — and my favourite."

The next day, when the excitement of the welcoming celebration was over, the two women had more time to talk.

"You're a duchess now, Lina. Must I call you 'Your Grace'?"

"Do, and I'll go into hysterics," Catalina joked.

"So how is His Majesty, your father?"

"Papa has the various sufferings of an old man. His joints ache sometimes, and there are other things. But that is not the worst of it — even worse are the burdens he bears, with troubles in the Netherlands and in the Americas. While he was in Aragon for my wedding, we heard about that English pirate, Francis Drake, capturing two ports in the Caribbean. That was after Drake had sacked the town of Vigo."

"Yes, we heard about that. The nerve — sacking a town right on the Spanish coast!" Sofonisba said.

"Last year, when El Escorial was finished, Papa was so emotional, he wept," Catalina said.

"Ah, the Escorial. I was there when the first stones were laid. What an old woman that makes me." Sofonisba patted the grey hair that had overtaken her auburn strands.

"It is a beautiful place, señora, the library, the monastery, the gardens — and I enjoyed seeing your paintings on its walls every day."

Sofonisba smiled with deep gratification, letting a few memories dance in her mind. "And your sister Isabel — how does she fare?"

"Isabel is quite well, and she helps Papa a lot, keeping his endless papers sorted." She paused, and noticed that Sofonisba was staring at her. "Señora — what's wrong?"

"Oh, sorry, nothing's wrong, it's just that, just now, you reminded me so much of your mother, may she rest in peace. You have her voice, and her dark hair," Sofonisba said.

"I don't remember her."

"Well, you were a babe of just one year when she left us," Sofonisba said. "I can tell you that she was kind, and generous, and she had a good mind. She loved parties, games, theatricals. Indeed, she made the court a lively place. She also liked to draw and paint and play the clavichord."

"I'm glad to know these things," Catalina said.

At home in Genoa, Sofonisba recalled what Catalina and her sister had meant to her. Lavishing attention on them had helped her bear her grief over their mother's death, and her impatience as she waited to marry. She decided that the self-assured Catalina would make a fine duchess.

She also decided that Catalina was a young woman of good taste — after all, she had asked Sofonisba to paint her portrait. In it, Catalina wore a dress of purple brocade, with bands of intricate gold embroidery down the front and around the hem and the over-sleeve edges, which stopped above the elbow. The undersleeves were a pale gold, with spiky lace at the cuffs, as on the wide neck ruff. Sofonisba considered it the best painting she had done since leaving Spain, and the one that gave her the most pleasure.

Sofonisba's painting class was humming with creativity when Orazio's form filled the studio doorway. His expression made her eyes grow wide.

"We'll be ending the lesson a little early today, please. Until tomorrow then," she announced. Her pupils filed out, saying goodbye to her while smiling to themselves, *Of course, her husband's just back from another sea voyage.*

"Orazio."

"Dearest," Orazio began, and her trepidation increased. He called her that only when he had something difficult to say. "I have lost my post."

"What?"

"I am no longer captain of a Genoese Republic galley," he said, his features hardening. "While coming home from Palermo, a pirate ship appeared, along the east coast of Corsica. Normally I try to evade them, but this time I chased them, I had them on the run." He gazed off and made two fists. Sofonisba grew pale and slumped deeper in her seat.

Orazio reached over and squeezed her arm. "Love, I realize what any mention of pirates means to you, but this time, no one was hurt. We gave them a good scare, and after a short while they caught a wind that pulled them south. Then we continued toward Genoa. Some of my men found the chase exhilarating, and cheered along with me when the pirate ship fled, but others were frightened. Cowards! Those men — if I can still call them that — spoke to the naval officials when we landed, and convinced them that I had put the galley and its cargo at risk, and so, I was dismissed."

After a moment, calmer, but with her brow still furrowed, Sofonisba asked, "Did you explain yourself?"

"Of course. I said that everyone on board, and the galley, and the cargo, were never in any danger. That in fact, we had to do something bold against the pirates. But it didn't help. The weak little bastards," he snarled.

"How awful."

"But the good merchants of Genoa and Palermo, they understand," Orazio said. "I saw a group of them as I was leaving the naval offices, and they offered me command of their private ships. The Lomellini will not be kept ashore! Sonia? Now what's wrong?"

She had untied her apron and flung it to the floor, and untied the neck strings of her chemise. Her face, throat and décolletage were sweaty. She leaned back in her chair and fanned herself with a piece of parchment.

"We'll be all right, love, please don't take it so hard," Orazio said.

"It's not *that*," Sofonisba said, and the bizarreness of the timing of her paroxysm almost made her laugh. "I'm just having one of my 'old woman' episodes." She let out a long breath. "There, I feel better." Her fanning slowed.

"I didn't know you still had those," her husband said.

"Actually they are rare now."

"Should I call a physician?"

"No, I'm all right. So tell me — when will you go to sea again?"

"I don't know, but soon, perhaps. Now why are you looking at me so strangely, my love?"

Sofonisba was gazing thoughtfully, studiously, at her husband's seated form. "I've drawn you many times, and painted your portrait, but there's one thing I've never done, a certain way I'd like you to pose," she said.

"What way is that, pray?"

"In the nude, my lord."

Orazio's eyebrows shot up, but he gave her a sly smile and said, "You certainly are feeling better," as he began to unbutton his jacket. By the time Sofonisba had bolted the studio door, closed the shutters, and lit two lamps, Orazio had removed his clothes and was reclining on his side on a rug, with one knee bent. "How's this?" he asked.

"Ah, lovely," Sofonisba smiled as she picked up a piece of chalk and parchment. She sketched quietly for a while, admiring the firm muscles of his chest and the long planks of the thighs.

"Why didn't I think of this when we first married? To draw a nude male has been a missing part of my art education."

"How pleased I am to fill it in," Orazio said jauntily.

She sketched him in reclining and standing poses, then said she had kept him long enough and handed him his stockings and shirt.

But Orazio set the clothes aside and pulled her to him, and began to unhook the back of her bodice.

⌒

The Record of the Convent of the Holy Virgins
Church of San Vincenzo, Mantua
October 13, 1587

One of our beloved sisters, known to us as Suor Monica, born into this world as Elena di Amilcare Anguissola, of Cremona, was called by God to everlasting life in His heavenly kingdom on this day, quite unexpectedly, but with time to receive the sacrament of Extreme Unction. Suor Monica was a painter of great skill, and she left behind many holy books illustrated by her talented and devoted hand. With great sorrow we grieve for her, and we will always remember her sweetness and patience.

Sofonisba took to her bed, crying inconsolably and refusing food. "Orazio," she howled, "it is more than I can *bear*."

She took out the gold pendant Elena had given her and stared at it, as if to memorize its every detail all over again. Then she closed her fist around it and squeezed it in her palm until her arm ached.

On the third morning, Orazio was surprised to see that a breakfast tray was gone from the table outside their bedroom. He entered to find the tray half-empty, the shutters open, and Sofonisba seated at her dressing table while her maid arranged her hair. The maid put in the last hairpin and left the room.

Orazio sat down on the bed. The red and swollen look of his wife's eyes startled him. "My love, I'm so sorry. I know you and Elena were especially close."

Her words came slowly. "When Papa arranged for me to have painting lessons, he said she could go, too, because he wouldn't dream of separating us."

"Your father was a wise man."

"People said it all the time, 'Ah, of all those Anguissola sisters, that Elena is the most beautiful.' And they were right." She inhaled deeply, let it out. "She had brown eyes, so large and bright, and dark-blond hair that I always wished I had."

"Would you like to go to Mantua?"

"There's no reason for that, now."

"Why don't you have a Mass said for her? It might make you feel better. I'll walk you to the church."

Sofonisba's face darkened. "A Mass. Such a small gesture … Oh, why wasn't I there?"

"There was no time," Orazio said.

They sat in silence for a while. Then Sofonisba said in a low monotone, "Well, yes, then, let's schedule that Mass." She pulled a lacy black veil down over her face. "And I must light a candle, or ten."

After two weeks, Sofonisba returned to the studio. She did a few sketches and carefully prepared a canvas. She depicted the mystical marriage of St. Catherine: the saint knelt before the infant Jesus, who placed a ring on her left hand, while the Virgin, St. Joseph, and St. Anne looked on in wonder. Sofonisba gave the saint Elena's dark blond hair and robust figure. As a nun, Elena, like Catherine, had been a bride of Christ. Sofonisba felt her grief gradually recede with her brushstrokes.

AUGUST, 1588

"O *Dio*, her *breast* is showing!" Orazio nearly shrieked.

"Yes it is. So what do you think?" Sofonisba asked.

"I don't know what to think," Orazio stammered, his eyes fixed on the large oval canvas. "Isn't it a bit, well, unseemly?"

"Some will see it that way. But all I've done is paint the Virgin nursing her Son. How could showing the Virgin's breast be wrong? The early Christians saw nothing wrong with depictions of bared breasts."

"The early Christians did not have to get the approval of popes. Aren't you worried about your reputation?"

"Orazio, I am in my fifty-sixth year now," Sofonisba said. "I'm too old to worry about my reputation. Not too long ago, painters used to depict nursing Madonnas. Even if things have changed and Pope Sixtus denounces me over this painting, I trust that the nobility here in Genoa will still want me to do their portraits. And the painters, well, I think they will still want me to teach them."

"Whew, Sonia. I just don't know," Orazio said. "I like the bright, rich colours, and the Virgin's expression, very tender. And the tones of the Child's skin, and the modelling of his body — it is simply exquisite."

"I've taught you well," Sofonisba smiled. "About painting, that is."

"Everyone will admire those good things — *if* they can see anything other than that bared breast." Orazio stepped back to take a longer view. "You may be overestimating the open-mindedness of the nobility here in Genoa. Who commissioned this, anyway?"

"Giovanna Spinola. She's a very astute art patron. She ordered an oval-shaped Madonna and Child for her bedroom. Other than that, she didn't say how I should handle it, she only said, 'Sonia, be creative.'"

Orazio guffawed. "Well, you've certainly been that! Wait'll she sees exactly how 'creative' you've been!"

Sofonisba paused and looked at the painting thoughtfully. "When I painted at King Philip's court, I had to follow the rules of court portraiture. And they were so limiting! Now that I can be liberal in my work, I want to challenge the idea that expressing purity requires shame of the naked female body. I believe that the Virgin's purity is still evident, even if she is not ashamed that her breast shows."

"I see," Orazio said. "So, when will you show this to Signora Spinola?"

"She asked me to present it at a salon, so I'll do it this afternoon. Please carry it down to the sitting room for me."

⁓

That afternoon, when Sofonisba pulled off the white silk cloth covering the painting, she was greeted with gasps, "Ohs," "Ai-yees!" and chirps of surprise, in varying tones of approval and incomprehension.

Giovanna Spinola was the first to say anything intelligible, and when she did, the room went deadly silent. She said that a mother nursing her child was an intimate act, and that Sofonisba had made it more so, but that she had used sensitivity, and had created something rare and beautiful. Spinola also said she saw the sweetness of Correggio in the painting, and concluded by saying she would be proud to hang it in her home.

At that, everyone began talking at once, congratulating Sofonisba and echoing Spinola's praise. The painter smiled graciously, and Orazio, at the edge of the crowd, regarded her with love and admiration. In the weeks ahead the painting continued to raise spirited debate whenever painters and art patrons gathered. Some judgments were critical and some complimentary, but Sofonisba saw no decline in the flow of commissions and students to her door.

A few weeks later, word reached Genoa of an event that eclipsed any number of bare painted breasts. To turn England from Protestant to Catholic, and to stop English pirates from seizing Spanish galleons full of treasures from the Americas, King Philip had sent an armada of one hundred thirty ships toward England. But the ships, outmaneuvered and incompetently commanded, ended up burned and wrecked off the coasts of Scotland and Ireland. Genoa, as a seafaring city loyal to Philip, talked about it endlessly, in words full of mourning, anxiety, and anger.

MAY, 1591

Sofonisba received a letter from Turin, dashed off with Catalina's usual enthusiasm: "My first daughter is now two years old. Her father gave her a dwarf as a birthday gift — do come and see them!"

"You see, Lina herself had a dwarf as a companion in Madrid. Such a clown! Lina and her sister were devoted to Magdalena," Sofonisba explained to Orazio. "I'm guessing that Lina wants a portrait of her daughter and this new dwarf. I haven't seen her in six years. I'd like to leave for Turin tomorrow."

"Perfect. I'll be heading back to sea tomorrow."

Catalina did indeed want a portrait of child and dwarf. While Sofonisba worked, Catalina read to her from letters she had received from her father, King Philip. He had sent her dozens of them, beginning the day after she left Spain.

"Poor Papa. He's been counting the days since then. I'm saving every one of these letters. He talks about all the things that worry his 'poor head,' and about his son Philip. Then here he says that I might find it better to give birth lying in bed rather than in a birthing chair, and that when it comes to childbirth, he has seen it all."

JULY, 1591

Sofonisba finished the painting and returned to Genoa. She and Orazio, newly returned from his sea voyage, were in their sitting room when a servant, her face tense, appeared in the doorway.

"Well, what is it?"

"It's a message for my lady."

"Bring it here." Sofonisba took the folded parchment from the servant, who ran off.

"I've got to talk to her again about not running in these halls, it makes the whole household chaotic ... Sonia? *O Dio*, bad news?" Orazio asked.

"My mother is dying," Sofonisba gasped. "I must go..."

"We can leave at once. I'll arrange a carriage."

The ride seemed interminable, over roads alternately muddy and rutted. Sofonisba prayed the rosary until she could no longer stand the feeling of the little beads between her fingertips, and she shoved the rosary deep into her single bag.

Early one morning, just east of Piacenza, when she dared to imagine that the tower of Cremona would soon come into sight, the carriage jolted so hard that she was thrown from her seat.

"Sonia, are you all right?" Orazio asked, helping her up.

"I'm all right, just find out why we've stopped," Sofonisba ordered.

An especially deep rut had snapped the rim off one of the carriage wheels. The driver said it would take him a day to have the wheel repaired in the nearby village.

"I can't wait!" Sofonisba wailed. "I'll just take one of the horses."

"Riding the rest of the way? It's nearly fifteen miles!" Orazio said.

"Orazio, you know I'm an excellent rider. I'm going, and that's an end of it." She instructed the driver to unhitch one of the carriage horses and fit it with a bridle. Then she placed a folded blanket on its back. "I'm coming with you," Orazio said, arranging a horse for himself, and they took off down the road. She had travelled the path before but always in a carriage, and could not remember so many hills.

It was evening when she arrived at the family palazzo. Covered with dust and wracked with exhaustion, she cursed the stiff legs that would not quite let her race up the stairs to her mother's room, where Asdrubale and Anna Maria held a candlelit vigil.

"Mama." Sofonisba knelt beside the bed and took Bianca's hand. The greyness of her mother's face stunned her.

"Sonia," Bianca whispered, looking into her daughter's eyes.

"You made it."

"Of course I did, Mama."

"How?"

"On a swift horse."

Bianca closed her eyes. Asdrubale and Anna Maria moved closer. Then the brown eyes flew open.

"Ach …" Bianca's chest rose, and she exhaled her last breath. Sofonisba, still holding her mother's hand, sat back and let the tears rain down.

⌒

Bernardino Campi, now an elder of sixty-nine years, was among the many who came to the Anguissola palazzo to mourn.

"I now live here in Cremona once again. Anna wanted to be near her people, and there was good work for me here," Campi said. "I am so sorry about your mother." He coughed violently.

"Thank you." Sofonisba wanted him to talk on and on, so that she could fully absorb his startlingly changed appearance. Campi's figure was a bit stooped, his beard and thinning hair were grey-white, and many lines spread out around the warm brown eyes.

"I know, you're thinking your former teacher is such an old man now," he said. "Well, more than thirty years have passed."

"The years have been no kinder to me, I'm sure," Sofonisba said.

"Can you get away?" Campi asked. He coughed again. "I'd like to show you something."

They rode in his carriage out the Via Marmolada to the church of San Sigismondo. "This is where your father hired me to be your teacher," Campi said as they walked down the vast nave. "At the time I was painting those frescoes." He indicated Saints Filippo and Giacomo on a chapel vault.

He then led her into a side chapel, where for the altarpiece he had painted St. Cecilia, patron of music, playing the clavichord, watched over by St. Catherine, both elegantly bejewelled and dressed in sumptuous shades of rose, green and blue. On another altarpiece, St. Jerome paused in his studies to gaze heavenward.

They moved back into the nave and stood under the central cupola. "But most of all, I wanted to show you this," Campi said, pointing. "*The Glory of Paradise*. It took me seven months."

Sofonisba looked up to see a complex scene of saints with their symbols, and blessed souls joining the saints in heaven. The whole, even with dozens of figures, achieved a pleasing harmony, and Campi had used perspective masterfully.

They sat down. "Signor Bernardino, all your work here is superb, excellent—" She caught her breath and stopped. "Oh, how arrogant of me, the pupil praising the teacher…"

"Not at all," Campi said. "Sonia, compliments from you mean more to me than any other compliments I will hear, because, well, we both know…"

"Oh, signore, please don't…" Sofonisba said, dreading the road Campi was headed down.

"It's all right, really, how could I not have known it for years? Ever since I saw that double portrait, I knew. How brilliant! A portrait of the teacher painting a portrait of the pupil. What *invenzione!* 'Worthy of Titian of Venice,' I said to Anna. It was clear to me then that you had surpassed me, and I have made my peace with that."

Campi coughed again, and then they sat silently a few moments.

"Signor Bernardino," Sofonisba said, "you told me that a painter must travel, and then you set me on my way. I will never forget that."

Campi smiled. "The good fortune went both ways. Now let's get back inside the city walls before nightfall."

LATE SUMMER, 1591

Sofonisba, while sorting out her mother's things, had found a self-portrait miniature she had done before going to Rome. She took it with her back to Genoa. A few weeks after she returned she received a message that Bernardino Campi had died, while painting frescoes in a church in the town of Reggio, at age sixty-nine.

His death sounded a gong of gloom in her head, seeming to cause all the small bodily difficulties Sofonisba had tried to ignore over the years to suddenly rise up in undeniable revolt. She would soon turn sixty. She cursed the extra time it took her to climb the stairs to her studio. She had to keep her easel near the window, and sometimes painted out on the gallery, to have enough light to help her aging eyes. She let her willing pupils prepare her canvases and grind the pigments for paints.

In honour of her mother, she painted a large but warmly intimate domestic scene with soft-edged figures — *Holy Family with St. Anne and St. John*. Both St. Anne and the Virgin smiled at the curly-haired infant Jesus. The painter placed in one corner a symbol of sadness: a small dog, lying down and ready for sleep. Sofonisba signed her name and the date — 1592 — near the dog's head. She hung the painting in her bedroom.

⌒

Sofonisba resumed the salons. One afternoon Pietro Francesco Piola, a student and frequent guest, handed her a drawing, one of many being passed around the room. "You'll especially like this one," he told her.

The drawing stopped Sofonisba cold. It showed a young man with one bare shoulder poking above his shirt. His forehead was squinched and his mouth was agape as a lizard bit his right hand.

"Who drew this?" she asked the assembled guests.

"Michelangelo Merisi. He goes by 'Caravaggio,' the name of his hometown, east of Milan," Piola said. "He must have been inspired by your drawing of a child bitten by a crab. You know, copies of that sketch have been going around everywhere for decades. Congratulations, Sonia — he's paying you quite a compliment here."

"Caravaggio," she repeated. "Just looking at this, I'd say he shows great promise. And not just because I inspired him!" They all laughed.

"I'd like to meet him some time," Sofonisba added.

"That's inevitable. It seems as if every painter in Italy finds their way to this palazzo eventually," Piola said. "But beware of Caravaggio — they say he has a violent temper."

NOVEMBER, 1597

Sofonisba found herself once more on the muddy road to Turin, *for the last time*, she reflected morosely. Catalina Micaela had just died after giving birth to her tenth child, who also died. Catalina was only thirty years old. Reports arrived from Madrid that King Philip, Catalina's father, was so enraged and broken by grief that he wept and howled and stomped around El Escorial in a way quite uncharacteristic for him, indeed, that no courtier had ever seen before. It was whispered around the palace that the shock and despair would damage Philip's own health, which was dangerously weak.

In the fall of the following year, 1598, lying in his tiny room at El Escorial, surrounded by the treasured holy relics he had long collected, and holding a crucifix, Philip died at age seventy-one, setting off many days of mourning.

Just a few months before, the king completed his last official act. He resolved the long-troubling situation in the Netherlands by making it a separate, semi-independent state and ceding the land to his beloved daughter, Isabel Clara Eugenia. She would rule that country alongside Philip's nephew, Archduke Albert of Austria, whom she married in Valencia in the spring of 1599.

The couple stopped in Genoa on their way to the Netherlands. Twenty colourfully dressed horsemen greeted them at the dock. The city honoured Isabel and Albert with a series of receptions, theatricals, and jousts. Sofonisba and Orazio were among the hosts who held lavish banquets.

"I'm so sorry about your sister and father, may they rest in peace," Sofonisba told Isabel as they sat on a terrace of the bishop's palazzo. "You're the last person left now, of all those I was close to at court."

"Thank you," Isabel said. "I still miss them both, so much."

"Remember when Magdalena Ruiz taught you both how to turn somersaults? It wasn't easy, in your long dresses, but both you and Lina took to somersaulting down the palace corridors. I could hardly keep up. Once, you two rolled right into your father's study," Sofonisba said, and laughed.

"I do remember. Papa couldn't stop laughing. When we were older, Lina and I used to take our meals with Papa, just the three of us."

"After your dear mother died, may her soul rest, you and your sister were the people His Majesty loved more than any others, make no mistake about that," Sofonisba said. "That never changed, even after he married again and fathered more children."

"I'm so glad I could be with him at the end, but señora, it was terrible!" Isabel covered her face with her hands for a moment. "He gave me Mama's wedding ring and told me to keep it always. Then he — oh, his mind went in and out," she moaned. "But he was awake at the very end, just as he wanted to be."

"Now you are left to carry on his work, dear Isabel. It is fitting somehow," Sofonisba said, sitting back and giving the infanta a painterly assessment. "Your dark grey eyes always matched his, and I suspect you have his capacity for hard work. That will serve you well in the Netherlands."

A servant entered and placed a tray on the table. Isabel poured them each some wine and passed a plate of small cakes.

"Papa told me many times how much he admired your work, and that he appreciated your companionship with Mama," Isabel said, taking a sip. "Some years ago he commissioned another woman painter, Lavinia Fontana of Bologna, to paint a Holy Family panel for El Escorial. Did you know? And that's all because of you."

Sofonisba's heart leaped, and she wished she could, too. "Oh Isabel, I can hardly tell you how much it pleases me to hear that," she said.

Isabel then gave Sofonisba's pride another boost. "Señora, I want you to paint my wedding portrait," Isabel said. "Several court painters at El Escorial offered to do it, but I turned them down. I wanted you."

They talked on about the past, then about Isabel's wedding, and Sofonisba's life in Genoa. Finally, Isabel, confident in the closeness between them, said, "Señora, forgive this question, and don't answer if it offends you, but, how old are you now?"

"Ah, Isabel," Sofonisba said. "I am in my sixty-seventh year. My grey hair, my lined face, they show it, I know. But I never complain. You see, two of my sisters died so young…" She sighed. "I, on the other hand, inherited a strong body from some hardy relations. My long life is a gift from God."

In the life-sized portrait, Sofonisba gave Isabel a serious but not grim appearance, in keeping with the important duties that the infanta was about to assume. Isabel wore a dress of sober black velvet, but with a wide jewelled belt, and open sleeves revealing embroidered gold undersleeves. Her neck ruff, shaped from highly intricate lace, sat in many layers. In contrast with her necklace of large pearls, Isabel also wore a simple gold chain with a small statue of St. Anthony of Padua, a gift from her father. For Sofonisba's work, Isabel rewarded her with a gold chain containing rubies, emeralds, and sapphires.

As a new century dawned, fireworks exploded all over Europe, above city squares and streets filled with dancing revellers. After attending Mass, Orazio and Sofonisba stood on their upper gallery and watched Genoa's celebration burst over the harbour. Sofonisba did not regret that her body would not let her keep up with the

dancers below; she had danced enough in her youth. She squeezed
Orazio's hand.

APRIL, 1603

Spring brought a mysterious visitor to Sofonisba's sitting room. A
young noblewoman — or at least that was what Sofonisba concluded from her gown and feathered hat — asked her whether she
resembled anyone whom Sofonisba knew.

The painter took a long look, but her eyesight had not been keen
for some years, and she was in no mood for riddles.

"No, young lady, you do not."

The visitor smiled and said she was Juana, a daughter of Don Juan,
King Philip's half-brother, the hero of Lepanto. Then Sofonisba
remembered — Don Juan, that rake whom some thought was so
charming. She had not thought about him since leaving Madrid.
She asked Juana to sit down.

Juana was born in Naples and had spent the thirty years of her
life there. She explained that she was about to be married, and had
come to Genoa to visit some relations. While in the city she had
met Giovanna Spinola, who recommended that Juana commission
Sofonisba to paint her wedding portrait. Giovanna had told Juana
about Sofonisba's time at the royal court in Madrid.

Juana said she did not remember her father, being only in her
fifth year when he died at the age of thirty-one. Sofonisba told her
about painting his portrait when he was thirteen years old. She did
not tell her about her father's ardent pursuit of women, which at
that time was just beginning.

Sofonisba painted Juana full-length in a black velvet gown,
brightened by gold-embroidered red silk undersleeves. She wore a
thick and wide neck ruff. Sofonisba did not know how young women
could bear them, but that was the fashion. She held a folded fan in
her right hand and a handkerchief in her left. In the background

stood half of a Habsburg column and a distant view of a town.

Sofonisba considered it one of the best paintings of her Genoa time. She was surprised and proud she could do it at her advanced age.

AUGUST, 1605

The pounding on the palazzo door and subsequent shouting came late in the night, its sound so loud and persistent that it carried up to the third floor. Sofonisba and Orazio were well aware of it before a servant tapped with a frightened staccato on their bedroom door.

"Signore, signora, please come quick, a stranger is downstairs, and he may be a madman!"

"I'll go," Orazio said, pulling on clothes and shoes. "Jesus, Mary, and Joseph," he muttered on his way down the stairs. From his study he grabbed a dagger.

"Let me in!" a voice screamed, while fists continued pounding on the kitchen door. "Let me in, or by God, I'll kill you!"

"Quiet down, man, and don't threaten me at my own house!" Orazio yelled through the door. The servant, behind him, held up a lantern. Orazio unbolted the door and opened it a crack, holding the dagger high. "Who are you?"

"I am Michelangelo Merisi," said a ghost of a man, eyes wide with terror, his clothes dirty and tattered. "The painter called Caravaggio. This is the home of the woman painter from Cremona, Sofonisba Anguissola, yes?" the man asked.

"Sofonisba Anguissola de Lomellini, yes, and what could you possibly want with my wife?" Orazio said.

"They say she takes in painters. That they all come here. I am desperate. Please let me in."

Orazio looked over the absurd figure, noted the scraggly beard and wild hair. He opened the door and Caravaggio dashed inside.

"Thank you, thank you," the painter whispered.

"What in the world…?" Sofonisba had come down to the kitchen.

"This man says he is Michelangelo Merisi, the painter who calls himself Caravaggio," Orazio said.

"I *am* Caravaggio, signora, a poor and desperate painter," with one hand over his heart.

Sofonisba took the lantern from the servant and sent her to bed. "Now, signore, why are you so desperate?" she asked.

"There was trouble, you see," Caravaggio said, eyes darting. "A notary in Rapallo — we had words. For a notary, he certainly was strong. I had to defend myself, and then I had to flee."

There came another knock at the door, this one only a bit less panicked.

"Aaagh! They're coming for me!" Caravaggio whispered loudly. "Hide me!"

"Here," Sofonisba pointed to the dark corner behind a wine vat.

"I won't hide a criminal here!" Orazio said.

"It's just until we find out who's at the door," Sofonisba said.

The new visitor was a neighbour who had heard Caravaggio's uproarious arrival and worried about the safety of Orazio and Sofonisba. "Everything's quite all right," Orazio assured him. "Just a vagabond who we sent on his way." The neighbour left.

"Whew," Caravaggio said as he stood up. "Perhaps the Lord will let me live through the night after all."

"Excuse us a moment, signore," Orazio said, and he and Sofonisba stepped away. "He can't stay here, Sonia! If he's killed somebody, it's too risky!"

"Oh, I don't think he's killed anybody," Sofonisba said.

"You always think all painters are blameless."

"I do not! Didn't I ever tell you about Alonso Sánchez Coello?"

"Not now. Caravaggio can sleep out with the horses — I'll show him where. Then we'll deal with him in the morning."

As the bells of the nearby church tolled seven the next morning,

Sofonisba crossed the bright courtyard to the stables, accompanied by a servant carrying a tray of bread and butter and some fruit. "Please stay," Sofonisba directed the servant, recalling the stories told about Caravaggio. In the back of the stables they could see only Caravaggio's head where he stood behind a hay bale, facing the wall. Sofonisba said loudly, "*Buon giorno*, signore," and he walked toward them, adjusting his clothes.

"Ah, *buon giorno* good signora, how pleased I am to see you before I leave, so that I can thank you for your trouble."

The three sat down on hay bales. "Here, eat something," Sofonisba said, and the young painter eagerly cleared the tray. While he ate, Sofonisba studied his face, a lifelong habit.

"You see, signora, I do not sleep well, because of, ah, troubles I have…"

"Now, I truly don't care what happened in Rapallo," Sofonisba said. "If anyone catches up with you here, understand, I won't be able to hide you. But I must be certain about something else. Have you ever seen a copy of my drawing of a boy being bitten by a crab?"

Caravaggio smiled. "Now you've found me out, signora." He yawned and ran a hand through curly dark hair. "You must have seen my drawing of a young man's encounter with a lizard." Sofonisba nodded, and Caravaggio went on. "I think every painter in northern Italy, maybe the whole peninsula, has seen and admired a copy of your drawing of that crying boy. I took one look, and it was like a bolt went through me. I studied it for days, going over every stroke." The painter used his hands to help tell the story. "The boy's squinting eyes, his full round cheeks, the exquisite form of both his hands, the girl's arm around him in a gesture of comfort. I bow to your genius, signora. My drawing is a pale imitation. I also did two painted versions."

"It was you in your drawing, wasn't it? I remember now the thick hair, those full lips."

"It was indeed me. Like you, signora, I do many self-portraits," he said. Then he stood up. "I must go now. I've imposed on your household long enough."

"But where, pray, will you go?"

"Up the coast into France, and then, it depends which way the wind blows."

"Take this," Sofonisba said, and handed him some florins tied inside a cloth. "You'll need it."

"Ohhh, a thousand thanks, signora, you are too kind. I will repay you," Caravaggio vowed.

Sofonisba walked Caravaggio across the courtyard and through the gate to the street. "Thank you for the many compliments, and God be with you," she said, and watched as he blended into the animated crowd of the Genoese morning.

She found Orazio in his study.

"Caravaggio is gone. Now, let me tell you about the Spanish painter Alonso Sánchez Coello…"

MAY, 1610

King Philip III of Spain, who despite his poor health had succeeded his father, asked Sofonisba to send him a self-portrait. She portrayed herself in an unadorned black velvet gown and a white ruff. Her hair, now a dark grey, was pulled back under a white cap and filmy veil. In her left hand she held a book, and in her right, a card with writing on it: "To his Catholic Majesty, I kiss your hand. Anguissola."

"You don't spare yourself, that's certain," Orazio said. "Every wrinkle in your face and hands is there."

"Ha, no, I left out a few," Sofonisba said. "I do have a tiny bit of vanity. Anyway, I'm seventy-eight. I've no need to spare myself. And that ruff is not wide enough for the current fashion, but plenty wide for an old lady."

"The writing on that card — so your devotion to the royal family goes on," Orazio said.

"Well, we lived hand in glove, for many years. I won't forget that."

"My dear, this shows you as the dignified, elegant matriarch of painting in Europe. And it also shows that your old painting skills are still there," Orazio said.

"Ahhh, praise be, love, that's just what I intended."

10.

Sicily Reclaimed

I live, I die, I burn, and I drown.
I feel extreme heat in enduring cold.
Life for me is too soft and too hard,
I have great troubles mixed with joy.

—Louise Labé (1526-1566)

JUNE, 1615

Sofonisba sat on the deck of a galley taking her to her new home
in Sicily, a place she had long wished to never see again.

Orazio had retired as a ship's captain, having reached the age
when sailing the Mediterranean was too rigorous. Restless in Genoa,
he told Sofonisba that the winters in Sicily were warmer, and the
pace of life quieter, and surely that would appeal to her, although
he had other, more ambitious reasons for wanting to live there.

Sofonisba agreed with him about the appeal of calmness. She had
dearly loved her life in Genoa for many years, leading the artists
there, teaching and inspiring them. Someone had deemed her the
grande dame of painters. But as she grew older and her body faltered,
she could no longer help each painter in the way she wished. Fatigue always set in too soon, and her eyes became more and more
unreliable. She decided it was time to let the younger generation
of painters take her place.

She also agreed that Orazio deserved his own time. His real motive for wanting to leave was to run the ship chandlery he owned in Palermo, and to preside over the six hundred Genoese merchants who lived there. Also, he longed for public office, and in Palermo he had a chance.

It was all so sensible, so reasonable. Still, Sofonisba's memories made her hesitate. While her private life with Fabrizio in Sicily had been joyous, she had not forgotten the awful aspects of those years on that island, fighting with Fabrizio's relations over his inheritance. Her painting had suffered, and there was the frequent threat of plague. Finally came the worst pain of all...

Orazio reassured her that their lives would be different. While she had indeed experienced some painful years in Sicily, they were long past. The couple would live in Palermo, not Paternò as Sofonisba had before, and Fabrizio's family held far less influence these days. With Orazio's connections, he and Sofonisba would be the powerful ones.

A message from Palermo secured Sofonisba's confidence in the move. Orazio's son Giulio, a father of three boys, had just sired a daughter. Orazio had told Giulio much about Sofonisba, and even though the two had never met, Giulio wanted to name the girl after Sofonisba, and he asked the painter to be the girl's godmother. She simply could not refuse that.

In her chair on the galley deck, she noticed that the sky had turned an ashy grey. The wind smelled salty-fresh and felt pleasingly cool on her face and hands. She looked toward the Italian coast as the galley glided by. She loved that land, but found that she could sail away from it without distress. This separation from the peninsula of her birth and of her family did not feel like a wrench to the heart, as she had suffered when she departed for Spain long ago.

Now, she had so little family left. Four years before she had lost her last sister, Anna Maria, she of the dark hair and eyes. Of course, that dark hair had faded — Anna Maria had lived to her sixty-sixth year. Sofonisba thought back to the days when she taught her to paint in the studio in Cremona. She had rich memories of working with Anna Maria on a *Madonna with the Christ Child and St. John.* It was the best panel they had done together, and they both signed it. Then Anna Maria painted her own *Holy Family with St. John* for the church of Sant'Agata. But Sofonisba's favourite of all Anna Maria's works was her *Holy Family with St. Francis.* In it, the Virgin held her infant up on his feet, and his right heel was raised — a charming detail. Anna Maria poured sweetness into the faces of her subjects in that work, yet she was not afraid to include the death symbol: a skull. It still saddened Sofonisba that her youngest sister had died before her.

Anna Maria never had any children. Sofonisba counted the family who remained: Anna Maria's beloved husband, Europa's daughter Bianca, Asdrubale, and herself.

♾

To Artemisia Gentileschi of Florence
April 12, 1616

Dear Signora Gentileschi,

I am so pleased to hear of your many accomplishments as a painter in Florence. I first learned of them when I lived in Genoa, where copies of studies for your paintings often circulated among the many painters I knew.

My reason for writing is that I felt compelled to offer you my heartiest congratulations on having been elected to the Accademia delle Arti del Disegno of Florence. Your entry into that august group is much greater than any ordinary entry, because you are the first woman to receive that honour. It fills me with pride for our gender because, although women painters have much skill and are fully capable of displaying that prized quality — *invenzione* — we are not always fully recognized and appreciated. It is a situation I know all too well. Many years ago I applied to the painters' guild of Cremona, and was rejected solely because of my gender. There is no denying that it was a painful rebuff. While I never forgot it, I do not dwell upon it.

We women who paint are called marvels, or miracles, or wonders, as if we cannot create great paintings through talent and dedication, but rather require the help of some unnatural entity. Those who praise us are often quick to add comments on our moral virtue and goodness — two traits seldom valued in painters of the male gender. Do not be fooled, I beseech you!

You and I have in common the painting of many portraits and religious scenes. I, like you, have painted *Judith Slaying Holofernes*. The heroism of that story is irresistible! I also saw a sketch of your *Susanna and the Elders*. You handled the modeling and the twisted pose of her naked body so well — and painting nudes is sometimes considered beyond a woman's talents — and you convey powerfully the drama and tension of the scene. The tastes of art patrons change with the years, and I am glad that you are free to paint women's flesh so lavishly and unashamedly, in this and other works, a choice that was denied to me when I began as a painter many years ago.

Continue in your praiseworthy efforts, do not be deterred by anyone or anything. God grant you many happy and fruitful years ahead.

Sofonisba Anguissola de Lomellini

PALERMO, 1620

The studio was silent, as usual. Indeed, it had never rung with the voices and exuberance of students. It was on the palazzo's ground floor, to save Sofonisba's legs. On this day, Sofonisba thought that the stillness seemed especially appropriate, like the quiet of the tomb or a graveyard, because she was placing the last touches on her final painting. It had to be a self-portrait. Old age had made her sketching and painting methods more deliberate and labourious, so she could not expect anyone to pose. She set the easel next to a window, sat down and pulled the easel so close that the canvas was inches from her eyes. Beside the easel sat a mirror, almost as close.

She portrayed herself in a simple black dress, seated against a plain grey-green background, with a long black shawl pulled over her shoulders. Her grey hair was parted in the middle and partly hidden under a white silk cap.

When she showed it to Orazio, he was so moved he feared he would break down. "As usual, you don't spare yourself," he said, forcing his voice not to crack. *The eyes, they're of different sizes — she can't see herself well in the mirror. Her vision is worse than I thought.*

"The hands are delicate and lovely," he added. *Not at all realistic, but she's entitled to flatter herself.*

"Thank you, Orazio. Now let's go out to the garden."

An eager young painter from Antwerp, Anthony Van Dyck, a passenger on a Genoese galley, bided his time at sea by writing in his journal.

May 12, 1624

At last I'm sailing toward Palermo. What finally put me on this awful ship was an invitation from Emanuele Filiberto, viceroy of Sicily. He wants me to come to Sicily to paint his portrait, to commemorate his appointment as viceroy. But I anticipate an even greater joy in Palermo: meeting the Cremonese woman painter, Sofonisba Anguissola.

I heard much about her in Genoa while I stayed there with my uncles. It seems she was the matriarch, if I can use that word, of Genoa's artistic community. She was without a doubt the city's leading portraitist, and she painted many members of the nobility, showing insight and unsurpassed skill. Artists also told me about her generosity as a teacher, and her extensive hospitality. She gave many a struggling painter not only encouragement, but a discreet "loan" of a roll of coins. There's even a story about her helping that knave, the late Michelangelo Merisi, the one they call Caravaggio, when he fled from Rome or somewhere after yet another foolish tussle. I decided I had to meet this extraordinary woman, who has now lived in Sicily for several years.

May 15, 1624

We have dropped anchor well off Palermo and don't dare come in to dock because of horrible news — the plague has broken out, and has begun to ravage the city. Many passengers are refusing to go ashore, and according to custom, the captain cannot require them to disembark. We sit here in a state of floating confusion as everyone tries to decide what to do. In my eagerness to meet Signora Anguissola, I would have been the first one off this ship, but now...

May 30, 1624

Plague or no plague, I can stand it no longer. The passengers on this stranded ship are crazed with anxiety, the food and fresh water are running low, and restlessness is overtaking my fear. My people are hardy Flemish stock, so maybe I can evade the plague long enough to paint the viceroy and meet Signora Anguissola. The captain said a rowboat will take me and a few others ashore at dawn tomorrow.

June 15, 1624

It's a strange and hideous thing to be in a city under the siege of plague.

Nearly all normal traffic has disappeared from the streets — even the disposal of the dead must wait. If a stray cat or dog toys with the rags used to wrap the dead, that poor animal will shortly suffer convulsions and death.

I am now installed at the viceroy's country villa. It is the nature of the plague that there are occasional brief respites, and when one occurs, I will send a message to Sofonisba Anguissola, to request a meeting with her. Until then I concentrate on the viceroy's portrait, and pray that God spares Signora Anguissola long enough for me to meet her.

July 11, 1624

And now at last the lull, although no one would say that the danger has lifted completely. The pause allows the bodies of the dead to be hauled away. On some days there are too many to carry off, or no one wants to touch them, and they are left lying in wretched piles on the street.

I am taking advantage of this pause to go into the city to meet Sofonisba Anguissola. The viceroy understands my eagerness, and doesn't mind a slight delay in my finishing his portrait. A carriage will take me to the city's southern gate.

The young man hurried through the streets, pressing a perfumed handkerchief to his nose. His stomach lurched at the sight of dead bodies still lying in doorways. The few living people he saw, also hurrying and silent, carried flowers or bundles of herbs or spices, which they breathed into against the pervading stench. He wondered if he were smelling hell itself — a putrid blend of decaying flesh and acrid garbage. Above it all hung an eerie quiet. Where were the cries of the fishmongers, the fruit sellers, the dozens of other street vendors? Where were the carriages, the beggars, the running children? Even the stray dogs and cats had fled, revolted at last.

He passed the church of San Giorgio dei Genovesi. In the church-yard, bodies lay stacked in ghastly disarray, outnumbering the people left to bury and mourn them. None of the dead would have the dignity of a separate grave. Two desultory phantoms, gloved and masked to reveal only their vacant eyes, moved among the defunct, throwing and pushing them like dead goats into a deep trench.

The young man was relieved to arrive at an impressive three-story palazzo of massive rusticated stones in the ancient Arab quarter. As the maid led him up the stairs, he removed his cap and tried to put in order his mass of wavy brown hair.

"Step over here, to where I can see you." It was a voice creaky with age, but audible and decisive. The old woman sat framed between two inlaid wooden tables.

Van Dyck set down his bag and walked across the red-tiled floor.

"So, Signor Van Dyck, you wanted to see me so much that you braved this horrid plague," Sofonisba said. "I'm honoured." She wore a black gown and a white linen veil that trailed down both shoulders, pushed back just far enough on her head to reveal a bit of grey hair.

"Signora Anguissola, I'm the one who is honoured. Please ex-cuse my poor Italian." As he took her outstretched hand in both of his, Sofonisba thought, *Ah, the long, tapering fingers of a painter.* Van Dyck, for his part, noticed her bulging finger joints, and how the backs of her hands were veined as if with mad strokes of blue paint. *But these hands held the tools of her brilliance*, he told himself, and they did not tremble.

"It's a thrill to have a young man pay me a call." Her speech had a slow cadence. "And a painter at that. Now do sit down, right there. How are your people in Antwerp?"

"They're fine, thank you, signora. Now, all the painters I knew in Genoa said they missed you, and they highly recommended that I try to meet you. You're still quite legendary there. And pray tell, how are your people in Cremona?"

"Hmm. 'My people in Cremona,'" Sofonisba said without bit-terness. "It's kind of you to ask — my five sisters are all gone, and my only brother, Asdrubale, died last year…" she sighed, "in the spring, may he rest in peace — now, in Cremona, I have only a niece, who is getting on in years but is quite well, God be praised." She exhaled heavily.

"Indeed, God be praised," Van Dyck said, shifting awkwardly. He thought he could spend hours studying the paintings and tapestries he saw everywhere.

"Did you know that I turned ninety-two this year?" Sofonisba continued. "I don't paint anymore. The eyes — it's the cruellest thing for a painter. I was able to design the decoration of this room." She took one of her frequent pauses for breath. "But I couldn't carry it out myself. Orazio hired some painters, and it was great fun to order them about. They did all that." Sofonisba waved a hand toward gaily painted flowers and leaves bordering windows that admitted some July sunlight.

She adjusted the flat starched white collar that set off her pale, lined face, with its sunken cheeks and fleshy jawline.

"How I miss painting," she sighed. "I loved getting inside my subject, finding some aspect of — personality, then conveying it in their expression and posture — and that's what you must do, young man." She paused, then took a deep breath and let it out slowly. "I loved planning all the — details of costume, the objects, the background. Then applying the pigment just so," she raised an imaginary brush in her right hand. *Cough.* She shook her head and dropped her hand. "Ah, I miss it all, even the smell of a fresh canvas! Then when it's finished, ah, the joy of standing back to behold it — now, I have to hold things close to see them — and I'm not sure I could handle a brush for long." She flipped one hand dismissively. "Ach, here I am, already going on like an old lady! Ha! Tell me, Signor Van Dyck, how goes your portrait of the viceroy?"

"Oh yes, he sends his regards. The portrait is going rather well. He was a very patient sitter for such a busy man. I want to get the engraved detail in his armour as beautifully precise as you always did in your portraits of prominent men, the same as you painted the designs in the fabric of women's dresses. I saw many of your portraits in Genoa."

Sofonisba smiled. "You're very kind, signore. I knew Emanuele as a baby in Turin — oh, that was long ago — when I used to visit his mother, the infanta, um … yes, Catalina, that's it, God rest her soul … I painted her portrait several times — and her first daughter, now what was her name … 'M' something, Minerva? No, that was my sister — she died so young…" She hesitated and looked away. "Margaret, maybe."

"Yes, the viceroy spoke about you, and how close you were to his mother," Van Dyck said. He had noticed that Sofonisba's left eye was red-rimmed.

"Ah, I feel it, now you're giving me the artist's eye, just as Maestro Buonarroti did when I first met him," she said.

Van Dyck's brown eyes widened. "You met *il Divino?*"

She nodded. "I was twenty-two, and he was seventy-nine. Do you see a miniature self-portrait on this table? Should be there — that's how I looked back then. I wanted to see Rome, of course, like any painter, but the real reason for the journey was to meet him." She coughed and cleared her throat. "I was so afraid he was just indulging me to be polite. But I took lessons from him every day for months — *his* idea! Even though his gout was bothering him."

"That must have been just wondrous and magnificent," Van Dyck said, and sighed.

"Ye-es, it was wondrous and magnificent." Sofonisba chuckled. "He helped me with — anatomy, perspective, composition. That, too, was a long time ago. I've forgotten some things, but you don't forget meeting such a man."

Van Dyck looked at her with renewed admiration. "Signora, may I sketch you while we talk?"

Sofonisba cocked her head. "Did I hear you right? You want to sketch me, an old woman of ninety-two?" She inhaled deeply.

"Not an old woman, but Sofonisba Anguissola, *la Maestra*."

"Ah, once again, signore, you are very kind. Well, all right then. Just don't get too close — and don't sketch me from too high an angle, or too low. If you do, my wrinkles will show too much."

Van Dyck retrieved his bag from across the room. He pulled out a sketchbook, opened a jar of ink, and lifted a quill.

11.

Farewell

Palermo, November 17, 1625
To Her Grace, Governor of the Spanish Netherlands
Archduchess of Austria, Isabel Clara Eugenia

Your Grace,

Often we have heard here in Palermo of your most able rule over the Low Countries, despite the recent troubles. I praise your dedication and talents in government, no doubt inspired and taught by your highly esteemed father, our late King Philip II, may he rest in God's embrace.

My own world has unfortunately gone dim and silent, for my dear wife and companion, my Sonia, has left it for the next. She died in my arms after making her peace with God. She had spent nine decades on this earth, and it was enough. We were together as husband and wife for nearly forty-six years.

We buried my Sonia yesterday in our church of San Giorgio. I plan to have a memorial built for her, a simple marble tomb that will tell all who see it that she was among the illustrious women of the world.

Sonia often spoke warmly about being your companion and teacher in your earliest years, and how much she treasured the time she spent in Spain at your father's court. She loved you dearly, and was exceedingly proud of the woman you became. Her visit with you when you passed through Genoa shortly after your wedding was a precious gift of our years in that city.

One special joy of her final years was the visits she received from Anthony Van Dyck, whom you wisely chose as your court painter. I am sure he told you about the long, collegial conversations that he had with Sonia — she was glad to share her love and knowledge of painting. She told me that Van Dyck flattered her without fawning, which she would have hated.

May you continue in your just and capable government, Your Grace, alongside your honourable husband, and may God grant many happy years to both of you.

Your most humble servant,
Orazio di Niccolò Lomellini

Epilogue

The first two words of Wendy Wasserstein's 1988 play *The Heidi Chronicles* are "Sofonisba Anguissola." They are spoken by the title character, an art history professor who, during a lecture, laments that even though Anguissola was considered in the seventeenth century to be on a par with Titian, she is not mentioned in the textbooks that the professor's students use.

Those seventeenth-century observers may have been overstating Anguissola's abilities, although some of her works were misattributed to Titian and other painters. In any case, there is no denying Anguissola's great achievements, and for most of her life, her work was well-known throughout Europe and she enjoyed international celebrity. A few references to women artists appeared in writings on painting in the 1500s and grew in the 1800s and the early part of the twentieth century. Anguissola and Rosalba Carriera of Venice are mentioned in *A Short History of Italian Painting,* written in 1914. But women artists were left out of the major surveys of Western art written in the 1950s and 1960s. So what happened? Why did Anguissola and other women artists disappear from the written record?

Women were never included in art history in the same way that men were. Giovanni Boccaccio, writing in the 1300s in a book praising accomplished women, said about a woman artist of antiquity: "I thought that these achievements merited some praise because the art of painting is mostly alien to the feminine mind and cannot be attained without that great intellectual concentration which women, as a rule, are very slow to acquire" (251). When writers on art throughout the 1600s and 1700s described Anguissola, they all mentioned her nobility; some noted she was beautiful and well-educated, was paid large sums of money and received lavish gifts. By contrast, descriptions of male artists rarely mentioned their social class, appearance, or education. Little was said about Anguissola's abilities as an artist, perhaps because many of those writers had not seen enough of her works. They quoted Giorgio Vasari and mentioned that Michelangelo admired Anguissola's drawing of the boy with the pinched finger.

In the 1700s, academies in Rome and Paris became centres for art education. Women were, for the most part, barred from academy membership, a situation that isolated them from intellectual and theoretical debates in the arts. They could not take life drawing classes, an exclusion that left them insufficiently trained to do history painting, thereby closing them out of the genre considered by the nineteenth century to be the most significant and praiseworthy.

At about that time, the categories of "woman artist" and "female school" began. Separate paths of art history were written for men and women. The Victorian view was that men could design great buildings, carve monumental sculpture, and create paintings in the respected genres. Women, on the other hand, were innately untalented, and nature had predisposed them to "feminine" subjects and techniques: portraits, pastels, miniatures, and flowers. Once women artists were separated in this way, it was easy to ignore them altogether. Portraiture and still-life — genres considered proper for women — were regarded as too unchallenging to be significant.

Art history in its modern form, born in the twentieth century, largely carried on Victorian notions about women and art, and maintained that women were naturally of lesser ability and therefore of no historical importance as artists. In 1915, art critic Claude

Phillips sank to the lowest level of commentary on Anguissola when he wrote: "Sofonisba painted with something of that tepid rose-tinted sentimentality proper to the woman-painter, then as now" (Cook 235-36). According to art historian Ann Sutherland Harris, women artists confronted the belief that women simply did not have the potential for artistic genius (Harris and Nochlin 28).

It was not until the second wave of the modern women's movement in the 1960s and 1970s that feminist art historians retrieved Anguissola and other women artists. Art historian Ilya Sandra Perlingieri said in a 1988 article that despite years of studying art history, she had not heard of Anguissola until she saw one of the painter's self-portraits in a Los Angeles exhibit of women artists in 1976 (54). Anguissola is now mentioned in first-year art history courses, and women artists are now to be found in commonly used textbooks, including recent editions of textbooks that once excluded them.

Anguissola's second husband, Orazio Lomellini, did build a tomb for her, in the church of San Giorgio dei Genovesi in Palermo. The date in the inscription is 1632. That suggests that Anguissola's birth year, much debated by art historians, was 1532. Lomellini could well have chosen to build the tomb in the year that would have been the centenary of her birth.

The epitaph in the white marble says that she was beautiful and gifted and a woman of accomplishment. It also mentions her husband's sorrow over losing her, and says that her talent as a portraitist was unequalled.

As a woman, Anguissola found herself restricted to certain genres such as portraiture, but she took that limitation and turned it into a triumph. The faces still intrigue us — a king, queens, nobility, clergy, children, soldiers, her family, a servant. She also excelled with her numerous and thoughtful self-portraits, from teenager to octogenarian, full of revealing iconography and in a variety of formats, situations, and sizes. She painted them at a time when self-portraiture was still fairly rare and novel, and she contributed greatly to the establishment of that genre. It later became an important area of art activity for such male painters as Rembrandt. Unsurprisingly, when done by a male painter, the genre gained respect. It is an unjust irony that the diminished position of women painters in Anguissola's time was partly due to their pursuit of portraiture, one of the few genres open to them.

Anguissola dared to go beyond portraiture of individual subjects, to try unusual, more complex compositions. Before her, no one had thought to place upper-class subjects in informal domestic settings. With her painting of her sisters playing chess, she innovated the genre of intimate household scenes in which subjects posed naturally, a century before it became a staple of Dutch and Flemish painters (Perlingieri 1992: 210). Another example of her progress beyond individual portraits is her group painting of Minerva, Amilcare, and Asdrubale.

It is a testament to her achievement that Anguissola had a strong influence on other painters, both women and men. Caravaggio's painting of a young man bitten by a lizard is an early example. Anguissola's portrait of Elisabeth of Valois served as the model for the 1606 portrait of the Marchesa Brigida Spinola Doria by Peter Paul Rubens. Anguissola may have met Rubens in Genoa.

Anguissola's painting of Margaret of Savoy as a child with her dwarf served as the forerunner for two paintings: Diego Velázquez' *Prince Balthazar Carlos with a Dwarf* from 1631, and the renowned *Las Meninas* of 1656, now a treasure of the Prado collection. Anguissola's 1561 portrait of Alessandro Farnese was copied in a fresco at the villa of his uncle, Cardinal Alessandro Farnese, at Caprarola, north of Rome.

It was common for portrait painters at royal courts to copy portraits that were considered especially good. Juan Pantoja de la

Cruz, who became the official painter to the son and heir of King Philip II, copied some of Anguissola's.

When King Philip II asked Lavinia Fontana of Bologna to paint a Holy Family for El Escorial in 1589, he was making a request that could not be imagined if Anguissola had not spent so many years in Spain, paving the way for women painters. Fontana also painted several large altarpieces. A patron once asked Fontana for a small, round self-portrait in the same vein as Anguissola's 1552 miniature now in Boston, and Fontana revelled in the connection with the celebrated Anguissola.

We will let Fontana have the last word. In a time when the Italian word *virtù* did not signify moral rectitude but excellence and extraordinary ability, Fontana (in a letter of 1579) acknowledged "the virtue and worth of the Signora Sofonisba" (Murphy 26).

WORKS CITED

Boccaccio, Giovanni. *Famous Women*. Ed. and trans. from Latin by Virginia Brown. Cambridge, MA: Harvard University Press, 2001. Print.

Brown, Alice Van Vechten, and William Rankin. *A Short History of Italian Painting*. London: J.M. Dent & Sons Ltd., 1914. Print.

Cook, Herbert. "More Portraits by Sofonisba Anguissola." *The Burlington Magazine for Connoisseurs* 26 (144) (March 1915): 228-36. Print.

Harris, Ann Sutherland, and Linda Nochlin. *Women Artists, 1550-1950*. Exhibition catalog. Los Angeles County Museum of Art, 1976; New York: Alfred A. Knopf, 1989. Print.

Murphy, Caroline P. "The Economics of the Woman Artist." *Italian Women Artists – From Renaissance to Baroque*. Exhibition catalog. National Museum of Women in the Arts, Washington, DC, 2007. Milan: Skira Editore S.p.A., 2007. 23-30. Print.

Perlingieri, Ilya Sandra. "Strokes of Genius." *Ms.* 17 (3) (September

1988): 54-57. Print.

Perlingieri, Ilya Sandra. *Sofonisba Anguissola: The First Great Woman Artist of the Renaissance*. New York: Rizzoli International Publications, 1992. Print.

Wasserstein, Wendy. *The Heidi Chronicles and Other Plays*. San Diego: Harcourt Brace Jovanovich Publishers, 1990. Print.

List of Works

An "Anguissola tour" would take the traveller to several countries, mainly in Europe. In addition to being the first Italian woman to achieve fame as an artist, Anguissola is also the first for whom a substantial collection of works remains. Unfortunately, some of them, in Europe and elsewhere, are not on display in the museums that possess them. Attribution of some of the works is in dispute, and the year of creation is an estimate for many of them.

1545 — *Self-portrait with Old Woman*, chalk sketch, Gabinetto dei Disegni, Uffizi Gallery, Florence, Italy.

1548 — *Self-portrait*, chalk sketch, Gabinetto dei Disegni, Uffizi Gallery, Florence, Italy.

1550 — *Pietà*, oil on canvas, Pinacoteca di Brera, Milan, Italy.

1550 — *Bernardino Campi Painting Sofonisba Anguissola*, oil on canvas, Pinacoteca Nazionale, Siena, Italy.

1551 — *Portrait of a Nun*, oil on canvas, Southampton City Art Gallery, Southampton, England.

1552 — *Self-portrait*, oil on canvas, Uffizi Gallery, Florence, Italy.

1552 — *Self-portrait*, oil on copper miniature, Museum of Fine Arts, Boston, Massachusetts, USA.

1554 — *Boy Being Bitten by a Crab*, sketch, Gabinetto dei Disegni, Museo Nazionale di Capodimonte, Naples, Italy.

1554 — *Self-portrait*, oil on panel, Kunsthistorisches Museum, Vienna, Austria.

1555 — *Self-portrait at the Clavichord*, oil on canvas, Museo Nazionale di Capodimonte, Naples, Italy.

1555 — *The Chess Game*, oil on canvas, Museum Narodowe, Poznan, Poland.

1555 — *Portrait of a Dominican Astronomer*, oil on canvas, formerly in The Caligaris Collection, Terzo d'Aquileia, Italy; current whereabouts unknown.

1556 — *Self-portrait at the Easel*, oil on canvas, Muzeum Zamek Łancut, Łancut, Poland.

1556— *Portrait of Asdrubale Anguissola*, oil on panel, Museo Civico ala Ponzone, Cremona, Italy.

1556 — *Portrait of a Lady* (possibly Bianca Ponzone Anguissola), oil on panel, Museo Civico ala Ponzone, Cremona, Italy.

1556 — *Portrait of a Dominican Monk*, oil on canvas, Pinacoteca Tosio Martinengo, Brescia, Italy.

1556 — *Portrait of a Monk*, oil on canvas, private collection, England.

1556 — *Portrait of Giorgio Giulio Clovio*, oil on canvas, Zeri Collection, Mentana, Italy.

1557— *Portrait of Massimiliano Stampa*, oil on canvas, The Walters Art Museum, Baltimore, Maryland, USA.

1557 — *Portrait of Three Children*, oil on panel, Lord Methuen Collection, Corsham Court, Wiltshire, England.

1557 — *Portrait of Amilcare, Minerva, and Asdrubale Anguissola*, oil on canvas, Nivaagaards Malerisamling, Nivå, Denmark.

1558 — *Portrait of a Nun*, oil on canvas, Borghese Gallery, Rome, Italy.

1558 — *Portrait of an Old Man*, oil on canvas, Burghley House, Stamford, Lincolnshire, England.

1558 — *Portrait of a Lady*, oil on canvas, Staatliche Museen zu Berlin, Berlin, Germany.

1559 — *Holy Family*, oil on canvas, Accademia Carrara, Bergamo, Italy.

1560 — *Portrait of Don Carlos*, oil on canvas, Prado Museum, Madrid, Spain.

1561 — *Self-portrait*, oil on canvas, Pinacoteca di Brera, Milan, Italy.

1561 — *Self-portrait at the Clavichord*, oil on canvas, Earl Spencer Collection, Althorp, England.

1561 — *Portrait of Queen Isabel de Valois*, oil on canvas, Pinacoteca di Brera, Milan, Italy.

1561 — *Portrait of Queen Isabel de Valois*, oil on canvas, Kunsthistorisches Museum, Vienna, Austria.

1561 — *Portrait of Alessandro Farnese*, oil on canvas, National Gallery of Ireland, Dublin, Ireland.

1561 — *Portrait of Princess Juana*, oil on canvas, Isabella Stewart Gardner Museum, Boston, Massachusetts, USA.

1563 — *Portrait of Queen Isabel de Valois*, oil on panel, Prado Museum, Madrid, Spain.

1564 — *Portrait of Minerva Anguissola*, oil on canvas, Milwaukee Art Museum, Milwaukee, Wisconsin, USA.

1570 — *Portrait of the Infantas Isabella Clara Eugenia and Catalina Micaela*, oil on canvas, Royal Collection, Buckingham Palace, London, England.

1570 — *Portrait of King Philip II*, possibly completed by Alonso Sánchez Coello, oil on canvas, National Portrait Gallery, London, England.

1570 — *Portrait of Husband and Wife*, oil on canvas, Galleria Doria Pamphilj, Rome, Italy.

1570 — *Portrait of Anne of Austria*, oil on canvas, Stirling Maxwell Collection, Pollok House, Glasgow Museum and Art Galleries, Glasgow, Scotland.

1571 — *Portrait of Margarita Gonzaga*, oil on panel tondo, Captain Patrick Drury-Lowe Collection, Locko Park, Derbyshire, England.

1572 — *Portrait of Don Sebastian of Portugal*, oil on canvas, Fundación Casa de Alba, Madrid, Spain.

1572 — *Portrait of a Lady*, oil on canvas, The State Hermitage Museum, St. Petersburg, Russia.

1580 — *Portrait of a Soldier*, oil on canvas, Accademia Carrara, Bergamo, Italy.

1580 — *Portrait of a Nobleman and his Son*, oil on copper, Pinacoteca Nazionale, Siena, Italy.

1587 — *The Mystic Marriage of St. Catherine*, oil on panel, formerly collection of the Count of Pembroke, Wilton, England, current whereabouts unknown.

1588 — *Madonna Nursing her Child*, oil on canvas, Museum of Fine Arts, Budapest, Hungary.

1592 — *Holy Family with Saints Anne and John*, oil on canvas, Lowe Art Museum, University of Miami, Coral Gables, Florida, USA.

1595 — *Margaret of Savoy with her Dwarf*, oil on canvas, private collection, Madrid, Spain.

1599 — *Portrait of the Infanta Isabella Clara Eugenia*, oil on canvas, Prado Museum, Madrid, Spain.

1610 — *Self-portrait*, oil on canvas, Gottfried Keller Collection, Bern, Switzerland.

1620 — *Self-portrait*, oil on canvas, Nivaagaards Malerisamling, Nivå, Denmark.

Selected Bibliography

Acidini, Cristina, et al. *The Medici, Michelangelo, and the Art of Late Renaissance Florence*. Exhibition catalog. New Haven and London: Yale University Press, 2002. Print.

Amezúa y Mayo, Agustín González de. *Isabel de Valois, reina de España (1546-1568)*. Madrid: Gráficas Ultra, 1949. Print.

Baldwin, Pamela Holmes. *Sofonisba Anguissola in Spain: Portraiture as Art and Social Practice at a Renaissance Court*. Diss. Pennsylvania: Bryn Mawr College, 1995. Print.

Basile, Fiammetta. "Sofonisba Anguissola, gentildonna e pittrice." *La musica e le altre arti* (Jan.-Aug. 2006): 131-154. Print.

Battersby, Christine. *Gender and Genius: Towards a Feminist Aesthetics*. Bloomington: Indiana University Press, 1989. Print.

Battilana, Natale. *Genealogie delle Famiglie Nobili di Genova*. Bologna: Forni, 1971. Print.

Bergmans, Simone. "The Miniatures of Levina Teerling." *The Burlington Magazine for Connoisseurs* 64.374 (May 1934): 232-6. Print.

Boccaccio, Giovanni. *The Decameron*. Eds. and Trans. Mark Musa and Peter E. Bondanella. New York: W.W. Norton and Co. Inc., 1977. Print.

Braudel, Fernand. *The Mediterranean and the Mediterranean World in the Age of Philip II*. Vol. I. Trans. Sián Reynolds. London: The Folio Society, 2000. Print.

Braudel, Fernand. *The Mediterranean and the Mediterranean World in the Age of Philip* II. Vol. II. Trans. Sián Reynolds. Berkeley: University of California Press, 1995. Print.

Brown, Alice Van Vechten, and William Rankin. *A Short History of Italian Painting*. London: J.M. Dent & Sons Ltd., 1914. Print.

Capatti, Alberto, and Massimo Montanari. *Italian Cuisine: A Cultural History*. Trans. Áine O'Healy. New York: Columbia University Press, 2003. Print.

Caroli, Flavio. *Sofonisba Anguissola e le sue sorelle*. Milan: Arnoldo Mondadori Editore, 1987. Print.

Carr, Matthew. *Blood and Faith: The Purging of Muslim Spain*. New York: The New Press, 2009. Print.

Chadwick, Whitney. *Women, Art, and Society*. London: Thames and Hudson, 1990. Print.

Christadler, Maike. *Kreativität und Geschlecht: Giorgio Vasari's "Vite" und Sofonisba Anguissola's Selbst-Bilder*. Berlin: Reimer Verlag, 2000. Print.

Cole, Bruce. *The Renaissance Artist at Work: From Pisano to Titian*. New York: Harper & Row, Publishers, 1983. Print.

Cremona: Pictures of an Italian Province in the Po Valley. Supplement to *Sofonisba Anguissola and her Sisters*. Exhibition catalog. Cremona: Leonardo Arte, 1995. Print.

Croft, Pauline. "Why Court History Matters." *History Today* 46.1 (January 1996): 10. Print.

Defourneaux, Marcelin. *Daily Life in Spain in the Golden Age*. Trans. Newton Branch. Stanford: Stanford University Press, 1979. Print.

De Tolnay, Charles. "Sofonisba Anguissola and her Relations with Michelangelo." *The Journal of the Walters Art Gallery* 4 (1941): 115-9. Print.

Ferino-Pagden, Sylvia, and Maria Kusche. *Sofonisba Anguissola: A Renaissance Woman*. Washington, DC: National Museum of Women in the Arts, 1995. Print.

Freer, Martha Walker. *Elisabeth de Valois, Queen of Spain, and the Court of Philip* II. Vol II. London: Hurst and Blackett, Publishers,

1857. Print.

Gail, Marzieh. *Life in the Renaissance*. New York: Random House, 1968. Print.

Garrard, Mary D. "Here's Looking at Me: Sofonisba Anguissola and the Problem of the Woman Artist." *Renaissance Quarterly* 47 (Autumn 1994): 556-67. Print.

Garrard, Mary D. "Renaissance Innovator." Rev. of *Sofonisba Anguissola: The First Great Woman Artist of the Renaissance*, by Ilya Sandra Perlingieri. *Art in America* 80.9 (Sep. 1992): 33-5. Print.

Greer, Germaine. *The Obstacle Race: The Fortunes of Women Painters and Their Work*. London: Secker and Warburg, 1979. Print.

Hale, J. R., ed. *A Concise Encyclopaedia of the Italian Renaissance*. New York and Toronto: Oxford University Press, 1981. Print.

Handbook for Travellers in Northern Italy. 8th ed. London: John Murray Publishers, 1860. Print.

Harris, Ann Sutherland and Linda Nochlin. *Women Artists, 1550-1950*. Exhibition catalog. Los Angeles County Museum of Art, 1976; New York: Alfred A. Knopf, 1989. Print.

Heller, Nancy G. *Women Artists – An Illustrated History*. 4th ed. New York: Abbeville Press Publishers, 2003. Print.

Italian Women Artists – From Renaissance to Baroque. Exhibition catalog. Washington, DC: National Museum of Women in the Arts, 2007; Milan: Skira Editore S.p.A., 2007. Print.

Jacobs, Fredrika H. "Woman's Capacity to Create: The Unusual Case of Sofonisba Anguissola." *Renaissance Quarterly* 47.1 (Spring 1994): 74-101. Print.

Jensen, De Lamar. "French Diplomacy and the Wars of Religion." *The Sixteenth Century Journal* 5.2 (Oct. 1974): 23-46. Print.

Kamen, Henry. *Philip of Spain*. New Haven: Yale University Press, 1997.

Lapunzina, Alejandro. *Architecture of Spain*. Westport: Greenwood Publishing Group, 2005. Print.

Martin, Elizabeth, and Vivian Meyer. *Female Gazes: Seventy-Five*

Women Artists. Toronto: Second Story Press, 1997. Print.

Mee, Charles L., Jr. *The Horizon Book of Daily Life in Renaissance Italy*. New York: American Heritage Publishing Co. Inc., 1975. Print.

Michelin Tourist Guide – Italy. Harrow: Michelin Tyre PLC, 1988. Print.

Moray, Professor Gerta. Personal interview. May 12, 2011.

Musolff, Meghan Jane Kalasky. *Sofonisba Anguissola's "Double Portrait."* Diss. East Lansing: Michigan State University Department of Art and Art History, 2003. Print.

O'Malley, C. Donald. "Andreas Vesalius' Pilgrimage." *Isis* 45.2 (July 1954): 138-44. Print.

Parker, Geoffrey. *Philip II*. Chicago: Open Court Publishing Co., 2002. Print.

Parker, Rozsika, and Griselda Pollock. *Old Mistresses: Women, Art and Ideology*. London: Routledge & Kegan Paul, 1981. Print.

Partner, Peter. *Renaissance Rome, 1500-1559: A Portrait of a Society*. Berkeley: University of California Press, 1976. Print.

Perlingieri, Ilya Sandra. "Lady in Waiting: Rediscovering the Forgotten Brilliance of an Illustrious Renaissance Painter." *Art and Antiques* 11.4 (April 1988): 67-71, 116, 118-9. Print.

Perlingieri, Ilya Sandra. *Sofonisba Anguissola: The First Great Woman Artist of the Renaissance*. New York: Rizzoli, 1992. Print.

Perlingieri, Ilya Sandra. "Strokes of Genius." *Ms.* 17.3 (Sept 1988): 54-57. Print.

Pinessi, Orietta. *Sofonisba Anguissola: un "pittore" alla corte di Filippo II*. Milan: Selene Edizioni, 1998. Print.

Piperno, Roberto. E-mail correspondence. June 19, 2007.

Pirovano, Carlo, editorial director. *I Campi e la cultura artistica cremonese del Cinquecento*. Exhibition catalog. Milan: Electa Editrice, 1985. Print.

Pizzagalli, Daniela. *La Signora della Pittura: Vita di Sofonisba Anguissola, gentildonna e artista nel Rinascimento*. Milan: Rizzoli, 2003. Print.

Politi, Giorgio. *Aristocrazia e potere politico nella Cremona di Filippo II*. Milan: SugarCo Edizioni, 1976. Print.

Rodríguez-Salgado, M.J. "The Court of Philip II of Spain." *Princes, Patronage, and the Nobility: The Court at the Beginning of the Modern Age, c. 1450-1650*. Eds. Ronald G. Asch and Adolf M. Birke. London: German Historical Institute; Oxford University Press, 1991. 205-15. Print.

Ruiz, Teofilo F. *Spanish Society, 1400-1600*. Harlow: Longman, 2001. Print.

Saslow, James M. *The Poetry of Michelangelo, an Annotated Translation*. New Haven and London: Yale University Press, 1991. Print.

Sofonisba Anguissola e le sue Sorelle. Exhibition catalog. Cremona: Leonardo Arte, 1995. Print.

Speroni, Charles. *Wit and Wisdom of the Italian Renaissance*. Berkeley: University of California Press, 1964. Print.

Spotti, Marina. E-mail correspondence. Oct. 7, 2013.

Stone, Irving. *The Agony and the Ecstasy*. New York: Penguin Books Inc., 1961. Print.

Stortoni, Laura Anna, ed. *Women Poets of the Italian Renaissance: Courtly Ladies and Courtesans*. Trans. Laura Anna Stortoni and Mary Prentice Lillie. New York: Italica Press, 1997. Print.

Strathern, Paul. *The Artist, the Philosopher, and the Warrior*. New York: Bantam Books, 2009. Print.

Tinagli, Paola. *Women in Italian Renaissance Art: Gender, Representation, Identity*. Manchester: Manchester University Press, 1997. Print.

Vasari, Giorgio, and Giovanni Masselli. *Le Opere di Giorgio Vasari, Pittore e Architetto Aretino*. Florence: D. Passigli e socj, 1838. Print.

Vasari, Giorgio. *Lives of the Painters, Sculptors and Architects*. Vols. I and II. Trans. Gaston du C. de Vere. London: David Campbell Publishers Ltd., 1996. Print.

Vigué, Jordi. *Great Women Masters of Art*. New York: Watson-Guptill Publications, 2002. Print.

Warnke, Martin. *The Court Artist: On the Ancestry of the Modern Artist*. Cambridge: Cambridge University Press, 1993. Print.

Wasserstein, Wendy. *The Heidi Chronicles and Other Plays*. San Diego: Harcourt Brace Jovanovich Publishers, 1990. Print.

Wolf, Robert Erich, and Ronald Millen. *Renaissance and Mannerist Art*. New York and London: Harry N. Abrams Inc., 1968. Print.

Web Sites

Accademia Nazionale di San Luca. "Ritratto di Sofonisba Anguissola" by Bernardo Castello. Accessed Aug. 8, 2011.

Alacevich, Allegra. "L'Araba Felice. Sofonisba Anguissola." Accessed Dec. 19, 2007.

Ancora, Marco. "Sofonisba Anguissola: nuove importanti attribuzioni." *Agora Magazine*. Accessed Aug. 13, 2011.

Andrea Amati. Opera Omnia. Accessed Aug. 8, 2011.

Archdiocese of Toronto. Church calendar. Accessed March 1, 2011.

Bos, J. N. W. "Don Carlos of Spain," in Joan's Mad Monarchs Series. November 2009. Accessed Nov. 22, 2009.

Campi, Bernardino. "The Saints Cecilia and Catherine." 1566. San Sigismondo, Cremona. Accessed Aug. 13, 2011.

Carnet Photographique. Map of Spain. Accessed Aug. 13, 2011.

Catania – Sicilia. Paternò. Accessed Aug. 13, 2011.

Catholic Online. "Bernardino Campi." Accessed Aug. 13, 2011.

Chires, Krina. Types of Spanish flowers. Accessed Aug. 13, 2011.

Citta d'Arte della Pianura Padana. "S. Sigismondo." Accessed Jan. 24, 2007.

Ciudad de la pintura. "Alonso Sanchez Coello." Accessed Aug. 12, 2011.

Comune di Cremona. Mappa della cittá. Accessed April 11, 2011.

Cremona. *The Catholic Encyclopedia, Volume IV*. K. Knight, 2003. Accessed May 29, 2007.

Don Carlos of Spain. "The Ancient Standard." Accessed Nov.

15, 2009.

Encyclopedia of World Biography on Sofonisba Anguissola. Accessed Aug. 12, 2011.

Frescoes in the Cremona Cathedral (1520-22) by Pordenone. Web Gallery of Art. Accessed Aug. 12, 2011.

Holy Bible. King James Version. American Bible Society, New York, 1999. Bartleby.com, 2000. Accessed Sept. 26, 2010.

John of Austria. Answers.com. Accessed Aug. 13, 2011.

Kren, Emil, and Marx, Daniel. Web Gallery of Art. Biography – Pordenone. Accessed Dec. 5, 2007.

Map of El Escorial. "PlanetWare." Accessed Sept. 6, 2009.

Mastroianni, Paolo. "Gli sguardi di Sofonisba Anguissola riflessi nello specchio 'multiplo' delle sue sorelle." *DW press – Il quotidiano delle donne.* Accessed Aug. 8, 2011.

Medieval jousting history. "Medieval Life and Times." Accessed April 12, 2011.

Michelangelo Buonarroti. Web Gallery of Art. Accessed Aug. 8, 2011.

Milwaukee Art Museum. "The Artist's Sister Minerva Anguissola." Sofonisba Anguissola. Accessed Oct. 8, 2007.

Museo Nacional del Prado. Colección. "Following Victory at Lepanto, Felipe II offers the Infante Don Fernando to Heaven." Titian Collection. Accessed Aug. 12, 2011.

Office of Tourism. Cremona. Accessed Aug. 13, 2011.

"Palermo: identificate altre sette tele di Sofonisba." *Eco di Sicilia* Feb. 7, 2008. Accessed Oct. 7, 2010.

Pickle history timeline. New York Food Museum. 2003, Dana Terebelski and Nancy Ralph. Accessed Jan. 7, 2012.

Pinacoteca di Brera. Sala XVIII. Accessed Oct. 9, 2007.

"Portrait of Juana of Austria and a Young Girl." Isabella Stewart Gardner Museum. Accessed Aug. 12, 2011.

Renaissance Timeline in Fashion and Events. "Romance Reader at Heart." Accessed Aug. 8, 2011.

A Rome Art Lover's Web page. Casa di Michelangelo. Accessed Aug. 18, 2006.

Ross, John. "Spain and Portugal for Visitors. Aranjuez." Accessed Aug. 12, 2011.

Sicily on Tour. Paternò Castle – "A Turri." Accessed Aug. 13, 2011.

Suzuki, Jeff A. "Primero: A Renaissance Cardgame." 1994. Accessed Aug. 12, 2011.

Visual Lombardia. Cremona, Chiesa di San Sigismondo. Accessed Aug. 13, 2011.

What are the symptoms of smallpox? Health-cares.net. Accessed Aug. 12, 2011.

World Wide Arts Resources. "Artist: Bernardino Gatti." Accessed June 1, 2011.

Acknowledgements

Thanks go to The Bridgeman Art Library for the cover illustration, and to Italica Press for use of the works by Italian women poets. Also thanks to the American Bible Society, whose King James Version was the source of the Bible quotations.

The staff and collections of several research libraries were very helpful, especially the Toronto Public Library, the Boston Public Library, and the National Art Library at the Victoria and Albert Museum in London. The research and writings of Ilya Sandra Perlingieri were particularly useful. Special thanks go to Gerta Moray for sharing her knowledge of art history, and for her interest and encouragement. The Manuscript Evaluation Service of The Writers' Union of Canada helped to improve the first few chapters of the manuscript. Luciana Ricciutelli and her staff at Inanna Publications provided a thorough and useful evaluation of the completed manuscript, as well as valuable editing, fact-checking, and proofreading.

I owe by far the biggest debt of gratitude to my husband, Brian Deming, for his advice, practical help, support, and inspiration. *Grazie, caro mio.*

Carol Damioli, a native of Michigan, has lived in Boston, Chicago, San Francisco, Tokyo, Manila, Prague, Florence and Munich. She began as a newspaper reporter and worked in international radio and trade magazines. Her time in Florence led to the publication of her first novel, *Rogue Angel*, a historical novel about the Florentine Renaissance painter Fra Filippo Lippi, which was published in 1994. She and her husband moved to Toronto in 2007, where she lives and works as an editor and writer.